Judex

Judex

by
Arthur Bernède
&
Louis Feuillade

translated, annotated and introduced by
Rick Lai

A Black Coat Press Book

Visit our website at www.blackcoatpress.com

ISBN 978-1-61227-085-2. First Printing. March 2012. Published by Black Coat Press, an imprint of Hollywood Com-
ics.com, LLC, P.O. Box 17270, Encino, CA 91416. All rights
reserved. Except for review purposes, no part of this book may
be reproduced or transmitted in any form or by any means,
electronic or mechanical, including photocopying, recording,
or by any information storage and retrieval system, without
permission in writing from the publisher. The stories and characters depicted in this novel are entirely fictional. Printed in
the United States of America.

TABLE OF CONTENTS

Arthur Bernède in 1908

Introduction

The following novel, *Judex*, resulted from a screenplay coauthored by two remarkable men. The first was Louis Feuillade (1873-1925), one of the most influential film makers of all time. The son of a wine merchant, he was born in Lunel, a town in southern France. In 1898, he moved to Paris to continue his father's profession. The collapse of the family business following the death of his father in 1902 caused him to being a wine merchant. Employed by the *Revue Mondiale,* he briefly pursued a career in journalism. In 1905, he became a screen writer for Gaumont, the second largest film studio in France. Two year later, he was promoted to the position of Artistic Director for the entire studio. In his new capacity, he not only oversaw all Gaumont production, but also directed films himself. Before his death, he would direct over 800 films.

Initially, Feuillade fashioned a concept called *le film esthétique* (the aesthetic film). Essentially Feuillade promoted epic films with historical, biblical or mythological themes. Among the films directed by Feuillade in this category were *Prométhée* (*Prometheus*, 1908), *La Nativité* (*The Nativity*, 1910) and *L'Agonie de Byzance* (*The Agony of Byzance*, 1913).

Feuillade was versatile in multiple genres. He particularly championed the idea of a film series, His early film series were comedies featuring child stars. In this vein, he directed the successful *Bébé* series (1910-13) starring Clément Mary followed by the *Bout-de-zan* series (1913-15) with René Poyen. Feuillade even helmed realistic social dramas, which he dubbed his "Life as it is" films, such as *Les Vipères* (*The Vipers*, 1911) and *Le Nain* (*The Dwarf*, 1912).

However, it was a director of films about master criminals and sleuths that Feuillade became famous. In 1911, Pierre

Souvestre and Marcel Allain created the popular master criminal called Fantômas. Feuillade directed five films based as the murderous fiend: *Fantômas -- À l'ombre de la Guillotine* (*Fantômas: In the Shadow of the Guillotine*, 1913), *Juve contre Fantômas* (*Juve vs. Fantômas*, 1913), *Le Mort Qui Tue* (*The Murderous Corpse*, 1913), *Fantômas contre Fantômas* (*Fantômas vs. Fantômas*, 1914), and *Le Faux Magistrat* (*The False Magistra*te, 1914).

Movie audiences thrilled to the image of *Fantômas* in black tights and hood. Rather than pay royalties to Souvestre and Allain, Feuillade opted to create a gang of similarly dressed criminals in *Les Vampires* (*The Vampires*, 1915-1916), a serial in 10 chapters. The most significant character in this melodrama was Irma Vep (anagram of "vampire"), a leather clad villainess who was the forerunner of Catwoman from the *Batman* comic book. The character of Irma Vep may have inspired British writer H. C. McNeile (alias "Sapper") to create the recurring villainess Irma Peterson in his Bulldog Drummond novels. Evidence of McNeile's familiarity with Feuillade's thrillers resurfaced in *Temple Tower* (1929), a novel in which Drummond battled *Le Bossu Masqué*, a French master criminal whose costume resembled those of Fantômas and the Vampire gang.

Feuillade was criticized in the French press for creating movies that glorified crime. For his next serial, he needed to develop a hero who overshadowed the villains. He also wished to develop a moral uplifting theme that would evoke some of his earlier Biblical epics. In order to achieve this goal, he collaborated with Arthur Bernède (1871-1937). Bernède was a novelist, opera librettist, and playwright. As a novelist, Bernède had created a recurring French spy, Chantecoq, who appeared in such novels as *Coeur de Française* (1912), *L'Espionne de Guillaume* (1915) and *Chantecoq* (1916). Among the operas for which Bernède wrote librettos was *Sappho* (1897) by Jules Massenet (1842- 1912). There are two references to Massenet in the text of Bernède's *Judex*.

Together Feuillade and Bernède fashioned Judex, perhaps the first costumed hero in cinematic history. Judex is Latin for "judge." Also known as the "Mysterious Shadow," Judex wore a black hat and cape. The obvious similarities to the American pulp hero, The Shadow, are examined in an afterword following the novel. The title role was played by René Cresté.

Judex, a serial in 12 chapters, received limited release in late 1916 and a more general release in the following year. Concurrent with the debut of each installment, a novelization by Bernède was serialized in *Le Petit Parisien.* The entire text was subsequently published by Tallandier.

How much did Feuillade contribute to the storyline? He supposedly designed Judex's costume. The villainous Diana Monti is heavily reminiscent of Irma Vep. In fact, she was played by the same actress, Musidora. It's no surprise that René Poyen was cast as the Licorice Kid since that character is a virtual rewrite of the popular Bout-de-zan whom the child actor had portrayed in several comedies directed by Feuillade.

The film's theme of vengeance in the serial was heavily influenced by Alexandre Dumas's *The Count of Monte-Cristo* (1844). Edmond Dantès was framed for treason by four men. One of the conspirators was Baron Danglars, a corrupt banker. Following his escape from prison, Dantès abducted Danglars and imprisoned him in a secret prison. A very similar scenario unfolded in *Judex*.

Feuillade's serial was so successful that it inspired a sequel, *La Nouvelle Mission de Judex* (*Judex's New Mission*, 1918). Again Feuillade and Bernède collaborated on the screenplay. Like its predecessor, Judex's second adventure was novelized by Arthur Bernède.

In 1919, Bernède formed a partnership with actor René Navarre, the actor who played had played Fantômas in the five Feuillade films, and writer Gaston Leroux, the author of *The Phantom of the Opera* (1911). Together they created the *Société des Cinéromans*, a production company that would produce films and novels simultaneously. Of the later screenplays

9

written by Bernède, the most famous was for the serial *Belphegor* (1927) directed by Henri Desfontaines. The plot pitted Chantecoq, now a private detective rather than a spy, against a mysterious phantom, Belphegor, haunting the Louvre.

Bernède also wrote historical novels. Like Dumas, he sought to provide an explanation for a famous historical mystery in his own version of *L'Homme au Masque de Fer* (*The Man in the Iron Mask*, 1930). *Vidocq* (1923) told the story of Eugène-Francois Vidocq (1775-1857), the former criminal who founded the Sûreté, the French national police. In the novelization of *Judex*, the hero's dog was named Vidocq. *Mandrin* (1924) told the story of a famous French brigand of the 18th century.

After the Judex films, Feuillade made other crime serials. *Tih Minh* (1918) concerned a young Asian woman being pursued by a spy ring. *Tih Minh* is often inaccurately described as a sequel to *Les Vampires*. This is untrue. I've seen the serial in its entirety. The title character of *Barrabas* (1920) was a brutal master criminal in the tradition of Fantômas.

Judex was remade twice. A 1934 version was directed by Maurice Champreux, Feuillade's son-in-law. I haven't seen this remake. Jacques Champreux, Feuillade's grandson, co-authored a screenplay with Francis Lacassin for a 1963 version directed by Georges Franju. The film starred American magician Channing Pollock as Judex. While the original serial had vengeance defeated by forgiveness, this remake removed all the forgiveness and kept all the vengeance. The film also featured an unforgettable sequence in which Judex performed magic tricks using doves.

The following novelization fleshes out many of the characters who came off as very one-dimensional in the serial. This is particularly true of Daisy Torp, an independent woman as formidable as Emma Peel and Modesty Blaise.

Rick Lai

JUDEX

Part One: The Mysterious Shadow

1. Destiny's Vagrant

On the edge of the Seine between Mantises and Bonnières, nearly opposite the majestic Chateau des Sablons that
towered amidst immense foliage, stood a vagrant with a bag
and a walking stick. Ravaged by fatigue, he inspected the dark
confines of an old mill. Located alongside the river, the edifice
had long been abandoned. Three quarters of the structure was
covered by an inextricable mass of vines.

A painful sob erupted from the vagrant's chest.

"I have lost all! My poor wife! My son! My entire life!
My happiness! It would be better to end everything! But I
can't kill myself. I have to save my son. My son! I must be
brave. Yes, I must be brave!"

Erupting in tears due to the awakened memories of his
loved ones, the nameless man crossed the road. He stopped in
front of the monumental structure whose gilded paint gleamed
under the rays of the clear June sun. Gazing through the bars,
he eagerly contemplated the fine stone avenues, the punctuated flower beds and the beautiful alabaster statues. He was
dazzled by the imposing mansion and its vast marble pool
where swans dwelt magnificently among graceful waters worthy of the Palace of Versailles. From the distance, the rhythms
of an orchestra enveloped the grounds. Throughout the groves,
elegant couples were whirling in a romantic dance of spring.

The vagrant's tears dried. No longer did his eyes reflect
despair. His sorrow was replaced by hatred that threatened to
disrupt the festivities.

A white-haired man with a beard approached. Known as
Vallières, he possessed a distinguished, albeit deferential, appearance. He addressed the vagrant in a benevolent tone.

"What do you want, my good fellow?"

"To talk to the banker Favraux."

"Monsieur Favraux is very busy. I am his secretary . Maybe I could…"

Pulling some money from his pocket, Vallières extended it to the vagrant who objected with a virulent passion.

"I don't want charity. I want to speak to Monsieur Favraux."

Recognizing that he was confronting an obstinate man, Vallières decided to inform his employer.

Segregated from his guests, the banker was with a companion in a discreet arbor. They were viewing a splendid panorama to which the ruined mill in the foreground added a charming and picturesque quality. Favraux leaned romantically towards a very attractive woman whose reserved mannerisms suggested a simple and honest nature.

"Monsieur," announced the secretary, "there is a stranger at the gates insisting to see you."

Combining a sturdy maturity and temperate elegance with a shaven face and a steely gaze, Monsieur Favraux conveyed the modern image of a prominent financier. He expressed impatience in his curt response.

"Who is this individual?"

"A vagrant, Monsieur."

"A vagrant! You disturb me for that?"

"This unfortunate man appears very excited. I fear that he'll create some disturbance."

Upon these words, a haze passed quickly over the banker's face. Exhibiting intense passion towards the enticing female near him, he moderated his natural abrasiveness.

"Will you permit me, darling?"

"Please do," answered the young woman while modestly lowering her deep black eyes.

Accompanied by his secretary, Favraux walked towards the gates. Upon seeing the stranger, Favraux immediately addressed him.

"What do you want, my good man?"

Throwing his tattered felt hat to the ground, the vagrant revealed a visage tortured by anxiety. "Don't you recognize me?" he yelled.

"I've never seen you before!"

"I am Pierre Kerjean."

"Pierre Kerjean!" repeated the banker, unable to suppress a slight shudder.

"Come on," continued the vagrant, "you remember me, Monsieur Favraux. I was once an honest man. I owned a mill and some land on the other side of the road. I lived happily with my wife and child. One day, you arrived in the country. You bought Les Sablons. To enlarge your estate, you wanted to buy my property. Seduced by your large offer, I agreed. Then enticed by your promises, I entrusted my money to you. Not only did you ruin me, but you persuaded me to commit risky and fraudulent speculations. I wasn't as fortunate as you. I acted too rashly. My impatience proved fatal. I was condemned to 20 years of hard labor. My wife died of shame. When I returned from the penal colony, I learned at the City Hall that my impoverished son had become a thief!"

"And now?" insolently asked the banker recovering his composure.

"I don't want any money," asserted the old man. "I don't even want revenge. I *demand* simply your help in finding my son and reforming him!"

" I don't know what I can do for you."

"You don't know!" roared the vagrant while shaking his fist through the bars. "You are even more evil than I dreamed!"

"If you have any claims to make, address them to a court of justice."

"Justice!" laughed the ex- convict. "Ah! I know justice! For 20 years, it cursed me, while you, the true guilty party, continued to enrich yourself ruining and destroying everyone in your path! And when I ask a little mercy, you refer me to justice! Do you want to thoroughly crush me? This is cowardly! Abominable! Since I have little time left, I will devote my life to hating you! Every day and every hour, you'll see me as a living indictment of your infamous crimes! You'll hear me constantly scream accusations! You're only a thief and an outlaw!"

Shrugging in an arrogant manner, Favraux moved away from the gates. With compassionate words, Vallières strove to calm Kerjean's anger. The old man had one final outburst.

"You are cursed, Favraux! Cursed forever!"

Retrieving his hat and lifting up his sack, he walked away.

"I will have my revenge! Yes! I will have my revenge!"

This ordeal had broken his spirit. Scarcely traveling a half kilometer, Kerjean paused. Collapsing on a rock pile, he dropped his bag and stick. Taking his head between his hands, Kerjean began crying. He evoked through a distant fog the happy years that, alas, had been quickly swept away!

Suddenly, Kerjean quivered. Rumbles of an automobile drew his attention. A hoarse cry escaped him: "Favraux!" Kerjean recognized his enemy seated behind the wheel in a luxurious car with a 40-horsepower engine. Next to Favraux was a man in a chauffeur's uniform. Overwhelmed by his hatred, the old man ran towards the car screaming with arms outstretched. "Scum! Scum!"

Clipped by one the vehicle's fenders, the unfortunate Kerjean fell under the wheels. Not even leaning on the brake pedal, the banker continued on his way without any concern for the bloodstained man lying deserted on the white road.

Almost immediately, Kerjean reopened his eyelids. Raising his head, he saw the car carrying his assailant disappearing in a cloud of dust. With glazed eyes and twisted lips, Kerjean turned his face towards the sky. He moaned as his body was besieged by monstrous spasms.

"God will punish you!"

II. The Mysterious Message

In his extravagant study occupying the entire ground floor of the Chateau's principal wing, Favraux had already spent more than an hour at work that morning . His labor was disturbed by a knock on the large double door of his chambers.

"Enter," said the banker with mild impatience. However, his face became joyful immediately upon the entrance of his visitors.

The beautiful brunette, with which whom he had behaved so intimately the day before, advanced holding the hand of a charming boy. This lad , nearly five years-old, looked like a blond angel from a fresco of Le Dominiquin or Andréa del Sarto.

The child swiftly ran towards the financier. Jumping familiarly on the banker's knee, he shouted, "*Bonjour*, Grandpa!"

"*Bonjour*, Jeannot!" replied Favraux. After kissing the child and placing him on the ground, the banker's eyes looked into those of his grandson's governess.

While the youngster moved towards the wide windows that opened on the park, Favraux passionately murmured to the young woman.

"Marie, I love you!"

"Monsieur..."

"I love you, and I want... Yes, I want you to be mine."

"Your mistress, never!"

"I want you to be my wife!"

"Monsieur Favraux!"

"Right after the marriage of my daughter," murmured the banker.

A feminine voice came from the other side of the door, "Can I enter, Father?"

"Yes, Mama," replied spontaneously the boy at the window.

17

A young woman with a gentle and tragic demeanor appeared on the threshold. Radiantly gorgeous, she was attired in a becoming riding-habit that emphasized her harmonious grace and frail suppleness.

"*Bonjour*, Jacqueline," stated Favraux coldly.

"*Bonjour*, Father," replied the banker's daughter before timidly kissing him.

"Are you going horseback riding this morning?" questioned Favraux.

"Yes," responded Jacqueline. "I'll be riding in the forest with Vicomte de la Rochefontaine."

Hearing this name, the naïve Jean squeezed his mother's hand.

"Mama, it is true that I'll have a new Papa?"

"Yes," replied the young woman blushing slightly.

"What will I call him?"

"Father."

"Is he as rich as Grandpa?"

"My dear, there are questions that children shouldn't ask," gently scolded Jacqueline. "My little one, it's time for Mademoiselle Verdier's lesson. Please be attentive and obedient."

"Yes, Mama. I promise."

The child departed with his governess while Jacqueline sighed with motherly pride.

"My sweet little angel, if only I didn't have to share you!"

"Enough!" interjected Favraux. "You still have ridiculous ideas."

"Father, you misunderstand me. Let me explain."

"You don't know what you're saying. You are foolish, my daughter. Foolish!"

Hearing this brutal sentence, Jacqueline sadly lowered her head.

Surrounded by luxury, the kindly heiress had never known happiness. Her meek mother had died when Jacqueline was a child. Madame Favraux's spirit had been crushed by her husband's neglect and the shame caused by the ruthless swindling of his clients. Once Jacqueline returned from convent school, her father coldly used her as a pawn to advance his own schemes. The banker forced her to wed Jacques Aubry, a young engineer without money or scruples.

Favraux had intended Aubry, a genius in his field, to be his associate (actually, his accomplice) in his financial manipulations. However, Aubry had perished in an automobile accident in America during a business trip undertaken on his father-in-law's orders. Jacqueline, already embittered by her father's domination, resolved to devote herself entirely to her child. For years, the banker's absorption in new projects had distracted him from interfering with Jacqueline's life.

Nevertheless. Favraux eventually desired to form a new alliance. The financier sought to expand his clientele to include the French aristocracy. The cultivation of a young penniless noble related to the most prominent families would be the means to achieve this goal.

Within a few weeks, acting like a tyrannical despot whose power conquers all, Favraux rushed the betrothal. For a second time. he imposed his will on his young daughter. The poor woman again succumbed to the iron authority that her father exercised like a force of nature.

Confronted now by the father who had always bullied her, she had inadvertently permitted him to glimpse the painful sorrow in her heart. She was about to excuse herself when the whistle of an acoustic tube sounded.

"Here's my secretary," said Favraux to his daughter. "The mail has arrived. Leave me and do your riding . Go! Try to be cheerful during lunch."

"*Au revoir*, Father."

"*Au revoir*."

Resigned to her father's domination, the submissive Jacqueline withdrew.

Jacqueline passed Vallières, who respectfully bowed to her. "My regards to the Vicomte," the banker said to his departing daughter. Alone with his secretary, Favraux spoke in whispers.

"Have you checked on the incident involving the vagrant?"

" Yes, Monsieur."

"Well?"

"I discovered that no one suspects you of being the involuntary author of this unfortunate accident."

"I prefer that."

"As for Kerjean, he was found by peasants and taken to the clinic of Dr. Gortais."

"Did Kerjean say anything?"

"No, Monsieur, and he will say nothing."

"Is he dead?"

"Tonight he fell into a coma without regaining consciousness. All the time that I was at the clinic, he showed no signs of life."

"All is well!"

Favraux designated the voluminous mail that a footman brought on a tray, "Now we take care of more important matters."

Once the servant withdrew, the banker opened his correspondence with a paper cutter. His eyes focused on a big yellow envelope whose address was bizarrely written in gothic and exaggerated characters.

To the Banker Favraux
Chateau des Sablons,
Mantises (Seine-and-Oise)
Urgent and Personal

Somewhat intrigued, Jacqueline's father unsealed the envelope and read it aloud.

"*Not content with ruining the people, you have opted to murder them. I order you to pay for your crimes by donating half your wealth to the Public Assistance. You have until 10 o'clock, tomorrow evening, to execute my commands.*"

The mysterious message was signed with a single name written in red letters and followed by an exclamation point drawn like a tear of blood: *JUDEX!*

"Judex! Judex!" repeated Favraux with surprise.

"It's Latin for 'judge,' Monsieur," said the secretary.

"Yes, I know." The banker muttered derisively between his teeth. "But what does this mean?"

III. The Gilded Merchant

Maurice-Ernest Favraux was one of those individuals who became inevitably a very great man or an enormous scoundrel. Such men are presented with the fundamental choice between good and evil. Favraux had chosen the second path only because it allowed him to swiftly attain the gratification of his unbridled appetites.

He had taken gigantic strides. His parents, modest merchants, had worked their fingers to the bone in order to give him a solid education. They even paid for their son to study in other countries. In the Stock Market, it was said that no one else had amassed such a large fortune so rapidly.

At 18, he was a minor employee in a credit company; at 25, he invested money with the help of a stock broker; at 30, thanks to the influx of large sums of cash from a mysterious source, he had founded the Modern Bank of Industry and Commerce on the Boulevard Haussmann. Under his vigorous direction, that financial entity had expanded mightily without any restraints.

Endowed with unmatched audacity, versatility, energy and talents of persuasion, this gilded merchant had skillfully maneuvered around legal regulations without being prosecuted. Anyone challenging him was mercilessly crushed. He shamelessly sacrificed all his superfluous accomplices. His growing fortune bought out competitors and purchased silence. Financially secured, Favraux achieved a morally irreproachable position in global commerce.

In the middle of his triumph, on the eve of the climatic marriage of his daughter to Vicomte de la Rochefontaine, he had been stunned by Judex's mysterious message.

"What does this mean? What connection does this odd missive have with yesterday's incident? You just told me, Vallières, that old Kerjean didn't speak to anyone. Who knows besides us? There's only Reste Martial, my chauffeur,"

"There's one thing I don't understand, Monsieur. If you intended to drive the car yourself, why take Martial as a passenger?"

"Martial is a first-class mechanic. My car is a delicate piece of machinery. I need him if the car breaks down."

"Are you sure he isn't Judex?"

"I have no doubts about his loyalty. Martial owes me too much. In any case, the young man's barely literate. If he wanted to blackmail me, he would never choose this Latin pseudonym of Judex."

"Evidently," concurred the secretary.

"Consequently," concluded Favraux, "it's only a bad joke which should be ignored." Then he laughed. *"Diable!* All goes well, my dear Monsieur Judex! Half my fortune to the Public Assistance! That government agency doesn't need my money to raise orphans and build hospitals! Tell me, Vallières, since you know most of my dealings, why shouldn't I suspect you of being the author of this message?"

"On my honor, Monsieur, no!" declared the secretary. "It's bizarre anyway!"

"Let's proceed! We have wasted enough time on stupidities. Back to work!"

With apparent serenity, Favraux resumed the perusal of his mail. Dictating his replies to his secretary, he occasionally displayed vague signs of unease.

After Vallières withdrew to compose the correspondence, the gilded merchant openly voiced his anxiety.

"Damn! I would give 10,000 francs to know Judex's identity!"

Prosper Cocantin was the new director of the Celeritas Detective Agency located at 135 Rue Milton. He had recently inherited the firm from his late uncle, Ribaudet, the renowned private investigator. Cocantin was overwhelmed with pride to see his office frequented by Favraux, one of the kings of European finance. Even bigger was his surprise when the banker with haughty brevity requested his services.

"Monsieur, on several occasions I discussed confidential matters with your predecessors. I was always very satisfied with their services. I hope that it will be the same with you."

Favraux displayed the Judex message to the private detective.

"I've just received this letter. I'm convinced it's the handiwork of a prankster, but I don't like to be ridiculed. I want you to undertake the difficult task of promptly unmasking the signatory. No one attacks a man of my status with impunity."

"Monsieur," replied Cocantin, "I consider it a godsend that you are entrusting me with this letter." With the fervor of a beginner, he spoke confidently. "Within 24 hours, I promise to establish the identity of your mysterious correspondent."

"Thank you."

"Where do you want to receive the results of my investigation?"

"Tomorrow, I'll be unable to leave the Chateau des Sablons because I'm giving a big dinner party. Could you telephone me?"

"No telephone, Monsieur! I must come in person. If the prudence is the mother of security, the telephone is the enemy of the investigator. I'll personally bring you the fruits of my research."

"Agreed."

The next day, at 2 o'clock precisely, the director of the Celeritas Agency arrived at the Chateau des Sablons. He was immediately taken to the study where Favraux waited impatiently. Since the reception of the letter signed Judex, Favraux's vitality had been drained by silent dread.

Several times in the past, he had received anonymous letters with similar warnings. He had always shrugged off such threats by throwing them into the trash basket.

Why did this letter invoke such despondency inside him? Why did his fingers tremble involuntarily whenever they touched the strange paper? Why did this word "Judex" disturb him in a way that he had never felt before?

The banker had called upon all his faculties to analyze the sensations bothering him. Searching his phenomenal memory, he could not find any plausible explanation. Despite all his efforts to relieve this haunting obsession, he felt more assaulted by this inexplicable mystery.

Against his will, he was compelled to vocally express his apprehension.

"Judex... Judex... what does it mean?"

A heavy burden would weigh on Favraux's shoulders until this mystery was solved. Once Cocantin appeared, a glimmer of hope appeared in the banker's eyes.

"Well, Monsieur Cocantin, do have something for me?" he asked affably.

Not having discovered even a faint hint of the truth, the private detective decided to bluff.

"Be calm, Monsieur, absolutely calm. In 24 hours, and possibly even earlier, I shall unmask Judex."

A footman brought the mail of the afternoon. As the detective got ready to leave, the banker, visibly disturbed, rose from his chair and delivered a peremptory order to his servant.

"Leave me alone with this gentleman. Let no one disturb us."

Cocantin had just noticed that Favraux held in his hands a yellow envelope similar to the one that contained Judex's earlier message.

The banker unsealed it. Scanning every word, he read it aloud:

"If before the stroke of 10 tonight, you don't relinquish half of your ill-gotten fortune to the Public Assistance, it will be too late. You will be punished mercilessly."

And it was signed: *JUDEX!*

"The joke continues," emphasized Cocantin with a humorous smile.

"It has lasted far too long," scolded the banker while raising his eyebrows.

"Don't be upset, Monsieur Favraux," implored Cocantin. "The guilty party is probably closer than we thought. I shall conduct a thorough inspection of your house and its surroundings. This sinister joke shall soon collapse due to my efforts."

Placing the second Judex message in his wallet next to its predecessor, Cocantin looked at the influential financier with eyes filled with a dark flame.

"I reassure you, Monsieur. I'll watch over you!"

After Cocantin's departure, the banker dropped into his armchair as if it had suffered a seizure.

From that moment, he was unable to disperse the nagging menace of the weird signature signed in red letters followed by the bloody exclamation point: *JUDEX!*

The financier recalled all the disasters and corpses that each argumentation of his wealth had left in his wake. He brooded over his premonition that this was not a stupid joke invented by an envious or mildly vindictive correspondent. The banker felt eclipsed by an atmosphere of death.

What if it's true? thought Favraux as panic conquered his brain. *One of my victims has returned full of fury and hate. From the shadows, he's waging a ruthless campaign against me? Half my fortune! If I yield, I'm lost! My remaining money will dissipate! No! No! It's impossible! I won't do it!*

He imagined an invisible hand reaching for his throat.

"Marie!" he cried hoarsely.

The image of the young governess appeared before him in an exquisite vision of unspeakable delight. His black eyes reflected the darkness of hellish temptation; the mirage of this desirable woman restored his courage.

"To yield to a simple injunction," he said to himself, "would be cowardice! Madness! If this enemy really exists, then I await his onslaught. I accept his challenge. The war begins."

Galvanized by his desire for Marie Verdier, he was flooded by memories of all the past battles where his avarice emerged victorious. His crimes had been unpunished in the past. They would be unpunished in the future.

"I no longer fear you anymore! I accept the fight! To the two of us, Judex! Whoever you are, we shall see if you can strike me down."

IV. When the Clock Struck Ten

The halls of the Chateau were decorated profusely with beautiful flowers and brilliant electrical lights as the gilded merchant greeted the guests arriving for his daughter's engagement party.

Beaming with pride, the magnificently handsome Amaury de la Rochefontaine was constantly at his fiancée's side. Jacqueline, who only cared for her son, listened absentmindedly to the charming platitudes lavished on her by the handsome Vicomte.

As for the banker, he circulated among his guests and received their congratulations. Exhibiting his customary haughtiness, he frequently glanced toward Mademoiselle Verdier, whom Favraux had gently persuaded her to attend the dinner. The youthful governess modestly remained aloof. She seemed overwhelmed to find herself in such a glamorous gathering.

Favraux acted as he was oblivious to Judex's threat. Impeccable in his evening frock coat, Cocantin had been closely scrutinizing the guests. With great solemnity, he whispered enigmatically into the banker's ear:

"All is well!"

The truth was that the sleuth had vainly searched the Chateau des Sablons from the cellar to the attic. He had explored the courtyard and its dependencies. Probing the thick shrubbery of the park, Cocantin had only discovered Favraux muttering tenderly to Mademoiselle Verdier under the shade. The detective could no longer bluff.

Double doors opened wide revealing an imposing butler. "Dinner is served!" he announced. The guests moved into the Chateau's superb dining-room where they beheld a spectacularly decorated table.

Amidst this pleasant atmosphere of celebration, the conversation promptly became sparkling and animated. Bursts of feminine laughter resounded though the active whispers of tangled gossip. Compliments, biting criticism and scandal mongering spread amongst the crowd.

In a neighboring salon, an orchestra played a rosary of slow waltzes.

Raising his hand, Favraux arose to make the customary toast. The monumental clock on one of the room's panels displayed two minutes before 10 o'clock. Silence slowly spread throughout the assembly. With a slightly impaired voice, Favraux began.

"Ladies and gentlemen, let us drink to the health of my daughter, Madame Jacqueline Aubry, and Vicomte Amaury de la Rochefontaine…"

Approving murmurs circulated throughout the assembly.

"As our joy is intensified by the presence of old friends," continued Favraux, "I wish you, my dear Amaury, as well as my dear child, all the happiness that vows of marriage can create…"

Suddenly, the banker stopped as if he had forgotten the words. Instinctively, his eyes sought out the clock, The hands had almost reached the time foretold by Judex. Jacqueline's father remembered the threat. Fear shook his mortal frame. His audacity momentarily deserted him as anxiety clouded his mind.

Can this be true? At this moment does the hand of the unknown judge linger over me?

Nevertheless, he regained his composure. The financier nervously resumed his toast to the young couple.

"Yes, all the happiness that vows of marriage can create."

The words strangled themselves in his throat. A cold sweat appeared to his temples. A convulsive tremor shook his hands. To conceal his discomfort, he brought his glass of champagne to his lips and drained it quickly.

The clock struck 10 o'clock. Favraux's face contracted in a hideous convulsion. His glass fell from his hands to break on the table. Thrice he waved his arms in panic. As a frightful moan escaped his throat; he collapsed. He had been struck down.

Judex had kept his word!

In the commotion, guests ran to Favraux's side. Carrying him to the salon, they placed him on a couch. He no longer exhibited any signs of life. Despite all the lavished care, Favraux couldn't be revived.

A doctor, a family friend attending the dinner, concluded that the financier had succumbed to an embolism.

Jacqueline's fiancé, as well as Vallières, vainly tried to console her during this sad spectacle. Faced with the horrible tableau, the sobbing Jacqueline knelt alongside her father's body.

Concealed behind a tapestry, Marie Verdier observed the banker's daughter. With a bitter expression, Marie viewed Favraux's corpse, The facial features of the gilded merchant were frozen in a grotesque grimace of superhuman fright.

V. Jacqueline

Hurriedly leaving the Chateau with the two Judex letters, Cocantin had returned to his office completely terrified. He was incoherently talking to himself.

"This is where I began. Here's my life story. What should I say? What should I do? I don't know anymore! This is horrible! I feel sick!"

This man was in total distress. Three weeks ago, he led one of the most cheerful lives as well as one of the most banal.

He had been resigned to his trade of a detective. Until he was 40 years old, Cocantin had lived off a rather large stipend paid to him by his uncle, Monsieur Ribaudet, the guiding founder of the Celeritas Detective Agency. He divided his existence between two passions, women and Napoleon. It was obvious that the first one had cost him infinitely more than the second. The money granted by Ribaudet had been appropriately sufficient to extricate his nephew from any difficulty. His uncle's will had required that Cocantin succeed him and assume all his duties. In order to defend his livelihood, Prosper Cocantin had been forced to take over the direction of the agency. Now, for his first case, he was embroiled in a drama more fearsome than any he could have imagined.

"I should go to the police," said Cocantin to himself. "They are the true detectives—the only ones that should exist!" As he was about to depart, he changed his mind. "If I reveal all to the Prefecture, they could suspect me of being Judex's accomplice—or Judex himself! It is better to keep silent about this dark affair. I must hold my tongue!"

He hoped to regain his peace and tranquility, but that didn't happen. For two days, he struggled against the haunting visions of Judex. For two nights, he was persecuted by brutal nightmares.

In order to escape this obsession, Cocantin prepared to tear up the two letters which had intoxicated him like a diabolical perfume. Then a thought swayed him.

Favraux had a daughter. Do I have the right to keep her in ignorance of the dire circumstances preceding her father's death?

Perplexed due to his scrupulous honesty, he continued to contemplate the two messages. Raising his head, he beheld a bust of Napoleon on a shelf. *What would HE do in my place?* wondered the detective. The response didn't take long to arrive. Cocantin imagined the Emperor's thunderous delivering an order.

"Warn the family!"

The director of the Celeritas Agency did not hesitate. Hours later, he arrived at the Chateau des Sablons, requesting Madame Aubry to urgently grant him a private audience. Having just attended her father's funeral, Jacqueline was in a state of mourning. Despite her emotional distress, she consented to receive the detective. After bowing respectfully, Cocantin explained his presence.

"Madame, I beg your pardon for disturbing your grief. Being in possession of a family secret affecting you, I would be negligent to remain silent."

With total frankness, Ribaudet's successor related to Madame Aubry the banker's visit to the Agency, as well as all the preceding and subsequent events. Displaying Judex's two letters to support his claims, Cocantin had satisfactorily put his conscience at rest.

"Madame, having done my duty, all that remains for me is to regretfully give you my deepest respect."

Having read the two messages, Jacqueline was overwhelmed with indignation.

"These letters are an infamous attempt at extortion!"

"Madame," protested Cocantin with extreme sincerity, "I swear that I'm completely incapable…"

"Monsieur," interrupted the banker's daughter, "I don't accuse you. On the contrary, I commend you for your loyalty. You must understand that my father's memory can't be besmirched even for an instance. It is imperative to clarify this matter."

"You are correct, Madame."

"If I need your services?"

"You can count on me completely," promised the director of the Celeritas Agency as he withdrew with Madame Aubry's permission.

Alone Jacqueline read the first notice again.

"Not content with ruining the people, you have opted to murder them. I order you to pay for your crimes by donating half your wealth to the Public Assistance. You have until 10 o'clock, tomorrow evening, to execute my commands."

And it was signed: *JUDEX!*

There was the other delivering its dire warning.

"*If before the stroke of 10 tonight, you don't relinquish half of your ill-gotten fortune to the Public Assistance, it will be too late. You will be punished mercilessly.*"

Also signed: *JUDEX!*

Gripped by a feeling of dread, the young woman remembered the banker's collapse precisely as the clock struck 10.

"There can't be any doubt!" she cried tearfully. "My father fell victim to a shadowy conspiracy. My father was murdered!"

Until this day, Jacqueline had never doubted the financier's integrity. Like so many others, she had heard vague accusations and dismissed them as hateful lies and foolish slander. With a sense of foreboding, she wondered with a sense of foreboding if these rumors had a basis in facts. She began to challenge her earlier beliefs.

Was my father a thief and an assassin? Of course, he loved money. He was greedy for profits and merciless towards anyone who stood in the way of his projects. But could he have committed such horrendous crimes? No, no, it's impossible. Father, dear Father, forgive me for sullying your memories with baseless suspicions.

Striving to regain her normal composure, Jacqueline rang for a servant.

"Bontemps, did Vicomte de la Rochefontaine leave the Chateau?" asked Jacqueline.

"Yes, Madame. He left for Paris by car about a quarter of an hour ago."

"Tell Monsieur Vallières that I want to talk to him."

Some moments later, Favraux's secretary appeared in front of Jacqueline.

Pale and silent, the banker's daughter stared at the secretary. Her sad eyes implored him to help her. The sincerity and even benevolence expressed by Vallières' face reassured her immediately. She energetically sought his counsel.

"Monsieur Vallières, my father esteemed you greatly. The day before of his death, he told me how you were highly recommended to him by his friend, William Simpson of New York. I have complete confidence in you." She presented the two Judex letters. "Here is what a confidential investigator has brought me. Read."

"Monsieur Favraux had made me aware of these," revealed the secretary.

"You knew?"

"Yes, Madame. I must add that your father viewed these letters as insignificant."

"And yet," shouted Jacqueline, "he succumbed exactly at the time predicted by them!"

"That is true!"

"I don't want to be bothered by uncertainty. I ask you to accompany me to police headquarters."

"Madame, do you want me to advise you frankly?"

"I will listen."

"Don't go to the Prefecture."

"Why?"

"Don't force me to explain."

"Au contraire," resumed Jacqueline, "I need this information."

"You were satisfied to mourn your father without delving into his past."

"His past!" cried Jacqueline. "Are the implied accusations in these letters true? Why were the existence of these two messages hidden from me? Why all this mystery? Monsieur Vallières, in the name of Heaven, speak!"

"Madame…," said the secretary quaking with emotion.

"You're torturing me horribly!" screamed Jacqueline. She burst into tears. "Tell me that my father is innocent! I beg you! In the name of my son, swear to me that there's not a word of truth in these accusations!"

Vallières sadly lowered his head before giving his answer.

"Alas, Madame, the accusations are true!"

VI. Revelations of the Secret Files

Burdened by this new knowledge, Jacqueline fell on a couch ready to faint.

"Madame!" exclaimed Vallières. "Why did you force me to reveal these things?"

The young woman called upon all powers of resilience to reply.

"Don't leave! I'll recover. Don't blame yourself, Monsieur Vallières. You were right. Yes, you were right to warn me. Now, finish! I want all to know all. It's my right and my duty!"

"In that case, Madame, please come with me," said Vallières offering his arm to Jacqueline. He escorted her to the banker's study.

While the young woman sat down in her father's sanctum, Vallières approached a sculptured woodwork decorating a wall panel. He touched a secret spring inside. The panel moved disclosing a secret compartment in the wall.

"This is where Monsieur Favraux concealed his confidential documents," declared the secretary. "Only a short while ago, he revealed to me the existence of this hiding place. He made me swear to burn all the papers if he died. I was going to do so, Madame, the moment you summoned me."

Jacqueline found the courage to study minutely the voluminous file that Vallières deposited in front of her. It contained the indisputable proof that Favraux's criminal maneuvers had cleverly provoked the crash of Continental Consortium, the bankruptcy of Universal Revenue, the failure of Delta Phosphates, and the arson at the docks of New-City. The dossier documented several thousands of ruined families, many suicides and even the death of more than 100 workers by fire.

"You knew all this, Monsieur Vallières?" asked the sobbing Madame Aubry. "How could you, an honest man, remain my father's secretary?"

Reacting to these words, a strange glimmer appeared in Vallières' eyes. Bowing his head, he replied in a choked voice.

"I wasn't always an honest man."

Disturbed by this abyss of infamy engulfing her, Jacqueline had a simple request.

"Leave me, Monsieur Vallières."

"Madame," said the secretary, "this will always remain a secret between us."

With the melancholy of a man without anything to hope for on Earth, he prepared to depart.

Jacqueline delayed the secretary's departure.

"Monsieur," she said with admirable dignity, "the honesty which you recently shown erases any sins committed in the past."

Vallières leaned forward. Two distant tears appeared in the far corner of his eyes. More bent than usual, he left.

The banker's daughter gave free rein to all his despair.

"Thus," she said to herself, "the father whom I loved and feared, who appeared so superior to the public, was only a miserable man responsible for the ruination and death of countless innocents! This fortune left to me and my son was baptized by blood and tears! What an abomination! I shall hear continually the echoing curses and cries of his victims. Already they scream at me: 'All this gold isn't yours or your father's. It's ours. Your father stole it!'"

A cry of sorrow escaped her,

"My son! My beloved Jean!"

An even more horrendous fear devoured her thoughts.

Judex! Is this man so powerful that he can strike at a fixed time in the middle of a party? Was there nothing that my father could do to avert his destiny? Who knows his plans? Following his trail of vengeance, he might strike at me or even my child? It doesn't matter! I am prepared for anything! But my child! Have mercy on him! Have mercy on him!

A monstrous thought vibrated though her mind.

Did my father have mercy for the innocent? Mon Dieu! *How to divert the sword suspended over our heads? How to forestall Judex?*

Jacqueline's face froze in terror until a mystical fervor illuminated her eyes. A sublime determination shattered her fears. The flimsy and distraught creature was transformed miraculously into a vibrant woman full of nobility and courage. Seizing the secret files, she squeezed them against her chest and took them into her room.

"I know what must be done!" she shouted.

VII. Ill-gotten Gains

In his bachelor's quarters at of the Rue de Prony, the handsome Amaury de la Rochefontaine reclined on a divan. Smoking a perfumed khedive, he was enraptured by his delightful prospects. Convinced that the banker's death only delayed his marriage a few weeks, Amaury conceived magnificent projects. In the selfishness of his hedonistic existence, he had exiled Jacqueline's charming image to a nebulous region of his mind. Incapable of caring about his fiancée' hardships, his contemplations were interrupted by the ringing telephone.

Nonchalantly, Amaury rose and picked up the receiver.

"Hello!" he yelled impatiently into the device. His voice quickly softened. "My sweet Jacqueline, how are you?... Still sad. I understand... You want me to come over right away to Les Sablons?... You know that I am always at your beck and call... Nothing serious, I hope?... You can't tell me now... I'll rush!"

Hanging up the phone, Amaury became concerned. He wondered what had happened. Jacqueline's contracted voice suggested that she had just learned of some catastrophe. If her son was sick, she would have mentioned it. For the first time since the banker's demise, the Vicomte became worried. Could she have changed her mind about their marriage?

Using the telephone, Vicomte de la Rochefontaine asked his club to provide a car to drive him directly to Les Sablons.

Jacqueline received him in a small parlor. Her ravaged expression revealed all to the Vicomte.

"Some calamity has happened," he said. "Jacqueline, my darling... Is it your little Jean?"

"Jean's fine," reassured Jacqueline. "Amaury, you love me, don't you?"

"Do I love you!" exclaimed the Vicomte with great emotion. "Your father's tragic death has only intensified my feelings for you."

"Thank you." Jacqueline continued in a hushed voice. "Now listen carefully. I've just made a horrible discovery. I've received irrefutable documents. They are now hidden in a place known only to me. Yesterday, I learned that my father won his fortune by illicit, even criminal, means.

"No longer will I prosper from money illegally obtained. I have decided to relinquish my inheritance to the Public Assistance. Maître Vigneron, my solicitor, is here, accompanied by two witnesses. They're waiting in the salon for me to sign a document of donation. As for my son's portion of my father's legacy, I have no right to dispose of it. It shall remain in a trust administered by the solicitor. When Jean attains his majority, I shall inform him of the reasons that provoked my decision. It's my firm hope that he will refuse such ill-gotten gains and give them to the poor. Amaury, this is what I needed to tell you!"

Listening to this noble declaration that demolished his selfish plans, Vicomte de la Rochefontaine became pale. He formulated a plan to advance his interests.

"My dear Jacqueline, I accede to your generosity. I applaud your intentions. Nevertheless, will you allow me to give some friendly advice?"

"Speak!"

"Before finalizing this grave decision, you should take time to reflect. After all, you are not responsible for your father's errors. It's unfair to benefit strangers by stripping yourself of your entire fortune."

"Collected in filth and shame!" interrupted Jacqueline. "Monsieur de la Rochefontaine, how can you imagine for a single instant that I could preserve the least bit of such an inheritance? I want no part of it!"

"I beg you, calm down!"

"Calm down! I expected a different response from you. I felt that you would tell me: 'What you're doing is right. I love you more than ever. I want to be your companion for life.' Instead, after expressing disappointment and almost anger about the millions about to elude your grasp, you dare to dissuade me from an act that would make me a woman of stainless integrity and a mother above reproach!"

"Jacqueline!"

"Desist, Monsieur! I have taken your sincerity into account. You only wanted this fortune that I disavow. Despite any infamy attached to it, you would have accepted it. You never loved me."

"Madame!"

"I only accepted your proposal to placate my intimidating father. With a feeling of great relief, I return your pledge and your liberty."

"Listen to me…"

"Not a word, Monsieur. I beg you! I leave you without malice. You are already forgotten!"

Jacqueline went inside in the salon where the solicitor waited. Her face fervently reflected the total acceptance of her grand sacrifice. Approaching the table where Maître Vigneron had placed the act of donation, the banker's daughter with a steady hand surrendered all her wealth to the poor.

Crazed with anger, Amaury left the estate.

VIII Towards the Unknown

Without delay, Jacqueline had resolved to abandon the Chateau des Sablons. Once the solicitor had left, she assembled her servants. She affectionately thanked each of them for their long service. Giving them severance pay, she dismissed them. When she conferred with Vallières, the secretary renewed his sincere pledge of absolute discretion before withdrawing. Jacqueline bade a courteous farewell to Marie Verdier whose conduct seemed above reproach. The banker's daughter regretted the circumstances forcing their separation. Presenting a modest demeanor, the governess sadly replied with a few banal pleasantries. Once she crossed the threshold of the parlor, however, cruel resentment enveloped her face.

The most painful moment had come for Jacqueline. She met with her old footman, Bontemps, and his daughter Marianne, formerly Jean's wet nurse. Jacqueline talked to them with touching simplicity.

"My dear Bontemps, you told that your savings allowed the purchase of a small country house outside Paris. Do you and your daughter intend to retire there?"

"Yes, Madame."

"I'm ruined, completely ruined. I have no money. I must find work."

"Is this possible?"

"I'm not frightened for myself. However, I won't be able to support my son anymore. I implore you to take him with you. I'm making an extreme sacrifice by separating myself from the son whom I love more than life. It is regrettable but necessary! Listen to me, Bontemps and Marianne. More than anything, I want my son to be an honest man. He can't be in better hands than yours. I entrust him to you. I thank you in advance for what you shall do for him."

"Believe me, Madame," asserted Bontemps, "we are very touched."

"Yes," declared Marianne nearly collapsing into tears.

"Do you accept?"

"With all our hearts," said Bontemps. "You can count on us. We love this dear child. He's so sweet, so good, and so beautiful!"

Jacqueline felt her heart about to break.

"Take him as early as tonight. That will be best. As soon as I find lodging, I'll mail you my address. I will go to see him often. You will raise him for me, won't you?"

"Yes, Madame," said Marianne. She was saddened by the plight of her mistress.

Courageous to the end, Jacqueline finished.

''Maître Vigneron will send you a periodic remittance to pay for my son's upbringing. Come closer. Kiss me, Marianne, and you too, Bontemps. You are my true friends."

Her son had been playing in a neighboring room. Calling him, Jacqueline placed him on her knee. She concealed the emotional pain that tormented her.

"My darling, I'm forced to take a trip."

"Will you take me with you, Mama?" asked the boy.

"No, my dear child, it's impossible."

"Will you be gone long?"

"A few days only. During that time, you will live in the country with Bontemps and Marianne."

"You'll be happy with us, Monsieur Jean," promised Marianne. "You'll have lots of fun. There's a small donkey with a pretty cart."

"A small donkey!" said the child with the charming excitement of his age. "I want to go right away. Right away. You'll let me, Mama?"

"Yes, yes, my angel. Go, enjoy your self. Be happy."

She hugged him against her breast for one last time.

"I love you! I bless you!"

She turned towards Bontemps and his daughter.

"Take him. I can't delay any longer. Enough! I'll see you soon!"

Alone in the Chateau, the banker's daughter prepared her departure. She drew on her heroic resolve to see this task to the end. As the evening arrived, she was ready to go to the train station.

A ring resounded in the small parlor. The young woman wondered who was telephoning at this hour. Picking up the receiver, she listened.

"My daughter! My daughter! Forgive me!"

Her face contorted. She nearly screamed. Jacqueline had just heard the voice of his father!

Convinced that she was the victim of a horrible hallucination, she fled through the large empty rooms into the park. Disappearing under the trees, she shrank little by little into the night closing around her.

At an early hour of the next day, a young woman in mourning clothes carried a suitcase along a deserted street of Neuilly. Panting as she walked, the woman suffered oppressively from fatigue. At several points, she had to stop in order to regain her breath.

Suddenly, a shadow appeared. Its mysterious origin was impossible to explain. This shapeless entity relentlessly attached itself to her trail This bizarre being stopped when she stopped.

Was it a guardian angel from Heaven? Was it a herald of further misfortune and disaster? What was this mysterious shadow?

30 Centimes   Tous les Jeudis

LES ROMANS CINÉMA

JUDEX

Par ARTHUR BERNÈDE et LOUIS FEUILLADE

DEUXIÈME ÉPISODE

L'EXPIATION

Part Two: The Atonement

I. The Piano Teacher

"A letter for you, Madame Bertin."

"Thank you, Madame Chapuis."

"How are you feeling this morning? Not well? Your eyes are very red. You must have cried again last night."

"No, I slept very well."

"It isn't necessary to deceive me, my child. You're full of sorrow, you poor girl."

Holding herself extremely erect, Madame Chapuis, an affable 40 year-old woman, gazed benevolently at the younger woman. Clothed in an austere black dress, the other woman stood behind the opened door of her bedroom.

"You've only been my lodger for a short while," observed Madame Chapuis. "You don't need to hide things from me. I know that you're an honest lady, and I won't trouble you any longer."

"You are very kind," replied the young woman.

"I have to answer the telephone now! Good-bye, my child, and be brave."

The young lady closed the door. Her room was austere and clean. Sitting at a table, she unsealed the letter and read:

Dear Madame,

We're very happy in our new home. Jean is having a wonderful time. The first few nights, he cried and asked for his Mama, but we consoled him by promising to take him to see you. He joyfully dance when I read him your letter. I had to give it to him. He keeps it close to his heart! He is truly an Angel of the Lord. We're happy that you've settled in a nice boarding house in Neuilly and that you're giving piano and English lessons. In any case, Madame, you can rely completely on our devotion and our discretion.

My father joins me in giving you our regards.
MARIANNE BONTEMPS.
The Orchard
Loisy (Seine-et-Oise).

These lines were followed by a postscript. It was awkwardly printed in large letters:

Marianne holds my hand to make these words. I want to see you soon, my one true Mama.

Your son that loves you,

Jean

The woman kissed the naive scrawl. Her eyes stared at the portrait of her son.

"My cherished Jeannot," she murmured. "I love you! You are my life, my beloved son!"

Consoled by maternal love, the woman put on a modest hat with a veil. Grabbing a portfolio of music, she left after blowing a long kiss to the radiant picture of his child. She went out on the street. Walking briskly, she suddenly stopped. A name escaped her lips.

"Monsieur Vallières!"

A man of about 60 approached her. He held his hat to the hand in an attitude of affectionate deference.

"Madame, forgive me for bothering you. This meeting is a surprise. I was performing an errand in this neighborhood. I never expected to run into you. How are you and your son?"

"My son is in the country with the Bontemps family," replied Jean's mother. "As for myself, I'm doing as well as possible. What about you, Monsieur?"

"Luckily, I found a new position. It's far less lucrative than the one that I occupied with your father."

"Monsieur Vallières, you were a loyal friend under rather difficult circumstances. I shall never forget that! As far as the world is concerned, Jacqueline Aubry, the daughter of the banker Favraux, no longer exists. She has been replaced by Madame Bertin, piano teacher and English tutor. I held to my principles. I work for a living. Pride hasn't destroyed my happiness."

"You are the noblest woman whom I've ever knew," asserted Vallières bowing respectfully in front of Jacqueline.

"Excuse me, Monsieur Vallières, I have an appointment, and I don't want to be late. Visit me when you have the time. I reside in Neuilly, 10 Impasse Saint-Ferdinand. Not a word to anyone else, I implore you."

"Your wishes shall be respected. I promise."

The banker's daughter continued along the road. Absorbed in the alarming memories that her encounter with Vallières had just reawakened, she hadn't noticed the young man following her. With an elegant physique and an aristocratic walk, his pretentious haughtiness suggested a narrow-minded shallowness.

The moment Jacqueline reached Avenue Neuilly, the stranger accelerated as if he wanted to pass her. Realizing that he shouldn't approach the woman openly in the street, he halted. Contemplating her with a look of unhealthy passion, this shallow creature proceeded to the streetcar station of the Saint-Germain-Porte-Maillot line. In a moment of insolent self-conceit, he muttered under his breath:

"She shall make a charming mistress."

Locating a car parked at the corner of Rue Saint-Pierre, he talked urgently to a chauffeur in an impeccable maroon coat with gold buttons bearing the image of a marquis' crown.

"Teddy, go to the Rue de Varennes, and be quick."

Resting on the gray cushions in the back seat of the car, the stranger made a promise to himself.

"Even though it will take time and money, this woman shall be mine!"

II. The "King of Petticoats"

The individual who had just cynically decreed Jacqueline's conquest (or rather disgrace) was none other than Marquis César de Birargues, Vice-President of the Polo Club, Treasurer of the Sports and Arts Circle, golf champion, prince of the tennis court, and "King of Petticoats."

All these titles did not prevent him from being an unbearable elitist and the most useless person on Earth.

The Duc de Birargues, his father, was an exemplary gentleman. He had vainly sought to arouse in his son's soul the family traditions of honor and chivalry. The Duchesse, a noble woman of admirable virtue and captivating charms, had also tried to reform him with sound advice.

Reaching his majority, César had left the sumptuous abode in the Faubourg Saint-Germain occupied by the Birargues since the 17th century. Installing himself at a luxurious apartment in the Avenue Henri-Martin, he enjoyed for two years a dissipated existence, interrupted occasionally by a rare visit to his relatives.

To his sister's surprise, the Marquis visited her at 10 o'clock in the morning. Gisèle de Birargues received her brother in the vast salon where she had been practicing chromatic arrangements and arpeggios on her magnificent piano.

"*Bonjour*, César!" said the pretty Gisèle. She ran to kiss her brother. Blind to his scandalous life, she could only judge him through the virginal clarity of her soul.

"*Bonjour*, darling," replied the tennis champion. "You're studying. I should leave."

"No, stay" begged the kindly Gisèle. "We meet so rarely. I wouldn't ignore you even for Beethoven or Mozart."

César sought to ingratiate himself with his sister.

"I am even more flattered since you love music."

"It's a most admirable art."

"How are you progressing?"

"Madame Bertin commends my playing."

"Madame Bertin?" questioned the "King of Petticoats" with the hypocrisy of a rake.

"My new teacher," explained Gisèle. "I'm waiting for her arrival. She'll be pleased to tell you about my progress. She's very sweet."

"I have a pressing engagement," asserted César de Birargues.

"Please remain a while," insisted Gisèle. "I have much to show you. Madame Bertin is a very distinguished person. She supposedly once had a large fortune. Abbé Villetot, the curé of Saint-Philippe-du-Roule, recommended her. You should learn the piano. If you hire her as your tutor, it would be to your benefit. For this young lady is extremely talented."

"Piano lessons are not my forte," replied the "King of Petticoats" pretending indifference.

A door was opened by a chambermaid. "Madame Bertin," she announced. Jacqueline entered. Gisèle gracefully performed the introductions.

"My brother, Marquis César de Birargues... Madame Bertin, my teacher."

César was deferential in his greeting. "My sister, Madame, speaks highly of you. I'm very glad to make your acquaintance."

"Mademoiselle Gisèle has known me only a short time," said the banker's daughter. "I fear that she exaggerates my merits."

"*Au contraire*," protested César, "my sister is not mistaken. Every hour that you're here allows her to discover more of your precious qualities."

At this compliment, somewhat direct for a first meeting, Jacqueline reddened slightly. After curtseying with a discreet ease that revealed a worldly education, she deposited her music portfolio on the piano.

"And now, my lesson!" joyfully proclaimed Mademoiselle de Birargues.

"Should I leave?" asked César.

"Not at all!" decreed Gisèle.

"Then let's begin," said the banker's daughter gracefully.

Jacqueline had studied music at the Conservatory. She showed herself not only an excellent teacher, but also a versatile artist. Her talents exacerbated the passion already inside César.

The lesson almost was finished when the chambermaid announced that Baronne d'Orsel wanted to talk to Mademoiselles Gisèle on the telephone.

"This is for our charity sale," declared Gisèle. "You'll permit me, Madame Bertin?"

"Certainly, Mademoiselle."

"My brother will keep you company."

Scarcely had she left that César, unable to restrain himself, openly revealed his amorous intentions to Jacqueline.

"Madame, you may think me the most awkward and insane of men, but I can no longer conceal the feelings that you inspire in me."

Upon receiving this brutal and unexpected declaration, Jacqueline's response was to reject it.

"Monsieur," she stammered rising from her chair, "cease from making such a vicious joke..."

She didn't finish. Yielding to the natural enthusiasm of his lust, César seized the young woman forcefully. He ranted his shameless passion.

"Listen to me; I implore you! The first time that I saw you arriving at this house, I was so enraptured that I waited until you left. I secretly followed you to Neuilly. Yes, to the very door of the boarding house where you live in a room unfit for even a common laborer. Without your knowledge, I regularly observed your movements. I have experienced with you the Hellish existence of a penniless woman supporting herself in Paris. Your quiet courage and your touching resignation only intensified my feelings. For I love you, Madame. I love you to a point that I don't know how to express myself. I've become mad. I've lost my mind. Since the prejudices of my class prevent me from bestowing my name upon you, I beg you to listen to me. Let me assure your happiness by becoming your lover."

Maintaining her honest serenity, Jacqueline had silently endured the fiery speech of the aristocratic seducer. Only after César had finished did she react. No longer talking with her naturally mellow voice, she spoke with icy contempt.

"Are you a gentleman, Monsieur de Birargues?"

"Of a proud and ancient line."

"Then, why do you behave like a boor?"

"What are you saying?" shouted César. He was enraged by this virulent insult.

"I'm saying that you have abused my subordinate position to make an outrageous proposal in your parents' house. Your conduct is unworthy of a true gentleman."

"Don't be stubborn! Yield to me!"

"Withdraw, Monsieur, or I shall leave!"

Intimidated by the natural authority expressed in Jacqueline's speech, César Birargues retreated.

"I shall desist, Madame, but nothing will prevent from thinking about you. I can still hope."

Gisèle returned smiling. Resuming instantly to his usual demeanor, César defused the situation.

"It's time for me to leave, little sister. The short time that I passed with Madame Bertin has increased my desire to know her better." His lips formed a sinister smile before his departure.

Gisèle sat down at the piano. She played the first arrangements of Werther's *Clair de Lune*, which Jules Massenet, the great lyricist, believed to be the divine fulfillment of human kindness. As the music flowed forth, the student gleefully smiled. Jacqueline's face reflected sorrow as she leaned over the keyboard. When tears fell on the white keys, Gisèle raised her head.

Dismayed by her mentor's sorrow, Gisèle instinctively placed her arms around Jacqueline's neck. The young student looked firmly into the distressed eyes of her instructor.

"What's wrong, Madame?"

"I was thinking about my son!" said Jacqueline as her head fell on her pupil's shoulder.

After running errands all day long, Jacqueline returned to Neuilly around 7 o'clock in the evening. Before going to her landlady's dining-room, she entered her room. Opening the door, she was greeted by a surprise. In the middle of the table was a wicker cage with two white pigeons cooing benevolently. The young woman removed a letter attached to the bars of the cage. Reading it, she was plunged into a state of depression:

Madame, if someone threatens you, free these pigeons. I will rush to your rescue. I watch over you!

JUDEX

"Again Judex!" muttered the banker's daughter. "What is this new mystery? If I only knew! What good would knowing do? Much better to forget! My guilty father suffered a terrible punishment. I can only pray for his soul. This unknown judge, my father's persecutor, today pretends to be my defender, but I don't want anything from him. No matter what happens, these birds will remain forever confined in their cage."

Jacqueline gazed kindly on the two pigeons who both gracefully beat their wings.

"It's odd! I feel at peace."

Voluntarily resigned to her current existence, she clasped her hands in prayer.

"Thank you, my God. My son is happy. I don't have the right to ask you for anything more!"

III. Singular Individuals

In the late hours the night after the funeral of the banker Favraux, an automobile with its headlights off stopped opposite the small cemetery of Les Sablons.

Two men quickly alighted. One was a tall man draped in an ample black cloak. His aristocratic profile invoked an unyielding tenacity. He wore a soft felt hat with its brim raised in a cavalier style. His smaller companion, a wiry man with a sturdy and muscular frame, wore an elegant, gray velvet suit. A cap of the same hue crowned a face reflecting both fervent youth and precocious maturity.

"Roger," said the hushed voice of the first man, "are you sure that we weren't followed?"

"Absolutely sure."

"Did you forget anything?"

"Nothing, Jacques."

"Then proceed!"

The road was deserted. No sounds escaped the countryside. Large clouds veiled the Moon and the stars. Barely 200 meters in the distance, isolated houses revealed the sleeping presence of a town.

Choosing from an elaborate ring of skeleton keys, the man in the black cloak unlocked the cemetery gate. His companion carried a yellow leather satchel and a long narrow package wrapped in green serge. The duo penetrated the place of eternal rest.

The two mysterious individuals made a swift salute to the departed, a sign that they weren't common burglars or filthy grave robbers. Without any further hesitation, they advanced towards a small chapel containing the Favraux family vault.

Using a second selection from the collection of skeleton keys to open the door, they secretly worked inside the mortuary monument. At the conclusion of an hour, they departed carrying a body wrapped in a white shroud. They carefully deposited it in the back seat of their car.

The man in the gray velvet suit returned to the cemetery where he remained a long while. Having retrieved his satchel and package, he returned to the car and addressed his seated comrade.

"Everything's in order. No one will suspect anything."

"Let's leave!" said the man in the black cloak curtly. He apparently was his associate's superior.

After cranking up the motor, Roger jumped into the car. Grabbing the steering wheel, he maneuvered the car with the quiet skill of an accomplished driver.

An hour later, the vehicle stopped at the foot of a hill dominating the valley of the Seine. The hill was surmounted by the ruins of an ancient and vast abode. In the tradition of the bloody dramas that unfolded during the Middle Ages, this structure was named the Chateau Rouge.

The car was secreted in a garage concealed under a thick coat of ivy. Operated by a hidden mechanism, its metallic door could withstand any assault. Gifted with remarkable physical vigor, Jacques and Roger removed the corpse, They ascended the craggy path that ended in the imposing remnants of an antique feudal den.

The duo crossed several sections of crumbling walls and broken arches where many crows nested. Finally, they arrived in front of a crevice where sturdy pillars of granite supported a heavy solid arch that had originally sheltered the basements of the castle.

One of the men leaned on a concealed spring. A wide flagstone tipped open revealing the uprights of an iron ladder. Solidly set against the wall, the ladder led downward into the Earth. After Jacques and Roger entered with their burden, the flagstone automatically closed behind them.

"Brother," said Roger, "you are resolved to restore life to this miserable cur?"

"Perhaps," enigmatically replied the man in the black cloak.

In the distance, an owl flew madly among the ruins. It hooted ominously.

The next evening, the duo was in a vast luminous laboratory worthy of an expert chemist. Surrounded by elaborate electrical devices and scientific instruments, Jacques and Roger examined Favraux's body. The shrouded banker was spread inertly on an easel serving as an operating table.

"Is everything ready?" asked Jacques whose face generated mystical authority,

"Yes, brother," said Roger.

"You believe that he can be resurrected?"

"I'm sure!"

"Well?"

Roger hesitated before responding.

"Why do you want to reverse the punishment that this wretch deserved a hundredfold? You should have let him awaken inside his sealed coffin. Why permit his eyes to see daylight again? Why should his lungs freely inhale the pure air of life?"

"Because it must be done!"

"Remember our oath!"

"Roger," solemnly declared the older of the two brothers. His black cloak, buttoned to the collar, generated the legendary allure of a hero. "My friend, my brother, I entreat you. For now, don't question me. Soon you'll know, and you'll approve! Before that time, I take full responsibility! Revive this man!"

With nothing more to say, Roger moved towards a glass cabinet. Choosing a flask of milky liquid, he filled a Pravaz syringe. Seizing the frozen arm of Favraux, Roger gave it a strong injection.

Ten minutes passed before the banker gave the least sign of life. Slowly in unperceivable jolts, the heart began to beat once more. The blood circulated again. A long sigh exhaled from his mouth. The eyelids opened and closed many times as a lifeless flicker grew into a vague glimmer. The brain regained awareness.

Favraux didn't remember anything, but he began to perceive his surroundings. The haughty outline of Jacques became more and more distinct in this enigmatic milieu. Vaguely feeling that he had awakened from a dreamless sleep, Jacqueline's father finally stammered with a stiff voice.

"Where am I?"

"In my power," answered Jacques.

"Who are you?"

"I am Judex!"

Hearing this name, the banker gave a cry of terror. He remembered the frightful minute when his body failed him, the toast to the betrothed, the clock striking 10, and finally the nothingness of the void. He had died! Now suddenly, he was alive. He was face to face with his executioner! Judex!

He wanted to attack, but the powerful grip of Roger quickly immobilized him. After leaning on an electric button, Jacques placed in the banker's face a telephone device connected to a secret line.

"Favraux!" ordered Jacques. "Beg your daughter for forgiveness!"

"No, no... leave me alone," foamed the banker. "This is a trap. A monstrous outrage. You don't have the right!"

"Beg your daughter for forgiveness!" insisted the implacable judge.

The banker's will was overwhelmed by the force of his captor's personality. Hypnotized by the flame shining in Judex's eyes, the financier was rendered powerless. He yelled in the useless vehemence of despair:

"My daughter! My daughter! Forgive me!"

Jacqueline had been wrong in believing that she was the victim of a horrible hallucination. It was indeed her father who had spoken that night!

IV. The Verdict

The banker was morally crushed by this tremendous ordeal. Broken physically by his efforts to release himself, Favraux again lost consciousness. How long had he been deprived of any notion of life? When he recovered his senses, he had been incapable of determining the duration.

He was spread on a cot in a narrow penitentiary cell with a strong oak door and a barred window. Even stranger, he was clothed in a statutory uniform of a convict.

I am lost, he thought. *This man holds me. He will never release me.*

An immense sigh inflated his chest. A hoarse cry escaped three times from lips covered with a bloody foam.

"Judex! Judex! Judex!"

Falling back on his bed, the banker, was haunted by desire for freedom and his excessive passion for Marie Verdier. He remember her large eyes and seductive voice. He then had a flash of hope.

Who knows? Perhaps these people don't want to punish me for my crimes? They could have confined me to extort money.

Ignorant that everyone, except his two jailers, believed him to be resting in a grave in the cemetery of Les Sablons, the financier analyzed his plight.

Yes! that must be the truth. All these melodramatic gimmicks were created solely to intimidate me. These masters of fear want to deprive me of the resources which a wealthy man possesses even in the most secured prison. We shall see. If this is a question of ransom, I'm ready to discuss it. I'll pay a million... two... even three if necessary. I'll recover my money by force afterwards. But I'll leave here alive!

From the other side of the wall, the prisoner heard defiant laughter. The sinister mirth mocked him. Favraux knew the laughing persecutor was without pity. Jacqueline's father quivered as the sound filled his ears. Getting up from his cot, he inspected his cell. Soon he recoiled with fright. His throat dried . His forehead burst with sweat. At the top of the wall, above an outfitted table containing a water jar and a sandstone bowl, was a metallic mirror. Maneuvered by an invisible hand. it served as an electronic eye that never allowed him a solitary moment of respite. The mirror would follow all his movements including his minutest gestures. It would be impossible to escape its unending supervision.

The banker roared like a stalked beast. He understood that this mirror was there to allow his tormentors to feast on his suffering. The fiends were reveling in his slow agony!

His complex captivity consisted of a new torture in which a prisoner is weighed down by a jailer's constant surveillance day and night. Stripped of any human contact, the inmate wasn't even permitted the consolation of solitary meditation. Forbidden any form of comfort, he was consumed by the bitterness of despair!

In a crisis of proud fury, Favraux rebelled against this new ordeal.

"No! No! Not that! Not that!"

Seizing a towel on the table, he stood on his toes and covered up the mirror. The linen flared up as a flame quickly incinerated it. Drunk with rage, the banker jumped forward in a tremendous leap towards the mirror in order to seize it and smash it into pieces. A strong electrical current repelled him. For the second time, there arouse the diabolical laughter that caused the banker to shudder with terror.

"This is Hell!" stammered Jacqueline's father with a grimace of the cursed.

A scream erupted from his throat. From the wall opposite him came a crackling sound. Fiery letters appeared on the wall section close to the door:

Banker Favraux,

I had condemned you to death. Your daughter's generous donation of her inheritance to the Public Assistance, saved your life; but I condemn you to eternal imprisonment.

JUDEX!

"Eternal imprisonment!" repeated the gilded merchant gashing his teeth.

Favraux grasp fully the horror of his position. His crimes were being punished by a self-anointed judge. Misery overpowered the banker. He could not doubt anymore. He could not hope anymore. He wasn't the hostage of bold outlaws ready to release him for ransom. The sole mission of his unknown tormentor was vengeance!

I'm finished, thought the desolate banker. *No more haggling. No possible escape. This is my jail for eternity. Impri-*

soned for life between these four walls and under the gaze of that terrible mirror.

He began crying. This gilded thief cried not from remorse. This unscrupulous banker cried in anger. He cried for his lost life of luxury and power. He cried for the woman he desired. She inspired morbid passions sufficient to pervert nobler hearts. Rarely in his confusion did he stop to the think about the daughter sacrificed for his greedy appetites. For a moment, the exquisite picture of the charming Jean purified his tears. But it was only a flash. Selfishly his thoughts returned almost immediately to his own plight.

Shaking his fist towards the wall where the letters of fire had materialized, he shouted before collapsing to the ground.

"Judex! Judex! I know now why you didn't kill me!"

In the laboratory, Judex left the electric machine that allowed him to project the verdict into Favraux's cell. He rejoined his brother. Thanks to the movable mirror that Roger maneuvered using a hand-lever in a concentric arch, both of them could watch the gilded merchant. Prostrate on the flagstone floor, his shoulders shook convulsively without stop as he plunged into despair.

Judex solemnly leaned towards his companion.

"Well, Roger?"

"Brother, you were right," replied the young man cryptically. "*She* couldn't ask anything more from us!"

V. At the Callyx Bar

The Callyx Bar was situated in a street near the Place de La Madeleine. For years it had been a shrilly luxurious establishment in Paris. Operated by an unscrupulous owner and frequented by a shady clientele, it provided haven to the conspiracies of vagabonds and fugitives.

Its ultra-modern decor attracted hedonists in search of dubious companions. Delighting in the usage of hideous slang, these "good Parisians" romanced women of questionable virtue. Sitting on high stools, the female patrons drowned their moral misery in liquor.

Around 3 o'clock in the afternoon. the Callyx Bar was almost empty. In a remote corner was a handsome man whose age was between 28 and 30. His attire was of doubtful taste as demonstrated by his gaudy rings and over-sized tie. He sat at a table with a young brunette of rare beauty. Her dark eyes were plunged into a deep trance. The woman's remoteness was tolerated by her neighbor.

Distractedly, he grabbed a newspaper that someone had left on a stool. He scanned its pages with indifference. Suddenly, his attention piqued. His eyebrows contracted. His mouth opened in bitterness. Handing the tabloid to his companion, he pointed to a story on the first page.

"Read. This is very interesting."

Nervously the young woman seized the newspaper. Her eyes soon reflected savage hatred. Her lips stirred automatically repeating every word of the brief article.

"The death of the banker F. had a mysterious epilogue. Breaking her engagement with Monsieur de la R***, the daughter of the deceased financier disappeared after giving all her fortune to charity. It is rumored that she has entered a convent or left for America. What an enticing mystery!"

The dark beauty shrugged. "All that won't resurrect Favraux or give us his millions."

"What will we do in the interim?" asked the man visibly depressed.

"Our plan failed," continued Marie Verdier. "Favraux was totally infatuated with me! He was going to marry me, his grandson's governess! His will would have been rewritten to leave me millions! Six months later, I would have been a widow!"

She lustfully contemplated at her lover.

"We were so close to success!"

Instead, the ex-governess had returned the life she had led a year earlier. She was once more the glamorous Diana

Monti, the siren of the cosmopolitan nightclubs and the Mediterranean casinos.

"It's now a matter best forgotten," concluded the brunette. "For the moment, we must think of the future. You have an appointment here with Marquis César de Birargues?"

"He'll be here soon."

"Who is this Marquis?"

"A young egotist whom I've known for some time from the gambling circle of the Rue Washington. One night that he lost big, I had some extra cash, so I lent him 50 louis that he paid back the next day. We became friends. Knowing me as Baron Moralès, he's unaware of my true name and my police record. Pampered by his father, this bachelor is a reckless libertine. More importantly, he's colossally rich and stupid enough. If we cultivate him skillfully, we can swindle him out of a large sum."

"Perfect! Perfect!" exclaimed Diana.

"He told me the other evening," resumed Moralès, "that he was infatuated with a 'honest' lady who adopts a pose of unassailable virtue."

The gambler stopped talking. César de Birargues advanced towards him The aristocrat mitigated his natural impertinence by adopting an agreeable smile. Moralès greeted him with effusion.

"Dear Marquis, permit me to introduce you to my friend, Mademoiselle Diana Monti, the songstress whom I mentioned earlier."

"Mademoiselle, my compliments. I'm delighted to meet you." Staring at Diana behind his monocle, the "King of Petticoats" was an accomplished connoisseur of feminine beauty.

"Please join us," said Diana.

While César sat opposite her, Moralès talked to him with unrestrained familiarity.

"Did you succeed in your romance?"

"That didn't go as planned," answered the "King of Petticoats" whose lack of judgment equaled his pride.

"Gentlemen," said Diana, "if you have to talk about intimate matters, allow me to withdraw."

César objected. "As the personal friend of Baron Moralès, I trust you just as I trust him."

Prompted by a quick glance from his mistress, the gambler took advantage of the situation.

"You're very wise, my friend. Diana can give you excellent advice."

"Let me confide in you," said César. Demonstrating the full extent of his brazenness, he told Diana and Moralès about his meeting with Jeanne Bertin. He concluded with a pompous declaration:

"You will tell me that I'm a complete idiot. It's quite possible that I'm behaving like a schoolboy in love. If this woman continues to reject me, my life will become absolutely unbearable."

"This woman is your sister's piano teacher?" asked Diana.

"Yes."

"How did your sister hear about her?"

"She was recommended by Abbé Villetot, the curé of Saint-Philippe-du-Roule. She also advertized in the newspapers."

"Where does she live?"

"10 Impasse Saint-Ferdinand, in Neuilly."

With an incredible composure, Diana made a proposal. "If you listen to me, Marquis, within 48 hours, this woman shall be yours."

"Is it possible?" wondered César.

"You can have confidence in Diana," injected Moralès. "She is an extraordinary woman."

"I'm convinced," acknowledged the "King of Petticoats." Nevertheless. I am anxious to know how Mademoiselle will do it."

"That will cost you 10,000 francs," cynically added Diana.

Diana thought it ironic that César de Birargues was completely stunned.

"You'll see how simple it is," explained Diana. "The woman will be kidnapped. Don't worry, it will be done gently by people whom I know. I vouch for their tact and discretion. We inform you where the woman is. You arrive. You rescue her. She thankfully embraces you as the curtain falls."

"You see!" argued Moralès, "It's easy."

César pensively hesitated. He was silently torn between fear of the consequences and his bold desire.

"Maybe," observed Moralès, "10,000 francs is too expensive for you?"

His vanity wounded, César balked.

"Not at all! This is not a question of money. But a kidnapping is a serious matter!"

"First, the lady's safety will be a priority," reassured Diana. "Second, everything will be handled so discreetly that your role as instigator of this plot will never be suspected. It's the only way to achieve you goal. It's a classic scenario. Nine times out of ten, it's successful. You would be foolish to refuse."

"I see your point."

"Such matter must be executed promptly," pressured Diana. "If you concur, everything could be done as early as tomorrow."

"As early as tomorrow?"

"If you accept, we will telephone you the location where the woman is held."

"I need to think this over."

Understanding that it would be foolish to rush things, the ex-governess consented. She extended her hand.

"Marquis, you can count on us."

Following her departure from Les Sablons, Diana had taken residence at her lover's apartment at the Avenue de Villiers. Around 10 o'clock that evening, Moralès received a letter:

60

My Dear Baron,

As stipulated, I enclose a check of 5000 francs for the execution of our project. You will be paid a similar sum upon delivery.

Cordially yours.

CÉSAR DE BIRARGUES

"And now," said Diana, "we have work to do!"

VI. Diana Monti

Around 4 o'clock in the afternoon, Jacqueline finished her lessons and returned to Neuilly. After blowing several kisses to Jean's portrait, she was feeding the two pigeons when there was a knock on the door,.

It was the gentle Madame Chapuis. She joyfully announced that a very fashionable lady had arrived downstairs. The visitor wanted to hire the alleged Madame Bertin to give piano lessons,

"I didn't want her to come up without checking with you first. She must be a wealthy person because she arrived in a fancy car."

"Madame, tell her that I'm available."

Shortly thereafter, Diana opened the door. Two names were uttered simultaneously.

"Mademoiselle Marie!"

"Madame Aubry!"

The banker's daughter extended her hand towards Jean's ex-governess. Diana was shocked to discover herself in the presence of Jacqueline.

"Mademoiselle Marie, I'm happy to see you! How did you learn my address? Only Monsieur Vallières and the Bontemps family know it, and I can't imagine them disclosing it."

Having regained her composure, Diana hypocritically adopted an affectionate pose.

"Dear Madame, please don't slander your friends. I didn't talk to either the Bontemps family or Monsieur Vallières. I am employed as a governess for a wealthy American family that recently settled in Paris. They asked me to find a piano teacher fluent in English for their children. Reading a newspaper advertisement, I decided to secure the services of a 'Madame Jeanne Bertin.' I'm pleasantly surprised to discover that it is you."

More determined than ever to fulfill her infamous contract, the adventuress continued to deceive her former employer.

"You can't imagine how much I bless the Providence that brought me here."

Moralès' mistress reached an even greater height of hypocrisy when she saw Jean's photograph.

"This adorable angel! Pardon me, Madame. I was so astonished that I forgot to ask you about him."

"He's doing fine, thank you." Jacqueline was completely fooled by her ex-governess.

Diana played her role with infinite skill.

"I'm happy to repay all the kindness that you showed me! My employers, the Hopskings, are extremely rich. You'll be able to charge them 20 francs an hour. Be assured that I'll respect your incognito. They will know nothing. I promise not tell anyone. The children are excellent students. They're very kind. They'll be delighted to know you. Dear Madame, I have a request: may I kiss you?"

Jacqueline gave her permission. After receiving the kiss of treachery, the banker's daughter heartily expressed her spontaneous congeniality.

"Mademoiselle Marie, I shall never forget this recent proof of your affection."

"Isn't this wonderful?"

"When will you take me to your employers?"

"Right away. The Hopskings reside in Auteuil. We can be there in half an hour. Everything's arranged. Come!"

Taken aback by the sudden proposal of the adventuress, Jacqueline hesitated.

"Let's go, Madame, or I'll remove you by force," said Diana, pretending to be joking.

"In that case, I'm yours," agreed Jacqueline. Ironically, she was full of gratitude towards the deceitful trickster who was leading her like a lamb to the slaughter.

Dressed as an elegant sportsman, Moralès waited on the sidewalk. When Diana and Jacqueline appeared, he advanced towards them with his cap in hand.

"Madame Jeanne Bertin," said the adventuress, "this is Monsieur James Hopskings. He kindly consented to accompany me."

The anxious Moralès helped the young teacher climb in the luxurious limousine parked in front of the Chapuis boarding-house.

Diana sat close to Jacqueline. Moralès sat behind the wheel. The car quickly passed the Bois de Boulogne, crossed the Avenue de Longchamp, and reached the Lakes road. Instead of continuing along the road, the chauffeur forked to the right in order to enter a deserted avenue.

Diana then jumped on Jacqueline and pushed a wad of chloroform against her nose and mouth. The unfortunate woman didn't have the time to cry out. She vainly tried to resist. Diana held her while the narcotic did its work. She was soon nothing more than an inert lump.

The triumphant Diana savagely kissed her lover. "Do you know who this woman is?" she asked.

"No."

"This is Jacqueline Aubry, the daughter of the banker Favraux!"

"Did she recognize you?"

"She recognized me."

"And you still want to go through with this?"

"Be quiet! Now that we embarked on this journey," giggled the adventuress, "we must reach our final destination!"

"Papa Julian, when is Sunday?"

"In four days, my child."

"And I won't see Mama before then?"

"Alas, no, Jeannot."

"Why can't she come earlier?"

"Because she works, the poor sweet lady!"

"Yes, but why can't you take me to see her?"

Filling a horse-drawn cart with cabbages, Bontemps explained:

"My darling angel, we also have a lot of work. Don't fret, four days shall pass quickly."

"Four days! Four days!" repeated the boy counting on his fingers. Two tears formed in his soft eyes. "My poor dear Mama!"

For the rest of the afternoon, despite the repeated efforts of Bontemps and his daughter to cheer him up, Jeannot remained sad. Only after going to go to bed did he regain his childish joy. As Marianne maternally tucked him in after delivering a kiss, Jeannot's eyes filled with mischievous enthusiasm. Closing his eyelids, he appeared to fall instantly asleep. Leaving on a nightlight that benevolently illuminated the child's room, Marianne withdrew.

Jeannot was actually awake. His ears listened as the noise in the house slowly abated. When all around him became silent, he stood up and slipped out of his bed. Walking on his tiptoes, he stuck his ear to the door that connected his room with Marianne's.

Reassured that she was asleep, the boy got dressed. He carefully avoided bumping into any furniture. Walking stealthily, he went downstairs into the kitchen. Opening the window with meticulous care, he jumped outside. Finding the cart loaded with produce, he climbed in with some difficulty. He buried himself under the huge cabbages. In this secure hiding place, he felt asleep with absolute assurance that he would soon reach his ultimate goal.

While it was still dark, Père Mathieu drove the cart to the Food Market in Paris. As he traveled his normal route to the capital, he never suspected that the pile of vegetables hid a child dreaming quietly of his mother.

Towards dawn, the cart reached the Food Market. After entering the city gates, Mathieu stopped at a wine merchant in order to have a drink with his breakfast. Scarcely had he gone that a street urchin appeared. No one in Paris really cared where such children slept and how they ate. The boy had high boots, an old torn cardigan, a bag with a shoulder strap, and a gray hat covering his ears. He prowled around the cart. Noting that the street was deserted, he abruptly grabbed a cabbage. He was about to flee with his loot when the head of a cute blond child appeared before him.

"I don't believe it! They say that kids grow in cabbage patches, but I never expected to see it!"

Assuming an attitude of authority, he interrogated Jeannot.

"What are you doing there, you little brat?"

"I'm going to look for Mama," answered Jean.

"In a cart?" asked the urchin, playing with his bag.

"I hitched a ride last night."

"Didn't you have any money to take the train?"

"No. My foster parents wouldn't let me go alone to Paris."

"So you ran away?"

"I want my Mama!"

"What's your name?"

"Jean. What's yours?

"They call me the Licorice Kid."

"What sort of kid?"

"Licorice! The people in the neighborhood gave me that nickname because I'm as black as a mole. We can't stay here. We have to leave. If a cop catches us, he'll ask us too many questions Get out!"

Helping Jeannot descend from the cart, the Licorice Kid took him by the hand to guide him through the city.

"Where does your mother live?"

"I don't remember. Do you know how to read?"

"A little. Not a lot. And you?"

"I know my letters." Jeannot pulled out of under his vest his mother's message. Sitting closely together, each held an end of the paper. Both gazed at the paper trying to read every word with each other's help:

My beloved child,

I am very happy to learn that you are fine. Next Sunday, I shall be visiting you. Give my regards to your foster parents. Here is the address where I can be reached: Madame Jeanne Bertin c/o Madame Chapuis, 10 Impasse Saint-Ferdinand, Neuilly-sur-Seine.

"Neuilly! Neuilly!" repeated the Licorice Kid after a half hour of deciphering had ended. "You haven't knocked at the front door, farm boy. You're at La Villette. You have to cross almost all of Paris. Do you have any dough?"

"Dough?"

"Money."

Jeannot searched in his pocket and triumphantly drew out a coin worth two *sous*.

"That isn't much," noted the Licorice Kid. "It's not enough to pay for a streetcar, the tram, or even the Metro. You can forget about a taxi. You're in a real mess, my poor rabbit."

Jeannot began to cry.

"Stop sniveling," said his companion. "I'll drive you to your Mama."

"Are you telling the truth?" asked the boy

"You have two faces," asserted the urchin. "Sometimes, you haven't any manners, and sometimes, you act like a good chap. We have to shift for ourselves. We can travel in record time. Before you know it, you'll be in Neuilly!"

Jeannot was persuaded by his new friend's confident bragging.

"But what will your parents say?"

"My parents? I don't have any. I never had any. I work for the tramps who live in the ruined forts outside Paris. They

66

found me when I was a baby. I was too young to remember my parents."

He lowered his voice.

"I have to avoid their beatings. I always leave early for the market. When I don't return with my arms full of vegetables stolen from the carts and displays, well... I catch colds a lot, and worse yet, I have to run down to the city to collect cigarette butts in cafés. I've been living like this for years. I sometimes take a day off from my tasks .Come, little buddy, never fear. The Licorice Kid is here!"

Passing his arm under that of his protégé, the Kid added enviously.

"You're lucky, little buddy, to have a Mama!"

Madame Chapuis was astonished. A boy, almost in rags holding the hand of another clothed like a peasant, rang her door around 6 o'clock in the evening,

"Excuse me, Madame," politely asked the Licorice Kid. "Is this your boarding house?"

"Yes, my child. What do you desire?"

"Madame Bertin, if you please? I've brought her boy."

"This is Jean?"

"Yes, Madame," answered Jacqueline's son. Although tired by his escapade, Jean had begun to imitate the boldness of his fearless companion.

"This poor rabbit was unhappy because he couldn't see his mother," said the Kid. "Then he took a train to the Market, well, more like a cart of cabbages! I met him there this morning. He didn't know where to go. He asked for my help. Your place really isn't far. It's just not easy to get to. We found a taxi cab loaded for Neuilly. We could have arrived tomorrow. But I'm a smart kid. I let my buddy grab the back fender, I grasped the other, and here we are!"

"It's wrong to act like that," said Madame Chapuis. "Your mother, Jean, will scold you."

"No," retorted Jean. "She will kiss me. Where is she? I want to see her."

"She went out, but she will return."

In fact, an hour had passed since Jacqueline had yielded to Diana's trickery and left by car.

Madame Chapuis grabbed Jeannot. "Come darling, don't remain in the street."

The child hesitated. "What about him?" said Jean pointing to his friend.

"Don't worry," said the Licorice Kid. "Go with the lady. I don't want to spoil things. I'll go back to my hideout. I have a return ticket. *Bonsoir!*"

"*Au revoir*, Licorice!" shouted the banker's grandson who hugged the other boy.

"*Au revoir*, little buddy. You couldn't have done anything more for me." The proud gatherer of cigarette butts departed.

Still stunned by this incident, Madame Chapuis took Jeannot to the room of Jacqueline. With a touching frankness, the child related everything to her. Moved to tears, the worthy landlady did not have the heart to scold him anymore. She kissed him. Then the telephone stridently rang.

"My dear, I must leave. Your Mama will return soon. You must wait here."

Alone, Jeannot looked around him. "It's not as pretty as Grandpa's, but it's still pretty because my Mama lives here."

He walked to the open window in order to see the return of his mother. A joyful cheer escaped him. "Pretty little pigeons!" The child had in fact has just noticed the two birds. He moved towards the cage. The pigeons cooed softly as if they were acknowledging him as a friend.

"They're so pretty that I want to pet them." Suddenly, he stopped smiling. His face became serious as his eyes reflected compassion. "Mama, you've told me many times that birds should never be in a jail." He gently opened the door of the cage. "Leave, my little ones, leave. Fly quickly. Find your parents!"

The two pigeons joyfully flew out of the window. Gaining their sense of direction, their flight veered towards the ruins of the Chateau Rouge. Jeannot's eyes followed them. Ignorant that his act of mercy might save his mother, he was lost in rapture. Clapping his hands together, he yelled at the faithful messengers of Judex:

"*Bon voyage*, my little white pigeons. *Bon voyage!*"

Part Three: The Amazing Dogs

I. Vidocq

Around 8 o'clock in the morning, a tall man with an aristocratic bearing arrived at the boarding house at 10 Impasse Saint-Ferdinand, in Neuilly. Draped in an ample black cloak and holding the leash of a superb police dog, he asked to speak to Madame Bertin.

"Madame Bertin isn't here," replied Madame Chapuis. Her drawn features and red eyes testified to a night where sleep had been replaced by worry.

"She isn't here?" exclaimed the stranger with an astonishment that could have appeared false to a neutral observer.

"No, Monsieur!" replied the landlady, startled by the grand mannerisms of the stranger. However, she was reassured by his intelligent face.

"Are you a relative?" she asked.

"I am a friend of the family," said Judex. He spoke in a precise tone that dispersed all of the landlady's doubts.

"Come in, Monsieur." The landlady escorted the visitor into a small parlor on the ground floor. "Forgive me for receiving you like this. I'm extremely upset. I fear something tragic may have happened. She was a nice person. Very easy to live with. Never complained about anything." The landlady burst into sobs. "The poor woman!"

"Be calm, Madame," counseled Judex. "Tell me what happened."

"Yesterday, Monsieur, near the end of the afternoon, a lady came to see Madame Bertin for a piano lesson. I had never seen this woman before. Madame Bertin received the visitor in her room. Fifteen minutes later, they went downstairs. They had to have known each other a long time because they seemed very friendly. When Madame Bertin passed in front of

71

my lodge, she told me while hanging her key on the hook: 'I'm going shopping, but I'll be back before dinner.' She didn't return. I waited all night! If she was staying overnight somewhere else, she certainly would have telephoned. It's possible that she had an accident. Paris is dreadful with all those trams and cars spinning like bats out of hell. Since last night, I haven't slept. I've been up all night waiting for her. I prayed for her return, but nothing happened! An even worse calamity is that her son arrived last night. You think that he would have stayed in the country with those very nice friends of his mother. He's only four and a half. Can you imagine? I knew only a little about him. He didn't want to go to bed before kissing his Mama. Finally, he went to sleep. The poor darling! When he wakes up and doesn't see her, I don't know what to tell him! Everything is making me sick is worry! Too much stress!"

Judex had attentively listened to Madame Chapuis.

"Madame, may I ask you some questions?"

"Gladly, Monsieur. I don't know you, but you're a friend of Madame Bertin."

"Did you notify the police of your tenant's disappearance?"

"No, Monsieur. I always hoped that the poor lady would return. If you wish, we could go together to the station?"

"Let's wait a little longer. Did Madame Bertin receive any other visitors?"

"No, Monsieur."

"Did you ever see suspicious people prowling around?"

"Never... At least, not recently. There used to be a young man, rather fancy, who stopped several times in front of the house."

"And this woman who asked for Madame Bertin, please describe her."

"A very pretty girl with dark locks and big eyes. Well-dressed, even elegant. Madame Bertin called her Mademoiselle Marie."

Judex concluded that the visitor was Marie Verdier.

"Did you notice anyone else?"

"I don't know. My memory is failing me I'm too upset. Wait, Monsieur! This girl, Marie, arrived in a fancy car, the sort owned by a wealthy man. It was parked in front of my house. There was also a driver... A young man. He paced up and down the sidewalk and then drove off in the car with Madame Bertin and the brunette."

"Was this young man the same one that you saw earlier outside your place."

"No, Monsieur! I'm sure that he wasn't the other fellow."

Judex listened to the landlady's declarations impassively while displaying the courtesy of a true gentleman.

"You mentioned that Madame Bertin's son was here?"

"Yes, Monsieur. I put him in his mother's room."

"Could you take me to him?"

"Very gladly!" said the landlady totally captivated by the man in the black cloak. Nevertheless, she glanced anxiously at the superb dog whose leash the visitor held.

"Rest assured, Madame," said Judex, "Vidocq is only vicious towards vicious people. Otherwise, he's a gentle and intelligent animal—almost a human being."

"Then, please, come, Monsieur."

A few minutes later, Judex entered Jacqueline's room. Jeannot had just awakened. Seeing this stranger, the child was briefly scared. The presence of Madame Chapuis reassured him. Seeing the police dog sparked a cry of instant admiration.

"What a handsome doggie!"

"You can pet him, my lad" said Judex approaching the bed. "He's very sweet and loves children when they treat him kindly."

Jeannot petted the beautiful animal's head. He already considered it an affectionate protector. Then, remembering his anxiety, he became tearful.

"Madame, did Mama return?"

"Not yet," said the landlady.

"But she won't be gone for long," declared Judex. He kissed the forehead of the angelic child. Judex spoke gravely as if making a sacred oath. "I promise you, my child, you shall see your mother soon."

Turning towards the landlady, Judex whispered authoritatively.

"Your tenant is alive."

"May the Good Lord bless you."

"I personally will conduct the search, but not a word to anybody, you hear me? The safety of Madame Bertin depends on your silence."

"Count on me."

Taking a glove that Jacqueline had left on the table, Judex had his bloodhound sniff it. With his ears erect and his pupil on fire, the dog seemed to say to his master: "I understand!"

"*Au revoir*, Madame," politely said the mysterious visitor.

"Where do you think she is?" asked the landlady.

"It's Vidocq who will tell me," replied Judex while pointing to his agitated dog. Stretching his neck muscles and smelling the ground with his nose, Vidocq was ready to start the hunt.

When the man in the black cloak walked out on the street, Madame Chapuis watched him moved away.

"I didn't ask his name. Seeing how he kissed the boy, I know that he's an honest man."

Upon reaching the automobile where his brother waited, Judex fell prey to genuine anxiety. He had earlier investigated Marie Verdier's antecedents and unearthed her criminal past.

Why had the notorious Diana Monti abducted Jacqueline?

II. Diana, Moralès and Company

In a vaulted cell, daylight penetrated through an oval window outfitted with iron bars. A woman was prostrate on a rustic bench. Jacqueline Aubry had just regained consciousness. She realized her plight when she saw the massive locked door. She tried to get up, but her strength failed her. She fell back on the bench. Attempting to shout, her words became garbled in her throat.

"I'm a prisoner!"

Her mind was flooded by a question that she was incapable of answering. *Why?* Remembering all the details of her abduction. she was perplexed. *I've only shown kindness and sympathy towards this Verdier girl. Why did she spitefully attack me? I'm no longer wealthy. No one could hope to extort money from me. There is only one explanation.*

A name escaped from her lips.

"Judex!"

The banker's daughter was consumed by an irresistible foreboding.

Is he responsible for me being here? Is he still following his path of relentless vengeance? Did he lull my mistrust by sending me those two pigeons and declaring himself my protector? Has he engaged my son's governess as an accomplice? Was it through this woman that he was able to strike at my father?

Incapable of suspecting César de Birargues, Jacqueline's doubts evolved into certainties. Her impassioned brain remembered the terrifying events that she had experienced. She falsely concluded that Judex was her victimizer. Marie Verdier was only the enforcer of this mysterious figure.

She trembled for her child.

"My adorable Jean!" she shouted in her despair. "They will kidnap him. Nothing will dissuade this monster. Nothing! Not even the innocence of my angel! Not even the smile of a child! Who will defend you, my dear, from the attacks of our enemies? Why am I not there to protect you! I should have kept you by my side! *Mon Dieu*! It's horrible! I didn't believe that my world would transformed into a living Hell! Why's this happening! I never did anything wrong! I am ready to sacrifice my last breath of life for my son!

"My Lord, if, in your justice, you have decided that I must pay for the sins of my father, strike me down without mercy. But your anger must stop there. Don't be as cruel as the Jehovah of the Old Testament. Don't hound us even into the third generation. Have pity, save my child!"

Kneeling on the ground with her head bent and her hands clasped, she prayed with all the force of her desolated soul. Never did a more fervent petition gush from a maternal heart.

An excessive fever had seized her. When she raised herself up, she was shivering. Thirst dried out her lips. On a heavy table of wood, there was a carafe, filled with water, and a glass that the young woman just noticed. Taking a large gulp, she eagerly drank.

A tranquility swiftly descended on her. Her tears ceased as a progressive torpor caused her to lie down. Calmly lapsing into sleep, she smiled.

"My Jeannot, my precious…"

Shortly thereafter, the door silently opened revealing the silhouettes of Diana Monti and Moralès.

"She is asleep," said the latter.

"Yes," replied the adventuress, "and she won't awaken soon because I used a strong dose. It's much better that she stay that way. That will avoid needless explanations. Let's leave. Everything's going as planned. Besides, your friend must have received our telegram. We must not delay!" She added one final sarcastic comment. "May this angel rest in peace!"

After carefully closing the vault door, the two conspirators ascended to the ground floor. Their residence was a small villa at the edge of the forest of Chevilly (Seine-et-Oise), close to the picturesque road that runs from Médon to Vernouillet. Sufficiently isolated, the villa served as a refuge to the duo whenever they needed to avoid the attention of the police. Thanks to its remote location and their clever precautions, the outlaws had always succeeded in escaping detection.

The salon was furnished with a gaudy elegance. A bay window opened on a superficially maintained garden. Lighting a cigarette, Diana sat in a rocking-chair. Looking out the window, her lover impatiently waited for the arrival of their client.

"You understand what to do?" said Diana. "I can rely on you?"

"Yes," replied Moralès. "But don't you worry that our friend will think that we were too rough on the girl?"

The ex-governess expressed her annoyance by shrugging her shoulders.

"My little Moralès," she said bitingly, "you should know that I dislike cowards. If you want to remain my partner, you must take risks without displaying any fear or squeamishness."

"Diana, you know that I would die for you!" shouted Moralès, passionately grabbing his mistress.

"Take your hands off me!" She pushed him away. "We must discuss serious matters. You have done all that I told you?"

"I'm sure that you'll be pleased."

"Very good!"

"May I ask a simple question?"

"Speak."

"Once she's free, won't the banker's daughter accuse us."

"So?"

"But that's very dangerous!"

"Idiot," snickered the ex-governess, "we have the means to defend ourselves."

"Explain."

"César's letter for a start."

"And?"

"I will tell you when the occasion presents itself."

"Diana," begged an alarmed Moralès, "when are you ever going to trust me?"

Monti made a nasty smirk, but she didn't have time for further debate. A door opened revealing a singular valet. His formal attire couldn't conceal the swagger of a man suited to criminal endeavors.

"The guest has arrived!" he announced in a guttural voice.

In fact, a car had parked in front of the villa.

"Show him in, and do it right away," ordered the adventuress.

"Yes, Duchess," stressed the ugly servant. He departed to open the gate of the wall that surrounded the villa. A few moments later, he introduced César de Birargues into the salon.

The "King of Petticoats" was visibly upset. He didn't regret his shameful actions. In the intoxication of his lust, he hadn't questioned his base conduct. César was worried about the final phase of this scheme. He feared his eloquence might not convince the young woman. Would she deduce his role in this infamous masquerade and treat him with contempt? But it was too late to back off.

Viewing Diana's triumphant smile and the restored composure of Moralès, César was soon reassured.

César de Birargues gallantly kissed Diana's hand. "My friend, all went well?"

"Admirably."

"She's here?"

"She's here."

"She doesn't suspect that you're in league with me?"

"Not at all," claimed Diana. "The affair happened so quickly that the dear child is in a daze. At this moment, she calmly sleeps, awaiting to be reawakened by her Prince Charming."

"You are not only very skillful people, but also very loyal friends," foolishly said the handsome César. He took 5000 francs out of his wallet. "Here the remainder of the agreed sum. Take me to my Sleeping Beauty."

"In a moment!" said Moralès inspired by the expressive grin of his mistress.

"Why delay?" questioned the young de Birargues sharply.

"Our expenses were more considerable than I originally thought," cynically professed the gambler. "That's not all; we ran some big risks. We're implicated very deeply. You must pay us an additional 5000 if you want our captive."

"10,000 francs!" repeated César, stunned by this unforeseen demand.

"Take it or leave it," coldly concluded Moralès.

De Birargues experienced a shivering rage. In a second, the light had been extinguished in his spirit.

"I've been swindled!" he raged. He assumed an air of offended dignity. "You two are scoundrels!"

"Marquis!"

"Yes, two scoundrels. I give you five minutes to set Madame Bertin at liberty. Otherwise, I will go and report you to the Public Prosecutor."

"You would file a complaint? Against whom?" questioned Diana ironically

"Against you two."

"And then what?" said Moralès, putting under César's eyes he letter that he had imprudently written the day before.

My Dear Baron,

As stipulated, I enclose a check of 5000 francs for the execution for my project. You will be paid a similar sum upon delivery.

Cordially yours.

CÉSAR DE BIRARGUES

While rereading this letter, to which he had not attached any importance, the young rake understood the dreadful trap in which he had fallen.

Quaking with fury, he made a threatening gesture to strangle this bogus baron who had unscrupulously cheated him. "Scum!" he yelled. "You will relinquish this letter or else…"

"Come and take it," replied Moralès as he phlegmatically stuffed the envelope back in his pocket. "My dear Marquis, if you don't want to be needlessly harassed, I suggest you don't involve the police in our affairs. If you're short of cash, we'll give you time to raise it since we have a hostage."

"Hum. That's acceptable," said César at last. "Wait for me here. I will go to Paris and get your money."

"Very good!" emphasized Moralès.

Diana pushed the electric button activating the bell summoning her uncouth servant.

"Crémard, accompany the Marquis back to his car!"

"Diana," said Moralès when César had gone, "are you pleased with me now? Did I learn my lesson?"

"Not bad! Not bad at all!" The adventuress looked as if she was lost in a dark dream. "I think that I shall make something out of my little Moralès after all!"

III. Honor or Nothing

"Mariette," said Gisèle de Birargues to her chambermaid, "are you sure that Madame Bertin didn't telephone?"

"Yes, Mademoiselle. Quite sure."

"It's odd! She was supposed to be here at 10 o'clock and it's now 11:30. She was always scrupulously exact. She must either be ill or have had an accident."

"Does Mademoiselle want me to ask the footman?"

"That's unnecessary. If Madame Bertin doesn't show up, I'll send you this afternoon to inquire at her address."

The charming Gisèle in her exquisite and perfect dress evoked one of these graceful pictures of Latour, the wonderful artist of the 18th century. Entering the salon while waiting for lunch, she got ready to decipher a delicious composition of Lully when she froze on the threshold.

She had just noticed her brother collapsed on a couch. His head between his hands, he had fallen prey to an extreme depression.

"César, what's wrong?" she asked with emotion.

"Gisèle!" shouted the Marquis de Birargues with a face full of tears.

"Why are you crying?" questioned the girl. "Did something happen to our father or mother?"

"Oh, no!" said the young nobleman. "It's me... only me."

He stopped himself. He withheld a shameful confession as his chaste sister stretched out her hands to offer him unconditional support.

"Speaks, I beg you," entreated Gisèle. "You can completely trust me. I always told you my small sins; you can reveal your big tragedies!"

"Not to you!"

"Why?"

"Because it's monstrous!"

"I can't stand this uncertainty. Tell me. What happened?"

"It's... I'm a miserable sinner!"

"You, my brother!"

"Yes... me!"

"That's impossible!"

"My poor sister, if only you knew..." stammered the unfortunate man, crazed with remorse and shame.

With the noble character belonging only to exceptional beings, Gisèle consoled her brother.

"César, listen to me. I'm aware that for a long time your behavior has upset our parents, but you aren't evil. You'll always have a special place in my heart. If you committed a wrongful act, I can help you atone. You must tell me. Don't worsen your sin by hiding it from me. I'm no longer a child sheltered from the ugliness of life. I'm 20 years old, and I'm your sister. Whatever you've done—and I refuse to believe than you're as guilty as you believe—I'm here to offer forgiveness advice. I can save you. You're a Birargues like me. We're the same blood; the same race. Our motto is: *Aut honor aut nihil*. Honor or nothing. In the name of the honor that every generation of ours has shown, I beseech you, my brother, to tell me the stark truth!"

Sharply moved by this appeal at once so proud and so touching, César de Birargues recovered.

"Gisèle! You make me understand my unworthiness. Yes, my infamy! You want to know what I did? I will tell you. I know now that the story of my weakness, actually my crime, could never tarnish your purity."

"My poor brother!"

"Don't console me! I suffer, yes, I atrociously suffer; but I deserve to suffer a hundred more times!" In a panting, jerky voice, the Marquis continued. "Madly infatuated with a young respectable woman, and unable to overcome her rejection, I ordered her abduction. I paid 5000 francs in advance to her kidnappers. Today, they demanded another 10,000 to relinquish my victim."

While Gisèle was torn apart by anguish, César resumed with the intense excitement of a criminal making a full confession.

"I don't have another 10,000 francs. It's unlikely that I could raise it. These criminals possess a letter from me proving that I was the instigator of their crime. In other words, their accomplice. These rascals will blackmail me relentlessly. They already began. At any price. I must break free from their clutches by rescuing their hostage!"

"Who is this unfortunate?" asked Gisèle.

"Jeanne Bertin," disclosed the repentant abductor.

"It's horrible! This poor woman! So sweet! So good! Brother, you did this?"

"You know that I'm a miserable sinner! I see the abyss opening up in front of me. You've heard everything. Advise me. I no longer know what to do. I'm afraid of going mad. When you came, I was wondering if I should kill myself. Yes, kill myself!"

"Brother, don't say those things. You must live to make amends."

"I'm ready to do that! It's shameful for me to confess my infamy to a stranger! Where should I go? Tell me! Among our friends, who's the best man to confide in. Who is strong enough to defeat these criminals? I don't know anyone."

" I know the man!" energetically answered Gisèle.

"Who?"

"Our father!"

"Our father!" shuddered César. "He's the last person to whom I would go."

"He's the only one that can help you."

"He'll disown me!"

"He'll save you. Come!"

The Duc de Birargues received his children in his study, When he saw Gisèle's anxiety and César's depression, he knew that the latter was here to seek forgiveness for some misdeed. However, he never suspected that the act would be so heinous as to place their family honor in the hands of blackmailers.

The Duc de Birargues was nobility personified. He lived as more than a man of wealth. Much of his life had been devoted to the study of important social issues. His natural generosity was enhanced by an impartial sense of justice. If fate had entrusted him with a title and rank, he would exercise his privileges to perform exemplary deeds.

Always the master of any situation, he looked successively at César with severity and Gisèle with kindness. "My son, you are here to have your cause pleaded by your sister. I warn you, Monsieur: this is the final time that I will help you. My patience is exhausted. How much money do you need?"

Throwing himself at the Duke's feet, César stammered:

"My father, forgive me."

"Save him," implored Gisèle.

Worried even more by these words, the Duc de Birargues stood firm.

"Monsieur, rise up and speak. I command you!"

Full of intense emotion and burning regret, César, told his father the full details of the deplorable affair.

The Duc de Birargues had the admirable strength to listen to his son without interruption and without revealing any emotion on his face.

When César had finished, the Duc spoke with sovereign authority.

"Where is Madame Bertin?"

Unable to look his father in the eyes, César replied:

"In Chevilly-sur-Seine... Villa Brossard... on the road from Médon to Vernouillet."

"That is sufficient." Keeping his anger in abeyance, the Duc behaved with incomparable dignity. "I dare to hope, Monsieur, that you want to expiate your abominable actions. Your wrongly believed that your birth and your fortune gave you only rights, when they actually impose duties. The higher you are, Monsieur, the less you must descend. The more you have, the more you must strive to improve himself. For the only road to happiness is to conquer egotism by serving our fellow man. If our class had always put this maxim into practice, perhaps there would have been less aristocrats guillotined under the Revolution, and we would occupy a higher place in the world and in the nation!

"You admit that your sister counseled you to come here. She did well. For only I can avoid a scandal that would injure our entire family. All this must remain between us. Your mother must be kept unaware of your conduct, and I will gradually strive to obliterate any memory of it. As for you, Monsieur, you will leave this house for our estate in the Cévennes where you will await my orders. There, faced with your conscience, you will be able to measure the depth of the abyss into which you nearly fell. You must remember our motto: *Aut honor aut nihil.* Honor or nothing.

"Now, withdraw, Monsieur. I spoke to you as between gentlemen. Prove to me by your obedience that you are again my son! Go!"

"Father," resumed César, "I don't dare express my endless gratitude. I don't have the right to add anything to your pronouncements. Nevertheless, leave me to say a word, a single word..."

"Speak!"

"What about this young woman?"

84

The admirable Duc de Birargues responded simply to his distraught heir:

"Only I can save her!"

IV. Unexpected Visitors

Although very satisfied with the progress of their grand scheme, Diana and Moralès were impatient for César's return. The shrill doorbell prompted both of them towards the bay window that looked out on the garden.

"That must be him!" yelled Moralès.

"What does this mean?" exclaimed the adventuress. She had just noticed a white poodle hanging by his teeth from the metal chain of the doorbell on the gate. The animal's frantic movements had caused the ringing.

"Is this a stupid joke?" said the incensed Diana.

She started to go outside, but her pseudo-valet, Crémard, had anticipated her. Cursing the prankster, he went outside to open the gate. A scream of terror escaped him. While the poodle departed like a flash, a pack of 25 Vendean dogs invaded the garden. Their barks left no doubt as to their belligerent intentions. There was no human being present. It was as if the dogs obeyed the mysterious orders of an invisible master.

Some of the fearsome hounds chased the valet who barely escaped their fangs by running into the countryside. The remainder of the band ran towards the house as the wave of a headlong assault.

"What's going on?" asked Moralès turning pale.

"I don't know!" said Diana. She realized that an unexpected danger threatened both of them.

"Have we been betrayed?" said the false baron.

A noise of broken panes, followed by furious barking, resounded in the hallway.

"We're under attack!" shouted Moralès grabbing his automatic pistol.

Diana stopped him.

"Don't panic, Moralès. Birargues must have double-crossed us. He will pay!"

The dogs slammed their paws and their gnawing fangs against the door.

"Let's run!" shouted Diana.

Moving towards the vast fireplace, she pressed her thumb inside the sculptured wood. The fireplace, turning upon itself, disclosed of a stairway that led into the basement.

"Come!" said the adventuress.

"And the woman?" said Moralès.

"Forget about her." The amoral woman led her lover into the passageway. The fireplace automatically swung back into place behind them.

At the same instant, the door opened with a crash. Vidocq, followed by Judex and his brother, entered, After them came a magnificent white poodle whose sly expression contrasted with the feverish behavior of the bloodhound.

"Too late!" stated Roger. "Our nasty birds have flown away."

"Through there!" declared Judex, pointing to the fireplace in front of which Vidocq and the poodle simultaneously stopped.

The other dogs entered through the doorway. Becoming mute and motionless, they waited in the antechamber with gaping mouths.

Judex turned towards Roger. "Brother, look for Jacqueline," he said gravely. He shoved the lady's glove again into Vidocq's nostrils. The dog immediately ran away followed by Roger.

Approaching the fireplace, Judex easily noted that the two extortionists had not been able to flee up the chimney. He easily discovered the secret mechanism that concealed the escape stairway. He was about to descend the stairs with his poodle, when Roger returned.

"I found her!"

"Where is she?" questioned the man in the black cloak.

"She's lying in a prison vault."

"Did she see you?"

" No, she's been drugged."

"Take me to her."

The poodle prepared to follow his master.

"Maxime, stay here!" ordered Judex. "Remain with the other dogs."

Acting as a vigilant guard in front of the fireplace, Maxime took a seating position.

After having descending a narrow spiral stairway, the entry of which was concealed inside a pantry in the kitchen, the two brothers arrived at the vault that Vidocq had easily spotted.

Judex stood on the threshold, contemplating Jacqueline. Awaiting the coming of her savior, she rested. Leaning towards her, Judex deposited a sealed envelope on her chest. The bloodhound had followed his master. Judex pointed to the young woman.

"Guard her!"

Next to the feet of the young woman, Vidocq lied down

"Now that she's safe," said Judex to his brother, "we can deal with the others!"

When Jacqueline came out of the oblivion to which Diana and Moralès had consigned her, her eyes beheld a strange and unexpected spectacle. Seated close to her was a poodle with an intelligent gaze. A superb police dog, lying with his head on his knees, seemed be guarding her. Around her were grouped a pack of beautiful dogs. They contemplated her with friendly expressions.

The young woman believed that she was the prey of a hallucination. Finding the letter that her savior had left, she felt that the faithful eyes of the dogs were requesting her to quickly read it. She tore open the envelope and read:

Madam, you are free. No longer fear your abductors. I watch over you. You will be led outside by the good dogs that surround you. They will escort you through the forest until you are safe.

JUDEX

"I was wrong," said Jacqueline. "He kept his word. Yet the pigeons are still in their cage. By what miracle was he able to trace me? Why is my father's enemy so generous?"

While the young woman was lost in her deliberations, she suddenly felt a pull on the bottom of her skirt. The poodle was requesting her to depart.

Jacqueline left her prison. With Vidocq acting as a guide, she was accompanied by Maxime who never left her side, and followed by the handsome Vendean hounds whose long ears shook with goodwill. With her valiant escort, she crossed the house and the garden. Reaching the road and then the forest, she didn't notice the trace of another human being.

The pure air of the woods gradually restored her strength. All these noble dogs that yapped and frolicked joyfully around her revived her confidence and hope.

Happily embracing her liberty, she advanced with her protectors to a crossroad. Jacqueline was thinking of her son, her cherished Jeannot, when a luxurious automobile abruptly stopped near her.

Jacqueline intended to continue along the road, but a girl jumped out of the car. She ran towards the dogs waving.

"Madame Bertin! I'm happy to see you."

Joining his daughter, the Duc de Birargues respectfully greeted the piano teacher.

"Madame, once we learned of your peril, we rushed to your aid."

"How did you escape?" asked Gisèle.

"These brave dogs delivered me. I don't know who their master is. It's a mystery. How did you know that I was a prisoner?"

Without the least hesitation, the noble Duc de Birargues explained.

"It was my son. Falling into deep remorse, he confessed his crime to me. I humbly beg you to forgive him. Have mercy. Let me punish his evil. Save from disgrace a name without reproach and without stain. I swear, Madame, to revere you for all my remaining life."

"Monsieur," replied Jacqueline with dignity, "rest assured that there will be no scandal. I shall keep silent. As for your repentant son, I shall forgive him on the condition that he forgets me."

"Thank you!" said Gisèle embracing Jacqueline.

"Madame," said the Duc de Birargues. "I would be proud to call you my daughter!"

"On this Earth, Monsieur," answered Jacqueline, "I have only one right and one duty; to be a mother. I must belong to my child. It's the only goal of my life."

The Duc bowed respectfully to this unselfish lady.

"Tell me, Madame, where should I drive you?"

"To Neuilly!"

At the same instant, a strident whistle resounded in the distance. Instantly all the dogs jumped into the forest and disappeared among the dense foliage.

Everything had been heard by two men hiding behind a thick shrub. While the Duc's car traveled along the road, Roger had to prevent Judex from throwing himself in front of it.

"She's an angel!" said Judex.

Through an underground maze of ancient quarries that communicated with the Villa Brossard, Diana and Moralès had escaped from their unexpected visitors. They passed through the exit, a crevice in the middle of ivy-covered rocks. Suddenly, a loud noise originated from the corridor that they had just vacated.

"The secret passage have been discovered!" said Diana. "We've been followed!"

Pulling out their pistols, they placed themselves on each side of the underground doorway. Fingering their triggers, they were prepared to sell their lives dearly.

The noise came closer without revealing its exact nature. An exclamation of surprise escaped the two brigands. A fox-terrier appeared, carrying a wide envelope between his teeth. Standing on his hind legs, the dog dropped his burden in front of Moralès. He seized it immediately. It was addressed to Madame Diana Monti:

If you don't want to suffer the fate of the banker Favraux, never cross his daughter's path again.

JUDEX

The fox-terrier speedily ran away. Diana and Moralès were furious. They fired their guns several times at the retreating ball of fur.

The dog moved swiftly in the open field. The bullets couldn't reach him. When he felt completely out of range, the dog turned around and barked three times mockingly at his opponents. With his head held high, he disappeared behind an embankment.

"Judex! Judex!" fumed Moralès. "What sort of being is this man? What's his interest in the banker's daughter?"

"I must know—and I will," replied Diana.

V. Above Hate

At 2 o'clock in the afternoon, the Duc de Birargues's car arrived in Neuilly. After saying farewell to the Duc and his daughter, Jacqueline rang the doorbell of the boarding house. The anxiety of Madame Chapuis was replaced with elation.

"You, my child! I was so worried about you. I feared that you had an accident. You're here at last. That's the important thing. Where have you been? Come in. You can't stay outside. I no longer know what I'm saying. I'm so happy! I'm very fond of you. I told my older tenants this morning that you're like a younger sister to me."

Escorting Jacqueline inside, the landlady lavished attention on the younger woman.

"Can I get you something? You're very pale. You look tired and famished. You need to eat."

"Thank you, Madame. I'll have something later. Right now, I need to relax from my ordeal."

"Do what you want. You're home now. What happened to you?"

"I have just been through such a weird adventure that seems like a dream."

"I knew that when you failed to return on time, something extraordinary happened to you."

Thinking of the treacherous woman who had entrapped her, Jacqueline's eyes filled with tears.

"The villains! If you knew what I suffered!"

"My poor child!"

"You must have guessed that I was kidnapped!"

"That brunette tricked you?"

"Yes."

"And it was the man with the dog who rescued you?" asked Madame Chapuis.

"Did this man have a police dog?" said an astonished Jacqueline.

"He came here asking for you. A handsome man, between 25 to 30. Very distinguished. He said that he was a close friend of your family. When I told him that you were missing since yesterday, his face changed. I asked him to come with me to the police, but he refused. He told me an in a grave voice that I shall remember all my life: 'Not a word to anybody. The safety of Madame Bertin depends on your silence.' I didn't budge, and I was right since you're here."

Jacqueline reflected on the landlady's remarks. *Could this man be the mysterious Judex? How could he have known that I was in danger since I hadn't freed the pigeons?*

Madame Chapuis continued her comments.

"That man—I don't know how to describe him. A real gentleman even though he didn't tell me his name. He demanded a detailed account of what happened to you. I needed to show him your room. He kindly kissed your small boy. "

"My small boy?"

"Yes, Jeannot."

"Jeannot!"

"He's here!"

"How long has he been here?"

"Since last night. He was longing for you. He ran away from Loisy."

"*Mon Dieu!*"

"He came to Paris hidden in a cabbage cart. At the outskirts of the city, he met a very resourceful boy. He kindly brought your son to my house."

"Where is he?" said Jacqueline, galvanized by maternal love.

"I left him in your room playing with a box of soldiers that I gave him."

The young woman swiftly forgot all her anxieties and ran up the stairs. She opened the door to her room.

Leaving the toy soldiers aligned on the table, Jean threw himself into his mother's arms.

"Mama, it's wasn't nice to keep me waiting.'"

Jacqueline didn't have the heart to reproach her child. She hugged him and squeezed him fiercely against her heart.

More than ever, she felt that her entire life was this beautiful cherub whose two small arms were around her neck. She lovingly kissed him.

"Dear Mama," Jean said, "four days was too long for me to wait. Papa Bontemps didn't have the time to take me to you. I left. It was very nice in the cart. It was like sleeping in bed. I was bothered when the lady told me that you weren't here. Look at the pretty soldiers that the lady gave me. She's almost as good as Marianne. See the soldiers. They have rifles. Look at them!'"

With the charming manner of a child, Jeannot narrated his exploits.

"I met a very kind boy. He's called the Licorice Kid. He promised to visit me. He dresses funny. He wears a gray hat like those Papa wore at the races. The Kid always laughs. I want him always with me. Mama, can you have two sons?"

"Now, Jeannot, I must scold you."

"Me, Mama. Why?"

"It was very naughty to come here," said Jacqueline. "To leave your foster parents! Yes, very naughty. You worried those nice people once they noticed that you left. I'm sure that they looked for you everywhere. They must be very sad. My little Jean, you could have gotten lost on the road. You could been crushed by a car or taken by nasty people. What would I have done then?"

Her son lowered his head with its mass of blond curls. It was painful for Jacqueline to maintain a harsh tone, but she continued.

"Jeannot, you deserve to be punished. This time, I will forgive you, but I want you to reflect on the consequences of your thoughtless acts. If you do something like this again, instead of leaving you in Loisy, I'll be forced to put you into a distant boarding school where I might see you only three times a year. Do you understand me?"

"Yes, Mama."

"You will never do this again?"

"Never! Never! Never!"

As the child wiped away his tears with a small handkerchief, Jacqueline made an unexpected discovery. She noticed the empty cage in a corner of the room. The small door of the wicker bars still remained ajar.

Raising his head, Jeannot saw the surprise on his mother's face.

"Mama, I let loose the pigeons!"

"That was you?"

Fearing that he would be scolded again, the child hesitantly explained.

"Yes, Mama, you had told me that it wasn't right…"

He never finished. Jacqueline had taken him in her arms. Crazed with happiness, tears streamed from her eyes.

"You don't have to explain. You need no excuses, my beloved child. You saved your mother!"

The next day, Jacqueline decided to resume her life of maternal self-denial. She accompanied her son to the Saint-

Lazare train station. In a taxi with them was Marianne Bontemps. Notified by telegram of Jean's presence in Neuilly, she had arrived earlier to take the boy back to his foster home.

Scarcely had the car stopped at the station that the occupants saw a unusual sight. Dressed in a bizarre outfit, a small boy appeared.

"Good day, ladies and gentleman."

"The Licorice Kid!" shouted Jeannot clapping his hands.

Returning to the boarding house to visit Jean, the mischievous urchin had noticed his young friend climbing into the taxi with his mother and his foster mother. Then climbing on the back of the car, he had arrived at the same time as Jean.

"How are things, my old rabbit?"

Jeannot quickly hugged his friend.

"Mama, this is the boy who brought me to Neuilly."

"This is him?"

"Yes, Mama."

Looking kindly at this brave child who had navigated her son around Paris, the banker's daughter took a coin from hers purse and offered it to the Licorice Kid.

With comical dignity, the urchin showed Jacqueline his bag full of half-smoked cigars and cigarettes.

"Madame, I don't ask for charity, I'm a tradesman!"

Jacqueline smiled at this witticism.

"Is it true that you are alone in the world?"

"Yes, Madame."

"Did you ever know your parents?"

"Never!"

"Did someone adopt you?"

"The people who beat me up."

"They beat you?"

"And how!"

"Would you be happy to leave them?"

"I wish!"

Jacqueline felt compassion for this poor underprivileged youth. Despite the atmosphere of wickedness in which he always lived, the Licorice Kid had kept his benevolent nature intact. She was about to continue her questioning when Jeannot yielded to one to a sudden impulse.

"Since he's alone with no parents, could you be his Mama a little?"

"A lot even!" said the Kid

"Take him with us!" begged Jeannot.

" But, my little one…" replied Jacqueline.

"I don't want to leave him! We will stay together!"

"Great!" shouted the Licorice Kid. "I'll have a family!"

Jacqueline hesitated. Of course, it would be painful to separate these two small children whose firm friendship had grown from a chance encounter. On the other hand, she dreaded that Jeannot, so charming and pure, might be led astray by constant contact with this boy who, despite his good qualities, was still a child of the streets.

The kind Marianne decided to offer a solution. She intended to strike a sensible cord within Jacqueline.

"Madame, don't worry. We must learn from our recent experience. Day and night, night and day, Jeannot will remain close to me. I swear it! I also believe that we should take his friend with us. This child deserves to be saved!"

"You're wise, Marianne," approved Jacqueline.

"Does that mean you'll adopt me?" asked the Licorice Kid.

"Where are the people you lived with?" asked Jacqueline.

"Over by the old forts."

"What are their names?"

"The man is named Tortillard and the woman is called Pomme-Cuite."

Jean laughed at the woman's name which meant "Baked Apple."

"You will wait for the train with Marianne and your friend Jeannot," decided Jacqueline, "but if you don't behave…"

Pulling off his hat, the kid kissed the hand of his bene-factress, Reacting to his first real contact with kindness, he replied from the bottom of his heart:

"Madame, I'll behave because I'll be happy!"

"Poor child!" said Jacqueline.

Some minutes after on the platform of the train station, Jacqueline waved as Jeannot and the Licorice Kid blew kisses from the window of a train slowly departing.

While darkness covered the ruins of the Chateau Rouge, Judex was in his laboratory. Thanks to the moving mirror placed in the prison cell, he obstinately watched Favraux. The prostrate banker was crushed by his severe punishment.

Abandoning his observation post, Judex sat down in front of a table. Maneuvering a mechanism to open a secret drawer, he pulled out a photograph. He contemplated it with a fierce intensity.

It was a portrait of Jacqueline.

How had this framed photo from a piano in the large sa-lon of the Chateau des Sablons come into Judex's hands? Only he knew. Usually hard and ruthless when they were directed towards his enemy, his eyes softened with regret and melan-choly.

"Yes, she's an angel... an angel!"

At the end of a long meditation, he returned the portrait to its hiding place. He remained motionless. He appeared lost in a dream.

By a whim of destiny, Judex had fallen in love with the banker's daughter.

Part Four: The Secret of the Tomb

I. Pierre Kerjean

Dr. Gortais, the director of a famous clinic in the vicinity of Mantises, entered his office every morning at 9 o'clock precisely. After perusing his mail and putting on his medical garb, he was ready to examine his patients. His porter brought the business card of a visitor:

M. ROGER-JACQUES

Attorney-at-Law

Rue Michel-Ange, Paris.

"What that does he want," said the irritated doctor, "just when I'm about to make my rounds? Tell this man to return at 5 o'clock. Wait! Roger-Jacques! How could I forget his name? I'm available! It's all right! I was about to act like a fool! Joseph, fetch this man!"

Beneath a gruff exterior, Dr. Gortais was a good man devoted to his patients. Sitting at his desk, he took out a medical bill from a file. Joseph escorted a young man into his employer's presence. The well-dressed visitor had a clean-shaven face and an athletic physique.

"Please take a seat, Maître Roger-Jacques," invited the clinic's director.

Judex's brother moved slightly forward.

"Doctor, your secretary informed me that your patient, Pierre Kerjean, was completely cured. At the same time, I received your bill for his medical expenses. It amounts to 945 francs and 75 centimes."

"That is correct, Monsieur."

"Here are 1000 francs, Doctor."

"I will get your change."

"Unnecessary. The surplus can be a bonus for the nurses that took care of my client."

"You're very kind."

"Now, Doctor, allow me to congratulate you for saving this unfortunate man's life."

"When you brought me this poor devil, his condition was very critical. I was initially convinced that he would not survive the night. I did what I could."

"More than that, Doctor."

"The sly devil, although 60, is endowed with an iron temperament which nothing can crush!"

"You're too modest. Kerjean owes his life to your skill!"

Dr. Gortais was moved by these congratulatory words.

"You'll find that Kerjean is recovering beautifully. He's an old oak that has rediscovered its roots. Do you want to see him?"

"Before I do this, Doctor, I need to ask you a few questions."

"I'm at your disposal."

"Does Kerjean still know nothing about me?"

"You wanted me to be discreet. I closely followed your instructions."

"Does he remember the details of his accident?"

"He says that he fell from exhaustion on the road. Before he could lift himself up, an automobile quickly ran over him. He claims not to have noticed the occupants of the car."

"Thank you, Doctor. You can now show me this brave man."

"Will you take him with you?"

"If he consents."

Some moments later, Pierre Kerjean, completely cured, entered the doctor's office. He wore a modest suit that was meticulously clean. His hair and beard had been cut.

"My friend," said Gortais, "let me present Maître Roger-Jacques, a lawyer from Paris. Finding you on the road, he drove you to my clinic. You owe your life, Kerjean, to him more than me."

Upon first seeing the young man, the old vagrant's initial reaction had been mistrust. Quickly, his face relaxed. He spoke with genuine emotion.

"Often, Monsieur, I asked the doctor for the name of the generous person paying for my care. He replied always that he couldn't tell me, and I was content to bless my unknown benefactor. Since you have finally revealed yourself, Monsieur, you have my eternal gratitude."

Roger and Kerjean shook hands.

"I have no regrets about saving your life."

"You have a good heart, Monsieur. Thank you."

"I was just acting like a human being."

"Again, thank you."

"Now, Monsieur Kerjean," said Judex's brother, "what do you plan to do?"

"I don't know," replied the ex-miller. "At my age, it's very difficult to find work."

"I'm offering you a job for the rest of your life. You will also be given some time off to sort out family matters."

The astonished Kerjean considered these words.

"Monsieur, I'm confused by all your kind actions. What did I do to deserve them?"

"You have suffered hard times."

"It's true," said the old man. Lowering his head, he bitterly added, "But you don't know me."

Judex's brother stood up.

"You are mistaken, Kerjean, I know you. It's because I know you that I want to hire you."

Kerjean raised his head. Remaining silent for an instance, he stared at Roger before replying.

"Monsieur, I am yours!"

After saying farewell to Dr. Gortais, Judex's brother and the old man left the clinic. They climbed into a powerful automobile that took them directly to the Chateau Rouge.

"You will see things that will surprise and delight you," foretold Roger. "For the moment, I can't say any more. Trust me as I trust you."

More and more intrigued, the vagrant docilely followed Roger.

They climbed through the ruins and its maze of underground corridors. Reaching the laboratory, Roger introduced his brother.

Superbly imposing, Judex was even more enigmatic in his cloak of black velvet. His attire emphasized his statuesque bearing and handsome face.

"Kerjean," said Judex, "outside of my brother and myself, you are the only living person to have entered this room. As my brother has told you, we're resolved to ensure your happiness."

"My happiness is irretrievably lost," said the ex-convict.

"I shall do everything possible to restore it."

"You think I deserve this?"

"I am sure because you suffered."

"Do you know why?"

"I know that you're a victim of the banker Favraux. That alone evokes my sympathy."

"Do you hate him also?"

"More than you hate him."

"Why couldn't I have punished him?" roared Kerjean "Why did death cheat me of my vengeance?"

"Favraux isn't dead!" solemnly pronounced Judex.

"Favraux isn't dead?" repeated Kerjean. "Monsieur, I read in a newspaper that he had succumbed suddenly during a big dinner."

"And I tell you that Favraux is alive!" said Judex.

Seizing Kerjean by the arm, Judex brought him to the metallic mirror that viewed the cell of the banker. Roger slowly maneuvered the device to display Favraux dressed like a convict.

Seeing his enemy prostrate on the flagstones of his cell, the old Kerjean shook his fists. As blood rushed to his temples, he shouted furiously.

"It's Favraux! I recognize him! The thief! The monster! He's alive! Alive! Alive!"

While Roger retracted the mirror, Kerjean turned towards Judex. The superb figure crossed his arm to assume a dignified pose of silent vindictiveness.

The old miller of Les Sablons was dominated by the majesty of the mysterious figure.

"Who are you?" asked the old man.

"What you wanted to be, Kerjean. I am a judge!"

II. Face to Face

As Kerjean was rejoicing at the images in the metallic mirror, Favraux was gradually recovering from the shock of his imprisonment. At the same time, all the horror of his situation flooded his brain. The cell, the convict suit, the massive locked door, the fiery letters condemning him to a life sentence, and the omnipresent mirror would all comprise his eternal destiny!

The banker had no illusions. Judex would keep his word. He would never forgive. He would never relent. The sentence of punishment was final.

The miserable prisoner realized that he could live for years inside the four walls of this jail constructed to be an instrument of torture. He remembered stories of convicts confined as youths in prisons like the Bastille, Pignerol or Sainte-Marguerite. Inmates often left their incarceration as corpses with white hair.

He had recently read a book which vividly detailed the suffering of men condemned to life imprisonment in countries where the death penalty was abolished. Like the author of this study, he had reached the conclusion that it was better to die a hundred times than endure such a bleak existence.

Nevertheless, a last hope existed in him. It was inspired by his burning love of life as well as his instinctive fear of the beyond. His proud lack of scruples had previously prevented him from contemplating the afterlife.

Although Favraux had been plagued by mortal agony, his brain had not remained idle. For the first time in his life, the banker had truly examined his conscience. A list of crimes had flashed before his eyes. Before this day, he had glossed over the ruination and death caused by his actions. He had never been bothered by all the sorrow, bloodshed and misery associated with his financial ventures. This formerly incredulous materialist began to wonder if the justice of man was superseded by the justice of God.

All these thoughts had resulted in a cowardly desire to destroy himself. He formulated an ominous vow: *Let me embrace madness!* A state of insanity would satisfy his eagerness to forget his physical and mental degradation. The futility of such a desire plagued Favraux.

I won't even have this consolation. My brain is too healthy to ever produce a liberating lesion. I am fastened by a chain that only time will erode. How long will this last? 10 years, 15, years, 20 years!. Do I know? This must not be! Even if judgment awaits in another world, it's impossible to for divine retribution to be worse than my current fate. Why am I thinking like this? These beliefs are for spiritual weaklings. I ceased believing in such nonsense when I was 15 years old. I abandoned all the illusions of my youth. Why should I foolishly return towards a faith which I denied in my adolescence? No! There is no God! There is no Judgment Day! There is no Hell! There is nothing after death. There's only the end of all! The eternal sleep! The forgetfulness of the void! Much better to die!

For long time, Favraux searched for the means to extinguish his life. Should he starve himself to death? That wouldn't work. His jailers would force feed him. Strangle himself with a piece of his clothing? That would necessitate lengthy preparations that the metallic mirror would expose to its viewers.

Favraux would resort to the only swift means of suicide available. He would break his skull against the wall of his cell. Mustering all his forces, he prepared to pound his head against the granite when a roaring scream escaped him.

"There must be a better way! Since they can see me, I must have time to kill myself before they arrive!"

He slowly sat down on his wooden bed. Fifteen minutes of reflection only reinforced his prior resolution. Getting up, Favraux paced in a wide loop. Quickly he stood on his toes. Reaching towards the ceiling, he grabbed a sharp thimble from the electric bulb illuminating his cell. Favraux intended to use the glass fragment to cut his throat.

He didn't have time. Abruptly the door opened. Pierre Kerjean threw himself on the banker. Favraux was paralyzed by a vigorous stranglehold.

"Do you recognize me?" asked the ex-miller of Les Sablons.

"Kerjean!" shouted Favraux.

"Yes, it is I!"

Full of anger, Kerjean gazed contemptuously on the gilded merchant. "I foretold God would punish you, scum! Finally your rampage has been halted by a man stronger than you! All your victims are avenged! Your reign is finished, banker Favraux! The champion of justice has arrived! You will view the minutes as days, the days as years, and the years as centuries. Do you feel remorse? No. You are incapable of such a feeling.

"You smothered prosperity! You sowed misery! You instigated countless crimes! You destroyed families! You sent men to their graves! Do you regret the corruption spread in your wake? Your daughter is a noble and valiant lady voluntarily impoverished out of shame. She has been abandoned by your chosen bridegroom, a man only interested in money. She is reduced to supporting herself and her child, your grandson, amidst all the pitfalls threatening an honest woman alone in the streets of Paris. Do you care about her? None of that matters to you. You only care for yourself, scum!"

"I care very little for myself," said Favraux. "I want to die."

"As a coward! To flee your punishment... to escape pain." Kerjean looked down on the banker."I also lost everything important to me. My wife, my child, the old mill that was my private corner on Earth. All this you stole from me. I also was in prison, but I didn't want to die. I hoped for liberty. I endured those 20 years in the penal colony where I had been condemned for one reason. I needed to live not only for my loved ones but also for myself.

"I had to live to expiate the sins that I committed. Once I regained the ability to sleep at night, I didn't go to bed without asking forgiveness from God and the people whom I wronged. When I was freed, I looked the world squarely in the eye. I was purified of my crime. I returned to society as an honest man!

"In the isolation of this cell, freed from your temptations and insatiable appetites, why don't you fight to remake your soul? Why don't you strive to resurrect in your ulcerated heart an ounce of virtue?"

"You had the hope, the certainty to be free one day!" shouted Favraux in despair. "Not like me! No! No! You can't compare your sufferings to mine! I beg you to let me die!"

"We don't want that!"

"Have pity!"

"Did you pity me," angrily responded Kerjean, "when you knowingly sought to cheat me of my property by teaching me the art of fraud? Did you pity me doing my trial? With a single word, you could have persuaded the judges to show leniency. Instead, your court testimony transformed me from a petty forger into the worst from of criminal. Did you pity me when I begged you to help find my son?

"No! That why I can't forgive you. To let you die would be to forgive you. You will live, banker Favraux. You will live a, miserable life under my guard. Judex made me your jailer. As long as I, Kerjean, am here, you will never find freedom through death."

Upon hearing these words, the banker collapsed on the flagstones of his cell.

III. The Empty Coffin

Right after their misadventure of the Villa Brossard, Diana and Moralès put a safe distance between themselves and the hounds of Judex. They returned to Paris in a state of rage because their scheme had failed. The 5000 francs that they had been paid in advance by the Marquis de Birargues was scarcely enough to pay Moralès' large debts. The lovers moved out of the bogus Baron's rented apartment into a house owned by Diana.

"What will we do?" asked the gambler.

Reclining on a divan, his mistress pensively blew blue clouds of smoke from a cigarette.

"We're in a real mess!" he continued. "What if de Birargues denounces us to the police? We'll be arrested. I'll be sentenced to at least 10 years. Listen, Diana, you have to stop planning. You have to act. We can avoid the police by fleeing the country. Let's take what little money we have and leave without delay. Let's pack our trunks and flee tonight. I don't care where we go... Spain, Italy, Morocco, America... provided I'm with you."

"Idiot!" laughed Diana. Depositing her cigarette in an ashtray, she rose to confront Moralès. "You've forgotten that we are in possession of a document that identifies César as our accomplice. I'm convinced that instead of denouncing us, he will be more than happy to negotiate the return of this compromising document."

"It's possible! What about the woman?"

"Jacqueline? We don't have to fear her. In order to move against us, she would have to admit that Jeanne Bertin is really Jacqueline Aubry, the daughter of the banker Favraux. She has even more reasons to preserve her incognito and ignore us. Besides, she will have to deal with me if her silence is broken."

After stressing her implied threat, the adventuress changed the subject.

"There is in this moment something that worries me a lot more than César and Jacqueline."

"What's that?"

"Judex's letter."

Pulling of her blouse the mysterious message that the white poodle had deposited, Diana read it aloud:

If you don't want to suffer the fate of the banker Favraux, never cross his daughter's path again.

JUDEX

"Well!" exclaimed Moralès, "we can leave the woman alone."

"Read carefully the first sentence," suggested the adventuress.

Seizing itself paper, Moralès obeyed. "*If you don't want to suffer the fate of the banker Favraux...*" He was silent for a brief moment. "I see your point. Favraux must have been murdered."

"Not so quick," said Diana. "Now pay attention without interrupting."

"Speak!" said the gambler sitting down on the divan vacated by his mistress.

Lighting another cigarette, she sat on a stool opposite him. Diana's shrewd reasoning that was devoid of scruples.

"First, who is Judex?"

"Yes, who is Judex?"

"I had never heard of him before. Clearly, he possesses both formidable resources and reliable sources of information. After learning that we had captured and confined Favraux's daughter, he was able to trail us to our refuge. For the moment, let's ignore that. I want to focus on his letter. It tells us clearly that Favraux was struck down, and it hints that his assassin was Judex!"

"Maybe he's lying to scare us?" mused Moralès.

"That is what I first thought," said Diana, "but viewing this message in the context of certain events that unfolded at the Chateau des Sablons during the 48 hours preceding the banker's death, I must conclude that Judex wrote the truth."

"What events are you talking about?"

"First, I noticed that Favraux, in contrast to his normal behavior, was extremely nervous. Remember, he was behaving this way when his life seemed sweeter than ever. I know that he had secretly gone to Paris to consult the Celeritas Agency. The next day, its director, Cocantin, went to Les Sablons. He prowled around the house and the park acting like a detective searching for clues. There's one final detail which is significant. That evening, Favraux's cheerful mood struck me as artificial. As we entered the dining room, he whispered to me: 'My dear Marie, I really wish that I was older by two hours.'

"It was 8 o'clock when he pronounced this sentence. It was 10 o'clock when he collapsed! The day following the funeral of her father, Jacqueline abandoned all her fortune to charity, renounced her name, left her home, and confided her beloved child to former servants. If you factor in Jacqueline's actions, you will conclude that a disturbing mystery hovers over Favraux's death."

"You're right," said Moralès.

"I want to solve this mystery."

"Why?"

"Because I 'm convinced that the possession of this secret will not only enrich us, but also serve as a powerful weapon against those who struck down the banker."

"Aren't you afraid that we're treading on dangerous ground?"

"I'll dare anything!" Diana's eyes radiated a tragic audacity. "Must I remind you about what I said earlier. I don't like cowards. Take it or leave it. Walk with me or walk alone."

"Diana, don't talk to me like that!"

"Then show yourself worthy of me."

"I've already told you, I'm ready to die for you."

"It is not a question of being ready to die… but to live… and to live happily."

"Have you already unraveled this mystery?"

" I will!" shouted Diana. With savage determination, she made a diabolical pledge. "I shall learn how Favraux died by opening his grave!"

During an early hour in the morning, an automobile appeared in front of the small cemetery of Les Sablons. This vehicle contained four men and a woman. It parked in the exact place occupied earlier by Judex's car.

With the exception of the driver, all the passengers left the car. A muscular brute with wide shoulders carried a bulky package under his arm. He was followed by a slender dark man with a pointed beard and a sickly complexion. The bearded man wore a pince-nez over his excited eyes. These two men climbed the cemetery wall. Their companions, Diana and Moralès, concealed themselves in the thick foliage overlooking the embankment of the road. The driver moved the car to a side road situated 100 meters from the cemetery.

The night was dark and cloudy. Save for the distant baying of dogs, there was silence everywhere.

"Are you sure of these men?"asked Moralès.

His mistress was annoyed. "You are knocking me senseless with your questions… your doubts… your fears."

"We've never done something like this before."

"You believe that I should trust this task to newcomers? You know Crémard."

"I'm not worry about Crémard. It's the other fellow."

"Doctor Pop? I vouch for him also. I know his history in San Remo. A mere word from me to the authorities would cause him not only to lose his clientele but also his freedom."

"You're sure that he can diagnose exactly the cause of the banker's death?"

"He was one of the most brilliant students at the school of medicine in Montpellier. Wait! I hear noises."

"Maybe they're returning?"

"Already? That's not possible!"

"But it's them!"

In fact, Crémard and Dr. Pop had crossed over the cemetery wall. Diana, followed by Moralès, ran towards them on the road.

"Well?" asked the adventuress.

"You had me come here for nothing!" exclaimed the doctor.

"For nothing?" said Diana

Being a hoodlum raised in the ruined forts outside Paris, Crémard explained with blunt precision:

"The coffin is empty!"

IV. A Dark Affair

This revelation stunned both the reluctant Moralès and the bold Diana. She was naturally the first to regain her self-control. During the drive back to Paris, she ignored her lover's questions and launched herself into a deep meditation.

Her reflections apparently bore fruit. Upon returning to her place with Moralès, and paying the other members of the expedition with cash in sealed envelopes, her lips formed an enigmatic smile. Her large black eyes glimmered intensely.

"What do make of all this?" asked Moralès once he was alone with his mistress.

"For the moment, don't bother me. I need to straighten out all the ideas bubbling in my head. Be content to know everything is better than you suspected, and that even I had hoped. I need rest. Tomorrow morning, we leave for the countryside. Understand this, my little Moralès, if you obey me and show some backbone, the millions of Favraux residing in the coffers of the Public Assistance will be ours."

"What are you telling me?"

"The truth."

"But Favraux is dead."

"Favraux is alive!"

"Alive!" yelled the overwrought Moralès. "What's going on?"

"The corpse of a murder victim wasn't removed from the cemetery of Les Sablons. The grave robbers abducted a sleeping man."

"How could you believe something so incredible?"

"I remembered something that I had originally dismissed as unimportant. When Jacqueline renounced her fortune, I secretly spied on her. I saw her shocked by a telephone call. She became pale and trembled. Gashing her teeth, she stammered these words. 'My father's voice. He begs my forgiveness!' Believing that she was either mad or hallucinating, I quickly hid. If you analyze all the facts, you will come to the same conclusion. The banker wasn't a corpse stolen from his tomb, but a living man in the hands of his kidnappers. Certain pieces of information are lacking to completely confirm my deductions, but I know where to find them. As early as tomorrow, I shall have proof. *Bonsoir*, my little Moralès. Sleep soundly. Lose yourself in the rapture of a beautiful dream. I shall make your dream a reality."

The next morning, at around 10 o'clock, the two criminals went to the Celeritas Agency, Rue Milton.

Since becoming the director, Cocantin had seen the Agency's clientele progressively diminish. So he welcomed the visitors.

Dressed fashionably, Diana proceeded to parse the sleuth.

"Monsieur Cocantin, you probably don't remember me?"

"*Au contraire*, you're Mademoiselle Marie Verdier, former governess of Les Sablons." Full of admiration for the young woman's beauty, Cocantin was easily charmed by her during their casual talk.

"My dear Monsieur Cocantin, I had always hoped to see you again. I am not called Marie Verdier anymore. Embarking on a theatrical career, I have taken the name of Diana Monti."

"A very pretty name," approved the detective, even more captivated.

"And now," resumed the dangerous temptress, "allow me to introduce my friend, Baron Moralès. He was gracious enough to accompany me. We have a very delicate matter to discuss."

"Mademoiselle, Baron, believe me, I will listen with the utmost attention."

"Monsieur Cocantin," declared Diana, "I can be blunt with you."

"You are correct, Mademoiselle," replied Ribaudet's nephew. He pointed to the Imperial bust on his shelf. "Having applied to the modern private detective agency the principles and methods of the Napoleonic police..."

Cocantin was about to embark on a long doctoral dissertation, but he never finished his lecture. Rising from her chair, Diana placed her hands on Cocantin's desk and leaned forward. Her face was thrust into the detective's.

"Monsieur Cocantin, where is Favraux?"

"Favraux!" exclaimed Prosper Cocantin. He had never expected such a question. "He's dead!"

"Then why is his coffin empty?" objected Diana.

"His coffin is empty?"

"I learned this last night at the cemetery of Les Sablons."

"Mademoiselle, I don't care for this sort of joke."

"I'm being seriously. Monsieur Favraux no longer occupies his coffin."

Cocantin had no penchant for the trade that he inherited. He stared with gaping eyes.

"It's unheard of! It's crazy! It's insane! You must be mistaken."

"I repeat," insisted the adventuress, "that Favraux is no longer in his grave."

Then Moralès, whom his mistress had coached, shouted at the distraught detective.

"The man who abducted Favraux is Judex, and you are Judex!"

"Me! Judex!" The accusation was causing Cocantin's head to spin.

"Yes! You!" screamed the gambler.

"Cocantin, what did you do with Favraux?" hammered Diana.

The naive detective was too inexperienced to suspect the trap that was being laid for him. He was incapable of concealing his feelings.

"I would give two years of my life not to be involved in this dark affair."

Hopelessly gazing at the bust of Napoleon, he imagined his idol yelling at him: "*Cocantin, defend yourself!*"

Somewhat consoled, the director of the Celeritas Agency clumsily strove to act offended. "I protest, Baron. I protest, Mademoiselle. Prosper Cocantin is neither a vampire nor an assassin!"

"You are Judex!" insisted the two outlaws.

"I am hardly Judex," asserted Cocantin. "I was hired to find him."

"By whom?" questioned Moralès.

"By Favraux himself!"

"That can't be true!" said Diana.

"I'll prove it."

The detective decided to clear himself of the accusation. Taking a small key attached to his watch chain, he unlocked a desk drawer and withdrew two sheets of paper.

"Before his death, Monsieur Favraux had received two letters. I returned the originals to his family, but I kept copies. You can examine them."

At peace with his conscience, he showed the papers to the two visitors.

"You must realize that, if I had been Judex, I would have retrieved the originals of these two letters from this unfortunate banker's daughter."

"Certainly, Monsieur Cocantin," hurriedly declared Diana. She was pleased with the knowledge learned through trickery. "Our accusation was inexcusable. Please forgive us! How can we make it up to you? What do you want us to do? We were lead astray by rumors."

"What rumors?"

"One hears so many things," hinted the adventuress politely. "No one can prevent the circulation of libelous gossip."

"To accuse me of such things," said Cocantin indignantly. "My close associates know that I'm incapable of harming a fly."

"The world is so cruel."

"To paint me as a man that secretly kills people and steals their corpses! It's abominable! How can I halt such slander?"

"There is only one way," suggested Diana. "Help us unmask Judex!"

"I swore to wash my hands of this case."

"It's in your interest more than ours," argued Moralès. "In order to stop all this stupid gossip, the best course for you is to expose this man of mystery."

"The Baron is right," said Diana. "This scoundrel is still at large. It is essential to cut this evil out at the roots. By helping us, Monsieur, not only will you be helping yourself, but you will be providing a valuable service to humanity."

"You have persuasive arguments," acknowledged Cocantin.

"Can we count on your help?" asked Moralès.

"Before reopening this serious matter, I need to review the case file."

"My dear Monsieur Cocantin," said Diana Monti staring romantically at the private detective, "you don't imagine for an instant that I'm engaging your services solely by flashing my pretty eyes?"

"That alone would suffice," Cocantin said gallantly.

"Any labor merits compensation," replied Diana. "There are 100,000 francs for you, Monsieur Cocantin, if you succeed."

Overcome more by the flirtatious gaze of the ex-governess than by the promise of a large sum, Cocantin seized Diana's hands o and kissed them with more fervor than "Baron" Moralès.

"It's agreed," stated Prosper Cocantin. "Count on me. I'm your servant."

"Very good," approved Diana. "Absolute discretion."

"Discretion and speed!"

"Perfect!"

"What must I do?" questioned the detective naively.

"Await my orders!" declared the adventuress while continuing to bewitch Cocantin with her smile.

"All is well," said Diana triumphantly to her lover in the street. She leaned over and whispered into his ear. "I wasn't bluffing when I said we could recover the banker's millions."

"But first, it's essential to find Judex," noted Moralès.

"Naturally."

"And you believe that this Cocantin is competent?"

"Him!" cynically laughed Diana. "He is no more a detective than I'm an honest woman. I used him to obtain the necessary information for my plan to succeed. Now that's he provided it, I have no further need for him."

"Then why confide in him? Why promise him 100,000 francs?"

"Simply because I need a man who serves me with docile loyalty, and yet is incapable of penetrating my stratagems. Furthermore, he can act as a scapegoat if necessary. Cocantin is the ideal minion. He will serve us well!"

"You're a genius."

"No, but I'm very hungry. Take me to a good restaurant. We will then return to the house. My darling, we have much to do!"

V. The Obsession

Diana Monti was restless. Constantly looking at the street from her window, she mumbled to herself.

"It's essential to find Judex! It would be fatal if we don't. There's not a moment to lose. Favraux's millions! Mine at last! What revenge!"

The adventuress quickly remembered her life. She was the product of one of those shady households whose members lack any definite profession. Such families spend most of their existence avoiding the police and the courts. When this precocious beauty informed her parents that she wanted to be a dancer, they sent her to Italy to learn the trade. At the age of 16, she was wooed by Prince Martelli, one of the wealthiest aristocrats in Rome. Crazily infatuated with the young ballerina, he placed this girl of modest means on a pedestal. The Prince showered her with magnificent gifts and gave her a very thorough education. For several years, she had a luxurious life. Everything changed when Martelli died unexpectedly without taking the time to assure the future of his mistress.

She had to sell her possessions. Money soon melted in her hands. As her wicked instincts gained dominance, she evolved into one of those "flowers of evil" that live only for the moment. She voluntarily chose a life filled with shameful idleness and artificial pleasure. That existence changed when luck placed her in the presence of the banker Favraux. He saw her in Nice on a bench on the Promenade des Anglais. Rendered penniless by ruinous gambling, she was stranded in the French city. She didn't even have the resources to sell her jewels pawned long ago at the Mont-de-Piété.

Favraux imagined Diana to be an impoverished woman. He questioned her. Diana recognized the famous gilded banker. He had passed her several times in the casino without giving her a moment's attention. She only partially lied to the powerful financier. She identified herself as Marie Verdier (her true name), but she misrepresented herself as a teacher without position or relations. Of course, she hinted at her desire to be rescued from this unfortunate situation. However, she created the impression that she would rather die than owe her livelihood to immorality. She manipulated Favraux so skillfully that he began to fall in love for the first time in his life. Soon, she was installed as the governess of his grandson.

The banker was too smitten to suspect her fraudulent nature. His initial impressions were reinforced by the forged documents provided by Marie Verdier to support her claims. Thoroughly infatuated by the beautiful siren, the gilded banker believed her to be full of the austere virtues purged from his own soul. Consequently, he didn't want her to be his mistress, but his wife.

She had been very close to attaining her goal. After the disillusion of her monumental failure, she hoped to revive her dream. All her soul was committed to this outrageous desire. She would resurrect her moribund scheme of marrying the man whom she had already bent to her will. The Machiavellian plan forged by this formidable woman began to unfold. It can be summarized in the following steps. First, locate Judex. Second, force him to return Favraux. Third, have the banker reclaim the millions surrendered by his daughter to the Public Assistance. Fourth, marry Favraux. Fifth, assure herself of his fortune by killing him. More than anything, she was resolved to accomplish all her objectives.

She was sprawled on her divan with her chin supported by her hands. Her eyes hypnotized by the pit of infamy into which she was falling, Diana's face bore the monstrous rictus of a savage beast! The doorbell's ring interrupted her meditation. Moralès had returned.

"You were gone a long time," reproached the agitated Diana.

"It wasn't my fault," argued the gambler, browbeaten by the earlier tongue lashings of his mistress. "Crémard wasn't at home. I searched for two hours. I finally found him playing cards with friends in a small bar near the northern train station."

"Will he come?"

"Tonight. He promised to be here at 6 o'clock with Le Coltineur." The alias of Crémard's associate was a French term for a coal heaver.

"All is well," said Diana. "Thank you."

Between the two lovers, there was a gloomy silence which glided like death. Removing his hat, Moralès took his mistress by the hand.

"Diana, you will brand me a coward again…"

"Why?"

"I don't doubt your plan's success. We'll find Judex and Favraux, but you've forgotten something…"

"What?"

"Favraux has a daughter. She knows you're a crook. She'll talk."

"She won't."

"Why?"

"Because tonight she dies!"

"No! No! Not that! I don't want that!" Moralès became pale.

"What are you saying?"

The gambler's conscience had reawakened. "I'm a thief, but I'll never be an assassin!"

"Who's asking you to kill her?"

"You!"

"You're crazy! Since Crémard and Le Coltineur will be there, your hand won't be the one delivering the fatal blow."

"That's unimportant! I'll be an accomplice. Tomorrow you'll give another order that will incriminate me even further."

"My little Moralès, takes care!" threatened the adventuress. "I don't waste my time with useless words. You can do what you want. You can remain here, or leave. But remember this: If you refuse to obey me, the world will know that Baron Moralès is really Robert Kerjean, the son of the miller condemned to 20 years for fraud, and the man wanted by the police for various robberies. Now, choose!"

Diana's lover sat down in despair. Although the burden of dreadful crimes weighed on his soul, he spinelessly surrendered.

"You win! Favraux's daughter will die tonight."

At the same moment, Judex left his prisoner under the guard of Pierre Kerjean and Roger. The man in the black cloak departed the Chateau Rouge for an unknown destination. He was totally oblivious to the new danger that threatened Jacqueline.

VI. The Ambush

While preparing for dinner, Jacqueline Aubry read a letter from Gisèle de Birargues that had been delivered this morning:

Château des Aigles, Florac
My dear friend,
Arriving here after a long and difficult trip, I rushed to inform you about my family.

My brother was sincere in his remorse. Mother and I found him to be a very different man. He developed a strong fever. Without being extremely concerned, the doctor ordered him to rest. César begged me to tell you that he is humbled by your admirable generosity.

Following his recovery, my brother asked our father for permission to take a trip to the Far East.

And you, dear friend, how are you coping? Write me. I'll be happy to hear from you. I'll visit you as soon as I return.

GISÈLE

Suddenly, there was a knock on the door. Jacqueline stopped reading the letter. It was Madame Chapuis. Huffing and puffing, she breathlessly waved a blue paper

"A telegram for you, Madame Bertin."

"A telegram!" said Jacqueline. She was filled with anguish upon reading it:

Come quickly, Jean is very gravely ill.

"I'm being tested again!" shouted Jacqueline. "Lord, I thanked you too soon!" Regaining her composure, she made a fateful decision.

"It's 6:15. There must be a train around 7 o'clock for Loisy. I just have time to make it. While I pack, Madame Chapuis, could you summon a taxi?"

"Yes, my child! I'm sorry that I can't accompany you. The poor darling! I hope this isn't serious."

Jacqueline feared that this laconically brutal dispatch hid the full truth. She worried that even worse news awaited her.

Climbing into the taxi destined for the train station, a thought gnawed at her.

Could he have been coached into some new escapade by that boy who prowled the alleys of Paris? Marianne promised to supervise them, but an accident may have quickly resulted. If I lose my son, I'll have no reason to live! The banker's daughter strove to repress her tears. *I'm coming, my angel. Your mother will be at your side. My beloved son!*

The train ride seemed an eternity. Jacqueline was anxious to see her son and hear his voice. Once she was close to him, she hoped that her fears would be allayed. When the train stopped at the station, she immediately alighted. Jacqueline walked very quickly. When possible, she ran. She approached the bridge over the Seine that led to Loisy.

All was calm as dusk fell. Silence dominated the bridge. The structure was generally deserted during the dinner hour. Two men slowly advanced with hands in their pockets. They stopped in the middle of the bridge to observe two children fishing in a boat close to the shore.

"Are we going through with it, Crémard?"

"Yes, Coltineur."

"But what about the children?"

"They don't matter. They can't see us."

Still distracted by thoughts of her son, Jacqueline came within range of the two brigands. The criminals seized her. They threw a black hood over her head. Before the young woman could defend herself, they threw her over the parapet into the Seine.

The two killers were satisfied that their audacious and violent crime was a success. While Jean's mother disappeared under the waves, Crémard and Le Coltineur quickly rejoined Diana and Moralès, who waited in an automobile on the other side of the bridge.

Jeannot was extremely happy. Inseparable from the Licorice Kid, he went every day with him to the local school.

The two children were very well-behaved. Jeannot had profited from the lessons learned from his mother. The Licorice Kid gratefully appreciated the enormous advantages of a country life. Nothing to the world could prompt him to commit even a minor prank capable of endangering his new situation. He was fed regularly and given a comfortable bed. He had traded his eccentric garb for the clothing of a small peasant. Comfortable in his new surroundings, he demonstrated a strong loyalty towards the young friend responsible for his happiness. This gratitude translated into a deep affection.

One Saturday, Jean had returned from school having earned a Good Conduct Medal. The Licorice Kid had reaped a harvest of goodwill by working on the farm. Papa Bontemps and Marianne were both laboring in the garden. Confident in the good behavior of their two charges, the adults gave permission to the children to play hide and seek with their friends.

Doubtlessly, the two kids had already hatched one of those childish plots that delights fathers and frightens mothers. For after exchanging a quick wink, both of them deviated from their authorized route to the City Hall where the golden youth of Loisy normally played together. They followed a path that led to the Seine. After cutting two poles of modest dimensions in a hedge, they migrated towards a small shop normally visited on Sundays by Parisians who relieved their boredom through fishing.

The Licorice Kid was both negotiator and cashier for his young associate. Marianne had rewarded Jeannot for his winning the Medal with money that his mother had set aside for him. Entrusted with this small fortune of 20 *sous* by Jeannot, the Licorice Kid purchased two fishing lines and a handful of worms before rejoining his companion on the riverbank. The children climbed him into a small boat moored near the bridge that crossed the Seine. The Licorice Kid skillfully attached the lines to the fishing poles.

"Now we only have to catch the fish!" predicted the Kid handing a pole to his friend.

Their fishing had lasted a long while without any tangible results other the children's lines becoming entangled two or three times. The Kid unraveled the lines with remarkable dexterity.

"Over there!" cried the Licorice Kid. "There's a lady in the water!"

With their eyes focused on their hooks, the two children had been unaware of the vicious drama that had just unfolded on the bridge. Both of them saw a human form sinking in the river.

Jeannot let loose a cry of terror, but the Licorice Kid rapidly made a decision.

"Don't do anything, little buddy. Don't stir, and let me handle it. When I worked along Auteuil, I helped bargemen pull drowning victims out of the water. This isn't easy. You're either strong enough—or you're not!"

Unmooring the boat from the bank, the Licorice Kid rowed vigorously towards the area where the victim had disappeared. The moment the small boat arrived near the first battery of the bridge, Jacqueline came back to the surface.

"There!" shouted the Licorice Kid. Seizing a boat-hook located at the far end of the small craft, he was able to grapple the clothing of the unfortunate woman as she was sinking for the second time.

"Here, Jeannot," ordered the resourceful child, "hold on to the wood, and don't loosen the hook. If she sinks again, we won't be able to find her."

Energized by his friend, Jean seized the boat-hook and employed all his strength to execute his assignment. Without losing a second, the Licorice Kid rowed to the distant shore that was three or four meters away.

At last, thanks to the Kid's efforts, the boat reached the shore with the body of the woman in tow. Unconscious of their heroic act, they called for help. As no one replied, the Licorice Kid removed the hood covering the poor woman's face. A grasp escaped his lips. With a gesture, the Kid pushed Jean away.

"Go to the house for help," ordered the former street urchin. "Run, little buddy, run!"

The Kid had recognized the mother of his friend. He intuitively didn't want Jean to see his mother until it could be determined that she was still alive. Having seen the bargemen in action, he hurried to imitate the rhythmic movements designed to reignite the breathing of the drowned.

The brave child sweated blood and water. Out of breath, he still refused to give up. Finally, a first breath escaped from Jacqueline's lips.

"Are you feeling better, my good lady?" asked the triumphant Licorice Kid, adding to himself, "You'll be extremely happy to learn that I saved your Mama, little buddy!"

123

30 Centimes   Tous les Jeudis

LES ROMANS CINÉMA

JUDEX

Par ARTHUR BERNÈDE et LOUIS FEUILLADE

CINQUIÈME ÉPISODE
LE MOULIN TRAGIQUE

M. ARTHUR BERNÈDE

Photo Gaumont

Part Five: The Mill of Misery

1. Is This a Crime?

"Messieurs, I don't know who you are, and I don't want to know. Not only did you save me, but you also avenged me by striking down the man who stole my honor and destroyed my family. I belong to you, body and soul. Command me. I want to be your servant. I need to be your slave."

These were the words of thanks that old Kerjean delivered to Judex and his brother.

"But I want you to be my friend," replied Judex extending his hand.

Trembling with emotion, the liberated convict seized the hand that had been generously offered.

"Thank you!"

Better than a flowery speech, this simple outburst of gratitude proved to Jacques and Roger that they had found in the ex-miller of Les Sablons a man willing to die defending the door of his master. They entrusted him with the duty of guarding their prisoner during their absences from the Chateau Rouge,

Kerjean scrupulously performed his tasks because he enjoyed seeing the brutal punishment of the man that he abhorred more than anyone else in the world.

Several times during the night, he awoke to leave his quarters close to the banker's cell. His sole purpose was to listen to the moans of the prisoner. Every morning, he awoke early in order to enter Judex's laboratory. There he maneuvered the metallic mirror to observe Favraux crouched like a stalked beast counting the hours of eternity.

One morning, Kerjean perused a book at random from Judex's table. As he opened it, a picture fell out. It was the photograph of Jacqueline. Surprised by his brother, Judex had hidden the picture in this volume rather than restore it to his secret drawer.

Who is this pretty woman? wondered Kerjean. The old man was captivated by the expression of melancholy on Jacqueline's face He scrutinized the graceful countenance. There were signs of teardrops on the portrait. Holding the picture between his hands, he felt towards this unknown woman a sympathy born without rhyme or reason.

Kerjean was slipping the portrait back into the volume when the secret door accessing the iron stairway opened to admit Jacques and to his brother.

"Is everything going well?" asked Judex.

"Very well, Monsieur," answered Kerjean.

"The prisoner?"

"More and more desolated."

"He could live a long time like this!" commented Judex as he peered into the mirror.

Judex intended to gauge the ex-miller's morale.

"Kerjean, are you happy?"

"Yes, Monsieur. Thanks to you, I can hope again."

"My brother is already searching for your son," resumed Judex.

"You are so good to me!"

"I have nothing definite to tell," explained Roger, "but be patient and brave. We will certainly find him!"

"Yes, we will save him," energetically asserted Judex.

Strongly moved, the liberated convict looked at Jacques and Roger with religious fervor.

"You are good, both of you! Not only do you personify justice but also compassion. I had stopped believing in anything because only hate gnawed inside me. Now I'm a better man because you have shown me friendship."

Kerjean paused to scrutinize the faces of his audience. Encouraged by the benevolent attitude of the two brothers, the old man resumed.

"I want to revisit my old mill where my son was born and where my wife died. It's not that far away. Now that you

126

have revived hope inside me, I want to see this house where I left my soul. If I sit next to the silent wheel, I can dream about my child and his mother."

"Go, Kerjean, go," authorized Judex.

"When?"

Whenever you want!"

"Will you let me go right away?"

"Heartily."

"I shall return tonight."

"Don't worry, Kerjean. Leave, my friend."

The ex-miller was overwhelmed with joy. Thinking of the former home where his happiness had both blossomed and withered, he departed carrying his stick

"What a stout fellow!" said Roger to his brother. "You judged him well. We can trust him. He will never betray us."

But Judex was no longer listening to his brother. With a gesture that seemed absent-minded, but was really conscious, he opened the volume. He looked at Jacqueline's portrait with unmixed adoration. He was not the lover that tenderly contemplated a voluptuous woman. He was the religious devotee in ecstasy before the image of a saint.

After furtively glancing at Jacques, Roger withdrew discretely to a corner of the vast laboratory. Settled in an armchair, he removed a morning newspaper from his jacket pocket.

"Brother!" he exclaimed after perusing the newspaper.

"What did you find?" asked Judex.

"I just found this on the second page. Let me read it to you: *Is this a crime? In Loisy-sur-Seine, two small boys pulled a woman in mourning clothes, Madame Jeanne Bertin, out of the river...*"

"What did you say?" shouted Judex. Grabbing the newspaper out of his brother's hands, he read the item that finished thusly: *...A piano teacher from Paris, the unfortunate lady is in a coma and could not be questioned.*"

"It's horrible! 48 hours ago, we rescued this poor woman. Once again, she's the victim of an assault. Who are these miscreants persecuting this noble lady? They are doubtlessly the same people that wanted to deliver her to César de Birargues! Now to silence their victim, they cowardly plot her murder!"

Filled with magnificent indignation, Judex became as radiant as an archangel who has conquered a demon.

"I must crush these criminals! For them, there shall be no mercy! No extenuating circumstances! Only death! Roger, you agree with me? Only death!"

A sort of mystical intensity enveloped Judex.

"I must go to her aid. Will I be able to save her? God, who miraculously revived Kerjean to serve our designs, will not want her to perish. That would be an unspeakable tragedy. We would have on both our consciences the murder of this innocent woman. Our mission of sacred justice would remain forever tarnished by an indelible spot. We must ensure at any price that she's protected from her enemies. Remain here, Roger, and wait for me. I'll telephone you. *Au revoir!*"

"Do you love her?" shouted Roger grasping the hands of his feverish brother.

"Be quiet!" said Judex.

"Brother, I know you," continued Roger. "I know you are too proud to fail in your duty. Yes, you will be faithful to our sacred oath of vengeance! Let me tell you…"

"Speak!"

"Your love for the banker's daughter must not make you forget our hate for the father."

"Be assured," shouted Judex while holding his brother in his arms. "Since you read my heart, let me reply in turn. Fear nothing. I shall do my duty. Nothing but my duty! Even if I must rip out my heart! I swear it!"

After a long embrace with his brother, Judex disappeared by the secret door and franticly climbed the rungs of the iron ladder.

"I want her to live! She shall live!"

II. The Ambulance

"Wake up, Mama!"

Jeannot had climbed into his mother's bed. Kneeling close to her with clasped hands, he sobbed.

"Wake up quickly. Wake up!"

Helped by two neighbors, Marianne and her father had transported Jacqueline to their house. Nevertheless, she remained unconscious. It was difficult for Marianne to contain her sorrow. The Licorice Kid was equally dismayed.

"I did what I could!"

Suddenly Jean issued a cry of joy. Jacqueline groaned and half-opened her eyes. It was only a flash, but it was sufficient to be noticed by the child.

A very soft sigh exhaled from her lips. Her arms shifted lightly as if they wanted to hug the child. Jean smothered his mother's frozen face with kisses. Jacqueline closed her eyes.

The Licorice Kid gently approached the bed.

"Come, get off the bed and let her rest. You see that she's getting better."

The country physician, Doctor Pelet, arrived with Bontemps. The farmer had hastily gone to fetch him earlier. The general practitioner closely examined the young woman.

When he had finished, the doctor turned towards Marianne. He pointed affably towards the two children huddled in a corner.

"Are these the two young heroes who prevented the unfortunate drowning?"

"Yes, Doctor."

"You're superb, my little ones," declared the doctor. He patted the two children on the head. "If she had stayed under water a minute longer, she would have died." Pelet turned his attention to Jeannot. "You already have earned a Good Conduct Medal. Both of you should be awarded medals of valor. You've earned them."

"And Madame Bertin?" questioned Marianne.

"She's out of danger," diagnosed the doctor, "but she's very weak. I am prescribing medicine that must be administered with the greatest care. Hopefully it will restore her strength." He wrote the prescription. "These two boys are magnificent. Who are they? Her sons?"

"That one," volunteered Marianne pointing to Jeannot.

"And I'm her adopted son," volunteered the Licorice Kid. He was elated that his foster mother was improving.

"Here!" concluded Dr. Pelet handing the prescription to Papa Bontemps. "I will return early tomorrow morning to gauge the medicine's effects. Good-bye, my brave friends! Good-bye, young heroes! Let me hug you!"

The night went very badly. Bontemps, Marianne and the Licorice Kid alternated watching Jacqueline. She had a delirious fever.

The unfortunate woman relived in a nightmare all the ordeals that she had just experienced. She heard the distant voice of her father, the voice from the tomb that implored her forgiveness. She remembered her abduction by Marie Verdier in the car and her attack by the two unknown assailants who threw her into the Seine.

Pleas for mercy and cries of terror arose from her lips ending in a final outburst.

"To me, my Jean! My child!"

Towards the morning, the devoted Marianne delivered a dose of the medicine. The banker's daughter dozed off into a calm sleep. When Dr. Pelet returned, he examined her again.

"All is not well," said the doctor gravely.

"Doctor, we did everything that you ordered," replied Marianne.

"There is neither any threat of congestion nor pleurisy. However, there is a nervous breakdown provoking an overall weakening. She is predisposed to multiple complications that I better not describe."

While Marianne wiped away two tears, the doctor reflected an instant before resuming.

"I don't doubt for a single instant that Madame Bertin is under vigilant care here. Nevertheless, I consider her state serious enough to warrant her transfer to a hospital."

"*Mon Dieu*!"

"Don't grieve, my brave woman. This isn't a death sentence. It is an urgent precaution that I recommend."

"The doctor is being wise," interjected Papa Bontemps. "You see, Marianne, we must follow his advice. We must not reproach ourselves."

"I shall telephone Paris," declared the doctor. "I'm friendly with the director of the Beaujon Hospital. He'll send an ambulance. I'll apprise him of my diagnostic. Be calm, your friend will be cared for like a princess."

"Thank you again, Doctor," said Marianne. "We love Madame Bertin! She's such a good woman! It would be tragic if she died!"

"Courage and trust," said Dr. Pelet, squeezing Marianne's hand.

As the doctor left, she wiped away her eyes. While she was outside, a man about 40 years old approached her. Tall and elegantly attired, he addressed her in a cordial tone.

"Do you have an invalid at your place?"

"Yes, Monsieur."

"Your husband maybe?"

"No, a lady."

"Is this the young woman whom two children rescued last night in the Seine?"

"Yes, Monsieur."

"Is she recovering?"

"She's not doing well. Dr. Pelet is telephoning Paris for an ambulance to take her to Beaujon Hospital."

"Poor woman!" muttered the passerby. "She must have tried to drown herself."

"Monsieur, that's not true!"

"What happened then? Do you think it was an accident?" asked the stranger.

"I don't know, Monsieur. Madame Bertin hasn't regained consciousness."

"Let's hope that everything will sort itself out. *Au revoir*, Madame."

While Marianne returned to the house, the stranger went to the post office where he passed Dr. Pelet on his way out. The stranger mumbled between his teeth.

"If we want to arrive first, there's not a minute to lose."

Before 11 o'clock, an ambulance stopped in front of the Bontemps home.

An orderly quickly got out and conferred with the Bontemps. The orderly and the driver were taken to Jacqueline. Pale and motionless, her eyes were completely closed. She had no notion of what was happening around her. With a lot of precautions, the two men carried her on a stretcher to the car where a nurse waited in the interior.

Bontemps, Marianne, the Licorice Kid and Jean sadly formed a small procession behind the stretcher. Jeannot was told that his sleeping mother needed to go somewhere else to recuperate. Despite this explanation, the child was still upset. As he walked, his eyes focused on the patient. When the men put the stretcher on the ground before slipping it inside the ambulance, Jeannot planted a very soft kiss on his mother's cheek. Minutes later, when the procession moved away, the child burst into tears.

"Don't fret, little buddy," consoled the Licorice Kid hugging his friend. "You will see your Mama again!"

Jeannot's response invoked a bittersweet memory inside Bontemps and Marianne.

"They're taking her away like they took Papa. And Papa never returned!"

The Licorice Kid tried to divert his friend's sorrow.

"Come! Let's play with the nice soldiers that Madame Chapuis gave you."

"I don't want to play," refused Jeannot. "I want to cry."

"What! You're not a man. You're a little girl."

"No, I'm a big boy."

"Well, big boys don't cry."

Seeing Bontemps wipe a tear, Jeannot objected.

"Look at Papa Julien, he also cries. He's not a little girl."

"Don't be stupid, little buddy!" exclaimed the Licorice Kid. "Come! If you won't play with soldiers, we can feed the rabbits and the donkey."

Placing his arm around Jean's waist, the Licorice Kid moved him towards the shed. Suddenly Jeannot yelled.

"Monsieur Vallières!"

The austere form of the likable ex-secretary cast a shadow on the threshold of the front gate.

Right away, Bontemps and Marianne went to greet him. After embracing Jeannot, Vallières raised his hand benevolently.

"I read in the morning newspaper that Madame Bertin had a serious accident."

"Alas!" replied Bontemps. "It's true."

"I just passed an ambulance."

"They took Madame."

"Is she very ill?"

"Jeannot," said Marianne, "go play with your friend."

The two children moved away. With her father's approval, Marianne told Vallières everything she knew.

"Madame must have been attached by thieves! Filthy scavengers! Assassins!"

"Last night," confirmed Bontemps, "she said in her delirium that some men assaulted her. She also mentioned Mademoiselle Verdier, Jean's former governess. Madame mixed up everything. I couldn't understand her. The important thing is that she's gets better."

"The doctor has hope," emphasized Marianne. "For some time, Madame has been plagued by bad luck."

The loyal girl had scarcely pronounced this sentence when another ambulance parked near the house. Slightly different from the first, it displayed the insignia of a red cross. An orderly got out of the seat next to the driver's.

"Are you Monsieur Bontemps?"

"Yes, Monsieur," said Papa Julien.

"We've come from the Beaujon Hospital for a Madame Bertin."

"This is crazy!" exclaimed Bontemps. "Madame Bertin has just left a quarter of an hour ago in another ambulance from Beaujon."

"Monsieur, that's impossible!"

"It's the truth."

"This is too much," said the astonished orderly. He was joined by a young nurse.

"The director couldn't have sent two cars at once," she said. "Were you given a hospital admittance form?"

"Not at all."

"The others definitely said they were from Beaujon?"

"Clearly."

"This is odd!" stressed the nurse. "I beg your pardon, gentlemen and lady. We shall return to Paris and report to the hospital administrator."

The pensive Vallières saw the ambulance depart. He turned towards Papa Julien and Marianne.

"Don't worry. I'll go straight to the Beaujon hospital. I'll send you news of Madame Jacqueline."

As the ex-secretary moved away himself, Jeannot and the Licorice Kid ran towards him.

"*Au revoir*, Monsieur Vallières," said Jean.

"*Au revoir*, little one."

"My friend wants to meet you. Can he?"

"Of course."

The Licorice Kid grasped the hand of the banker's ex-secretary.

"Are you a friend of Jean's Mama?"

Vallières replied with a kindly smile.

"Yes, little one. Perhaps her best friend."

III. To the Edge of the Abyss

After the town of Loisy, the ambulance carrying the unconscious Jacqueline didn't take the road to Paris. Instead it followed the road along the edges of the Seine to Meulan. Shortly before arriving in Bonnières, the car stopped. The orderly seated next to the driver turned towards the nurse in the back with Jacqueline.

"All is well?" he asked.

"Yes," replied a commanding voice.

"You still want to go to the mill?"

"More than ever."

"I would rather…"

"Leave me alone. Pay attention to the road."

The driver, Crémard, put the car in gear. "She's in a bad mood this morning," he whispered to his male colleague. "She worried that we'll end up in a ditch." While Moralès remained silent, Crémard continued to speak. "Everything is working beautifully. Our lady boss knows how to run a business. She never hesitates. She always skates on thin ice. She puts fire in your belly. She's a bold one."

In fact, Diana had just succeeded in an audacious scam worthy of the greatest criminals of the past and present.

She had dispatched Dr. Pop to Loisy to gather information. As soon as Pop telephoned her and repeated his conversation with Marianne, the adventuress had made her decision.

"Moralès," she had ordered, "find Crémard right away. He must be at home. Tell him to find an ambulance and bring it to my door within an hour."

"Within an hour? If we ask him now…"

"He's resourceful. I'm sure that he can do it. You must return immediately."

"I would like to know…"

"We must be in Loisy before 11 o'clock. There! Are you happy? And now hurry. We don't have a second to lose."

Moralès had punctually executed the instructions of his mistress. Always prepared, Crémard promised to be on time. In fact, at 10 o'clock exactly, he arrived at Diana's door driving an ambulance that he "borrowed" from a Passy garage which he had long kept under observation. While Moralès, disguised as an orderly, was seated in the front, Diana, dressed as a nurse, took her place to the interior. It was this ambulance that arrived a quarter of an hour before the real one from the Beaujon Hospital.

Once more, the criminals had abducted Jacqueline.

Moving at a very quick pace, the ambulance followed the road of Mantises to Bonnières. Before reaching the Chateau des Sablons, the former property of the banker Favraux, Crémard considerably reduced his speed to take a small route that led directly to the old Kerjean mill. The ambulance stopped opposite the courtyard, overrun by shrubs and weeds. Strutting boldly, the cynical Crémard got out of the car. So did Moralès. He was pale and visibly upset. Diana also left the ambulance. The two men retrieved the stretcher bearing Jacqueline. Still unconscious, she seemed close to dying.

"Moralès, take her into the mill," ordered the adventuress. "Crémard, get rid of the ambulance. Return here after dusk with a different car."

As Crémard departed, Moralès lifted Jacqueline in his arms. Crossing the court, he climbed broken down steps of antiquated wood. Entering a cold room on the first floor, he deposited his burden on an old bench.

Leaning towards Jacqueline, Diana listened to the breathing of the unconscious woman.

"I was hoping that she would die *en route*," said Diana, "but she breathes. She still lives. We must employ extreme measures."

Followed by her lover, she went into the neighboring room. It was a small storage room used to house flour bags. Raising a trap door, she looked into a rather deep pit that led to the river .As the water flowed, she heard the noise of an eddy.

Without pronouncing a word, she closed the trap door and returned to Jacqueline. Accompanying his mistress, Moralès became increasingly worried.

With an expression more merciless than the cruelest executioner, Diana looked at Jacqueline. She noticed the paleness of her accomplice.

"Moralès, is there something wrong with you again?"

"Diana, why did you have me come to this mill?"

The adventuress brutally explained.

"I learned of its existence during my tenure as the governess at the Chateau des Sablons. I planned to use it to eliminate Favraux when the moment was ripe. Now, it's the perfect place to dispose of his daughter. Such a possibility never entered your head. You're whiter than a sheet. Do you have any blood in your veins?"

"I'm recalling all my memories of this house," resumed Pierre Kerjean's son. "My parents. My childhood. I was happy in our home."

"A romantic interlude. No, my little Moralès, I really don't care for this kind of music!"

"Diana!"

"Let me be! We aren't here to dwell on the past, but to act in the present. This woman is an obstacle. Finish her once and for all!"

Like a barbaric priestess, Diana pulled out a clasp-knife hidden in her blouse, opened the folded blade, and extended the weapon hilt first towards Moralès.

"Take this and get to work!" she ordered

Moralès revolted by pushing back her hand. Diana adopted the domineering tone which often squelched her associate's scruples.

"Come on, strike! We'll get rid of the body by throwing it through the trap door! It's as simple as night and day! Why are you waiting?"

Moralès again hesitated. Diana yielded to the violent anger bubbling inside her.

"If you fail me now, you'd better watch out!"

All of a sudden, the son of Pierre Kerjean underwent a transformation. A flame of indignation ignited in his eyes. He seized the wrist of the hand in which Diana held the knife.

"Diana, I won't kill this woman. Not here, in the house where I was born... in this room that was my parents'... where my mother died..."

"Then," roared Diana, "I'll do the job myself!"

"No! No! You understand me! Not here! I won't allow it! I'll defend her!"

Moralès tightened his hold.

"Leave me! Let me go!" screeched Diana, foaming at the mouth.

"Drop that knife!"

"No!"

"Diana!"

"I'm not afraid of you!"

"We shall see!"

A savage fight began between the two lovers. While Moralès strove to disarm her, Diana became wild with fury. She tried to bite her lover's wrist and then his face. There were hoarse cries mixed with obscene insults as they battled like jungle cats.

The two outlaws were rolling on the floor in a furious embrace when the door opened revealing a sturdy old man. His harsh voice interrupted the two fighters.

"I am the former owner of this house. I won't see it soiled by any crime!"

At this unexpected intervention, Diana and Moralès separated from each other. They were mutually stunned by the dominating presence of the newcomer.

"I am Pierre Kerjean!" yelled the intruder.

Diana ran towards a neighboring room while Moralès was gripped by panic.

"My father!"

IV. The Convict's Forgiveness

For perhaps the first time in her eventful life, Diana felt the icy touch of fear in her veins. In the storeroom, she stuck her ear against the partition as Pierre Kerjean, without losing a second, bolted the crude lock on the door.

"I've caged this one!" said the old man. "Now for the other!"

Turning towards Moralès, Pierre Kerjean stood between him and Jacqueline. To the old man's surprise, his antagonist was a defeated man with a face full of tears.

Not daring to raise the eyes, the trembling Moralès questioned weakly.

"Are you Pierre Kerjean?"

"Yes!"

Diana's lover hesitated before an admission erupted from his lips.

"I'm your son!"

"Robert!" cried the old miller in despair. He struggled to master his emotions. "It was true what they told me at the town hall. My son! My Robert! I remember you as kind and caring. Your mother and I had such wonderful dreams for you. Now I find you about to commit an abominable crime!"

"Father!" shouted Moralès, "Father, I've disgraced you, forgive me!"

"I don't have the right, my son, to forgive you. If you became a thief, it was my fault. You followed my bad example. To my dying regret, I left you and you dying mother in poverty. My only legacy was for you to be branded the son of a convicted forger!

"I could argue that I was not as awful as I was painted. I could explain how I was manipulated by a man a hundred times more guilty than me, the banker Favraux, who used his tremendous power to hide his crimes from the law. I could use my ignorance and gullibility to portray myself as a victim.

"I'll avoid such excuses. For you, I endured my imprisonment and abandoned the ideas of suicide that haunted me after learning about your mother's death. Only for you! My son! As soon as I finished my sentence, I wanted to return to France to find you. I had hoped that you would remain an honest man. You had so much promise. I imagine that you would see your father gnawed by remorse and listen to my defense. When you would learn all the circumstances of my condemnation, then you would at least partially forgive me. Maybe you will even welcome me at your dinner table.

"I was deluding myself with false hope. I, the ex-convict, failed to arrive in time to prevent you from becoming an assassin!"

"No, father, no! I swear to you, I am not an assassin! Didn't you hear what was happening?"

"I was at the far end of our old garden. Lost in my painful memories, the cries from inside the mill summoned me. Then I found you fighting with a woman over a knife that must be intended for that poor lady over there!"

Kerjean pointed to the icy pale Jacqueline hanging on to her life in a coma.

Moralès protested with vehemence:

"No, Father, I didn't want to kill her. I was protecting her from that miserable woman. She tried to kill me when I refused to take the lady's life."

"Why?"

"Father, don't force me now to describe the monstrous abyss in which I nearly fell. Later, I will tell you all, but not now. I implore you. Not now!"

Moralès, or rather Robert, had hurled these words with such sincerity that Kerjean desisted.

"Who is this poor lady?" asked the old man approaching Jacqueline.

"This is Jacqueline Aubry, the daughter of the banker Favraux," revealed Moralès.

"The daughter of the banker Favraux!" repeated the ex-miller. "The daughter of…"

Suddenly, he paused. Astonishment registered in his eyes. Kerjean has just recognized the young woman on the bench as the subject of the photograph that he had found hidden in Judex's office. Judex had told him of Diana Monti's vendetta against the banker's daughter. The ex-miller realized that the other woman must be the treacherous ex-governess. Concealing his thoughts, he interrogated his son.

"Robert, you're not lying to me?"

"No, Father, I told you the truth! I committed crimes. Yes, I admit it. I did horrible things. If I became a dishonest man, it's because I was seduced by the woman behind this wall. She's now certainly listening to us. I'm not afraid to scream the truth at her. She was my evil genius. She put me on this fatal slope. Abusing my passion for her, she made me the despicable and corrupt man that I am.

"But, Father, I hadn't totally deadened my conscience. I recovered just in time. At the height of her infamy, she wanted to place in my hand an assassin's knife. I finally saw everything clearly. I understood. I had degraded my soul. I wanted this knife to sink into my tempter's heart. If you hadn't entered, I would have killed her rather than do what she wanted. I would have then surrendered to the law. I couldn't do what she wanted. My only consolation is that I had not totally succumbed to evil!"

A devilish laughter erupted from the storeroom.

"Ah!" shouted Moralès angrily. "Father, please let me finish this monster! Let me crush this viper!"

"No, remain here!" ordered the elder Kerjean. "You don't have the right to right wrongs. It's a job that belongs only to the truly worthy. Listen to me. What I will say you is very grave. On your answer depends both our lives."

"Speak, Father," responded Robert humbly.

"Are you really determined to abandon this wicked woman?"

"Yes!"

"Are you ready to be an honest man?"

"I swear!"

The older Kerjean scrutinized his offspring intensely. He wanted to gauge the sincerity of his son's heart.

"I believe you. I entrust you with the banker's unfortunate daughter. Will you vindicate my trust?"

"Yes, Father!"

"I will inform the man who represents justice in my eyes."

"Father!" shouted Robert. His face was bathed in tears. "Father, what will you do with me?"

Pierre Kerjean spontaneously opened his arms wide to Robert.

"My poor wife, if you see us from up there, forgive me as I forgive him!"

V. The Judge Arrives

Some instants after the ex-miller of Les Sablons had left, his distraught son, Robert Kerjean, shook as he heard a knock on the storeroom door. A persuasive voice filled the air.

"My little Moralès, you have been very mean towards me. All those things you said to your father!... I heard everything, you know."

With crossed arms on his chest, Moralès implacably reviewed every word of his mistress. "So?" he said harshly.

"Listen to me, I beg you," Diana said softly. "You know that I love you. I want your happiness as much as mine."

"It's useless to say anymore."

"Why?"

"Because I now clearly see your game. You never loved me."

"Mora..."

"No! You only romanced me in order to enslave me. I was only a pawn necessary for your plans to become reality. If we had succeeded, you would have ruthlessly discarded me."

"You are unfair!"

"Enough!"

"I ask only one thing. Let me leave."

"Never!"

"Moralès!" implored the adventuress with true or fake sobs. "What you're doing is shameful. Hours ago, you held me in your arms. You showered me with kisses. You swore that you were ready to sacrifice your life for me."

"I was mad!"

"Release me. I beseech you. Don't surrender me, my darling. I love you!"

"Leave me alone!"

"Yes, I want to be with you again. I want to run away with you. Please, lover, don't deliver to this mysterious judge mentioned by your father!"

Full of remorse, Moralès, stifled within himself all the passion that he had ever felt towards Diana Monti. He kept an icy silence as she struck repeatedly against the door.

"Release me, I implore you! No! You can't betray me. These people will kill me. It's horrible! I promise you that I won't harm this woman. My only desire is to flee with you. We can go far away. Just the two of us. Have pity for your lover. I'm the woman that you adored... that you can adore again. You are again mine and will always be mine. You won't release me because you're afraid that I'll spurn you. You tremble that my tears will move you into breaking the oath that you gave your father. And what will happen, my poor Moralès? By saving me, won't you save yourself? Reflect. What will your life be like?

"You will have to hide yourself. You will either flee or surrender to the law. Do you want to spend the best years of your life trapped in a prison cell? Do you want to die in some filthy penal colony... far from everyone... far from me... the woman ready to sacrifice herself completely to your happiness? Moralès, Moralès, it is possible that you don't hear me; that you ignore my pleas? We have some money stashed away... and we can still pull off our blackmail scam with the letter from the Marquis de Birargues... Get 10,000, 20, 000, 50,000 francs maybe... With that, we will leave for foreign shores. We're clever. We work well together. Do you want to retire from crime? I want the same thing. I now know what I want.

"In the last minutes, I have examined my life. I've changed. I was wrong to be so ambitious. The lure of Favraux's millions drove me mad. From now on, we will be equal! Provided that you free me... provided that we are both free, both of us will remake our lives. Moralès, Moralès... my friend... my lover..."

The son of Kerjean persevered in his silence.

"You won't even answer me... It's monstrous!" shouted the adventuress.

Moralès had moved away from the door. He feared that the captivating temptation of Diana's voice would hypnotize him into liberating her. He heard the sound of a body dropping heavily on the floor. As stifled cries came from the storeroom, Moralès covered his ears, He understood that his passion was not completely dead. If he heard anything further, even for a moment, he might yield to his mistress and all would irreparably be lost.

Despite that knowledge, he was stirred by the heart-rending sobs that grew weaker and more and more despairing. He tried to divert his thoughts toward the other woman, the daughter of the banker Favraux, who was sprawled on the bench in the abandoned room of the old mil. Her hair undone around her Madonna-like face, the motionless woman seemed to be imprisoned in a sleep not of this Earth.

An enormous fear spread rapidly through this newly-regenerated soul. Was she dead? As much as Diana, he would be responsible for her murder! Understanding the extent of his cowardice, he moved closer to Jacqueline. He didn't dare touch her. He feared feeling a hand frozen by death. Hoping that she still lived, he waited with eagerness the least breath that would be exhaled from her lips. He would have given anything for her to open her eyes.

"Feel better," he said to Jacqueline. "I don't want to cause you any more harm. I now protect and guard you!"

144

But there were no signs of life. Her sleep seemed the absolute silence of the void.

Not able to master the guilt consuming him, Robert Kerjean knelt next to Jacqueline. Becoming bolder, he held gently the hand of the young woman. It seemed warm to him. The blood must still be circulating in her weak and unconscious body

Was this an illusion? No. Moralès soon felt some tentative heartbeats occurring intermittently. She was alive! Alive! She could be saved. She would be saved.

This depraved criminal felt rejuvenated into an honest man. He felt his heart softened by the first pure spark that had burned inside his heart since childhood.

He fervently tasted the sweetness of redemption. He believed himself to be saved. He abhorred and cursed his evil actions of the past. While Diana mysteriously remained silent, Moralès remained kneeling in front of Jacqueline. With his hand in hers, his face had a poignancy that seemed to be petitioning the Almighty.

This was how he was found by old Kerjean upon returning to the tragic room. He looked at his son benignly.

"Yes," said the old man, "I was right to trust you. Your eyes couldn't lie. When they cried, they were the eyes of your mother."

Vaguely aware of his father's presence, Robert rose

"Now, Father, I'm ready. The judge can come. I await him!"

Judex had scarcely arrived at the Chateau Rouge when he learned from his bother a possible clue to Jacqueline's abductor. The man in the black cloak was about to leave when the telephone rang.

"Hello!" said Kerjean's voice. "Come quickly to the mill at Les Sablons! You will find Favraux's daughter there."

Judex's eyes flashed with relief. Instead of asking details, he hung up the receiver.

"I suspected that Jacqueline wasn't far away. Marie Verdier knew of this mill."

As his intellect analyzed recent events, a fearsome indignation formed on his face.

"This woman and his accomplice had resolved to murder Jacqueline. They transported her there in order to easily dispose of her body. The monsters! But this time, they shall not escape me! And this brave Kerjean! Without him, I might have arrived too late! Brother, good fortune is spawned by generosity. I must leave. There isn't a moment to lose!"

"Will you return with her?" asked Roger.

"Maybe!"

After feverishly squeezing Roger's hand, Judex left the underground lair for the Seine. He climbed into a quick motorized dinghy moored to a pontoon by the shore. Turning on the motor, he descended the Seine towards the mill of Les Sablons which was a few kilometers away.

Judex easily maneuvered the he boat on the river. It sailed through the admirable landscape belonging to one of the most beautiful valleys in France.

The avenger wad lost in his thoughts.

Twice Jacqueline was almost murdered. She was saved the first time by children, and the second by an old man. These rescues resulted from chance rather than my intervention. Next time, I must anticipate events. I, and only I, must watch over her.

When the old mill finally appeared in the radiance of a beautiful summer sun, Judex felt his heart beat with hope. He quickly reached the shore. Mooring his dinghy to a tree, he ran to the mill where Kerjean waited him.

Right away, Judex headed for Jacqueline, ignoring Moralès. The gambler had meekly withdrawn to a corner of the room. Holding a flask of embossed silver, Judex poured a powerful restorative down the young woman's throat. Soon, a light coloring appeared on Jacqueline's face. Her breathing became stronger and more uniform. Her lips shook with a barely perceivable shiver. Her eyelids half-opened. Her gaze slowly wandered around her.

Did she notice Judex leaning over as he awaited her recovery? In any case, his image suddenly became blurred in the mist that clouded her thoughts.

Nevertheless, she intuitively knew that there was a protective friend with her. Her features relaxed into a serene expression. Her eyes closed, but not in death. They closed with the sleep of life.

"We must take her away!" said Judex to Kerjean.

The mysterious vigilante shifted his attention to Moralès. Judex ominously addressed him.

"Was it you who kidnapped this woman?"

Moralès lowered his head in disgrace. "Yes, it was!"

"Murderous scum!"

Kerjean placed himself in front of his son. The grief on the old man's face halted the vindictive voice of the self-styled judge.

"This is my son," pleaded the ex-miller. "An evil woman brought him to this pit of damnation, but he redeemed himself in time! Ashamed of his crimes, he threw himself on his knees to implore my forgiveness. I could not refuse him. As a final proof of his sincerity, he guarded this unfortunate lady and prevented this she-devil from fleeing."

"Where is Marie Verdier?" asked Judex bitterly. He stared searchingly at Moralès. The gambler understood that he faced a man whose will no one could resist.

"She's there!" he said, pointing to the storeroom door. "Take care! She's armed and knows how to defend herself."

With a contemptuous smile, Judex calmly unbolted the door and opened it.

The storeroom was empty. Diana Monti had disappeared.

How did the adventuress escape from the storeroom that was as tight as a mousetrap?

Her audacity was multiplied tenfold due to her burning desire to escape this "judge" whose coming had been foretold by Kerjean.

Understanding that she could not sway Moralès, Diana had acted decisively. She found the solution. The only means of escape was the trap door. There was the danger of drowning, but the reward was worth the risk.

Supple as a panther, and also an excellent swimmer, the double danger that she faced couldn't deter her. She never hesitated. Once she made her choice, her only thought was to execute it. She continued to groan and to sob. She feigned even falling down. While she was engaged in her subterfuge, the adventuress removed her clothing until only her undergarments remained. They would serve as an adequate replacement for a classical bathing suit.

After giving further false demonstrations of her helplessness, she put her plan into effect. Proceeding silently, she dived though the trapdoor. Skillfully, she passed through one of the wide paddles of the mill's wheel. Reaching the river, she made her way to the other bank where she hid among the reeds.

While noting Diana's escape, Judex had first directed his suspicious gaze towards Moralès. The gambler pointed to the clothing and boots of the adventuress on the floor.

"She threw herself into water."

"It's obvious," acknowledged Judex.

"What a formidable woman!" said Moralès. "I never imagined that she could escape! Be on your guard, Monsieur. She is very dangerous. You have an enemy who will defend herself by any means necessary' She'll never relent in her desire to destroy you."

The frankness of Kerjean's son convinced Judex of his reformation. Putting his hand on Robert's shoulder, Judex addressed the senior Kerjean.

"I was justified in telling you to hope. This boy seems sincere."

"I am, Monsieur, I swear," interrupted Moralès sharply. "I have only one desire: to have the opportunity to prove it to my father as well as to you."

"Perhaps," said enigmatically the man in the black cloak. "Yes, perhaps the opportunity will present itself earlier than you think. I restore you to your father. You will accompany us; but listen well. Judex remembers those who betray him as well as those who serve him. He knows how to punish as firmly as he knows how to reward."

"Monsieur," asserted Moralès with deep respect, "you will find me to be the most loyal servant."

"I hope so."

"And I," said the senior Kerjean, "I will act as his guarantor. If ever my son violates his oath, it is not you, Monsieur, who will punish him. It will be me!"

"Father, you will never have this sad duty," said Robert kissing his father's hands.

Judex went back to Jacqueline and wrapped her in his cloak. He took her to his dinghy followed by Kerjean and his son.

He cautiously placed the young woman in the boat. She gently rested there. While the sun began subsiding on the horizon, the dinghy moved away quickly in the direction of the Chateau Rouge. The boat passed through this sublime setting of nature that radiated happiness on all living things. Soon, the flimsy craft faded into a black speck before totally disappearing.

Diana Monti appeared from among the reeds. She swam once more in the river towards the mill in order to wait for Crémard's return. Reentering the old building, she dressed quietly in the storeroom. Going to the window from where she could watch the splendid panorama of the Seine, she gazed stubbornly with vengeful eyes towards the direction that the small boat had taken.

"Diana Monti shall have the last word!" she swore.

Part Six: The Licorice Kid

I. Tearing Away the Veil

In front of a hairdresser, an elegantly outfitted, beauty finished her toilette. Her pale complexion revealed a recent sickness. A chambermaid opened the door. Her face bore a sympathetic expression.

"Does Madame need anything?"

"No, Mariette," replied Jacqueline, "unless you're going to tell me where I am?"

"Madame will know soon."

"Why all this mystery?"

"'I have nothing to tell Madame."

Putting a finger to her lips, Mariette disappeared with an enigmatic smile.

Extremely puzzled, Jacqueline recapitulated all the events of the preceding days. Receiving a telegram that her small son was very sick, she had hurried to take the train for Loisy. In the middle of the bridge across the Seine, she had been assaulted by two brigands and thrown into the river.

From that moment, her memories became extremely confused. She vaguely recalled being a bedridden invalid attended by the Bontemps family. Her kneeling son had kissed her before she lost consciousness. She had faint thoughts of a trip in a fast automobile. Fighting to reawaken, she had been trapped in a paralytic coma.

She remembered the dazzling sensation of a brief awakening. Close to her had been a man dressed in black. She could not distinguish his face except for two large eyes that radiated compassion. Then the darkness of oblivion resurged. She had fallen again into the death-like sleep.

When Jacqueline regained consciousness, she was surrounded by unfamiliar objects in a luxurious room. Mariette was at her bedside. As soon as she had the strength to articulate some words, she questioned the maid.

"Where am I?"

"With friends sworn to protect you," replied the chambermaid.

"And my son?"

"You will see him soon. Don't speak. Rest. Don't worry. You will be cared for. Once you heal, you will know the truth, Madame."

Jacqueline, very weak, had obeyed her devoted nurse.

Every day there were new developments. One morning, Jacqueline had found on her night table her cherished portrait of Jeannot. Another time there was a small letter.

My lovely Mama,

I know that you are better and that we will be together soon. I am happy, I am behaving. I love you.

Your Jeannot

P. S. The Licorice Kid also sends you his love.

Every day Jacqueline had seen roses, her favorite flowers, replaced in splendid bouquets inside the Sèvres vases decorating the fireplace.

In this benign atmosphere, the banker's daughter, more morally drained than physically, had been rejuvenated.

Soon Jacqueline knew that she would learn who had driven her here. She would learn the identity of her unknown benefactors. She had no definite clues as to their identity. She had suspected the de Birargues family since her nurse had the same first name as Gisèle's innocuous chambermaid. However, Jacqueline remembered that the Duc and his relations had gone to the Cévennes. Furthermore, they had no reason to remain hidden from her.

For a moment, the name of Judex sprang into her mind. She quickly discounted the possibility, but it persistently returned. She brooded over being once more indebted to her father's apparent murderer. Her moral crisis was alleviated by gazing at the portrait of her son.

Mariette had told her. At last, Jacqueline would know the truth!

There was a knock on the door. "Enter," she said. She hoped that finally all her questions would be answered.

"You!" she exclaimed joyfully. The kindly Vallières, her father's ex-secretary, stood before her.

"I'm very happy to see you, my friend. Tell me where I am."

"Madame, you are in my home." Pulling a letter from his pocket, Vallières gave it to Jacqueline. "This will explain everything."

The banker's daughter read the letter:

Madame,

You are surrounded by so many dangers that I entrusted this letter to your friend. He shall fulfill all your wishes. I dare not present myself to you, but there is no one in the world more devoted to your welfare than myself.

JUDEX

After reading this, Jacqueline's eyes darkened. Her face was distraught. She shuddered as she spoke.

"Who is this Judex?"

"I don't know," said Vallières.

"Did you see him?"

"No. It was one of his servants who drove you here. In the name of his master, he asked me to give you sanctuary. Now, dear Madame, you are safe here. I must frequently be absent. As I earlier told you, I have a new position that requires me to work long hours. You know Mariette and my housekeeper, Madame Fleury. They will attentively see to all your needs. I only ask that you stay in this house until the threat hanging over you dissipates. Hopefully, that will be soon."

"And my son?"

"As early as tomorrow, he will be here."

"Thank you, my dear Vallières, thank you from the bottom of my heart!" shouted Jacqueline. Holding her protector's hand, she reproached him affectionately. "Why didn't you see me earlier? Why all this mystery?"

"It was necessary," replied the ex-secretary. "You suffered from a nervous concussion that the least strain could worsen. My doctor advised that you be kept ignorant of the truth."

"My friend, I will never forget what you have done for me."

Vallières protested modestly. "I did nothing but provide a refuge; the man who saved you was…" He didn't finish. He was afraid of injuring the young woman by pronouncing the fateful name.

Jacqueline did it herself.

"You were about to say Judex?"

"Yes, Judex," admitted the ex-secretary.

"And you know nothing of him?"

"No, Madame." The ex-secretary paused briefly. "Did you see him?"

"Me?"

"Yes. Do you remember any man when you opened the eyes in the Kerjean mill?"

"No," answered Jacqueline trying to muster her memories. "I don't remember."

She then questioned the veracity of her father's former assistant. "You didn't tell me the truth."

"Oh! Madame."

"Or at least you know a lot more than you've revealed to me."

"Why do you believe that?"

"How could you know all these details if this Judex had not taken you into his confidences?"

"I already explained, dear Madame. I only saw his servant."

"I want to believe you. Answer me honestly. Do you have the means to communicate with Judex?"

"Yes, Madame," replied Vallières.

"Will you write a letter to him that I will dictate?"

"Very gladly."

Vallières sat down at a table full of writing instruments. His hand trembled as it soaked a quill pen in an ink bottle.

"Madame, I await your orders."

Completely in control of the situation, Jacqueline began dictating:

Monsieur,

My friend, Monsieur Vallières has just put informed me how I was brought to his home. I gladly accept the hospitality of this excellent man. However, I will only stay here on condition that my son comes to stay with me.

"That was already understood," interrupted Vallières gently.

Jacqueline continued her dictation:

As for you, Monsieur, I owe you my life, but your mysterious name will always evoke the tragedy of my unfortunate father's demise. I dare not repeat it, and I can only read it with dread. I will ask Monsieur Vallières never to say it in my presence.

"Are you finished?" asked Vallières after Jacqueline stopped.

"Yes, I'm finished."

With an impassive and cold gesture, Vallières gave the letter to the young woman. She signed and returned it to her host.

"Believe me, my friend," said Jacqueline, "that I will never forget your loyalty."

"I only did my duty," said the ex-secretary. He bowed and respectfully kissed Jacqueline's hand.

Returning to the long antechamber, he walked into his private study. Seated at his desk, he touched an electric button activating a bell. He was staring on Jacqueline's letter which now rested on his desk. In response to the bell, there appeared a woman of about 50. Clothed in a black dress, she was the housekeeper, Madame Fleury. She revered her employer.

"Gabrielle," said Monsieur Vallières. "I have to leave. I insist on constant vigilance. Don't allow anyone to come here outside of the people whose names I gave you. You will scrupulously supervise Mariette. She's a very responsible girl, but she's also very young and pretty. She can be suborned. At the least suspicion of disloyalty, do not hesitate to send her packing. You can always telephone me at my other residence."

"Monsieur can rely completely on me," said Madame Fleury.

"And now, Gabrielle, leave me and let no one disturb me."

"Not even Monsieur Roger?"

"I said no one."

"As you wish, Monsieur." Turning round. the housekeeper turned left the room.

Vallières got up and paced around the room. He locked his door. Returning to his desk, he collapsed into his armchair. Holding his head between his hands, he sighed deeply. His shoulders shook. A name issued from his throat!

"Jacqueline!"

Suddenly Vallières rose. His bent posture rectified itself. His eyes shined intensely. He pulled off the wig and beard that had disguise the austere face of Judex.

"She will never love me!"

II. Crime Marches on

After the affair at the Kerjean Mill, Diana Monti had prudently decided to remain incognito. Waiting for events to unravel, she registered under a false name in a modest hotel outside Paris. For several days, no further setback befell her or her two enforcers, Crémard and Dr. Pop. Having been informed by her two associates that Paris seemed safe, Diana promptly returned to the capital.

The treacherous adventuress had not abandoned her plans. She was engaged in a fight to death with Judex. Coldly she weighed both the dangers and her trump cards in this deadly game.

These were the dangers. First, Judex was a powerful enemy whose true identity and nature was shrouded in mystery. Second, Jacqueline could upset her scheme to rescue the banker. With a few words, she could expose Diana's true nature to Favraux. Third, Moralès had turned informer due to fear and remorse.

Diana held these trumps. She knew that Favraux was alive in the hands of Judex. Her supreme ace was her willingness to employ any means, even the most brutal, in this ferocious fight. She couldn't be intimidated by any obstacle. She would play this game to the bitter end. Nothing would stop her from obtaining her goal, the millions of the banker.

Already her murderous brain had engineered a new plan, more diabolical than her earlier schemes. She confidently felt that success was guaranteed. The grin of a fallen angel formed on her lips. A flash of triumphant cruelty illuminated her deep eyes. After putting on the most stylish apparel, she had herself driven to the Celeritas Agency in the Rue Milton.

Once again, crime was on the march!

Around 10 o'clock in the morning, Diana Monti conferred with Cocantin. The detective was in total ignorance of the drama at the mill as well as all the circumstances that that preceded it. He courteously received the ex-governess. The sleuth couldn't resist the charms of the beautiful woman.

"Monsieur Cocantin," said the adventuress, "did you discover any clues to Judex's identity?"

The face of the detective darkened. The name of Judex had the ability to plunge him into despondency, and even the handsome fee promised by Diana couldn't stimulate his enthusiasm.

"Mademoiselle," he stammered, "in these kinds of cases, you are not unaware of…"

Diana interrupted immediately. "Monsieur Cocantin, don't say anything more. You've done nothing."

"That is to say…"

"It's useless to deceive me. I won't be swayed. Your behavior has been unkind, even unsavory. When you promised..."

To these words, Prosper Cocantin proudly glanced at his Napoleonic bust.

"Madame, I'm an honest man. All these complaints weary me."

"You know very well," recalled the ex-governess, "that you will earn 100,000 francs if we discover Judex and, through him, Favraux."

"100,000 francs is quite a sum, but my honor... my conscience..."

"Your honor and your conscience don't enter into this," retorted the adventuress giving a wink that caused Cocantin to forget all about Napoleon. "Think. What do we have to do? We must find a man held hostage. What do you risk? Absolutely nothing. You can earn a lucrative 100,000 francs fee while winning the undying love of a woman."

"Mademoiselle, what did you just say?"

"Monsieur Cocantin, you have captivated me," purred Diana. "It would be tragic if two people like us, so well suited to each other..."

There was a knock on the door. It was the porter bringing a visitor's card to Cocantin.

"Amaury de la Rochefontaine," shouted Cocantin with impatience. "Tell him to wait, I'll receive him after this consultation."

The adventuress wondered why Jacqueline's ex-fiancé had come here.

"Do you know this man?" said Diana whose soft voice was sending quivers through the private detective.

"I don't want to talk about him."

"He is a very refined aristocrat."

"I didn't tell you..."

"Very wealthy!"

"You are misinformed!"

Unnerved by Diana's clever stratagem, Cocantin lost all sense of discretion

"He's financially strapped. In fact, he's totally broke. The proof is that he's here to pester me into helping him secure a financial loan."

Prompted by a sudden inspiration, Diana arose.

"Monsieur Cocantin," said Diana moving her face close to the detective, "let me receive the Vicomte de la Rochefontaine."

"Why?"

"I'm in a position to render both of you a great service."

"But…"

"There is no 'but.' Let me do it. You won't regret it."

"Do you know my client?" asked Cocantin.

"Much better than you do. I'm in a position to perform the service requested of you. I will split the commission with you."

"I'm not sure that I can accept your offer."

"Do you want three quarters?"

"That's not what I'm saying."

"For the third time, I ask you to let me see him."

"You're very generous." Ribaudet's nephew was behaving like a lovesick youth.

"Please go into another room," said Diana.

"Is that essential?"

"It's necessary, my dear friend. You do want to be my dear friend?"

"Ah! You're exquisite."

Escorting Cocantin to an adjacent office, Diana issued an edict.

"Come out only when I tell you."

"You are divine!" exclaimed Cocantin.

As a precaution, Diana bolted the lock on the office door. Taking her place behind Cocantin's desk, she rang for the porter.

"Tell Vicomte de la Rochefontaine to enter," she commanded.

159

Finding himself alone in Cocantin's office with the ex-governess of Les Sablons, Amaury was extremely surprised. The graceful adventuress courteously smiled.

"Dear Vicomte, you never expected to find me here."

"You are correct, Mademoiselle."

"I'm delighted to see you."

"The feeling is mutual."

"I was about to write you." She lowered her voice. "I have a very interesting proposal for you." Totally in her element, Diana displayed her consummate mastery as a negotiator.

"Here's why I asked my dear friend, Cocantin, to leave us alone. Dear Vicomte, spare me five minutes. Your time will be well spent."

Somewhat suspicious, Amaury obeyed. *I must tread carefully*, he thought. *This bold lady seems formidable.*

"Mademoiselle, you have peaked my interest."

"First, I want your word of honor that all this will remain solely between us."

Amaury nodded his head in approval.

The adventuress demonstrated that her maxim was to aim straight for the heart.

"What would you say, Vicomte, if someone discovered a gold mine and offered to exploit it jointly?"

"Mademoiselle, I find your question odd."

"I see the necessity to dot every 'i.'" She began to speak in hushed tones. "I remind you of your promise of absolute secrecy."

"Yes, it's understood."

"The banker Favraux is alive."

"What are you saying?" exclaimed Amaury de la Rochefontaine.

"I have proof that Favraux no longer rests in his tomb."

"It's unbelievable!"

"Favraux was forced into a cataleptic sleep. He was later removed from his coffin by a mysterious figure that holds him currently in his power."

"This sounds like a work of fiction."

"This isn't fiction. This is reality. I have irrefutable proof. Listen to me…"

After briefing Vicomte de la Rochefontaine on the subject of Judex, Diana concluded triumphantly:

"Is this not truly a gold mine that we are about to exploit?"

Still distrustful, the Vicomte had an objection:

"Why, Mademoiselle, do you need a partner to exploit it?"

"I won't hide the truth. The venture is not without danger. I can't secure the services of a total stranger. But you can be trusted. Here's why. The breakup of your marriage with the banker's daughter puts you in a precarious position. Excuse my bluntness."

"I prefer that."

"I see that we understand each other. Cocantin could only help you obtain a few thousand pounds to resurrect your comfortable existence. I offer you the rare opportunity to place your hands on a large fortune. Don't let it escape. Let us walk hand in hand, united by the same lust for the same goal. Together, we can unmask Judex and rescue Favraux. All my cards are exposed on the table. Vicomte de la Rochefontaine, I have revealed my secrets. Give me your answer!"

Amaury now understood the nature of the woman facing him. He replied with the manner of a grand seigneur completely detached from the rest of humanity.

"Allow me, Mademoiselle, to speak to you as frankly as you spoke to me."

"I would expect nothing less."

"You have not concealed that this questionable venture would place us both in grave peril."

"That is evident."

"Of course, I don't doubt the success of our enterprise."

"Nor do I."

"You are sure to be rewarded. How do I profit by this affair?"

"Favraux would willingly pay millions for his liberty."

"You are unaware of what happened between his daughter and me?"

"I know only one thing," roared Diana unleashing her hate. "Jacqueline is my mortal enemy."

"Do you know how to deal with her?" asked Amaury.

"I do," fiercely avowed the adventuress, "and I won't hide it from you. More than you, I view her as major impediment to my plans. I now have the means to eliminate this obstacle, and I will do it."

Diana's vehemence made Amaury shudder.

"You don't want me to murder her?"

"Such crazy talk!" Laughing, Diana shrugged hypocritically. "Are people like us assassins? There are a hundred other ways to do it. Speak lower. We both know Cocantin is a fool. He doesn't need to know our secrets."

She was skillfully manipulating the impoverished nobleman. She continued to perversely tempt him in a soothing voice. Her infernal audacity broke down Amaury's indecision. The nobleman succumbed to his thirst for wealth.

Having secured victory over Amaury, Diana was ecstatic.

"Now that our negotiations are concluded, my lucrative proposal can be easily executed."

"And, as you told me, we shall forge a weapon to circumvent both Judex and Jacqueline."

"I wouldn't have it any other way," asserted Diana. Her vindictiveness would have terrified a more scrupulous soul than Vicomte de La Rochefontaine.

"Under those conditions," admitted Amaury, "the matter is settled."

"Then we are in agreement?"

"Completely," consented the penniless nobleman. The adventuress had dexterously entangled the amoral profligate in her nets.

"The success of our plan depends on its prompt execution. You must play the main role in the first stage."

"Understood."

"Let's act quickly. It's time to release Cocantin."

Her eyes shining with cruelty, Diana unbolted the lock. Slightly congested, Cocantin had been impatient to regain his liberty.

Without giving him the chance to say a word, Diana soothed the sleuth with pleasantries.

"Forgive me, my dear Cocantin, for making you wait, but Vicomte de la Rochefontaine and I had very important matters to discuss. Suffice to say, we reached an agreement. We have pressing duties to perform. We will return tomorrow morning to finalize everything with you."

The adventuress enchanted the detective with an adoring smile.

"Dear friend," she continued, "I will not forget you. You can rely on me more than ever. You hear me, more than ever! Come, Vicomte! Till tomorrow!"

"Till tomorrow!" replied the someway confused director of the Celeritas Agency.

Which new crime did Diana Monti plan? What new perils were going to endanger Jacqueline?

After escorting his two clients to the antechamber, Cocantin viewed their departure with puzzlement. "An eccentric woman," he mumbled to himself, "but that she is intoxicating! If she keeps her promises, I won't be sorry."

Galvanized by his hopes of romance, Cocantin returned to his office. He directed his eyes towards the bust of Napoleon. The detective quivered as he imagined his Emperor threatening him with a stare. The bust seemed to be saying "*Cocantin, I am unhappy with you*!"

Perplexed, he sat down and thought. A vague worry invaded his brain.

"Maybe it would be better to quit this detective business," he muttered. "This woman fills me with fear. Uncle! Uncle! Why did you bequeath me this agency?"

III. The Two Brothers

Judex was being torn apart by emotional turmoil. Brooding in his office, he was lost in a trance that veiled his handsome face with sorrow.

"There's nothing I can do," he murmured. "Nothing!"

Grabbing his wig and false beard, he was about to put them on again. Due to his expert makeup and the documents verifying his false background, he had flawlessly played the role of Vallières before the banker and his daughter. His preparations were interrupted by a knock on the door.

"Who's there?" said Judex impatiently.

"Roger."

"What do you want?"

"I need to see you."

Still undisguised, Judex opened the door.

Seeing his sibling's real features, Roger was startled. "You're being foolhardy."

"Be quiet," insisted the unmasked Vallières. After escorting his brother into the study, Judex closed the door.

"What's happened to you?" asked Roger with concern."You seem overwrought. Why suddenly remove the disguise that enables you to accomplish our mission of justice?"

"Read it," said Judex simply while handing him the letter that Jacqueline had dictated two hours earlier.

Roger melancholically returned the letter to his brother.

"Did you read it?"

"Yes, I read it!"

Judex had memorized the letter. He repeated it verbatim:

As for you, Monsieur, I owe you my life, but your mysterious name will always evoke the tragedy of my unfortunate father's demise. I dare not repeat it, and I can only read it with dread. I will ask Monsieur Vallières never to say it in my presence.

"Brother," said Judex, "do you understand how I'm suffering? I'm trapped in a nightmare!"

"Jacques, your duty demands courage," counseled Roger.

"Courage! I constantly repeat this word to myself. Will I have enough to see this mission to its end?"

"What are you saying?"

"Listen to me," continued Judex. "Our mission is justice, not vengeance. Like you, my brother, I swore to close my heart to romance until we accomplished our sacred trust. This vow was kept until I infiltrated Favraux's household in my disguise of Vallières. There, I gradually developed feelings for this sweet young woman. Despite my best efforts, she inspired friendship and sympathy. I realized immediately that she, like us, was a victim of her father's tyranny.

"These feelings threatened to weaken my resolve. I fought them until my resolve overwhelmed them. They didn't impede me in accomplishing my ruthless task. However, there followed a deeply moving scene with Jacqueline. I fully measured the nobility of her soul.

"Remember our conversation. 'Brother,' I told you, 'this unfortunate woman has just saved her father through self-sacrifice. After what she did, we can't leave this villain to awaken in a coffin. Even though his crimes are monstrous and our hatred is just, we no longer have the right to impose the hideous penalty of being buried alive!' Then you replied: 'Brother, you are the oldest child! You are the master. I shall obey your orders.' And you sanctioned my decision, Roger, because your conscience also dictated this merciful verdict."

"And because I realized that you were in love," replied Roger.

"Brother, you're wrong!" protested Jacques with a dark energy. "At that very moment, I only liked her. Now that I know her better, I fully savor her virtue. When I realized the perils endangering her, when I found her on the verge of death in the mill of Les Sablons, my heart was forever conquered. Roger, you will chide me. You may even curse me, but I must make this confession before it kills me."

Judex seized his brother in his arms.

"There are moments when I want to free her father."

"Jacques!" shouted Roger becoming pale. "Remember you that we are bound by our sacred and solemn oath."

"And if I violate it?"

"Do not harbor this delusion."

"If I try?"

"You shall be smashed by justified hatred."

Jacques became silent.

"My comrade…" said Roger

Judex suddenly raised his head; a new hope illuminated his face.

"Brother," he said, "I will be obliged to leave you for 24 hours. I will refrain from discussing our prisoner. Kerjean shall stand guard. During this time, find Jacqueline's child and restore him to her."

"I'll leave right away for Loisy," said Roger. He empathized with his brother's pain.

"Thank you."

"And remember, your duty demands courage!"

Marked by destiny, the two brothers embraced at length.

Roger whispered this mysterious sentence into Judex's ear.

"Kiss *her* for me!"

"I will!"

An hour later, Jacqueline recovering from his moving interview with her father's former secretary, received the following message:

Madame,

I am obliged to leave abruptly. In accordance with your wishes, your child will be here tonight or tomorrow. I beg you not to leave your room before I return.

Please accept, Madame, this expression of my sincere loyalty,

VALLIÈRES

"The gallant man!" said Jacqueline while bringing the letter to her lips.

IV. Jolts of Fear and Love

Arm in arm, bearing their backpacks, Jeannot and the Licorice Kid traveled their normal route to the country school.

"Is that Jeannot?" said a woman's voice.

The Licorice Kid was quickly deserted by his small companion. Jacqueline's son ran towards an elegant woman. Accompanied by an equally fashionably dressed man, she was standing next to a parked automobile.

Diana Monti grabbed the child and began to stroke his hair.

"I'm very happy to see you, Jean," said the adventuress.

"Where are you going?" asked Amaury.

"To school," answered Jean.

"We'll drive you there," proposed Diana.

"I'll go," replied Jean, "but you have to take my friend."

"That's fine. Climb in, both of you. Let's go."

"Swell!" yelled the Licorice Kid. "We're traveling like bigwigs!"

The open car moved at a fast pace. Jean was already chatting joyfully when Amaury decided to rid himself of a bothersome witness. The Vicomte cleverly pushed the Licorice Kid's hat. Taken by the breeze, it flew away. Once the car stopped, the Kid got out to recover his hat. The chauffeur, none other than Crémard, then drove off at full speed stranding the Licorice Kid on the road.

"Wait!" vainly hollered Jeannot. When the car passed the school towards an unknown destination, the boy screamed.

"I don't want to go with you!"

"Don't worry, my dear," proclaimed Diana. "Don't be afraid. We're very fond of you."

"Where are you taking me?" asked Jacqueline's son.

"To Paris."

"To see Mama?"

"Yes, we're taking you to Mama."

"Why didn't you wait for the Licorice Kid?"

"Be quiet!" said Amaury curtly.

The child began crying. His head rested on Diana's shoulder. She hypocritically caressed the boy's hair.

Once the car stopped in front of the Celeritas Agency, Jeannot was slightly pacified. Diana and her new accomplice got out to confer with Cocantin.

"We're here as promised," said the adventuress.

"Who is this handsome child?" asked the detective.

"A very nice boy whom we're returning to his mother," declared the adventuress.

After signaling Amaury to take the boy over to the window, she explained to the director of the Celeritas Agency:

"This is Jacqueline Aubry's son. We don't intend any harm. We only need you to mind him for 48 hours. During this time, the Vicomte and I shall inform Judex of the child's whereabouts. There's no doubt that Judex will come for the boy."

"And then?"

"Leave the rest to us."

"I don't understand what you're doing," declared Cocantin unenthusiastically.

"Remember that there will be 100,000 francs for you once we identify Judex." She then entranced Cocantin with a smothering glance that seemed more than a spoken promise.

"Everything is settled! Amaury, let us take our leave of Monsieur Cocantin."

At the same time, Jeannot ran towards the detective.

"No, Monsieur! Let me stay with you. They're mean!"

"You see!" laughed the ex-governess. "He wants to stay with you. Don't disappoint him, my dear friend."

"*Au revoir*," exclaimed Amaury following Diana into the antechamber.

Alone with Jacqueline's son, a flabbergasted Cocantin sought to console the boy. "Poor lad," said the detective. "You want to be friends?"

"Yes, Monsieur," replied Jeannot. "Will you take me to my Mama?"

"Where is she staying?"

"In Neuilly, with Madame Chapuis. I don't know the street, but I remember the house."

A true drama played itself in Cocantin's heart. *Obviously,* he thought, *I made a bad bargain. This Diana is a terrifying woman. Terrifying!*

Jeannot sensed in the detective a natural protector. As the boy jumped into his lap, Cocantin looked at the bust of Napoleon.

I can't be wrong, he told himself. *It would be best to return him to his mother.* Suddenly a jolt of fear ran down Cocantin's spine. Although Ribaudet's successor wished to validate the boy's trust, he had doubts.

If I back out of my deal with these people, they will turn on me with every trick imaginable. This child has nothing to fear. First, they promised not to harm him. You don't need to be a genius to see their game. They only want to use him to ensnare Judex and deliver Favraux, both praiseworthy goals. After all, I wouldn't be upset to see Judex unmasked. There is also my fee of 100,000 francs, Damn! In order to live a life of comfort, 100,000 francs would be a respectable sum.

Sitting on Cocantin's knee, Jean was talking about Papa Julien's donkey and ducks. Cocantin didn't hear him because he once more consulted his oracle, the Imperial bust. In defiance of his expectations, the detective didn't perceive the desired approval.

The Emperor doesn't order me to march. Therefore, I must return this lad to his family.

A new jolt impacted him. This was not a jolt of fear, but one of love. The image of Diana had just engulfed his mind. He heard again the voice that sang in his ears. He recalled her bewitching smile and smothering glances. He breathed again the subtle smell of her perfume. The detective was confused. Which guide should he follow: Diana or Napoleon?

Alas! The Emperor suffered a second Waterloo. Stifling his conscience, Cocantin was conquered by the brilliant mirage of a romance with Diana. Believing himself in love, Cocantin yielded inevitably to passion. He decided to keep the child.

To placate the last scruples residing inside him, he turned the third time towards the bust to make a solemn promise. *Sire, I guarantee you that no one shall harm a single hair of this child. He's under my protection!*

Having reconciled his duty and his desire, Cocantin spent the remainder of the day taking care of Jeannot. The detective greatly enjoyed playing games with the youngster. The boy finished his conquest of Cocantin's heart. When evening arrived, the sleuth surrendered his large bed to the child. Clothed in an evening robe, Cocantin made a makeshift bed out of two chairs. Both the detective and the child succumbed to the sleep of innocence.

V. The Exploits of the Licorice Kid

When the Licorice Kid retrieved his hat only to see Diana's car abandon him, he became virulently angry.

"Drat! I missed the boat!"

He ran screaming after the car. Realizing that he had little chance to catch the vehicle, he made a wise choice. After raising his fist to the kidnappers as they disappeared in a cloud of dust, he returned directly to his foster family. He told them what had befallen Jean.

Judex's brother had just arrived by car at the Bontemps residence. He had a letter with Vallières' signature. The ex-secretary begged them to let his emissary take Jean back to his mother. Distressed by the Licorice Kid's story, Papa Julien wanted to notify the police. Roger advised a different course of action.

"Don't do anything to alert these villains that we're on their trail. Let Monsieur Vallières and me handle it. If Marie Verdier and Vicomte de la Rochefontaine have abducted Jean, I guarantee you that we won't delay returning him to his mother."

"May the Good Lord bless you!" said Marianne.

As Roger went back to his car, the Licorice Kid had a re-quest.

"Monsieur, take me with you to find my pal!"

Judex's brother looked at Marianne and her father before replying:

"Only if your guardians consent!" replied Roger.

"Yes, kind sir," accepted Papa Julian.

"Send us news soon," said Marianne.

"Within 24 hours you'll receive word," said Roger. After installing the Kid in the car, Judex's brother sat next to him and ordered to his chauffeur to drive them to his expensive apartment on the Rue du Cirque near the Champs-Élysées.

Without losing a single instant, Roger embarked on his campaign to trace Diana and Amaury. To his dismay, he learned that for several days, neither of them had been seen at their usual haunts. Roger traced Diana to the house where she lived with Moralès, but she was no longer there. Amaury had vacated his apartment in the Rue de Prony for parts unknown. Roger suspected that Amaury had rented a new apartment for himself and Diana.

Despite all his efforts, Roger had not found any clue to the whereabouts of the kidnappers. Cognizant that Diana was a woman capable of the most abominable crimes, he con-cluded that she intended to use Jean as a hostage to ward off any attack.

After a sleepless night, Roger got ready to expand his in-vestigation. During lunch, he was listening to another rendi-tion of the abduction by the Licorice Kid. A valet brought the newspapers. Scanning them, Roger's attention was attracted by an advertisement.

JUDEX
If you desire news of the child,
contact the Celeritas Agency,
135 Rue Milton. Central 86-45.

"This time, I have something," muttered Roger. After he finished his examination of the Licorice Kid, he removed a cigarette from his case. Smoking it, he thought aloud.

"It was smart to let this youngster come with me. He will prove very useful."

Grabbing a telephone, Roger immediately called the detective agency. "Hello, is this Celeritas?... Very well... This is Judex on the phone... Yes, Judex." A scared exclamation vibrated through the receiver causing Roger to smile ironically. He then spoke with a sinister solemnity. "Hello! Monsieur Cocantin... Hello!... Are you there ?... Judex will be at your agency today at 4 o'clock."

Wearing a policeman's hat made of paper, Jeannot was pretending to ride Cocantin like a horse when Diana and Amaury arrived in the office. Embarrassed to be found in this position, Cocantin led Jean to a neighboring room. Adopting a pompous manner, he addressed his intimidating clients.

"I am pleased to announce that Judex telephoned me."

"Ah!" exclaimed Diana. "What did he say?"

"He'll be here at 4 o'clock."

"*Diable*!" noted Amaury. "There is not an instant to lose."

Ringing for porter, he ordered him to perform an errand that would take him to the other side of Paris.

"What are you planning?" protested Cocantin. "You don't intend to ambush Judex here?"

"My dear friend," soothed the perfidious adventuress, "remember our agreement."

"I must follow my conscience."

"Come on, Cocantin, don't mention what you lack," scoffed Amaury. "Besides, it's too late to back off. You're either with us or against us. Decide!"

"Be with us, dear Prosper," beseeched the ex-governess.

However, Cocantin seemed to have regained his virtue. The ghost of Napoleon was going to gain ascendency over this woman when fate intervened.

A dark intruder had arrived at the Agency. He beheld the inscription on the front door: *Enter without ringing.* Following its instructions, he walked up the stairs into the antechamber. Not finding anyone there, his first announced his presence by knocking on Cocantin's door.

"It's him!" said Diana. "It's Judex!"

Pulling out guns from their pockets, Diana and Amaury positioned themselves on either side of the door. "Enter!" said the terrified Cocantin dropping into his armchair. Slowly the door opened revealing the bold newcomer carrying a large envelope.

Cries of disappointment issued from the two conspirators. In disgust, Amaury deposited his gun on the desk.

"Monsieur Cocantin, please?" said the Licorice Kid with a sly smirk on his face.

"I'm him," stammered the detective.

"Here's a letter for you."

Opening the envelope, the director of the Celeritas Agency read the letter without emotion:

Monsieur Cocantin,

I don't trust you. There is no proof that you're holding the child that's the object of my search. If this child shows himself at the balcony of your apartment, I shall arrive within minutes to negotiate his ransom.

JUDEX

Consumed by intense anger, Diana and Amaury glared threateningly at the young messenger. The Kid taunted them with insolent bravado. In their fury, the conspirators were prepared to torture the boy, but Cocantin courageously grabbed the child.

"I forbid you to touch him!" exclaimed the detective.

Diana and Amaury were startled by Prosper Cocantin's unexpected audacity. Before they had the time to react, Cocantin pushed the Licorice Kid into the room containing Jacqueline's son. Grabbing Amaury's gun, Cocantin uttered the classical sentence that rebounds throughout famous melodramas.

"The hour is grave!"

In the shadow of his idol, Cocantin put his other hand inside the middle of his jacket in the classical Napoleonic stance. "I command you to drop your weapon, Mademoiselle Monti." Diana angrily tossed her gun on the desk. Cocantin felt the heart of a hero twitch inside him. He put his gun on the desk.

"And now, let's talk!" he said ominously,

Recognizing the Licorice Kid, Jeannot was ecstatic.

"You're here!"

"Yes, sonny!"

Jean smothered his friend with hugs.

"Enough, little buddy, enough!" said the boy from the fortifications. "The die is cast. We must fly with the wind."

Executing Roger's instructions with an intelligence equaled by his boldness, the Kid explained:

"You have to leave here, and fast. Unless we do that, my poor rabbit, you'll never see your mother ever again."

"I want to leave right away."

"Wait. Don't rush. We must shift for ourselves, little buddy."

Going towards a window that led to a balcony facing the street, the Licorice Kid opened it gently. Leaning outside, he made a quick sign to Roger who waited with three companions on the sidewalk. Returning to Jeannot, he took him by the hand.

"This is the time, my brother, to prove that you're no coward." Inducing Jean to walk out on the balcony, the Kid pointed to the rail. "Climb over! Go! No fuss! You have nothing to fear. Have fun! Don't worry, little guy! Jump straight into the street. There are men waiting to catch you."

Jacqueline's son closed his eyes. When a whistle sounded in the street, the Licorice Kid seized Jean and threw him into the air. After whirling two or three times, Jean fell safely into a blanket that Roger and his acolytes had stretched wide.

At the same instant, the door of the room opened, allowing the entry of Cocantin and the two conspirators.

"You can look for him," triumphantly announced the Licorice Kid, "but he has flown away."

Running to the window, Diana and Amaury saw an automobile with their hostage inside disappear around a street corner. Their fury knew no bounds. Grabbing the Licorice Kid, they brought him back into Cocantin's office. Diana bombarded the brave youngster with questions.

"Who is Judex? Where's hiding? Speak or I'll beat you!"

The Licorice Kid remained silent. In the throes of their anger, the felons might have injured the child if Cocantin hadn't intervened. He abruptly grabbed both guns on his desk and pointed them at his supposed clients.

"Hands in the air!"

When Diana and Maury didn't execute his commands, Cocantin fired a warning shot. The two conspirators ran into the antechamber and down the stairs. After closing his door and double-locking it, Cocantin turned towards Judex's messenger.

"You performed well. I'm honored to know you."

"Me too," replied the boy. "I'm honored to know you."

"What's your name?"

"The Licorice Kid."

"Your real name?"

"I don't have one."

"You have no family?"

"Probably."

Extremely moved, Cocantin took the Kid on his knees as he had taken Jeannot. Filled with admiration for the boy who had just given a lesson in valor, Cocantin contemplated him in silence.

"What are you thinking?" asked the Kid.

"I wish" said Prosper Cocantin, "that I had a son like you."

"And me," replied the Licorice Kid, "I wish that I had a dad like you."

Hugging the boy, Cocantin peeked victoriously at the Emperor's bust.

"He resembles the King of Rome! The very son of Napoleon!"

A half-hour later, Roger reunited Jacqueline and her son. The boy found refuge in her maternal arms.

As for Judex, he had not yet returned. What was the goal of his mysterious pilgrimage?

Part Seven: The Woman in Black

I. The Spouse

Located at the far end of a long, oak-lined avenue in the forest of Dreux, the Chateau de la Ferté had been constructed towards the end of the 18th century by a rich financier. He had secluded himself there supposedly to redeem his soul after a life of excess. More likely, he retreated to the edifice in order to recover from the damage done to his health by a hedonistic existence.

Situated in the middle of the country within 12 kilometers of the city, it was completely isolated. During the Revolution, the Chateau had become the property of Citizen Poussard, a merchant selling supplies to the army. Under the July Monarchy, it had passed into the hands of Comte de Mériel, who modified it into a hunting lodge. Soon abandoned, it had fallen in a lamentable state of ruin and decay. About 15 years before this narrative began, a woman in mourning, Comtesse de Trémeuse, had purchased the Chateau from its previous owner, Monsieur Forois, who had balked at the enormous expenses needed to restore the estate. With the allure of a grand lady, the Comtesse had a youthful face that contrasted with her magnificent snow-white hair.

Six months after the Comtesse had moved into her new residence, she had transformed the formerly luxurious residence of the farmer-general of Louis XV into an austere place of contemplation and prayer. Living in a state of complete isolation, she never received visitors. Her only companions were three old servants: a coachman, a valet and a cook. Her presence in this corner of the Earth only became noticeable due to her numerous donations to charities for the needy. She only left her home to take a solitary walk in her vast property or sit in the sunshine on the wide terrace overlooking the valley. In her mourning clothes, Comtesse de Trémeuse represented the personification of a sorrow shrouded in secrecy.

In the region, they called her the "Woman in Black." As no one knew anything about her, some gossips attempted to question her servants. Her attendants wrapped themselves in a silence that only served to exacerbate the curious speculation. As the years passed, the gossips had resigned themselves to unanswered questions. A respectful silence surrounded the strange chatelaine of La Ferté. No one paid any attention to this sad and beautiful woman.

On a morning when she was treading slowly on an obscure path, her valet finally found her after a long search. After apologizing deferentially for disturbing her mediations, he delivered a telegram. The dispatch contained only these words:

Will visit you at 11 o'clock. Your Loving son. Jacques.

A slight smile wandered across the mouth of the Comtesse. A brief movement had occurred in a face that had seemed permanently immobilized by grief. Resuming her grave demeanor, she returned to the Chateau and secluded herself in a stylish room full of beautiful furnishings. Looking at a table, her eyes focused on a photograph of two boys of 14 and 12. They were her sons. Picking up the picture, she kindly contemplated the image with admiration and pride.

She put the portrait on the table. Her brilliant eyes feverishly implied an eternal drought of tears. Motionless and haughty, the Woman in Black was absorbed in her dark dreams.

A horrible tragedy had ravaged her life. The last descendant of one of the oldest and most illustrious families of Corsica, Julia Orsini had married, at age 20, Comte de Trémeuse, an excellent gentleman who had not been satisfied to merely be born wealthy. He energetically strove to expand his fortune. Owning major mining concessions in America and the Transvaal, his business enterprises never distracted him from being

179

an incomparable husband. He deeply cared for his beloved Julia.

The birth of her sons, Jacques and Roger, two years apart, had completed her happiness. Several years followed without any cloud disrupting the ideal harmony of this family. It seemed to be blessed by the priceless treasures of affection and joy.

One evening, Comte de Trémeuse hosted a large dinner party. Among the guests was the banker Favraux. He had infiltrated the Comte's household in order to swindle it. Originally intending to extort money from Trémeuse, the scoundrel decided to betray his host by another means. The financier resolved to seduce the nobleman's wife. Captivated by the classical beauty of the Comtesse, the unscrupulous banker launched an amorous assault conceived in vulgar cynicism.

As early as his first interview with Madame de Trémeuse, he suffered the consequences of his false calculations. Scarcely had he risked a crude declaration of love than the stern Julia directed him towards her parlor door.

"Get out, Monsieur! If you ever dare to show yourself in my presence again, my husband, Comte de Trémeuse, will lower himself to throw you into the gutter!"

Knowing that the nobleman was a first-class duelist with both sword and pistol, Favraux retreated. From that day forward, he became the ferocious enemy of the Trémeuse family. He brooked no delay in making his hatred known.

Shortly thereafter, an obstinate string of mishaps stalked the nobleman. Several of his planned business ventures fell apart without any indications of the cause. Three big contracts, the basis of his finances, were not renewed. His credit had once been limitless, but gradually the securing of loans became more and more difficult.

One day, the workers of one of his most important mines went on strike. Although he had yielded to all their demands, his representative telegraphed him appalling news:

The miners voted to reject the contract. I fear violence.
Chief Engineer Bernard.

The next day, the Comte learned that his mine had been sabotaged to such an extent that it would cost at least a million pounds and six months of labor to repair the damage.

Facing payment deadlines that couldn't be met, the Comte searched for capital. He was ignorant of the scene that had transpired between Favraux and his wife. Not wishing to sully her own reputation, or upset her affectionate husband, the Comtesse had decided to keep the banker's scandalous conduct to herself. Totally in the dark, the nobleman appealed to the banker.

Three days later, the scoundrel sent him the following message disguised by the hypocritical veneer of sympathy.

Unable to find any investors interested in your mining corporation. Deep regrets.

FAVRAUX

On the same day that Monsieur de Trémeuse received the news of the mine having been repaired at tremendous cost, he also learned that it had just been flooded! The extent of the damage was devastating. He was ruined! Never in a hundred years did the Comte suspect Favraux of being the dark instigator of this calamity.

In a tearful scene, he revealed to his wife the stark truth.

"If he wanted, Favraux could save me. He is my only hope. I already asked for his support, but he refused. Maybe, today, if I accept all his conditions, I will be extricate myself and avoid the shame of bankruptcy. Without Favraux, we are lost. I will not hide the truth from you, my precious Julia, I may not have the courage to survive this collapse!"

The name of Favraux had shown Madame de Trémeuse the glimmer of truth. She understood all. With an infernal desire to repay the insult, this obscene knave had cunningly taken revenge for her scorn by ruining her husband and children.

The gallant woman staunchly accepted the terrible revelation of their financial peril. Hiding carefully her conclusions from her beloved husband, she replied calmly:

"Darling, you did well to tell me the truth. Now that I know the facts, I can remedy the situation."

"What do you intend to do?" asked Trémeuse.

With magnificent composure, Madame de Trémeuse made a declaration:

"You had enough faith in me not to hide the catastrophe threatening us. I know you are infinitely brave. Now, let me try to secure our happiness and save our family."

"I ask again: what do you intend to do?"

Without the least hesitation, the Comtesse answered with a heroic flame in her eyes:

"I shall see the banker Favraux myself!"

II. The Mother

While taking this grave decision, the proud descendant of the Orsini family had never yielded to fear. Instead, she obeyed her own internal counsel.

Find this man. Don't humiliate yourself in front of him. Raise your head proudly before him. Don't be timid. Be a grand lady that comes to settle accounts with a man who offended her. Shame him with his unworthy conduct. Force him to beg your forgiveness and make amends for all the evil he has caused. This Favraux can't be a total monster. There must be some honor remaining in him, or at least an ounce of mercy. He will certainly recognize the injustice of punishing a woman's scorn through the ruination of her innocent family!

Madame de Trémeuse had been born an Orsini. She viewed the idea of vengeance as a grand ideal, one of those traditional values unsoiled by pettiness or cowardice. She expected to be strong enough to confront the banker and force him to admit his odious conduct.

Confident as she had never been before, she was ready to fight to the end. Armed with limitless energy and a strong love for her husband and sons, she presented herself the next day at the banker's residence. Surprised by her unexpected visit, Favraux agreed to see the Comtesse.

Treating her with the most respectful courtesy, he escorted her to an armchair near his desk. His deferential correctness could almost foster the belief that he was ready to renounce his malicious campaign.

"This is a pleasant surprise, Comtesse. Why have you honored me with a visit?"

"You don't know?"

"Not at all, Madame."

"You must be aware that my husband has been for some time in financial difficulties."

"I do know that."

"I came to you to ask you to help us."

"Monsieur de Trémeuse must not have told you that he had already solicited my support. To my deep regret, I had to refuse him."

"He did tell me."

The sly Favraux struggled to conceal the burning passion that the Corsican beauty inspired in him.

"Comtesse, whatever my desire to assist Monsieur de Trémeuse, as well as yourself, it is absolutely impossible to reverse my decision. At this moment, all my resources are engaged elsewhere. Europe has entered a very serious financial crisis. Capital remains elusive, and I can't see any way to help you. Unfortunately, I can't spare you any more of my time. I deeply regret that I can't do more than merely extend my pronounced sympathy!"

"Then my husband is lost. My children ruined!"

The banker threw up his hands as if he was powerless.

Madame de Trémeuse could no longer conceal her thoughts.

"Monsieur Favraux, haven't you sufficiently gratified your vengeance by forcing me to cross your threshold? Haven't you done enough because of what transpired between us?"

"Comtesse, I don't understand what you're telling me."

"You understand very well. The author of the catastrophe besieging my family is you!"

"Me!"

"Yes, Monsieur Favraux. You are the instigator of the horrible conspiracy directed against my husband. You conducted a secret war against him. You compromised his credit. You organized the strikes. You bribed saboteurs to flood the mines. Yes, you did all this to break him. And why? Because once, when you attempted to seduce me, I hounded you out of my house. Don't try to deny it. You can't hide anymore. You just gave me the proof of my accusations. I read it in your eyes. How you tremble, Monsieur Favraux. You've become pale. Is this remorse? As if I would forgive you!"

Transfigured by the righteousness of her cause, she attacked with the fervor of an immaculate wife and mother.

"Do you realize the consequences of your recent actions? I doubt it. If you reflected on all the suffering that you caused, you wouldn't have the stomach to undertake another crusade of hate and death! You were blinded and intoxicated by your impulsive lust. Now that you are confronted with reality, you can see the injustice of your hate. You can tell yourself to stop. You must go no further. You must not break my husband because of my refusal. You must not ruin my children because of their mother."

"Comtesse, you are Corsican," resumed Favraux who had listened to Madame de Trémeuse with an impassiveness that was more artificial than real.

"Yes, I am Corsican."

"I'm very surprised to hear you talk this way. I imagined that you understood vengeance better."

"Monsieur Favraux!"

Losing all restraint, the financier shouted his guilt:

"Yes! Your husband is lost! Your children are ruined! You guessed correctly! I did it all!"

"Do you regret anything?"

"Nothing!"

Very pale, Madame de Trémeuse rose. Advancing towards her, the banker felt conflicting emotions of desire and fury compelling him to speak:

"You made me suffer! One doesn't wrong a man like me with impunity. You didn't understand with whom you were dealing. You didn't realize the extent of my injured pride. You see it now. And I'm not finished yet. As for morality, I mock it. As for honor, I know it not. I have only one guide: my desires. If I want something, I take it. I have only one principle: myself. When someone crosses me, I strip that person bare!"

"You're a monster!"

"If that is what you call a being who takes everything he craves from life, then, yes, I am a monster!"

"And to save my family," shouted Julia Orsini, "must I disgrace myself!"

"Why are you here?"

"You don't understand?"

"You want to save your husband."

"By causing you to realize your shame."

"You believe you could defeat me like that?"

"Yes, for I believed you still had a heart."

"I never had one."

"You are implacable."

"Just as you are."

At these words, Madame de Trémeuse sobbed. Favraux moved close to her.

"You really love this husband of yours?"

"Yes... I love him!"

"And your children?"

"I love them!"

"Well?"

The cynical banker brutally grabbed the arms of the Comtesse. Foul words sprang from his lips as he shamefully addressed her like some commodity to be purchased.

But Madame de Trémeuse released herself from Favraux's unwanted embrace. When the gilded merchant laid his hands on her again, the indignant lady slapped his face. The enraged banker leaped at her. He extended his hands forward as if to strangle her. Then he desisted. A flashing glare of contempt from the daughter of the Orsinis had intimidated him.

"Get out," he commanded. "I no longer want to see you. I hate you. I abhor you. I curse you!"

He opened the door of his study. Still proud and nobly repressing her tears, the Comtesse left the room where had transpired a tragic conflict whose stakes were the honor of a woman and the survival of a family. When she passed in front of the banker, he acknowledged his supremacy by making a disdainful prediction.

"I'll see you soon, Comtesse!"

Madame de Trémeuse refused to tremble under the threat. The worthy woman proudly exited. As she disappeared, the gilded merchant laughed like a hyena. If he had noticed the face of the Comtesse, he might have hesitated before completing his vile handiwork. For the eyes of Julia Orsini did not cry. Instead, they reflected all the terrible hate contained in the human heart.

The furious Favraux returned to his desk. Seizing his telephone, he began yelling into the mouthpiece. He punctuated every sentence by pounding his fist on the desk.

"Hello... Hello... Meyer... It's Favraux! Tell everyone to sell the Trémeuse stock... Sell! Sell! Sell!"

III. The Widow

Within a day, the collapse of Comte de Trémeuse's company was an accomplished fact. After the debacle, the Comte returned to his house. His wife welcomed him with open arms for she read on his face the appalling reality.

"Have courage," she said with sublime simplicity. "We will strive together to make our two sons worthy of the noble name they bear."

"Thank you," replied Pierre de Trémeuse, tenderly embracing the Comtesse. He tried to be calm. "Forgive me, Julia, for having failed you."

"Don't talk that way."

"Nothing will remain once this house is sold."

"That's unimportant! We'll always be together!"

"Yes, together," said the Comte in a hollow voice, "to carry the weight of shame."

"Shame?"

"My poor darling, you don't know public opinion. No one shall forgive my failure. The shareholders of my mining company will always be convinced that I'm a dishonest man."

"No, no, that's impossible," protested vehemently Madame de Trémeuse. "You're the most loyal man in the world! You're the victim of an infamous plot!"

The gallant woman stopped herself. Nothing in the world would prompt her to add to the tortures of her spouse. She couldn't have him know her dealings with Favraux, especially the ugly scene that had unfolded in the banker's study.

She tried to infuse the Count with the wonderful energy that burnt inside her. Her admiring eyes sought to communicate love and strength.

"I need you, and so do our children"

"I will do my duty!" said the nobleman. He planted a long kiss on the forehead of his spouse. "Thank you… my beloved."

Under the pretence of writing some letters, he withdrew into his study on the upper floor.

At this point in time, Jacques and Roger, accompanied by their tutor, returned from school.

With her characteristic firmness, Madame de Trémeuse judged that it was useless to leave her two sons in ignorance of the catastrophe. She brought them close to her. With calm simplicity, she apprised them of the situation.

"You are both old enough to understand your duty."

At these words, Jacques and Roger threw themselves into the arms of their mother. A single dry gushed from their generous hearts: "Poor Father!"

Suddenly, a deafening detonation reverberated from the upper floor.

Madame de Trémeuse grew pale. Her children remained frozen on the spot. She rushed upstairs into her husband's study. Comte de Trémeuse was lying on the ground. In his hand was a recently discharged pistol.

The panic-stricken Comtesse bent down next to him. She vainly tried to revive him. The bullet had entered his heart.

"He's dead!"

On the table was a letter in an envelope addressed to Madame Trémeuse. Upon recovering from her initial shock, she opened it and read:

My dear Julia,

Let it not to be said that Comte de Trémeuse survived his disgrace.

You will understand. You will condone my decision. Of this, I am sure! For I do not die a coward; I die an aristocrat.

Tell this to our sons. Use this terrible example to forge their hearts to survive any ordeal!

I give them my final blessing at the same time that I send you my last kiss.

PIERRE DE TRÉMEUSE.

An hour later, the young widow took her sons by the hand to the funeral bed where rested their father's corpse. All three knelt and prayed in silence for a long time.

Faced with his death, the mother once more became a daughter of the Orsinis. When she rose from the ground, there was no place in her soul for anything but vengeance. Showing her sons their dead father, she addressed them stridently.

"Your father is the victim of a criminal named Favraux. It is Favraux who ruined your father. It is Favraux who engineered your father's disgrace. It is Favraux who placed the fatal weapon in your father's hand. It is Favraux who murdered your father!"

Shaking with grief, she issued an order:

"My sons, swear to your father that you will avenge him."

Yielding to the Corsican blood in their veins, Jacques and Roger shouted a savage resolution:

"Yes, mother, we do so swear!"

Some days after this horrible drama, Madame de Trémeuse got ready to move with her sons to a modest establishment. But then, a young engineer, Monsieur Bianchini, insisted on seeing her about a very urgent matter. Upon hearing his name, the young widow was surprised. She remembered words that that her husband had spoken to his secretary a few days earlier.

"It's been three months since I had news of Bianchini," the Comte had said. "Some accident must have befallen him. My last hope is gone. "

Madame de Trémeuse immediately received the engineer.

"Comtesse," he said, "I just learned about your husband's demise. It is even more tragic because I bring good news. Monsieur de Trémeuse sent me, two years ago, to search for gold in Africa. It was a dangerous venture. I was nearly killed a hundred times. After a long and patient search, I discovered a fabulous lode."

A mournful cry escaped the Comtesse.

"Monsieur! Monsieur! Why couldn't you have told us earlier? My husband would still be alive!"

"Madame," resumed Bianchini taking great pains to restrain his emotions. "Do not condemn me before you have all the facts. Over there, I became certain that my movements were being spied upon by a certain Debord, an agent of a banker named Favraux."

"Again! Always this man!" The face of the Comtesse was filled with hate.

Bianchi continued his narrative.

"I had to take extreme precautions before wiring or writing the Comte. If I had made a wrong move in this distant country, all would have been lost. Those saboteurs would certainly have murdered me in order to steal my discovery. Ignorant of the dire events that unfolded here, I refrained from sending the Comte a message that could have been intercepted by his enemies. Instead, I believed it more prudent to come here myself. Madame, know this: I will never be able to console myself for failing to arrive in time. This will be the eternal sorrow of my life!"

"Monsieur Bianchini," said Madame de Trémeuse, "you acted according to your conscience. I cannot condemn you." She stifled a sob. "Then, we are rich?"

"The lode is worth more than 50 million francs."

"Monsieur," said Julia Orsini whose eyes shined with a strange fervor. "Your loyalty makes you our partner in this endeavor. As early as tomorrow, I'll finalize the details. You will set off for Africa once you are fully able. I know my sons will be able to count on your support."

Bianchini bowed to the gallant woman. "Their fortune is secure, Madame. I give you my word."

The engineer had not exaggerated. His discovery was truly phenomenal. Thanks to his intelligence, which equaled his loyalty, Bianchini was able to draw a profit from the enterprise earlier than expected. He more than exceeded the promises that he made to the widow and sons of Comte de Trémeuse.

The Comtesse consecrated herself completely to the education of her sons, She cultivated the idea of vengeance planted in their young minds. She succeeded in making Jacques and Roger not only into two men of the first caliber, but also two implacable avengers.

She artfully developed the special aptitudes of each son. Jacques's intelligence predisposed him to intensive study. He became a scholar open to all the modern and bold ideas, while refusing to become a cynical philosopher who placed himself above the common man. By contrast, Roger was an accomplished sportsman. Endowed with a stunning physique, he was a tireless and fearless athlete.

Jacques was the brain. Roger the brawn. Both loved each other. United by the same oath, they considered the least quarrel amongst them as a true sacrilege. Subservient to the will of their mother, they formed with her a true trinity of vengeance united in a single thought and fueled by the same spirit. Often the Comtesse had to moderate their impatience. She wanted to strike effectively. Not only must Favraux be punished, but the severity of the retribution must equal the infamy of his crime.

Jacques and Roger had for their mother a reverence bordering on fanaticism. They were firm in their conviction to unquestionably follow her guidance. Once the Comtesse judged her sons sufficiently prepared to undertake their mission, she told Roger: "You will obey your brother as your brother obeys me." Enthroned in her austere residence, she gave the signal for hostilities to commence.

For the first time since the tragic death of his husband, she was thrilled when she received Jacques's first letter:

Dear Mama,

Henceforth, I am called Vallières. I am old, stooped and gray-haired. I shall return as the personal secretary of Favraux. We shall be avenged!

JACQUES

At the end of only a year, she received this message even briefer that the earlier one:

The moment that I have awaited for years has come. Favraux will be stuck down at his daughter's engagement party!

J.

And finally this telegram, as terse as it was ominous:

It is done! J.

Madame de Trémeuse rose and clasped her hands. With her eyes directed towards the sky, she thanked God for allowing her to anticipate His justice.

Every day, the daughter of the Orsinis reread Jacques' three messages. She waited with a feverish impatience the day when she would hear from her sons the details of the vengeance that had been the cornerstone of her existence.

Her son had now wired her that, within hours, he would be close to her. The hours stretched. She was anxious to embrace him in her arms. She wanted to thank him in the name of the victim... in the name of her avenged spouse... in the name of the father who, in his grave, doubtlessly heard the terrible cries of mortal agony erupting from Favraux as he awoke, trapped for all eternity, between the nailed boards of a coffin!

IV. The Son

"How are you, my son?"

Such were the first words of Comtesse de Trémeuse when Jacques de Trémeuse appeared in the vast lobby of her Chateau. The grave concern on his face was a warning of bad news, or at least serious complications.

"Mother," said Judex after kissing tenderly the gallant woman, "you always raised me to believe in integrity and honor. I would be an unworthy son if I violated your trust."

Madame de Trémeuse was confused. "Jacques, what are you saying?"

Judex courageously made his request. "I ask you to release me from my oath."

Julia Orsini was shocked. "Your oath? You haven't fulfilled it? You wrote to me that justice had been done! Are you a liar? Are you a Trémeuse? Are you my own flesh and blood?

"Favraux is not dead!"

"*What?*"

"Favraux is in my power, confined in a prison from which no human being could escape."

"He still lives!" bitterly exclaimed the Comtesse. Her eyes gleamed with hate. "Why have you spared this criminal? Did he spare your father? Why have you and your brother broken faith?"

"Roger isn't party to my decision. I solely made it of my own free will. My mother, I assume total responsibility."

"Why? Why?" cried the Comtesse at the height of indignation.

"My mother," replied Jacques nobly. "I wanted to be a judge, but I lack the soul of an executioner."

"Jacques, you've betrayed me."

"Mother!"

"You've betrayed your father!"

"Let me explain."

"You failed in your task! You forgot you were my son! I will never forgive you!"

"Mother!" implored Jacques. His demeanor remained respectful yet passionately firm. "I entreat you to hear my plea."

"Speak!" consented the grand lady. Seating herself in a gothic chair, she seemed frozen in gloomy despair.

Judex solemnly began: "Only when Favraux was entombed in his grave did I question my right to leave him there. Even then, not for an instant did I hesitate. Not for a minute did my conscience challenge me. My soul remained as hard as bronze. My heart made me the inflexible judge that nothing could touch. Yet, an unexpected event caused me to be plagued by self-doubts. Following a conversation in which I exposed the crimes of the banker Favraux, his daughter generously abandoned her inheritance to the Public Assistance. My conscience told me: 'After such a gesture, you do not have the right to condemn Favraux to such a barbaric death.' I had him withdrawn from his coffin and restored to life."

"And, now, you want to save him completely?"

"Perhaps."

"Wretch!"

"Yes, mother, you are justified in to call me a wretch. I'm a wretch because the deepest corner of my soul is terrified by what I've done. I'm a wretch because, by striking down a guilty man who deserved punishment a hundred times over, I also imposed the most merciless suffering on an innocent woman who is a wonderful human being twice over... an incomparable mother... as close as possible to a true saint."

"His daughter!"

"Yes, his daughter," forcefully repeated Jacques de Trémeuse, "His daughter whose tears inspired me a pity that I initially succeeded in overcoming, but whose self-denial, courage and sacrifice eventually broke my will... a will that I believed to be made of steel since this will, my mother, was really yours. His daughter who appeared before me with an aura of touching agony that would soften even you... since she caused me to cry..."

"You love her!" shouted Julia Orsini staring at her son. Contemplating her son sadly, she darkened her voice with bitter disappointment. "I believed that I had attained my goal. I believed that that the hate soaked into your heart was impossible to overcome. What has happened now? You want to release your father's enemy? You want to return him to his daughter?"

"I want to be released from my oath," staunchly declared Judex.

"Never!" roared the Corsican woman. "I am unyielding! And as long as I live, you will either obey or commit treason. Choose!"

"Mother! You wound me!"

"Haven't you wounded me more?"

Jacques shouted forth his despair.

"Horror consumes me! Since I've seen this woman cry, I no longer believe vengeance to be a duty! Yes, I even doubt that we have the right to deliver justice."

"This criminal passion has destroyed your reason," proclaimed Madame de Trémeuse, devoured by an insatiable fire.

"Who knows if she has driven me towards the light? Who knows if she has not opened my eyes to the truth?"

"Jacques... you blaspheme."

"It's my conscience that speaks."

"Remember your father!"

"I haven't forgotten him! The more I think about him, the more I recall his generosity and humanity. Would Pierre de Trémeuse have sanctioned the actions of his widow and sons?"

"Silence! I never told you about all the nights when I awakened from horrible nightmares. In my slumbers, I heard the voice of your father scream: '*When will the coward who struck me down be paid in kind? When will this insolent outlaw, this infamous monster, no longer triumph? His execution is all the more sacred not because you must avenge me, but*

194

because you must stop the scourge of his crimes. You must save all those future souls whom he intends to ruin!' Jacques, my son, my child, what of the times that I dreamt of his voice! You wouldn't want it to return to haunt me… to reproach me for failure due to your weakness. I could not bear this ordeal once more. Yes, I would die!"

"My poor mother!"

Torn between the hate and love that had for years had exclusively molded her life, Julia Orsini shouted an appeal:

"Have I, at last, rediscovered my child?" A burning fever possessed her. "Listen to me, my son. Hold me tight. Forget this deceitful mirage of a love that cannot exist in your heart. It is so unnatural that you should reject it! Return to your earlier faith. Being a judge means being superhuman. Strengthen your faltering hand to grip the blade of inescapable retribution. Strike without pity. Strike without weakness. I will consent to keep this man in a prison that must be his tomb of despair. But to terminate your oath as you request… to allow this outlaw to run rampant in the world. Never! That would be both a crime and an act of insanity… A crime because you would be betraying the oath which no power on Earth can cause me to annul… An act of insanity because by liberating Favraux, you would cause your mother to hate you!"

Recognizing that nothing would dissuade his mother, Jacques surrendered to her stubborn cruelty.

"Favraux will remain a prisoner until the end of his days."

"Thank you, my son."

"Don't thank me, my mother! You have reminded me of my duty. I beg your forgiveness for having forgotten it."

The Woman in Black rose to her full height. In her somber dress with her white hair and tormented face, she appeared to be the personification of the legendary Nemesis, Daughter of the Night, dispenser of vengeance and justice.

"Jacques, I'll forgive you once you purge your heart of this poisonous flower."

Jacques bowed to his mother. No other word was exchanged between them.

The pact that Jacques wanted to break left this tragic test more intangible than ever. His soul was still tortured. His spirit was fastened by shackles that, with every step, pierced his flesh. The self-styled judge walked away overcome by a sense of futility.

After he had gone, Julia Orsini, wiped away two tears of anger that she had courageously contained during the argument. She approached her husband's portrait. Contemplating it in solitude, she committed herself to a task she viewed as inevitable and sacred.

"Since your sons have already betrayed their oaths, only I will avenge you!"

V. The Grandson

"Monsieur Vallières, when will I see the Licorice Kid again?" asked Jeannot.

Returning to Paris, Jacques de Trémeuse had resumed once more the personality of Vallières.

"As soon as possible, my boy," replied the banker's ex-secretary.

Also present was Jacqueline. Her face was full of affectionate concern.

"I'm only too happy to please you and your Mama," said Vallières.

Shortly thereafter, Prosper Cocantin received a mysterious telephone call that perplexed him His puzzlement did not prevent him from agreeing to the caller's request.

"Yes, I understand… 5 o'clock, Place Armand Carrel… I will be there!"

After consulting the bust of Napoleon several times, Cocantin fell into a deep slumber. Waking up later, he went out on his balcony. Leaning on the railing, he noticed the corner of Rue Lamartine and Rue Hippolyte Lebas. A roofless car was parked there. Next to the vehicle was a man of about 30. A hat worn low on his forehead and a raised collar obscured his features.

They're still there, the sleuth thought. *It's perfect. He who laughs last laughs best.*

Renewed by the fresh air, the private detective returned to his office and rang for his errand boy.

"Look for my big wicker trunk," directed Cocantin. "Bring it to the balcony. It needs to be aired out because it's been too long in the attic."

The moment the boy returned with the requested trunk, the Licorice Kid, who had prudently remained in the Celeritas Agency since Jean's escape, burst into Cocantin's office. Needless to say, the warm relations between the detective and the boy persisted.

"Hey, Coconut," shouted the kid, "are you going on a trip? Is that why you need a trunk?"

"Listen to me," said Cocantin "Your friend Jean misses you."

"That's grand!"

"I'm going to take you to him."

"Great!"

"After what happened here, we have to be careful," explained Cocantin solemnly. "Our enemies must not know where I'm taking you. Otherwise, awful consequences will befall both of us."

"You're making my hair stand up!" joked the Kid.

Taking the Kid by the hand, Cocantin brought him out on the balcony. The detective opened the lid of the trunk. "Hide inside."

"Then, what?" questioned the Licorice Kid. "You want to lug me around like dirty clothes? Are you going to take me out with the laundry?"

"Leave it to me and fear nothing," ordered Cocantin

"This is funny," said the Kid as he disappeared in the trunk.

After glancing at the still stationary car, Cocantin brought the wicker basket back into the office.

Minutes later, Cocantin's chambermaid helped him deposit the trunk in the front passenger seat of a taxi. A rope was tied around the trunk to keep it closed. The maid got inside the back of the cab. After giving an address to the driver, Cocantin returned to his office. He rubbed his hands with satisfaction.

Scarcely had the taxi started up, than the car waiting alongside the Rue Hippolyte Lebas followed in pursuit. After crossing the exterior boulevards, the taxi passed through the Boulevard Barbès and the Boulevard d'Ornano. Turning left at the Porte de Clignancourt, it took the Boulevard Ney along the line of the old ramparts of Paris.

Then an audacious act happened. The roofless car had been following at a respectful distance. Now, it accelerated at a sudden pace. Seated in the back was Amaury de la Rochefontaine. He was armed with a makeshift crosier made from a curbed pipe. Once the speeding car ran parallel with the taxi, Amaury use the crosier to grasp the rope around the wicker basket. Before the skilled taxi driver had time to react, the trunk was plucked in a flash into the other car. Piloted by Crémard, the 24-horsepower car carrying Amaury and the trunk disappeared in the direction of Boulevard Berthier. Running at full power, Amaury's car left the taxi in the dust.

"Bravo, boss," approved Crémard. "You behaved like you've been a thief all your life."

"My apartment, quickly!" ordered the Vicomte left breathless by this daring operation.

After zigzagging through various streets to evade pursuit, Crémard stopped in front of Amaury's residence, temporarily being used by Diana Monti as a hideout. Leaving the car, Crémard, carried the trunk on his shoulder.

"Who's the smart aleck now, Licorice Kid?" asked Diana's henchman.

"We've got better things to do than clown around," curtly said the Vicomte. He disliked fraternizing with lowlifes like Crémard.

"He says nothing," noted Crémard climbing the stairway. "The little devil is heavier than I thought."

"Well?" asked the adventuress impatiently after her associates had entered the apartment.

"He's inside!" informed Amaury pointing to the wicket basket deposited by Crémard in the middle of the parlor.

"Are you sure?" challenged Diana.

"I saw Cocantin hide him there."

"You should have seen the boss," interjected Crémard undoing the rope that surrounded the trunk. "He hooked it like a fish. It's amazing."

"You little rat," sneered the ex-governess, "now you'll pay!"

"I think he's lost his tongue," concluded Crémard. "He hasn't said a word since the boss fished him out of the car." He opened the trunk. "Jump out, you slimy toad, or I'll skin you alive!"

When nothing budged, Diana nervously seized the old patched blanket that seemed to conceal the child. An angry cry escaped her. The voluminous blanket contained only a large cement block wrapped in rags. Pinned to the rags was this message: *The Licorice Kid is no dummy.*

"Fooled by Cocantin," shouted Diana. "This is too much!" Pale with fury, she continued to scream. "I'll have my revenge! Yes! I'll have it! I'll have it!"

During this time, the director of the Celeritas Agency watched the two cars drive away. Once they were sufficiently distant, he left his place with the Licorice Kid going towards Place Armand Cerral. Roger de Trémeuse met them there. The detective related how he had outwitted his opponent. After Roger congratulated him on this trick, Prosper Cocantin radiated pride.

"There is nothing that I can't do. If Napoleon returned from the dead, he would make his Minister of Police. I would be the equal of Joseph Fouché!"

"Well, brother, are you happy?" asked Roger.

Disguised as the elderly Vallières, Judex's features hid the gnawing bitterness inside him. He replied first with an evasive gesture that expressed his deep depression. Finally he spoke.

"I'm tearing myself apart. I can't repress this devouring love. Whether I will be stronger than this passion, I don't know. I abstain from questioning the future. I must find the strength to silence my heart."

"Poor brother!"

"You were justified in criticizing me," sighed the older de Trémeuse. "Be happy that you have never been tested by a similar struggle."

"Or failure."

"I shall not fail. The anguish of my mother, whose desolate cries I shall always hear, shall dictate my duty. I don't know if she's right or wrong, but I will bow to her will until the day I die."

"I don't think less of you," said Roger with admiration. "I'm sure that the fulfillment of your oath will bring you consolation."

"I hope so!"

"Besides, didn't you win am undisputed victory over our mother by obtaining her permission to spare Favraux's life? Who knows if our mother's heart may soften someday and will concur with your... our... recommendation to set him free?"

"Let's not harbor any illusions," declared Jacques. "Our mother will never yield. She has lived too long with her hatred. It will only die with her. I don't see the possibility of her ever consenting to the return of Favraux to his family. Jacqueline could never forgive Jacques de Trémeuse for being Judex. My only consolation will be to continually protect her under the guise of Vallières, an old man devoid of passion. I will try to borrow his soul just as I have fashioned his body. The friendship that my alter ego inspires in Jacqueline may help me forget her hatred for the man who judged her father!"

"I'm proud to hear you speak like this," shouted Roger he strongly shook Jacques's hand. "Without closing the door to hope, I know that you'll remain standing inflexible on the threshold of duty."

While the two brothers confided in each other, the door of the office opened gently. Revealed was the disquieting outline of the austere Woman in Black.

After listening to Roger's last words, she slowly approached with an inscrutable smile.

"Come to me, my sons! Believing my presence needed, I came here."

Confronting Jacques, she spoke like a spirit from beyond. Her voice froze the two brothers in an aura of respectful awe.

"I reflected at length on what you told me, Jacques. Rather than reverse my decision, I must chide both of you for disobedience."

She was the embodiment of supreme authority.

"Where is Favraux?"

Jacques replied without hesitation. "Close to Andelys, by the Seine, in the Chateau Rouge, which you bought to be our headquarters for our mission of vengeance."

"Where is he confined?"

"In a prison cell in the one of the former jail cells of the castle."

"Who guards him?"

"A man whose loyalty is unquestionable."

"Tomorrow, you will take me to my enemy," dictated urgently the daughter of the Orsinis. Her eyes enlarged themselves in a sort of mystical trance. "Since you have shirked your task, I shall avenge your father myself."

Intimidated, Jacques and Roger kept silent.

"You reserved a room for me in this residence. I hope you will not forbid me from using it."

Without waiting for a response from her sons, she went into the hall and stepped towards the door of Jacqueline's room.

Jacques got ahead of her. "Mother, I beg you. Don't go in there."

"Why?"

"There's someone there."

"Who?"

"Favraux's daughter."

"Her! How dare you bring her here! Your sacrilege is greater than I imagined!"

"Mother, let me explain!"

"I want to see her!" demanded the Corsican.

The two brothers regarded her with mute despair.

"I assume," she said stridently, "'that you won't forcefully restrain me."

With her face contracted by hate, she deliberately opened the door. She stopped herself immediately.

Kneeling on the bed next to Jacqueline, Jeannot and the Licorice Kid, in their night shirts, had joined hands. With their eyes raised to the Heavens, they clearly repeated the prayer that Jacqueline had taught them:

"Give us today our daily bread. Forgive us our trespasses. As we forgive those who trespass against us."

This spectacle was so deliciously simple, so poetically moving, that, for the first time in many long years, the face of the implacable Corsican woman displayed a glimpse of mercy. Once the prayer was finished, Jacqueline glimpsed the woman in mourning clothes. The young woman directed towards Vallières an expression that seemed to ask: *Who is this lady, and why does she look at me so strangely?*

The Comtesse had read the heart of Jacqueline. The Woman in Black spoke in a voice that her sons did not know anymore. She spoke with a tranquility that suddenly seemed human.

"I am... the sister of Monsieur Vallières... I came to Paris for a few days... Forgive me for disturbing you..."

As Jacqueline was about to reply, the Woman in Black closed the door abruptly. She addressed her two sons in the antechamber.

"Leave me. I need to be alone."

In Judex's study, she remained in deep meditation. Her eyes had an odd acuity. Her lips trembled. Painful sighs escaped from her chest. An intense struggle had erupted inside her.

These two charming children had radiated virtue and this young woman feminine nobility. Suddenly she found herself praying for those who had offended them. Words of mercy had been transmitted from the innocent hearts to her heart of agony. "Forgive us our trespasses" had fallen from these children's lips and moved her spirit strongly.

Would the angel of mercy be triumphant over the god of vengeance? The outcome was in doubt.

A vision from the grave, a tragic evocation of irreparable heartbreak, rose in front of the Comtesse. Her features expressed a fanatical resolution as an oath escaped her mouth.

"*He must die! It's necessary! I demand it. And it is I who will strike him down!*"

Two cherubs then appeared suddenly as the door slightly opened without noise. Dressed in their long white shirts, Jeannot and the Licorice Kid had been sent by Jacqueline while Vallières and Roger remained in the antechamber. The children advanced in their bare feet towards the Woman in Black prostrate in her funeral meditation.

Taken aback, Jeannot stopped. The Licorice Kid encouraged his companion forward by pointing simply. With outstretched arms, the child advanced again.

"Madame, Madame," said Jean softly.

Julia Orsini raised her head.

Seeing this blond angel smiling at her, she quivered. She tied to defend herself against the mercy invading her soul.

"Madame," asked Jeannot, "don't you want to kiss me good night?"

She was faced with an innocence that she had forsaken, but still craved. Moved by this divine image of kindness, Madame de Trémeuse felt suddenly transformed.

As the day before, two tears flow on her cheeks. However, these weren't tears of vengeance. They were tears of mercy.

"Come, my little one!" she shouted while embracing Jacqueline's son.

The small child had won a victory that had been denied to the Good Lord!

Part Eight. The Caverns of the Chateau Rouge

I. Him!

"I want to see him!

"Mother!"

"I want to see him. Take me to him. I demand it!"

Spoken bitterly, these terms were imposed by Madame de Trémeuse on her sons. Jacques and Roger had no choice but to obey. Shortly thereafter, they left in an automobile with their mother for the Chateau Rouge. During the whole trip, the Comtesse remained in a state of bitter sadness. She was going to confront her nemesis, the man who had ripped her life apart as cruelly as a tiger feasts on flesh. All her ideas of vengeance, temporarily exorcised by Jean's pure kiss, reasserted themselves.

By this time, she no longer castigated her sons for violating their oath to her. No longer did she condemn them for abandoning the bloody road that she had mapped. On the contrary, a ferocious joy was beating inside her Corsican heart.

Soon she would gaze on her enemy entombed alive in an escape-proof prison. Caught in the brutal glitter of pride, she would finally proclaim to this miscreant lying defeated at her feet: "I have broken you in turn!"

In the distance, the majestic ruins of the Chateau Rouge dominated the valley of the Seine. Seeing it, an enigmatic smile wandered on her lips. She was about to experience the most significant hour of her life. Guided by her sons, she navigated the labyrinth in the old fortress. Traversing in the caverns, she reached the laboratory of Judex where the vigilant Kerjean ceaselessly guarded the prisoner.

"Who is this man?" questioned the Woman in Black.

"This is Pierre Kerjean," replied Judex. "Once Favraux's victim, now his jailer. He hates the banker as much as we do. We can rely on him."

Kerjean respectfully bowed in front of the grand lady.

"And *him*?" she said with a voice that sent shivers down the spine. "*Where is he?*"

"Look, mother," said Jacques. He pointed to the mirror that relentlessly followed all the captive's movements in his cell.

The daughter of the Orsinis was unable to suppress her surprise.

In the huddled heap on the cot, it was impossible to recognize the man who, weeks earlier, had been a master of finance, one of the lions of modern capitalism.

An untrimmed beard swamped his face. His overgrown hair covered his forehead. His convict suit endowed him with a sinister allure. A continuous cough began with a breath and evolved into a loud roaring. A hoarse rumble escaped from his foaming lips. His eyes were white and lifeless. His hands stubbornly hugged the knees that almost touched his chin.

"Him!… Him!…" repeated Madame de Trémeuse , She had had never suspected the state of physical and moral degradation into which the conscienceless criminal had fallen during his journey into despair.

Nevertheless, this terrifying vision did not placate Julia Orsini. She haughtily addressed Jacques.

"I want to speak him."

"Follow me," said Judex vacating the laboratory. He guided his mother through the maze of corridors.

Suddenly Favraux saw the imposing outline of the haughty Woman in Black, the desirable aristocrat whose indignant refusal had prompted his cowardly vendetta. She advanced towards the miserable prisoner. No longer did she speak as a woman. It was Vengeance personified who uttered as simple sentence that resounded under the arch as an echo of supreme justice:

"Favraux, do you recognize me?"

The banker slowly raised his head. His dazed eyes scanned around him. A hideous smile wandered on his lips.

"Favraux, look at me closely," said the grand lady. "I am Madame de Trémeuse."

Hearing these words, the prisoner didn't shudder. Nothing on his face revealed shock, anger or terror. There was only the same attitude of prostrate indifference.

Did he truly see the woman shouting at him?

Perhaps, but no memory had reawakened in his brain. His hands still gripped his knees and pulled them towards his chest. He remained stuck in the repetition of simple rhythmical gestures. To the accompaniment of nasal humming, his head wagged in a grotesque pantomime.

All of a sudden, Favraux noticed a piece of chain hanging on the wall. In a jerky gesture, he grabbed it. With a smile on his face, he stroked the chain. He began to whisper to it.

"He's mad!" exclaimed the Comtesse. She gestured to her son that she wished to leave the cell.

They returned to the laboratory. Overcome by her horrendous interview, she fell in an armchair. Judex respectfully addressed her:

"Mother, have we tasted enough revenge?"

The daughter of the Orsinis did not reply. For the first time since the death of her spouse, the implacable woman wondered if human vengeance had its limits.

Two visions clashed inside her. First, there was the image of this merciless butcher, this ravenous blackmailer, this assassin of morality, lost in absolute mindlessness as he drowned in the most ignominious morass. Second, she saw her beloved husband frozen in the grip of suicide on the floor of his study. The latter was sufficient to purge from her heart any vague desire of compassion and mercy.

Yes, the guilty one will pay, she thought. *He will remain there – a ferocious but chained beast – until the other justice, the verdict of God, decides that his punishment must end. She, the earthly judge, would come here to feast on this spectacle. She would watch the slow mortal agony of her enemy. She would count with him the torturous minutes. With the harshest fervor, she would hear his lips exhale an inexhaustible threnody of distress that resounds as an unconscious echo of fading memories!*

Madame de Trémeuse rose. She intended to return to the mirror. She wanted to see Favraux suffer again, as he would always suffer. However, she halted. She recalled the child whose sweet kiss pressed against her forehead. In the most divine of hallucinations, she imagined her enemy's grandson approaching her again. She fantasized him embracing her and curing her burning fever with a kiss.

This vision of innocence had occurred precisely when she began to drink once more from the font of vengeance. A conflict resumed inside her. Her maternal feelings, previously smothered by retribution, were resurrected in a mystical crisis. Stronger than hate, a new feeling invaded her. Irresistible and sweet, this emotion was represented by the clear eyes of Jeannot. His voice seemed to sing in his ear: "You want to kiss me, Madame?" She accepted this offer. She returned it. Wasn't this forgiveness? Wasn't this already a promise, a pact, between she and this child? Tears dripped from her eyes. Her heart beat faster. Returning to the mirror, she looked at Favraux who now seemed to lull a small child in his arms. Overcome by this sight, she leaned towards Judex. She spoke with a voice that her son had never known.

"I cannot leave this man in this tomb!"

II. The Eternal Delilah

Following a lengthy consultation with Kerjean, Judex had left the Chateau Rouge, accompanied by his mother and brother.

After bringing the prisoner his daily meal, the ex-miller of Les Sablons rejoined his son. The gambler waited in quarters assigned to him beneath the Chateau. Since the dramatic reunion in the mill, Moralès, or rather Robert Kerjean, continued to display sincere remorse. Nevertheless, despite the pardon of his father, and the favorable welcome of Judex, he remained despondent. For lengthy periods, he silently meditated with his hands over his face. This was the state in which old Kerjean found him.

"Robert, I'm very concerned about you. You constant depression worries me. I fear that your confession wasn't as complete as I thought."

"Nevertheless," declared Moralès, "I told you the truth."

"You're wrong to challenge me. I forgave you with all my heart. Judex told me yesterday that he was ready to provide you with a new career based on honest work."

"Father," said Diana Monti's ex-lover, "I will never forget the affection you just displayed. I shall always remain indebted to Judex for what he has done for both of us. But…"

Unable to master his emotions, Robert Kerjean stopped

"But?" asked the ex-convict. "Speak, my son."

Moralès remained silent.

"I begin to understand," said Pierre Kerjean. "This woman… You desire her again. Isn't this true?"

Without answering his father's question, the young man made a declaration:

"Father, I don't want to remain here anymore. It's necessary for me to leave. I must go far, very far away. There I will rebuild my life based on honor and duty."

"I hoped that you would stay with me!"

"I repeat that it's necessary for me to leave."

"You're more upset than I thought."

"Perhaps," sighed Moralès. He showed his father a letter that he had just written and addressed to Judex. "Read!" It was a laconic declaration seemingly dictated by an unshakeable resolution:

Forgive me for leaving the Chateau Rouge without seeing you. My father will deliver this letter. I intend to redeem myself in the Foreign Legion. Allow me to thank you again, and remain forever your devoted servant.

ROBERT KERJEAN

"My poor boy!" said Kerjean fighting back his tears. "I won't ask you to reconsider your decision. You would only have taken it after long deliberation."

"Yes, Father."

"Go… and return before I die. My sole desire is that the hand of an honest man, my son Robert, closes my eyes on my death bed."

"Bite your tongue," asserted Moralès. "Many years of happiness await you. Trust me."

"Kiss me, my son. Good-bye, and be brave!"

Robert Kerjean returned to Paris. Since it was late evening, he couldn't go to the recruitment office to fulfill his intention of becoming a new man. He had to delay that formality until the next day. After registering in a modest hotel, he opted to kill time by taking a stroll on the boulevard.

Pervaded by both a physical and a spiritual fatigue, he entered a café. Seated at a table, he ordered a glass of Port. He leafed mechanically through an illustrated magazine. He abandoned his disinterested perusal almost immediately. The younger Kerjean was completely absorbed in thought. By chance, he had entered an establishment capable of reviving a vivid memory. A bittersweet reminiscence began to consume him.

Some days earlier, he had stopped here with Diana. He looked at the table where they had sat side by side. He recalled that his mistress had never been more beautiful, more voluptuous or more captivating. What beautiful plans they had conceived together! Her voice seemed to whisper inside his brain. *We could be happy once more. We could be lovers again.*

Through a phenomenal autosuggestion, Moralès imagined Diana standing in front of him. Enraptured by her eyes and fascinated by her smile, he had a wild urge to get up and embrace her. However, reality instantly intruded. Finishing his drink, he left still obsessed by the vision of his lover. Her effigy continued to entrance him. He could mount no defense against her beckoning call. She exercised an attraction that no human will could withstand.

Almost involuntarily, he came to the house where she had moved shortly before their quarrel. Having left Amaury's abode, Diana had resumed residence there the day before.

A thought flashed through his mind. *If I enter, I am lost!*

He wanted to flee, but a hellish power forced him to remain rooted to the spot. His eyes shifted towards the window of the apartment hoping to see the adventuress one last time. Before leaving her forever, he wanted to engrave her eidolon in his soul. His renunciation of their love would be marked by this final farewell.

The curtain raised. She was there! The heart of the distraught Moralès began to ache once more. *The* woman! *The* woman he loved! He would always desire her! He fought against this lust. He was about to move away forever. He would be broken by a mad passion, but he would be purified by renunciation, the cruelest act of self-sacrifice. His desertion halted when he noticed another profile close to Diana. It was a well-dressed gentleman who smiled lovingly at the gambler's ex-mistress.

"She has a lover!" shouted the crazed Robert Kerjean. "A lover!"

Bitten by jealousy, the gambler jettisoned all his good resolutions. His stormy anger propelled him into the house. Rushing upstairs, he rang the doorbell. Jostling the chambermaid who opened the door, he invaded the parlor where Diana was flirting with her new conquest.

"You!" shouted a sharply surprised Diana.

"Diana," said Pierre Kerjean's son, "I want to speak to you alone."

Placed in an awkward position, she opted to save face. With a pleasant smile, she introduced the two men. "Vicomte Amaury de la Rochefontaine, let me introduce my friend Baron Moralès. I told you about him."

Without giving Robert any chance to say a word, she proceeded to defuse the situation.

"The Vicomte, as you recall, was Jacqueline Aubry's fiancé when I worked at Les Sablons. He's here to provide information about the death of Monsieur Favraux."

Placated by these words, Moralès acknowledged Amaury. After returning the greeting, Amaury noticed a sly wink by Diana. Guessing the meaning of this signal, he acted accordingly.

"I must leave you, Madame. Hopefully, we will talk again."

After kissing Diana's hand, he departed leaving the two lovers alone.

Instead of bursting into angry reproaches as Robert expected, the bewitching damsel advanced towards him. More seductive than ever, she wrapped her supple arms around him.

"I waited for you," she said softly. "I was patient. I knew you would return to me."

"I must say farewell before leaving you forever."

"Leave me forever!" exclaimed the adventuress feigning shock.

"Yes. After what happened, we can no longer be together. I'm joining the Foreign Legion."

"Why?"

"Because I won't become a killer!"

At these words, Diana Monti, a skilled actress, slowly released her embrace. She spoke with bitter regret.

"It's true. I was mad. Consumed by the desire to be rich, I wanted to create for us a life of happiness and joy. I lost any notion of common sense. I abandoned myself to the most careless extravagances. I almost dragged you with me in the abyss. Your desertion made me realize how insane I had been. I don't blame you for almost delivering me to Judex. You were in the right. I almost sent you to the guillotine."

Sitting down on a divan, she cleverly employed deceptive tears alongside her lies.

"I have changed in the last few days. I no longer am the same woman. I now have only a desire to live anonymously in a far corner of the Earth. The only person who can grant me the peace I crave is you."

"Me!" yelled Robert Kerjean. He struggled internally to resist this woman. "But I'm leaving you forever." The last statement was made without enthusiasm.

"Don't you love me anymore?"

Moralès ceased talking. The silence was more eloquent than a burning confession.

Feeling that she had the upper hand, Diana took his arm and moved closer to him.

"I love you," she said. Listen to me. I love you even more because of the evil that I have done to you. And you still love me. You don't have to defend yourself. You were unnerved by the sudden appearance of your father. I am certain that when you later searched your heart, you both forgave and desired me. Even now you forgive and desire me. As always, you shake with hesitation. In your soul, in your heart, you dare not even ask yourself if our love can be reborn. You must regain your courage not to strike at Jacqueline, but to help me to save her father."

"What are you trying tell me?" asked Moralès.

"I beg you again… for your happiness and mine… I don't want to say our love… since you have divorced yourself from me."

"Diana!" protested Robert.

"Our love… is… subject to your will."

"Explain."

"Promise to listen to me calmly, and to answer me frankly."

"Speak!"

"You know where Favraux is!"

"But…"

"You know it! If we free him… we'd make our fortune."

"Diana!"

"Let me finish! If we become wealthy, we can go far away to realize our dream of happiness. Our future depends on you!"

The brow of Moralès was wrinkled with stress.

"What you ask me is impossible."

"Impossible. Why?

"Because I promised."

"Promised what? Promised whom?"

"My father. I promised never to reveal to anyone else where Judex keeps Favraux prisoner."

Diana was thrilled with joy. Now that a breakthrough had been made, she no longer needed to engage in deceptive maneuvers. She knew how to strike her point home.

"I don't want to speak ill of your father, but he's an eccentric recluse. You have respect and loyalty for a man whom you didn't see for years. Furthermore, you have affection for a man who was condemned to 20 years of hard labor."

"Don't scoff at my feelings! My father's trying to transform me into an honest man!"

"I don't scoff. I merely observe. What a pity! If I asked you to commit a criminal act, I would understand. After all, breaking your word to a dishonest father in order to free a man wrongfully imprisoned is not a repugnant act. By refusing, you're sacrificing our happiness."

The eyes of Moralès flashed with indecision. He remained silent. The adventuress rose from the divan to deliver another thrust.

"You don't want to do it! I'm through trying to convince you. I know someone willing to do the job."

"Who?" asked Pierre Kerjean's son.

"Amaury de la Rochefontaine."

Upon hearing that name, Moralès reacted with anger. "Him!"

"Why not?"

"I don't want you to see him!"

"What right do you have to impose conditions on me. Love no longer binds us. There is nothing between us!"

"Nothing!" shouted Robert grabbing her hands. "Nothing! Can't you see how I suffer?"

"Where is Favraux?"

215

"He is… He is…" Moralès stopped himself. A chill went down his spine. "And Jacqueline?"

Diana shrugged her shoulders. "What about Jacqueline?"

"She knows several things. She knows that you wanted to kill her."

"So?"

"Then… I'm afraid…"

"Of what?"

"I'm afraid that you still want to…"

"Cease sprouting stupidities!" With an extraordinary self-control, the adventuress sought to overcome her accomplice's objections. "I shall find an intermediary to act for us. We can remain in the background."

"Cocantin, doubtlessly?"

"No, he's too stupid.

"Then who?"

"The man who was here earlier."

"De la Rochefontaine?"

"Yes, the Vicomte that you so foolishly took for my lover. In reality, he is a valued associate. I'm willing to have him do the things that we can't. Please, Moralès, be reasonable. I'm asking you to do a minor thing; and our future rests on your refusal or your acceptance. Help me deliver Favraux. You can! That's very easy for you. Very easy. I can be yours forever. Answer me, Moralès. Do you want to stop looking into my eyes? Why rob your mouth of my kiss? You prefer exile in a dangerous country where you would probably die a cruel and useless death? Soon after signing the enlistment papers, you would bitterly regret it. For you have me in your blood. If we are finished, you won't be able to forget me anymore than I will be able to forget you. Moralès, my love, do you want to condemn both of us to devastating sorrow? No, no, that will not be. We love each other. We mean so much to each other. Join me in an embrace which will bind us for eternity!"

The seductive siren had never been more enticing or more beautiful. She moved her face towards her lover's.

216

Searching for his lips, she delivered a burning kiss which no one could resist. It was a kiss combining exquisite delight with treachery and death.

The harlot had reclaimed the sinner.

Moralès was once more enthralled to her. He was once more capable of any act of treachery. All his good resolutions had melted under Diana's strokes like snow under the sun.

With a hoarse voice, a solemn vow was made by the man who had betrayed his father's trust.

"Give me three men and a fast car, and I promise to bring Favraux here tonight!"

III. The Scavengers of the Night

Very late in the evening, a powerful automobile stopped in the vicinity of Chateau Rouge. Three men vacated the vehicle. They were Moralès, Dr. Pop and the Coltineur. While Crémard stayed behind the wheel of the limousine, Moralès led the others up the path towards the ruins.

After being promised by his accomplices that his father wouldn't be harmed, Diana's lover prepared to fulfill the pledge that she had cleverly extracted from him.

His plan, subsequently revised by Diana, was brilliant in its simplicity and remarkable in its audacity. Driven by his passion, he intended to accomplish it without the least hesitation. No remorse could hinder him. The adventuress now so completely dominated him that his soul had been cleansed of all scruples.

First, he personally listened outside the door of father's sleeping quarters. He heard only uniform breathing, the indication of a deep sleep. All seemed well. Despite the lack of noise, he turned the key in the lock. He rejoined his associates already inside Favraux's cell.

Luckily for them, the exterior lock had surprisingly been left open. The criminals attributed this to negligence on Pierre Kerjean's part. Entering the cell, the doctor saw a sleeping man spread on a cot and covered in a blanket. The crooked doctor skillfully pressed a chloroformed gag against the prisoner's mouth while the Coltineur tied a rope around his blanket. Moralès remained in the corridor to act as look-out. The operation happened in less time than it takes to describe. Very satisfied with the rapid execution of his bold coup, Diana's lover guided his two associates carrying the banker through the passageways with a lantern. They eventually reached the exit and returned to the car.

"Go quickly to Paris."

"And you, boss?" questioned Crémard starting up the motor.

"I remain here."

"Why?" asked the Coltineur.

"That's my affair," curtly retorted Moralès. "The job's done. That's essential. Leave the rest to me."

"Let's go," said the sinister chauffeur. The car drove away.

Once the plan had been accomplished, Moralès had begun to fully understand the consequences of his infamy. Fearful that his treason would prompt reprisals by Judex, Robert Kerjean had resolved to create an alibi to fool his father. Again he climbed the path to the ruins. After traversing the caverns, he reached the door of the senior Kerjean's room. After turning the key to unlock the door, he knocked.

The door was opened almost instantly. Moralès had a surprise. He stood opposite Roger de Trémeuse.

"I thought you left!" exclaimed Roger. "Your father told me that you were going to join the Foreign Legion."

"Yes," explained Robert, "I haven't changed my mind, but I unearthed a plot to remove Favraux, so I quickly returned here to warn you."

"Did you see Diana Monti?" asked Judex's brother.

"Yes," answered Moralès hypocritically. "By pure chance, I swear. However, this chance meeting will luckily frustrate her latest scheme. I didn't hesitate to return to the Chateau Rouge. I didn't want you, Judex or my father to believe that I was still this woman's accomplice."

"You did very well," approved Roger with a slight reluctance. For Judex's brother had noted the consternation of Moralès, despite all his efforts to conceal it. Harboring suspicions, Roger spoke with the calm demeanor of a man with absolute trust in his companion. "Besides, we have nothing to fear, I stood guard." He pointed to a man completely concealed under his bed's blanket. "Favraux is here; he isn't about to leave."

"Favraux is here!" repeated Robert in shock.

"Yes," said Roger uncovering the face of the sleeping prisoner.

"How did he end up in that bed?"

"Due to his sad state, my brother and I took pity him. We moved him to this room. It's much better than his prison cell."

"And my father?"

"Tonight, he sleeps in Favraux's cell."

Moralès felt a cold sweat on his forehead. The man that he had just dispatched to Paris under guard was none other than Pierre Kerjean!

If not for an incredible effort, Robert would have fainted.

"Very good," he stammered. "Now there is no reason for me to stay. I can leave."

"One moment," said Roger. "I must go to the laboratory to check on a chemical experiment. Please watch Favraux. I'll return in a few minutes."

Not daring to refuse, Moralès seated himself in a chair. Consumed by terror, he contemplated suicide in the wake of these unexpected developments. He feared that it would be impossible to save his father. The car was long gone. There weren't any trains to Paris before 6 o'clock in the morning. A single course remained open to him. He could confess all to Roger. Must he condemn himself? The alternate was to inadvertently commit parricide!

Moralès was prepared to throw himself at the mercy of Judex's brother when a loud groan startled him.

Sitting on his bed, Favraux stared at Moralès with dazed and wild eyes. Seeing this living corpse, Diana's lover shivered. The banker giggled sinisterly. Frightfully, the lunatic rose from his bed. His dangling arms twitched nervously from delirium as he advanced. Pale with terror, Moralès got out of the chair and tried to reach the doorway.

"I want in to kill someone," moaned the madman. "I want to kill someone! It's good to kill! Yes! It's good! It's good!"

To escape the maniac's embrace, Robert Kerjean ran into the corridor and fled into the underground shadows.

In the throes of his murderous obsession, Favraux stopped for a moment. Should he pursue this victim? The banker stepped into the corridor. Almost immediately, he halted as confusion flooded his brain. His enraged face changed to reflect a distant joy. Falling into the chair just vacated by Moralès, he began humming a sluggish lullaby while his arms made the gesture of holding a non-existent child.

A vision of his grandson had appeared before the lunatic. Soon a name was added to the wordless song: "Jeannot!" Tears flowed on the ravaged cheeks of the prisoner. The captive became calm. He remained in the chair performing the same protective gestures as that of a loving grandparent. For the first time, the angel of remorse had brushed the banker with his wing.

The three criminals, Crémard, Dr. Pop and the Coltineur, arrived in Paris with their prisoner. Diana and Amaury waited impatiently for the results of the expedition. Crémard immediately informed them of their supposed success.

"We're back! The banker's outside in the car. The others will bring him up."

"And Moralès?" asked Diana.

"He remained at the Chateau."

"I hope he doesn't do something stupid!"

"That's irrelevant!" observed Amaury as Crémard moved away. "We have the banker. That's important. The rest doesn't matter."

"It does to me," noted the adventuress. Her eyeballs lit up with a murderous gleam. "At any price, I must rid myself of this Moralès. He's become too unreliable."

Amaury de la Rochefontaine nodded his head in approval.

"Let's forget him for the moment. We must greet our brave banker. He'll be happily surprised to be at liberty!"

The doctor and the Coltineur brought bound man into the middle of the parlor. They deposited him in a large and comfortable armchair.

"I gave him the maximum dose," explained the doctor. "That worked out well! He remained quiet and peaceful during the trip."

Loosening the bonds, the physician exposed the head of the alleged Favraux.

"It's not him!" exclaimed Diana staring at the ex-miller of Les Sablons. Under the influence of the doctor's powerful sedative, Kerjean remained in an absolute stupor. The adventuress erupted in an insane rage.

"I know this man! This is Pierre Kerjean! He's Moralès' father!"

"We've been betrayed!" said Amaury. He was no less furious than his associate.

"Betrayed by whom?" asked Diana. "Let's see. Certainly Moralès wouldn't have relinquished his father in place of Favraux. As for Judex, even if he intended to checkmate us, he wouldn't surrender such a devoted servant. He knows too well that I never spare my prey! This is certainly an inexplicable puzzle. Must bad luck always plague us? This may be a setback, but I refuse to be beaten. I will continue to fight!"

She pointed threateningly at Kerjean. "To begin with, this man must disappear. If his unbound body is found in the Seine tomorrow, his drowning would be judged an accident or a suicide."

"Diana!" interrupted Amaury.

"Silence!" she decreed. "You are either with me or against me. There is no middle ground. Half measures are beneath me. Choose!"

Browbeaten by the adventuress, Vicomte de la Rochefontaine lowered his head in submission. The impoverished nobleman acquiesced to his role of accomplice to these killers.

Pierre Kerjean was irrefutably condemned.

IV. The Revealing Nose

Since the comic-tragic scene unfolded in his office, Prosper Cocantin had undergone a moral transformation. Softened by the naïve sweetness of Jeannot and stimulated by the intelligent bravery of the Licorice Kid, he became a new man. Under the auspices of the eidolon of the man he deemed his master, Napoleon, Cocantin began planning the most audacious projects.

Reexamining his records of Judex, the detective concluded that the man of mystery had behaved in an exemplary manner. As a honest man and a respectful upholder of the law, Cocantin now considered it his duty to declare war against the people who tried to make him an accomplice to their crimes. As the saying goes, *he had seen the light*. He realized the dangerous role that Diana Monti, Moralès, the Vicomte and their cohorts had tried to manipulate him into playing during this unfortunate drama. Terrified by the consequences that could have resulted, he attributed his salvation to an opportune, or rather Napoleonic, intervention.

While Cocantin's heart caught on fire quickly, it also could be extinguished with just as much spontaneity. His passions were never long-term. When he realized that his adventures in love could force him into foolish acts, tedious diversions, or real dangers, he would *cut out the evil by the root*. These reversals were not a matter of willpower but of temperament. After lusting for Diana with an incandescent fire, he suddenly loathed her ferociously. He summarized his new state of mind in a single sentence from his notebook: "A woman capable of beating children can never really be in love!" From this moment onwards, the director of the Celeritas Agency had developed a merciless hatred towards Diana and all her gang.

Armed with a resolution to strike fearlessly, Cocantin had formulated the battle lines of his campaign.

From this day forward, he thought, *I won't not have a day of rest until I have tracked down these criminals. I must deliver them to justice. To achieve this goal, I will spare no expense. I will risk my life a hundred times. Nothing will stop me. Day and night, night and day, I will follow their trail. If necessary, I shall ensnare them in their own lair.*

Cocantin energetically proceeded to launch his assault. His plan was vague but it rested on a foundation of good intentions.

Rather than seek wisdom from Napoleon, his regular source of inspiration, the director of Celeritas Agency decided to model himself on the sensational popular exploits of policemen from the past and the present. For 48 hours, he researched narratives of varying degrees of authenticity. His skull became stuffed with all the fabulous legends that cast a halo around the heads of Eugène Francois Vidocq and his successors. Slightly scared, even confused by this mass of documentation, Cocantin learned only one thing. To be a good detective, you must be a master of disguise.

Cocantin purchased a large wardrobe in which every miscellaneous profession was represented. He tried on various wigs. He glued elaborate false beards to his face. However, after two days, he was forced to abandon his efforts to radically transform his appearance.

Pretending to be a plumber, he roamed the street like an old hunter stalking easy prey. When he passed an acquaintance, the detective was hailed ironically:

"Hello, Monsieur Cocantin. Where did you get this funny idea to wear a disguise?"

How did he recognize me? wondered the private detective.

Returning to his rooms, he spent long hours in front of the mirror in order to design other disguises imperious to detection. All his endeavors were in vain. No matter how elaborate the disguise, he was greeted on the streets by "Hello, Monsieur Cocantin."

A nagging question persisted in his mind. *Why does everybody recognize me when I can't recognize myself?*

Prosper Cocantin had failed to notice his most distinctive feature. He had a nose that was so uniquely immense that it could have traded places with the one lauded in the brilliant tirade from Edmund Rostand's *Cyrano de Bergerac*. Prominently attached to his face, this vast nose started by bending in a circular arch, continued in an imposingly upright line, and finished in a double bulge. The obtrusive nose tended to point crosswise towards the left side of the heart.

"Cocantin is a thrifty boy!" joked his friends behind his back. "For his retirement, he put his nose aside."

Now forced to search for the principal cause of his failed disguises by scrutinizing his face in a mirror, Cocantin realized the truth.

"My nose!" he shouted. "It's my nose! *Parbleu!*"

With a patient supply of makeup, he strove in vain to diminish its prominence and to lessen the character. Always it revealingly rose in the middle of his face.

"I can't cut it!" shouted Cocantin hopelessly.

Would this nose force him to abandon his plans? No. Fortunately, a thoughtful reflection on history calmed the psychological fears of Cocantin.

I never read anywhere that Fouché, Napoleon's famous Minister of the Police, ever concealed his features. That fact didn't prevent him from being the foremost detective in the world. I'll imitate him! I'll be a detective without a disguise. I'll be more elegant, more daring, and more French! I will provide myself me with all the defensive and offensive methods that modern science can put at the disposal of someone facing danger.

Therefore, Cocantin acquired an armored breastplate destined to repel the bullets and knives of his enemies. He bought four pistols, one for each pocket in his jacket and trousers. He slipped into his belt a long, thin dagger. He was equipped with American brass knuckles and a bludgeon capable of knocking an ox senseless. With this veritable arsenal in tow, he raised the collar of his overcoat and pushed his felt hat down to shade his eyes. He went off to war swearing to his Napoleonic bust that he would return either the victor or the vanquished!

First, he located Diana and Amaury. That was easy. Having accomplished this task, Cocantin was somewhat embarrassed. Doubts plagued him. What should he do next? A banal saying of classic import furnished him with a line of attack: "Luck is the policeman's god." Cocantin judged this maxim be appropriate since it was similar to philosophical phrase: "Wait for your luck to change!" He saw the only wise decision open to him.

"I won't let them escape."

Scarcely taking time to sleep or eat, he began to prowl the vicinity of the house where Diana lived. He awaited the opportunity to strike a blow for justice. His patience was soon rewarded.

During his nightly vigil near of Diana's house, he scanned the windows hoping to discover some important clue. His heart skipped a beat when he heard a noise.

An automobile containing three suspicious men stopped in front of the building containing Diana and Amaury. The driver got out and entered the house. Swiftly returning, he made an odd gesture to his companions. They carried a body wrapped in a blanket with a narrow rope tied around it. Their unusual cargo was transported into the house.

"This is it," muttered Cocantin. He had a premonition that big events would happen. As soon as the door closed behind the two men and their burden, Cocantin, moved out of the corner where he had concealed himself. He went towards the automobile to take the license number.

All of a sudden, he quivered. A vigorous hand just bore down on his shoulder. Cocantin turned around. A tall man in a black cloak and a felt hat stood before him. His face was harsh and enigmatic.

The disconcerted director of the Celeritas Agency could only stammer.

"Monsieur… Who are you? What do you want?"

"I am Judex!" stated Jacques de Trémeuse.

V. A Bold Maneuver

Prosper Cocantin was startled by the invocation of this mysterious name. His initial reaction was fright, but the benevolent gaze of this shadowy figure assured him. Feeing that he was in the presence of a man of principle, the detective concluded that he had nothing to dread from this strange and powerful inquisitor.

"You are Judex? I am Cocantin."

"I know."

"Monsieur Judex, I'm delighted to make your acquaintance."

"May I shake your hand?"

"I didn't dare ask you."

Spontaneously Cocantin extended his two hands to Judex who grasped them.

"I know, Monsieur," said Jacques de Trémeuse, "that you have acted in my interests. I thank you."

"I acted according to my conscience."

"We are in accord."

"Believe me that we are united and that there is nothing that I wouldn't do for you."

"In that case," resumed Judex, "please explain your presence here."

"I'm on a case," said Cocantin proudly. "I have sworn to expose Diana Monti and her gang."

"Which means," emphasized Jacques, "that we pursue the same goal."

"And which proves," added Cocantin, "that men of honor are destined to meet!"

Passing his arm under the detective's, Judex escorted him towards a car parked in the shadows nearby.

"Would you be willing, Monsieur Cocantin, for this night at least, to pool our resources?"

"Monsieur, I am both flattered and delighted."

"Then this is a collaboration?"

"Which I am deeply honored to join." Cocantin was filled with self-esteem. "I trust, Monsieur Judex, that you won't find me completely useless."

"Likewise."

Ribaudet's successor had never been so thrilled in his life. He spoke with a seriousness that amused Jacques de Trémeuse,

"At this moment, Diana Monti is engaged in some extraordinary enterprise. Shortly before we met, a car stopped in front of the house of this swine; for she is a swine, Monsieur Judex. There is no other expression."

"Continue, Monsieur Cocantin."

"Three men got out of the car whose license number I was writing down when you accosted me."

"What happened next?"

"These men transported inside the house a bulky package. It seemed to be a human being tied up in a blanket."

"Monsieur Cocantin," interrupted Judex, "say no more. Know that you have just done me a great service… and that I will never forget it!"

Judex's presence here merits explanation.

In the middle of the night, Judex was in his study in Paris. Seated in front of his desk, he vainly tried to escape, through reading, the nagging torture of his impossible love. Always Jacqueline's image appeared to his eyes; and always he heard her voice making a brutal proclamation that the name of Judex never be pronounced in her presence. More than ever, he understood the frightful tragedy imposed on him by his oath of vengeance.

The telephone linked directly to the Chateau Rouge rang. Judex seized the receiver. It was Roger on the line.

"Moralès has just returned under the pretence of needing to speak with his father. He vainly tried to conceal that he was worried. Suspicious of his behavior, I left to wake up Kerjean. Following your instructions, he had exchanged rooms with Favraux. Kerjean had disappeared. A strong odor of chloroform hung in the air. The door blocking the principal corridor had been opened, even though it can only be maneuvered by a secret mechanism. When I returned to question Moralès, he was gone. I searched for him in vain. Terrified by the consequences of his actions, he must have hastily returned to Paris. There's no doubt that Moralès betrayed us. By trying to remove Favraux, he let his father be captured instead."

Without losing an instant, Judex had telephoned a neighboring garage where night and day a powerful limousine, piloted by a chauffeur of unquestionable loyalty, waited at his beck and call. Reviewing all the vicissitudes of recent events, Judex had himself driven to Diana's house in the belief that the abductors had gone there. He hoped to arrive in time to save the unfortunate Kerjean from the reprisals of the formidable adventuress.

The information furnished by Cocantin proved to Judex that his first instincts had been correct. Undoubtedly Kerjean was with Diana. To save him, there wasn't a moment to lose.

Judex was a prudent man. His principle was to only risk his life after formulating the proper stratagems to defend himself as well as vanquish his opponents. He rapidly conceived such a decisive plan.

The detective respected the brief silence of the self-styled judge. Finally the man in the black cloak spoke.

"Monsieur Cocantin."

"Monsieur Judex."

"Are you armed?"

"To the teeth."

"We shall storm Diana's house and rescue her victim. Do you agree?"

228

Prosper Cocantin was astonished by his own courage. "Monsieur Judex! With a man such as you, nothing is impossible. We can go anywhere. We can beat anyone."

"Then... forward!"

After placing his dagger between his teeth, Cocantin held a gun in each hand. Judex advanced towards the door of the building until voices coming from inside caused them to halt.

"They're coming," said Jacques. He threw himself and Cocantin into the corner of the carriage gate that had earlier sheltered the director of the Celeritas Agency.

The door opened revealing Crémard. He jumped behind the steering of the car. He was followed by the doctor and the Coltineur, who deposited a securely bound Kerjean on the back seat. Finally, Amaury de la Rochefontaine sat next to the driver.

Scarcely had the car started up than Judex, without losing a second, ran to his own limousine with Cocantin. After murmuring some brief words into his chauffeur's ear, he addressed the detective seated next to him in the back of the car.

"I believe, my dear Cocantin, that we've been invited to an unusual spectacle."

The criminals' car moved at a steady pace. Judex's limousine kept a sufficient distance to remain inconspicuous. Nevertheless, it was consistently able to keep its quarry in view. Judex's chauffeur was an accomplished master of the road. It would have been child's play for him to catch up with the other vehicle and even pass it.

Obeying his very precise instructions, Judex's chauffeur continued to remain discretely behind the other automobile. The two cars passed through the capital, the Maillot gate, and the Bois de Boulogne. They headed towards La Muette at the edge of the Seine. Following Diana's orders, her accomplices had come there to throw Kerjean into the river. However, Judex didn't intend to give them the time to do it.

As the two cars rolled on the vast deserted roadway that descended towards the river, Jacques de Trémeuse uttered a simple word in the acoustic cone which communicated his commands to his driver. The limousine immediately accelerated. In a matter of seconds, it passed the other car.

In an extraordinary maneuver, the chauffeur sharply turned the limousine to the left, blocking the road. The shocked Crémard instinctively stomped on his brake. His car stopped some centimeters before the limousine.

Judex and Cocantin leaped from the vehicle. Armed with guns, they prepared to attack their opponents. Diana's underlings were men who never surrendered without a fight.

Jumping out of the back of the car, Amaury ran towards the other vehicle. Guessing the identity of the man in the cape, the Vicomte fired his pistol in the direction of Judex. At the same time, several other gunshots resounded.

It was the guns of Cocantin that spoke. At least one of his bullets reached its target. Vicomte de la Rochefontaine collapsed on the road, his forehead perforated with a large hole.

The doctor and the Coltineur fled into the night. They were quickly joined by Crémard who judged it prudent to abandon his car and its cargo.

Helped by their chauffeur, Judex and Cocantin transported Kerjean in their limousine. They then left for the Chateau Rouge.

Having rescued the ex-miller of Les Sablons, Judex strove, with the detective's assistance, to resuscitate the old man. Soon Moralès' father reopened his eyes. Seeing Jacques close to him, a serene expression spread on his face. It was shortly replaced by mortal anguish.

A cry gushed from his lips. "My son!"

"Rest, my friend," said Judex benevolently. "Favraux is still in the caverns of Chateau Rouge."

Hearing these words, Kerjean breathed more freely, His hand grasped feverishly the fingers of the man whom he recognized as his master. Kerjean's eyelids closed themselves. He seemed to fall once more into a deep torpor.

"The poor man!" said Jacques de Trémeuse. "How he will suffer when he learns the truth!" Cocantin continued to look at Jacques with boundless admiration.

It's astonishing how much this Judex resembles Bonaparte! he thought.

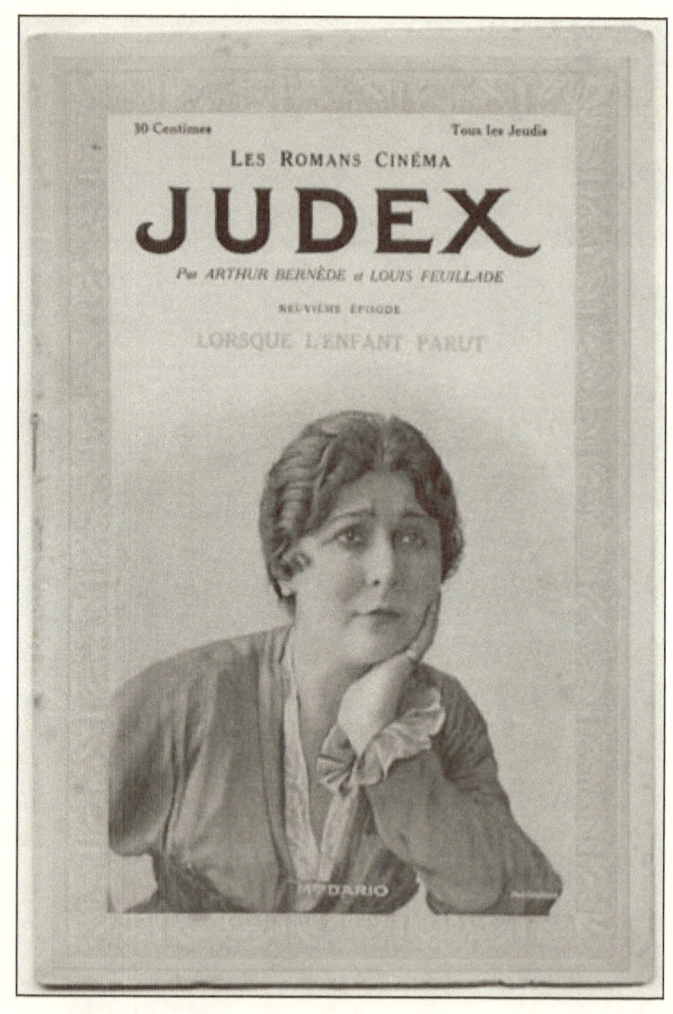

30 Centimes   Tous les Jeudis

LES ROMANS CINÉMA

JUDEX

Par ARTHUR BERNÈDE et LOUIS FEUILLADE

NEUVIÈME ÉPISODE

LORSQUE L'ENFANT PARUT

Mlle DARIO

Part Nine: When the Child Appeared

I. The Villa des Palmiers

Around 10 o'clock in the morning, under the dazzling clarity of a radiant sun, a large van sped down a dusty road. It parked in front of the main entrance to an expensive villa of the Mediterranean coast. The building was situated in the middle of the gulf of Saint-Tropez, a short distance from the small harbor of Sainte-Maxime.

Clothed in temperate elegance, a tall young man with an aristocratic profile had waited impatiently for the arrival of the automobile. He walked up to the car and greeted the driver who smiled at him affectionately.

"How was the trip, brother?"

"All went well."

"No difficulties?"

"None."

"And him?"

"He's as well as possible."

The skilled driver, Roger de Trémeuse, got out of the van. Judex opened the back door. He faced a white-haired man of advanced years. His bearded face was ravaged with stress. The passenger pointed to another man whose form was sleeping on a cot. Covered by a sheet, the unconscious man was dressed in a chauffeur's uniform and driving cap.

"As you can see, Monsieur, we completely followed your instructions. We have delivered your prisoner in the best possible condition."

"I had confidence in my brother and you, Kerjean."

Looking at Favraux whose carefully shaved face was perfectly calm, the ex-miller of Les Sablons elaborated on their journey.

233

"Thanks to the narcotic that we gave him before our journey began, he was very quiet. Since that night when he tearfully erupted, he's no longer the same man. His madness abated. Several times on the road, he awoke. We didn't hear any protest. He didn't make any angry gestures. He simply asked us if he could soon see his grandson. We told him that he would. He didn't say anything more and went back to sleep."

"Did anyone accost you during the trip?"

"We scrupulously followed the itinerary that you gave us," interjected Roger. "Avoiding the large towns, we drove mainly at night. We rested during the day in remote areas."

Favraux just reopened his eyes. Viewing the silhouette of Judex standing in front of him, he shivered slightly as fear spread over his face.

"We have arrived, Monsieur Favraux," said Kerjean softly

"Arrived…" stammered the madman still contemplating Judex with a continually growing terror.

"Be assured," said Judex, "that no evil will befall you. You will be given all the proper medical care you require."

The banker was surprised by the tone of the voice, which had been threatening in the past, but was now melancholic. Reclining on his sleeping cot, the distraught financier looked around him. Judex talked slowly in an effort to reach a mind riddled by confusion.

"Just as you owe you life to your daughter's sacrifice, you owe your betterment to the kindness of your grandchild."

"Jean!" murmured the prisoner clasping his hands.

Jacques de Trémeuse had just rekindled the only spark of sanity in the darkness shrouding the banker's mind.

"Come," said Judex with authority.

The docile Favraux got up. Leaning to the arm of Kerjean, he descended from the van and followed Judex into a garden surround by high walls. In the middle of the garden rose a vast house. The three men entered it.

After confining his prisoner in a comfortable room with a seaside view, the window of which was outfitted with solid bars, Judex took Kerjean aside into a neighboring room.

"I am honor-bound to tell you the truth," said Judex. "The discovery of our headquarters in the Chateau Rouge by our enemies didn't cause me to order Favraux transported here. I no longer believe in my right to cruelly prolong the suffering of this man. One punishes the guilty, but one does not torture the insane. Disgusted by the horrible punishment that we decreed, my mother supports my decision. Nevertheless, Favraux shall remain our prisoner. Therefore, it's essential that his presence here remain unknown. You must exercise the strictest vigilance towards him. Can I still rely on you?"

"You know well, Monsieur, that I'm your devoted servant body and soul."

"I know that. It's the reason that I feel secure."

"Your orders, Monsieur, will scrupulously be executed," promised Kerjean. "My hatred for this swindler is outweighed by my affection for you. I bow to your will." He sobbed slightly. "My loyalty hopefully will make you forget my son's treason."

"Your son's treason…" repeated Judex in a tone closer to sorrow than disapproval.

"Thank you," said the old man while shaking effusively his benefactor's hand.

Roger had just appeared with his mother. While Kerjean withdrew discreetly, Jacques moved towards Madame de Trémeuse. Still in mourning clothes, her tragic face reflected hope as well as wisdom.

"My son," she asked calmly, "are you happy?"

"And you, mother?" replied Judex.

The Woman in Black raised her eyes towards the Heavens.

"Your father will judge me."

"I already feel that he has vindicated you!" murmured Jacques de Trémeuse. He respectfully kissed his mother's hand.

"And Favraux?" she asked saying the name without expressing any hatred.

"He seems completely submissive," asserted Judex. "He has hardly any notion of past or present. Only when hearing the name of his grandson does he appears to come back to reality. Then his face saddens and he cries."

"Have you kept his transfer secret?"

"I took the proper precautions. Roger and I are on the alert against any suspicious activity. Kerjean will prove invaluable. He won't fail in his task. The prisoner won't try to escape. No one will know that the Villa des Palmiers is the last refuge of the banker Favraux!"

Judex's self-control was overcome by emotion.

"Mother, I thank you from the bottom of my heart. You have released me from a task that went against my conscience. The innocent must not suffer with the guilty."

"I also share that belief," said Roger.

For a moment, Julia Orsini kept silence. She gazed upon her sons with melancholy.

"I was wrong, my children. I should have executed my plans myself. Only a heart like mine, no longer open to love, can be so implacable. Today, I lament the consequences of my error. I had to yield to reality. I had to compromise. My conscience screeched at me: 'To avenge your husband, you don't have the right to torment your children!' For 16 years, the obsession of vengeance has reigned over my life with absolute dominance. The oppressive mastery of hate diminished and crumbled in the battle against myself."

"Mother!" shouted Jacques. He respectfully kissed the hand of the Comtesse.

"My sons, my sons, I don't recognize myself anymore. Not only did you persuade me to commute Favraux's death sentence, but you gain my compliance in his transfer from his prison cell. That's not all. I had to welcome him to my villa, which was to be our haven once our vengeance was secured. I even had to provide sanctuary to the daughter and grandson of this miscreant. I had to enact a farce that disgusts my very soul. I had to lie to them. I, Julia Orsini, Comtesse de Trémeuse, have grown to love these two beings whom I should despise because they are the blood kin of my enemy."

"But you understood," finished Judex, "that God had divorced them from the sins of the father by instilling in them the virtuous clarity of love."

As Madame of Trémeuse gestured to discourage this praise, Roger made his feelings known.

"Don't blame yourself! Your compassion for us has swayed your hatred. Jean's kiss has conquered you. You already feel your misery dissipating."

Madame de Trémeuse grasped the hands of her sons. For the first time in 16 years, she knew the sweet consolation of tears.

"And you," she said to Jacques, "what are your intentions towards this young woman?"

"She believes you to be the sister of Vallières."

"Do you view this deception as imprudent?"

"Why should it be?"

"First, for yourself."

"I know how to silence my heart."

"Didn't Jacqueline glimpse you at the mill at Les Sablons?"

"She told me, in my role of Vallières, that she doesn't clearly recall that fleeting vision."

"And the child," added Roger, "didn't you meet him at the boarding house?"

"I was wrapped in my cloak. The brim of my hat shaded my face. The child had just awakened. He scarcely looked at me because his attention was focused on our dog, Vidocq. The memories of the young are not that durable."

Judex concluded with a burning intensity:

"One thing is essential. The day will inevitably arrive when I will be forced to meet Jacqueline in my true guise. Our position towards her will become extremely delicate. Who knows whether such a meeting will awaken suspicions inside her. Not for anything in the world do I want her to learn that I am Judex. It is a final favor, my beloved mother, that I implore with all my reverence to be granted! I swore to you that I will not weaken. I swore that Favraux will only be pardoned with your concurrence. Don't hesitate to give to your son this supreme consolation!"

"Jacques! You want to court her!" said the Comtesse de Trémeuse with pain but without bitterness.

A furtive redness colored the handsome face of Jacques.

"You hope to gain my consent to this romance?" she asked.

Judex embraced his mother before making a final confession.

"Perhaps!"

II. Jacques and Jacqueline

Resembling a small forest, beautiful palm trees covered part of the superb garden that surrounded the splendid property that the Trémeuse family owned on the outskirts of Sainte-Maxime. In the shadow of this pseudo-forest, the banker's daughter knit a pretty work of embroidery while overseeing the frolics of Jean and the Licorice Kid.

She smiled with a slight sadness, but a joyous expression filled her eyes. Jacqueline almost felt happy.

The frightful memory of her father's supposed death still haunted her. The thought that his apparent demise had prevented him from atoning for his crimes plagued her. If not for that tragedy, she would have resumed a normal life filled with hope.

At present, she felt quiet and reassured. The affectionate devotion of the benign Vallières had already consoled her. She became especially fond of the woman who claimed to be the ex-secretary's sister.

Jacqueline had ascribed the initial coldness of the grand lady to a brief misunderstanding. The young woman took an excessive pleasure in seeing the older woman cajole Jean by stroking his hair. Jacqueline's feelings for Madame de

Trémeuse evolved from a discrete sympathy into an irresistible and tutelary friendship. Destiny had created a mysterious bond that had knocked down the seemingly insurmountable barriers erected by the tragedies of life.

Jacqueline's motivations remained unclear to her. Perhaps her feelings were inspired by a stronger will, the mystical power of the hidden Lord that influences our virtuous acts. For whatever reasons, Jacqueline was drawn to her father's victim without any knowledge of the suffering he had caused. She was influenced by the divine force of her own noble instincts.

For her part, Madame de Trémeuse, who believed in the invincibility of a hatred above any humanity, had not been able to withstand the child's charms. By taking her hand, the child had rendered the impossible love of Jacques sacred to her eyes. Her soul had been stifled by a natural haughtiness combined with a justified hatred. Now it had been rejuvenated by virtue that had seemed forever exiled.

The conversion of his mother from vengeance to mercy had resurrected hope in Jacques. Every day, his mother grew more attached to Jacqueline and her son. "Who knows what this miracle shall accomplish in the end?" he wondered

Another thought vibrated in his head. He must defend his charges against the schemes of Diana Monti. The diabolical adventuress was organizing a plot to ensnare the father and the daughter. Madame de Trémeuse had maternally closed her eyes to the dangers of this conspiracy.

There was nothing as blue as the waves of the Mediterranean and the gorgeous sky of the afternoon when Madame de Trémeuse joined Jacqueline in the garden. The Woman in Black didn't avoid the young woman, but regularly sought out her charming guest. Judex's mother had come to view Favraux's daughter and grandson as equal victims of the infamous banker. Gradually the spirit of Julia Orsini was exorcised of the initial hostility caused by her guests' shared blood with her contemptible enemy.

"Hello, dear Madame," said Judex's mother. She was caressing Jeannot and the Licorice Kid, who had interrupted their games to run into her arms. Julia Orsini looked benignly at Jacqueline.

"I have good news. Remember when I told my about my oldest son. Jacques has unexpectedly returned from his travels abroad."

"You must be very happy," said Jacqueline smiling sweetly.

"In fact," resumed Madame de Trémeuse, "Jacques is an excellent son who always treats me with respect and kindness."

"I would be delighted to meet him."

"He wants to be introduced to you."

"It would be my pleasure."

Impatient to be once more with Jacqueline, Judex had concealed himself behind a palm tree. He left his hiding place to advance towards the young woman. He greeted her with all the polite forms of etiquette. The banker's daughter simply allowed him to kiss her hand.

"Monsieur, I am happy to welcome you to this house where your mother has made me most welcome."

Suddenly she stopped speaking. Her eyes focused on Jacques de Trémeuse. A persistent question nagged her. *Where have I seen this man before?*

Noticing Jacqueline's reaction, Madame de Trémeuse became fearful that she had recognized Judex.

"Are you alright, my child?"

With her habitual frankness, the banker's daughter replied immediately. "Something inexplicable has happened. I have a feeling that this is not the first time I've seen your son."

"Nevertheless, Madame," asserted Judex exercising all his powers of self-control, "I've never been honored by your presence. It would be impossible for me to forget you."

Although disconcerted by this calm assurance, Jacqueline had only a very vague recollection.

"I am certainly mistaken, Monsieur. There's a reason you do not seem a stranger. Doubtlessly your mother's faithful description of you created the pleasant illusion that we had already met."

"Of course," said Judex.

"I present my son, Jeannot, and his young friend, the Licorice Kid. Come, children, meet Monsieur Jacques de Trémeuse."

The two children rushed forward immediately. For Judex, this was the more difficult test. With his habitual enthusiasm, the Licorice Kid ran towards Jacques right away and greeted him warmly. Judex embraced him immediately. Seeing Jeannot come close to his face, Judex didn't try to elude the danger of recognition. The child contemplated him for an instant.

"You appear to be very wise for your age," said Judex.

"Yes, Monsieur," replied the boy innocently. He put his arms around Jacques and kissed him on the cheek. The child then desired to resume his frolics.

"Monsieur, can I play with Licorice?"

"Of course," said Monsieur de Trémeuse putting Jean down. The boy rejoined his friend.

Judex was relieved. As he had foreseen, the child hadn't preserved the impression of his fleeting image. Now he was content. He was close to the one he loved. He would prepare untiringly the redemption that was henceforth the only goal of his life. A sublime bond of pure love was forged from the simultaneous birth of forgiveness in the heart of the victim and regret in the soul of the anointed executioner.

He gazed with luminous hope at his mother. Fearful that Jacques may have betrayed himself, Madame de Trémeuse decided to confer with him.

"Dear Madame Aubry, will you excuse my son and me? Since we have been separated for so long, we have many private family matters to discuss. Jacques, give me your arm."

As her visitors moved away, Jacqueline's doubts returned. Jacques's tall frame, aristocratic bearing, harmonious voice and especially his sympathetic eyes were somewhat familiar. She searched her memories, but found absolutely nothing.

Jacqueline was about to conclude that she was totally mistaken when Jeannot approached her.

"Mama! Mama!"

"What is it, darling?"

"The gentleman…"

"Which gentleman?"

"The one who was just here."

"Yes, well?"

"I know him."

Jacqueline shivered from a vague worry.

"How do you know him?" she asked drawing the child close to her.

"Yes, Mama. I waited to tell you because Licorice wanted to play. But I know him very well. I saw him before!"

"Where?"

Silently Jeannot attempted to remember.

"Try to recall," encouraged the mother.

After reflecting, the child replied: "I don't know!"

His mother was going to question him further, but the Licorice Kid interrupted.

"Hey, pal! Come on, let's play!"

Replying to his friend's call, Jeannot left his mother.

"It's strange!" murmured the concerned Jacqueline. She was lost in thought for a long time. No suspicion pervaded her mind. Nonetheless, she had a sensation that this new mystery would grow to cause her anguish. Entirely ignorant of the facts, she decided to record her feelings in a letter to Gisèle de Birargues. Collecting the children, she saw Jacques de Trémeuse walking along the path from the villa. He had changed his traveling suit for informal clothes that gave him a youthful allure very different from Judex. The banker's daughter was completely disconcerted.

"I was mistaken. I couldn't have met him before. Jeannot and I must have seen someone that resembled him. We are both in error."

242

Totally calm, she gracefully greeted Judex. "*Bonjour*, Monsieur."

"Are you pleases by your surroundings, Madame?"

"How could it be otherwise?" replied Jacqueline. "'This beautiful sun, this natural air, and above all, the presence of my son. I am have been so delicately looked after… You greatly resemble your uncle, Monsieur Vallières."

"He told me of your unfortunate experiences," said Jacques. "He has written to me at length on this subject. Even before I met you, I was concerned about your welfare."

"Thank you, Monsieur."

"If you permit me, Madame, I would like to join the ranks of those whose sweet duty is to help you forget a life of sorrow."

"I am confused by all this kindness," declared Jacqueline. Despite her earlier unease, she now felt enraptured by an atmosphere of happiness. "What have I done to deserve this?"

"What did you do!" shouted Judex. He could no longer silence the passion bursting within him. "Monsieur Vallières has praised your modesty as well. He has said… We all have said… My mother, my brother and myself consider you not only as the noblest of the women, but also the most admirable of God's creatures."

"Monsieur!"

"Let me tell you! Your sublime aura obliterates injustice and hatred. Do you believe in God's will?"

"With all my soul!"

"Continue to believe. Continue to pray. Continue to hope."

The handsome young man seemed mystically transfigured into an ancient prophet predicting a glorious salvation to a congregation kneeling before a holy shrine. Judex's voice vibrated with immense love and religious ecstasy.

"The Heavens do not have a monopoly on reward. The Earth can also render you happiness."

Jacqueline bowed her head. "No one has ever spoken to me like that."

A smile formed on Judex's lips. "Except Vallières?"

Except Vallières, thought Jacqueline, but she dared not repeat it. This deep voice burning with youth was new to her heart. It moved and charmed her. Once more, she became a mother. She lifted her eyes towards the beautiful sky as pure as her soul.

"If, as you say, I truly deserved a reward in this world, I in request only one, Monsieur. I wish for my son to be happy."

"He shall be," said Judex. He deposited a long kiss on the young woman's hand.

Both children had assumed the serious expression of supplicants about to address a serious request to an important personage. They advanced towards Jacques and Jacqueline.

"Monsieur…" began the Licorice Kid. Being naturally bold, he was inclined to speak first.

"What do you wish, my young friend?" replied Judex politely.

"We want…" risked Jeannot.

The request had to be of a delicate nature. Jean stopped himself immediately. The Licorice Kid felt uncharacteristically embarrassed.

"Please, speak," invited Jacqueline.

"Yes. What do you want, little ones?" questioned Jacques.

Mustering all their courage, the two kids shouted at the same time.

"We want Cocantin!"

"Cocantin?" repeated Judex feigning ignorance.

"Monsieur Cocantin," explained Jacqueline, "is a private detective extremely devoted to my son and his friend. He even saved their lives. They are both attached to him."

"What a splendid fellow!" said Judex.

"Indeed, Monsieur, but that's no reason for the children to be so insistent," noted the young woman.

Reacting to Jacqueline's reproach, Jeannot and the Licorice Kid impishly bowed their heads.

"*Au contraire*," declared Judex, "we'll be delighted to receive Monsieur Cocantin. I shall send him an invitation to spend some days with us at once."

"Oh! Thank you, Monsieur! Thank you!" The inseparable children had became ecstatic.

"He'll play hide and seek with us," rejoiced Jeannot.

"He's a funny one!" added the Licorice Kid. "There's his nose, Monsieur. It's as large as a quart of cheese."

"Please, Licorice," scolded Jacqueline gently. "You had promised me to never make such remarks."

"You're right, Madame. Please forgive me. I won't do it again." Humorously contrite, the youngster took Jeannot by the arm and moved away. Suddenly turning around, the Kid pointed at Judex. "That one is a prince!"

"A generous prince!" said Jacqueline. Her gaze made Jacques de Trémeuse want to kneel in front of her.

III. The Gazebo

Judex was sure of Cocantin. He had seen the detective work. His devotion and loyalty was unquestionable. When Judex had left for Sainte-Maxime, he had not hesitated for a moment to entrust the search for Diana Monti and Moralès to Cocantin.

The director of the Celeritas Agency had performed his task with fervor. Much more confident and determined, he had developed a unique affinity for the detective trade. In fact, he now regularly witnessed public executions.

However, his results didn't match his resolution. The adventuress and her lover had seemingly vanished from the face of the Earth. Perhaps discouraged by failure and fearful of Judex, they had abandoned their scheme. It was impossible for Prosper Cocantin to discover their trail. After several days and nights of intensive investigation, he wrote to Judex. According to the detective, the odds were overwhelming that Diana and Moralès had prudently fled Paris in the wake of their defeats.

Recognizing that the evil Diana was capable of doing the unexpected, Judex had reservations about the detective's conclusions. However, Jacques de Trémeuse considered the mission entrusted to Cocantin to be concluded. He sent a laconic telegram to private detective:

Come quickly. Regards. J.

Cocantin would have jumped into a fire for Judex. The sleuth quickly complied with the imperative command. Meeting Cocantin at the railway station of Saint-Raphaël, Judex took him to Sainte-Maxime. Putting his absolute trust in the sleuth, he briefed him on the situation during the journey.

"Staying at my mother's house is Jacqueline Aubry."

"The banker's daughter?"

"With her son and your friend, the Licorice Kid."

"Impossible!"

"The two children wanted to see you."

"Wonderful!"

"I didn't have it within my heart to refuse them this diversion."

"You're too kind."

"Monsieur Cocantin, I know that I can count on your discretion. I need your services during your stay."

"I await your orders."

Choosing his words carefully, the self-styled judge gave his instructions:

"Listen to me carefully. Never for an instant must Jacqueline Aubry suspect that Judex and Jacques de Trémeuse are one and the same."

"Naturally."

"My secret is in your hands, Monsieur Cocantin."

"I swear to you that it will be kept," asserted Prosper Cocantin gravely. "It's very beautiful what you have done here."

Proud to be the friend and confidant of a man such as Judex, Cocantin admired the splendid Mediterranean panorama that unfolded before his entranced eyes.

If the director of the Celeritas Agency had been endowed with the powers of divination, he would have been reluctant to travel to his blissful destination. While Cocantin had completely lost track of Diana and Moralès, the opposite was not the case. After noting that the mysterious tenants of the Chateau Rouge had abandoned their underground lair, the criminal duo had not ceased for an instant to discreetly keep the director of the Celeritas Agency under strict surveillance.

Informed by Crémard and the Coltineur of their fatal encounter with Judex on the road to La Muette, the adventuress realized that her adversary was now allied with Ribaudet's heir. Armed with this knowledge, she decided to roll the dice one more time.

"I have only to watch Cocantin. He'll lead me to Judex and Favraux!"

As events unfolded, the clever strategy bore fruit. Keeping tabs on the detective had been child's play for Diana. Learning of his train trip to the South of France, she decided to follow him. The same evening when Cocantin installed himself in a comfortable first-class compartment of the PLM train to Nice, an old man with a grey mustache and a young dandy with a supercilious monocle took their places in the neighboring compartment.

The old man was really Moralès, and his young companion was Diana Monti. Meticulously disguised, they never lost sight of the intrepid Prosper Cocantin for a single instant. Leaving the train at same time as their quarry at Saint-Raphaël, they saw him climb into an automobile with a man whom Moralès instantly recognized as Judex. From an agent at the station, they learned that Cocantin's companion was Jacques de Trémeuse. The same agent gave them the address of the villa where Jacques was staying.

In the cynical language of the underworld, Diana no longer had to play it safe. The criminals decided to take their revenge. Without hesitation, they drove to Sainte-Maxime. The conspirators realized the dangerous game that that they were playing. Judex was a formidable opponent. The essential

247

element was to remain scrupulously incognito. That stratagem assured them a big advantage, They avoided staying at a hotel where they would have been too conspicuous. After surveying the Trémeuse estate, they searched for a villa to serve as an observation post and a refuge.

They chose a coastal house with a rooftop gazebo that could be used to scan the countryside. After paying a month's rent in advance, they immediately moved into the residence under the false identities of Monsieur Blocalfred, a banker, and his son Albert. As early as the next morning, they spied on the neighborhood from the top of the gazebo.

Using binoculars, Diana studied the Villa of the Trémeuses. On a path, Jacques and Roger were walking with the attitude of people engaged in a confidential conversation. In a nearby garden, Cocantin played ball with Jeannot and the Licorice Kid under Jacqueline's gaze.

"She's also there!" exclaimed the female criminal. "Perfect! That simplifies things!" She made an infernal grin as she continued to scan with the binoculars. "We have cast our net beautifully. We did well to come to Sainte-Maxime."

Suddenly a cry escaped her. "Him! Him! I knew it. I was so sure. Now we have them all!" Passing the binoculars to Moralès, she pointed in a precise direction. "Look!"

Scarcely had Moralès looked through the lens that a disturbing paleness spread on his face. Contemplating new crimes to commit, Diana whispered into her lover's ear. "Favraux and your father!"

Diana was not mistaken. On a spacious terrace covered by flowers, the banker sat on a bench contemplating the sea. Next to him stood Pierre Kerjean. The ex-miller seemed attentive to every request made by his prisoner.

"Now," hissed Diana triumphantly, "I don't need any more information. I know what I must do."

"You want to remove Favraux?" questioned Moralès.

"Why else are we here?"

248

"But my father?" panted Robert. Once more under the complete domination of the adventuress, he shuddered at the new infamies that she would unleash.

"Your father?" laughed the sinister woman "You don't have to worry about him. In deference to you, I'll made sure he doesn't suffer any harm. He's lucky that you're his son. These sentimental issues must no longer delay us. Fortune smiles on us again. We can't let it slip through our hands. Come!"

The two criminals returned to the ground floor of the villa.

"I need to think," decided Diana. "Leave me alone. I don't want to be bothered."

She confined herself in her room. After two hours, she found Moralès in a balcony. Overcome by fear, the depressed gambler looked at the sea with eyes as dazed as those of the banker Favraux.

"You will leave immediately for Nice," ordered Diana. "Once there, go to the harbor and look for a brig-schooner called the *Eaglet*. It's definitely there. I just checked the harbor entries published in the newspaper. Ask to speak to Captain Martelli. Give him this letter. He will then tell you what to do. Return soon!"

Thoroughly enslaved, the submissive Moralès, hurried to obey his fearsome mistress As he moved away, a hellish flame lit up her large black eyes.

"My victory is assured! The banker's millions will soon be mine!"

IV. Grandfather

Jeannot and the Licorice Kid no longer had Prosper Cocantin to play with. Since he had arrived in Sainte-Maxime three days ago, Cocantin had endlessly presided over the young boys' recreation. The detective had gracefully catered to the children's ridiculous fantasies. Eventually, Jacqueline had to intervene to deliver the brave sleuth from his servitude.

Cocantin was allowed to explore the admirable corner of Provence that is the bay of Saint-Tropez. Sitting on a boulder, the director of the Celeritas Agency followed enthusiastically the graceful movements of the sails belonging to the ships in the harbor of Sainte-Maxime.

Meanwhile, Jeannot and the Licorice Kid still demonstrated that their love of games was limitless. In the garden of the villa, they joyfully played a soccer match. As we have already seen, the Licorice Kid was endowed with a reckless spirit. He loved exercise and adventure. The villa's garden seemed too confining to him. Every instant the ball was going to land into some massive flower bed.

"We're in a prison! There's hardly any room here. Say, Jeannot, let's break out."

"Break out?"

"Yes. If we do that, we would have more room. We also wouldn't hurt the geraniums and the roses. Your Mama wouldn't like it if we did."

Always ready to follow his friend's advice, Jeannot liked the idea but he had reservations.

"We won't be going far?"

"Far? Are you crazy? It's not far. Don't make me laugh?"

"What if Mama looks for us?"

"She'll call us. We'll hear her and we'll return right away."

"What if she scolds us?"

"Just kiss her!"

From Jean's point of view, the former gatherer of cigarette butts had managed to resolve the more delicate questions. Always shifting for himself, the Kid "knew what to do."

The two boys had left the garden by a small door spotted by the Licorice Kid. Two minutes later, they were playing a fabulous game of soccer. Suddenly the two friends cried in despair. Through a clumsy kick, the ball disappeared over the wall into a neighbor's property.

What could they do? The two children were perplexed. They looked at each other in shock. Already the sensitive Jeannot's eyes filled with tears. Soon a crafty smile lit up the face of the Licorice Kid.

"Don't be so sad. Come with me. I found a way!"

The little imp pointed to a wheelbarrow at the foot of wall over which the ball has just disappeared. A big cocker spaniel with long ears and a fat stomach slept there calmly.

"Hey! Get out of there, Rover!" shouted the Licorice Kid. The meek animal docilely left.

"It's up to us, sonny!" said the Licorice Kid to his friend. "Come with me into the cart. I will give you the short ladder. You will climb up the wall. Reaching the top, you can run down into the neighbor's yard and look for the ball."

Delighted to play the principal role in this new escapade, Jean followed his friend's order. Reaching easily the top of the wall, he made a quick inspection.

"All's well. I'm going down."

"Forward, little buddy."

Jean grabbed the vines hanging on a green trellis that outfitted the wall, After pricking his hands two or three times, he finally touched the ground. Almost immediately, he stopped. He noticed a bench shaded by a grove of palm trees. A man held the ball between his hands. He was examining it with a strange fixation. Jean approached him apprehensively.

"Monsieur, could you please return my ball?" he asked.

The man raised his head. Filled with shock and fear, Jacqueline's son shouted:

"Grandpa!"

It was the banker Favraux. Diverted by a ringing telephone, Kerjean had left his charge for an instance.

"Grandpa!" repeated Jeannot with sweetness and tenderness.

Confronted by this unexpected apparition, the banker's eyes lost their disturbing coldness. Upon seeing the blond cherub, they gradually softened. While this charming vision didn't cause the banker's reason to return completely, there was a beneficial tenderness. It was the first ray of sunlight after the night.

"My grandson, is that you?" he said with a trembling voice.

"Yes, Grandpa."

Jeannot approached. Completely reassured, he climbed on the knees of the banker. Hugging his grandfather, the child affectionately kissed him as he had done in the large park of Les Sablons. Through the exquisite love of a small boy, the miracle became complete. It was a tearful miracle of remorse. The banker's intelligence reignited. A torch illuminated the road of regret.

Favraux rose. His face was bathed in tears. Holding his grandson against his chest, he looked around and listened. A noise reverberated on the gravels of the pathway. It was Kerjean returning. Furtively he slipped himself around the massive tree to reach the foot of the wall. Convulsively he kissed Jeannot. Retrieving the ball, Favraux assisted the child to climb back along the trellis.

"Go," whispered the banker. "Tell your mother that you saw me. Go, my dear."

Once Jeannot disappeared behind the fence, Favraux returned to the bench where he had dreamed unconsciously before the brief dissipation of the funeral mist that had clouded his mind.

A worried Kerjean was there. Nonetheless, he did not hear or see anything. The banker gave him a voluntarily lifeless stare.

"Let's go inside," said Kerjean.

Without saying a word, lost again in distant dreams, Favraux docilely followed his jailer.

During this time, Jeannot rejoined the Licorice Kid waiting at the foot of the wall. He ran towards the Trémeuse Villa.

"Come quickly, Licorice. I must talk to Mama."

Jacqueline sat under a veranda that sheltered a wide marble terrace. Believing that the two children were still playing in the garden, she was surprised to suddenly see them rush towards her.

"Don't run, children, you might trip."

However, Jeannot rushed up the stairway that gave access to the terrace. He happily approached his mother.

"Mama! I saw Grandpa!"

Upon hearing these words, Jacqueline stood up and grabbed her son.

"Jeannot, what did you say?"

"I saw Grandpa."

"That's impossible."

"But I saw him. He spoke to me. He wants me to tell you he's there."

Jean pointed towards the neighboring Villa des Palmiers.

Although deeply troubled, Jacqueline couldn't doubt the child's sincerity.

"My dear, are you sure it was grandfather?"

"Yes," energetically asserted the boy. "He sat on a bench. He seemed very sad. He looked at my ball that had fallen by over the wall. When he saw me, he seemed happy, very happy. He took me in his arms. He caressed me; and then, I know not why... he began crying."

"And this was over there?"

"In the garden that is on the other side of the wall. Poor Grandpa... he seemed very unhappy ... you know, Mama."

Jacqueline remembered the ghostly voice on the tele-phone. She went shuddering towards the parlor of the villa where Madame de Trémeuse was with her two sons.

"Madame..." said Jacqueline with a choked voice. "My father is here. Jean has just seen him at your neighbor's. My son can't be mistaken."

Nearly fainting, she hung on to a drape while a wave of tears flooded her face.

Filled with anxiety, Jacques and Roger looked at their mother.

However, Madame de Trémeuse advanced compassio-nately towards the young woman. She no longer was Julia

Orsini, the savage Corsican, the ruthless widow sworn to vengeance. She was a pious mother hurt by her children's sorrow.

"Be peaceful, my darling." Her face assumed an expression of sacrifice and renunciation. "You must thank God for having returned your father to you."

Turning towards Jacques and Roger, she made an irrevocable decision. "My sons will take you to him."

Gazing on his mother with gratitude, Jacques de Trémeuse said simply to Jacqueline: "Come, Madame!"

They all went to the palm grove. Judex had planned to stand between the father and daughter. He would simply say "Judge me." However these words remained unspoken.

The swift Jean ran in front of the entourage consisting of Judex, Jacqueline, Roger and Madame de Trémeuse. He reached to the bench that the banker had occupied. But it was now empty.

The child gave a cry. He just noticed a gagged man tied to a palm tree. Judex, the closest of the adults, ran towards the tree. "Kerjean," he said, releasing the captive.

"I was taken by surprise. I don't know by whom. Favraux is gone. but he has…"

"Not a word in front of her!" implored Judex. He had just spied Jacqueline rushing towards him.

"What happened?" she questioned. The banker's daughter was overcome with frantic concern.

"Your father was there all the time," declared Judex, "but he's disappeared."

"*Mon Dieu!*"

Encouraged by the expression on his mother's face as she stepped towards him, Jacques de Trémeuse's voice revealed a love perhaps more powerful than any that had ever beat inside a human heart.

"Don't cry, Jacqueline, I shall return him to you. I swear."

V. An Infernal Plan

Diana Monti had not wasted any time. Since the morning, she and two sailors had been posted outside the Villa des Palmiers. Disguised as a man, she had awaited a favorable moment to invade the property and remove Favraux from his jailer's custody.

The garden had a small door that Judex and Kerjean had locked. Using a skeleton key, Diana and her two associates passed through that door. Concealed behind a thicket, they waited for the chance to strike.

Diana had seen Favraux seated on the bench. Subsequently, she had witnessed the banker finding the ball, taking Jean in his arms and accompanying him to the wall.

The adventuress wondered about the unexpected consequences of the meeting between Jean and his grandfather. Once she saw Kerjean return in order to escort his prisoner back to the house, she hesitated no longer.

The time to act had come. It was an opportunity that could not be wasted. She signaled her two companions. The sailors leaped on Kerjean. With remarkable speed, they gagged the ex-miller and tied him to a palm tree. Concurrently, Diana confronted Favraux.

"I am Marie Verdier, your grandson's former governess."

Dressed as a sailor, an anxious Moralès entered the garden through the unlocked door.

"This is my brother," said Diana pointing to her lover. "We're here to liberate you."

"You!" stammered Favraux whose reason had been jarred again by this unexpected intervention. "I saw my grandson. My daughter should be coming soon."

"Come with me," commanded Diana, "there's not a minute to spare. Judex lurks nearby. He'll kill you before your daughter arrives."

Stunned and disconcerted, the banker was dominated by the voice of this woman he had once fiercely desired. His terror at hearing Judex's name was skillfully exploited by the temptress. Favraux was induced to enter an automobile waiting outside. The car took a devious route towards the harbor.

"There's nothing to fear," said Diana. "We aren't driving blindly. We must make it impossible for your enemy to follow. Otherwise, you'll be lost forever. "

The infernal creature spoke with the same sweet voice that enraptured Jacqueline's father in the past.

"Your nightmare is over. You shall remain with us. We shall protect you. We shall avenge you." She leaned over to whisper into his ear. "You know that I still love you."

Completely assured, Favraux behaved like the survivor of a nearly mortal illness resurrected by the dawn of convalescence. He became silent. His eyes closed. Intoxicated by these clever words, he fell into a blissful dream.

Supported by Diana and Moralès, he embarked on a dinghy piloted by the two sailors. The boat headed towards a brig-schooner anchored a short distance from the shore. Coming aboard, they found the ship helmed by a bearded seaman built like Hercules.

"Captain Martelli," said Diana, "you wisely heeded my call. Our coup has succeeded. You shall be rewarded handsomely."

The amoral Martelli smiled with undisguised satisfaction. He had formerly been Diana's partner in a smuggling operation organized by her on the Italian coast. The two criminals, male and female, easily negotiated the terms of their new alliance.

Minutes after Favraux, Diana and Moralès were installed aboard, the *Eaglet* prepared to weigh anchor. Seated in the back, the astonished banker oversaw the preparations of the departure. Diana and Robert Kerjean had rejoined him.

"Where are you taking me?" asked the worried banker.

"To avoid any pursuit," said Diana, "we must quickly sail to either Sète or Port-Vendres. From there, we'll journey to Paris. There, you shall place yourself under the protection of the law. Through a malicious campaign of extortion, Judex coerced your daughter to donate your fortune to the Public Assistance. Once you reclaim your wealth, it will be completely and immediately restored!"

"I owe my liberty to you?" asked Favraux.

"My brother and I, together with our allies, these brave sailors, rescued you from your tormentors."

The banker was once more gazing at Diana with inflamed passion. "How did you locate me?"

"There isn't time to explain. Tomorrow, you'll be told everything. Know that we faced grave danger. This Judex is a monster! But I was determined to save you. I'm happy, yes, very happy to have succeeded,"

"Marie," murmured the banker, "I can't thank you enough, but I know how to repay my debt to you. Yes, I know!"

A triumphant glee illuminated the face of the adventuress.

"Are we leaving now?" asked Favraux

"Yes, we travel by night."

At these words, the banker's face darkened. The face of his grandson appeared before him. A deep sigh escaped his chest.

"Jean… Jacqueline!"

"What's wrong?" questioned Diana.

"I don't want this vessel to depart without my daughter and grandson."

The infernal creature spoke with hypocritical piety.

"I fully understand your feelings. I was about to offer to take them with us. We must act with extreme caution. Judex is really Jacques de Trémeuse."

"Jacques de Trémeuse!" shuddered Favraux. As his reason returned, he began to relive the terrible phases of his captivity.

"In order to divert suspicion, he pretended to be your daughter's protector. She totally trusts him."

"My poor daughter!"

"She isn't exactly his prisoner. However, your enemy considers her an invaluable hostage. Her freedom isn't totally restricted. We must quickly seize the opportunity to help her."

"You're right," approved the gilded merchant. "Tell me what to do. I'm so confused. I've lost the ability to think quickly."

"Listen carefully to me."

"Marie, I value you more than life itself."

With a captivating smile, the adventuress handed the banker a pen and a sheet of paper.

"Write your daughter to come here with your grandson. I personally will arrange for the letter to be delivered to her. In an hour, she will be close to you!"

"Again, thank you!"

Summoning all his will, Favraux hesitantly wrote some lines. Captain Martelli was preparing to depart. Diana interrupted him.

"We can't leave until tomorrow."

"Why?"

"I'll explain later. Tonight, around 10 o'clock. We'll talk on the quay."

"There's more to do?" questioned the brigand of the sea.

Diana laughed hysterically. "This time, my pretty Jacqueline, you and your heir shall not escape me!"

Part Ten: The Heart of Jacqueline

I. The Advice of Vallières

"Madame!" shouted Jacqueline Aubry. She sobbed in the arms of Madame de Trémeuse, "I beg you. Let me leave for Paris. There I can appeal to the authorities for help. They surely will solve this terrible puzzle."

"Calm down, my child," implored the Comtesse. "My son Jacques promised to find your father. I know him. He shall keep his word."

"Of course, I believe in him, but even a man of his courage and sincerity will be fighting an unknown force that seems unstoppable. How will he face such fearsome dangers? Will he be able to overcome them? Will he succumb to them? Will the hatred of Judex claim another victim? I have been silent for too long. The time has come to speak."

"You must stay silent, my poor friend," observed Julia Orsini.

"Why, Madame?"

"Because in the interest of your father, for his welfare and his honor, you can't involve the police in this matter."

The two ladies stood at the far end of a veranda overlooking the sea. Persuading the banker's daughter to sit next to her on a large wicker coach, Madame de Trémeuse explained with maternal affection.

"You confided your secrets to me. You told me earlier that your father's life was not above reproach."

"Alas!"

"It would be reckless to make this tragedy public. It must forever remain in the shadows."

"Madame... This is horrible. My poor father. He was here. So close. Was it Providence that sought to unite us? Did it drive my son into his arms? Did he show himself to his grandson because his sins had been expiated? Has the justice of men finally bowed to the justice of God?"

"Your father is alive," consoled the Woman in Black. "This reassuring fact must open your heart to hope."

"Of course, Madame, but Judex must have learned that he had been discovered. What if he has moved my father to a secret prison that no one can find?"

In accordance with the plan formulated with her two sons, Madame de Trémeuse made a forceful declaration.

"I'm sure that Judex had nothing to do with Monsieur Favraux's disappearance."

"Madame, what are you telling me?" exclaimed Jacqueline becoming pale.

Julia Orsini spoke with an authority tempered by affection. "My child, I know the truth! The man that we found tied up in the Villa des Palmiers told us everything. Seeking revenge on your father, Judex had resolved to kill him. Moved by your sublime gesture of generosity, his anger abated. For your son, and even more for you, Judex decided to spare your father and condemn him to life imprisonment. But your father soon fell ill... very ill..."

"*Mon Dieu!*"

"Judex, inspired by you, transferred your father secretly from his prison cell to the villa where your son found him. An unexpected event then happened. When your Jean, acting as Providence's messenger, ran to tell you that he had seen your grandfather, two individuals broke into the garden of the Villa des Palmiers. They overcame the custodian whom Judex had charged with guarding Monsieur Favraux. They spirited your father away. At this point in time, it's impossible to know his whereabouts."

"Do you know who abducted my father?"

"I do."

"Their names?"

"Diana Monti and Moralès. They are actually your ex-governess, Marie Verdier, and her lover. On three different occasions, they tried to murder you."

261

"It's horrendous!"

"Let me finish, my child. Armed with this information, Jacques and Roger are searching the countryside. They have already gathered precious clues. I can only repeat my advice. Continue to hope."

"Did Judex's servant reveal anything else?"

"He refused to give further details." The voice of the Comtesse trembled slightly. "Judex is not a man, but a family seeking vengeance." Madame de Trémeuse kissed the forehead of her enemy's daughter. "The jailer told us that remorse had entered your father's heart. There is no misdeed or crime that cannot be redeemed by contrition."

"Your words are so kind" exclaimed Jacqueline. She kissed the Comtesse. "Without you, what would I do? I no longer know. Although I'm ashamed of the crimes of the banker Favraux, I can't forget that he's my father. I want to help him secure redemption. I must hasten his deliverance. Fortunately, you are near me. If only your brother, the noble Vallières, was here. He would advise me what to do. Forgive me this momentarily failure. I suffer so much. Not only recently, but for a long time. I have always suffered. I didn't have a mother to console me. Mine died so young! I was a poor frightened child. I never asserted myself. I was intimidated by my father. Maybe my mother was the same. Did she die from lack of love? It's frightening. I was never treated with affection and devotion. I just wanted a sweet and peaceful life. I wanted to love and be loved. I am a daughter without a mother, a wife with a dead husband. I would have expired like my mother. If I didn't have my son, I would begged for death. My little beloved Jean is the true joy of my life, my only glimpse of happiness."

"He's the reason you must not drown in despair."

"You're very wise, Madame. The same advice had been given by my good friend Vallières. I want to tell him how wonderful you are. You are so good. I feel that I've know you are. It's strange. My heart was drawn to you immediately. And towards the your sons... Roger... Jacques..."

Pronouncing the last name, Jacqueline's voice quavered. Obeying an instinctive impulse, she added the following words as an unconscious confession.

"Yes, Monsieur Jacques especially."

Her spirit was overwhelmed by the conflicting distress and hope within her. Her head rested on the shoulder of Madame de Trémeuse as she sobbed in panic-stricken confusion.

"Forgive me, Madame, forgive me!"

Nearby, Jacques de Trémeuse had been hiding behind a cluster of roses. Having heard every word of the conversation, he was in ecstasy. His lips murmured an affirmation of his supreme passion.

"She loves me! She loves me!"

The Licorice Kid was sometimes studious during his moments of leisure. Seated in a comfortable rocking-chair, he was conscientiously reading *Le Temps*, Suddenly, a footstep on the gravel caught his attention.

Dressed in a frock-coat and a top hat, an old man had just appeared in the middle of the palm trees.

"My word! Papa Vallières!" shouted the Licorice Kid running towards the visitor.

Taking the ex-secretary by the hand, the Kid guided him towards the steps of the villa..

Attracted by the excited cries of the child, Jacqueline and Madame de Trémeuse ran to the source of the commotion.

Seeing her tall friend, Jacqueline's charming face beamed with joy.

"You're here! Just this morning, I told your sister how much I wanted to see you!"

"Your wish has been granted," replied Vallières.

"It's one of those amazing coincidences," said Jacqueline escorting Vallières into the parlor.

"I know, admitted Vallières. "I just met my nephew Jacques at the Saint-Raphaël train station. He told me everything."

"My poor father. I can't express, Vallières, my dear friend, how much kindness Madame de Trémeuse showed me. Never shall I forget…"

Her sentence remained unfinished because Jean interrupted.

"Mama, there's a man on the terrace."

In the parlor, Roger de Trémeuse stood opposite a sailor. After handing Roger a letter addressed to Madame Jacqueline Aubry, the seaman quickly disappeared. Roger brought the letter to Jacqueline. Unsealing the envelope, she read its contents aloud:

My dear daughter,

I am free at last. I want to see you. At 10 o'clock, meet me on the pier with Jean. You will no longer remain separated from your father.

I love you both.

MAURICE-ERNEST FAVRAUX

"It's settled," declared Jacqueline. "I will go to this meeting."

After the reading of the message, Vallières volunteered his advice with a serious tone.

"Of course, it's only natural that you want to answer the call of your father. I wouldn't try to dissuade you, except that I fear this letter conceals a trap."

"But this letter is in my father's handwriting…"

"How can you be sure that someone else wasn't guiding his hand? Your father could be the unwilling instrument to lure you into an ambush."

"Nevertheless…"

"Wait, Madame, let me ask you a single question. Who removed Monsieur Favraux?"

"Diana Monti."

"Otherwise known as Marie Verdier, the ex-governess of Les Sablons, a heartless enemy who, on multiple occasions, has eagerly sought to dispose of a bothersome witness."

Encouraged by approving nods from Madame de Trémeuse and Roger, Vallières continued:

"Therefore, I believe that you'll be committing a serious mistake in obeying this invitation of dubious origin. I should go to this appointment in your place."

"But what if it's a plot of my enemies?"

"I will know how to frustrate it. Stay calm. If your father appears at this designated place, I shall bring him back here to be reunited with here."

"My brother has just spoken with reason and wisdom," concluded Madame de Trémeuse.

"I have no other choice," conceded Jacqueline, "but to put my trust in you. Who knows? We may still hear news from Jacques." Her face reddened slightly. "Vallières, my dear friend, I have a premonition that he shall return my father to me!"

II. The Swimmer

While the events unfolded at the Trémeuses' villa, Prosper Cocantin, wonderfully pampered by his hosts, customarily performed his daily stroll. Being a very good walker, he became infatuated with this admirable coast, one of the purer jewels of our radiant Provence. He directed his pace towards the picturesque site called Beauvallon.

Always very attracted by the sea, he reached the shore by taking a small path though the palm trees. Choosing a boulder, he used it a convenient resting place. Seated there, facing the sea, his eyes were dazzled by the splendid panorama.

The wind soon rose from the south. A heap of big gray clouds accumulated in the sky. They covered the sun. The temperature soon dropped. Feeling chilly, Cocantin abandoned his observation post to walk along the beach.

"Brrr!" he said to himself. "It's too cold. The Midi is an odd country! It's nice and hot. You feel like one of those thick plants blossoming under an eternal spring, but then the sun hides itself. Instantly you're surrounded by the frozen coat of winter."

Continuing to reflect on the temperature variations of the Midi, Cocantin approached a villa built in the Gallo-Roman style. It was used as a bathhouse by a neighboring hotel. Stopping in his tracks, he noticed a large bath robe lying over a sandstone jar. The detective wondered about the owner of the robe.

That daredevil must be mad to bath in this freezing water.

He pulled out of his pocket a pair of small binoculars which he had bought in Paris before his departure. He inspected the horizon with awe.

"Ah! What a beautiful sight!"

Two hundred meters from the shore, he noticed a graceful form boldly swimming among the foam of the waves.

"It's a woman, and a very pretty woman at that," uttered the gallant Cocantin. He could not detach his eyes from the swimmer. His immense nostrils begin beating like the wings of a scared cormorant.

The swimmer came closer to the shore. Cocantin could clearly distinguish her pretty face covered by an elegant cap The headgear could not completely hide her abundant blond hair that gleamed like the momentarily absent sun. The young woman came closer. She emerged from the middle of the waves. Her superb body was impeccably encased in a bathing suit of black silk.

Nothing held Cocantin back. He quickly pocketed the binoculars. Seizing the bathrobe, he ran towards the charming water-sprite. Smiling she advanced towards him.

As passion bloomed in the detective's heart, the most eloquently gallant compliments were about to erupt from his lips. Suddenly he stopped as if petrified. He was pleasantly surprised.

"You?!"

"Yes! It's I!"

The director of the Celeritas Agency had recognized this daring beauty. She was Miss Daisy Torp, an American swimmer of the New Circus. Prosper Cocantin had once been infatuated with her. After a brief flirtation, they had lost sight of each other.

"My dear Prosper, how are you?" said Daisy.

"Fine. What about you?" Cocantin was dazzled by the entrancing beauty.

"Give me my dressing gown! It's cold."

"You were very brave to swim in such weather."

"Cocantin, you're so sweet!"

"Daisy, you're so charming!"

"This is totally unexpected!"

"I agree!"

Cocantin, was delighted to be reacquainted with the pretty girl who had, for several weeks, occupied his days and disrupted his nights. As Miss Torp prepared to enter the Gallo-Roman edifice where she had stored her clothes, Cocantin made a request.

"My dear Daisy, since chance has reunited us, can we see more of each other?"

"Certainly," concurred the pretty damsel. She had always appreciated the polite cheerfulness of her former admirer.

"Where are you staying?" asked the detective.

"At the Grand Hotel in Sainte-Maxime."

"We're neighbors. How come we didn't meet earlier?"

"I only arrived last night."

"What a coincidence! I'm happy to have found you! We could have a lot of fun together!"

Cocantin accompanied Daisy towards her dressing room.

"When can we meet again, my sweet beauty?" feverishly asked the sleuth

"I will be going on an excursion to Saint-Tropez," declared the swimmer. "I'll also be dining with friends at a villa, the Gabelle, a delicious retreat where we could go together."

"That would be fine!"

"Then, tomorrow?"

"Why not tonight?"

"You'll have to return to Sainte-Maxime very late."

"That's not important, Daisy. Your Cocantin is at your beck and call."

"You really want to meet tonight?"

"Yes."

"At 10 o'clock?"

"At 10 o'clock."

"On the pier of the harbor?"

"Agreed."

"You are divine!"

"I have to leave now. I'm freezing."

"Tonight."

"Tonight."

Before disappearing in the Gallo-Roman temple, Daisy dropped her bathrobe. Standing on her toes, she kissed Cocantin. In a state of ecstasy, the detective viewed her action as a promising preview of their evening dinner.

As she departed, the director of the Celeritas Agency stared after her.

"I'm lucky to be in Sainte-Maxime!"

III. The Truth

Upon learning of the letter addressed by Favraux to his daughter, Jacques de Trémeuse had decided on an appropriate strategy.

I won't go to this rendezvous wearing the face of Val-lières. It is Judex who shall arrive at the appointed hour.

Alone in his room on the upper floor, Jacques removed the false beard, wig and suit that rendered him unrecognizable. Putting on his felt hat and cloak, he looked out on the terrace. Hearing no noise from the direction of Jacqueline's room, he descended via a secret staircase to the ground floor where he ran no risk of meeting anyone at this late hour. Under the slivery radiance of the Moon, he crossed through the park. Passing through the gate, he reached the road to the Sainte-Maxime harbor.

The banker's daughter was not asleep. Leaning on the window sill, she recalled all the events that had plagued her life. While reviewing all her suffering, she wondered if, one day, her long ordeal would be replaced by the sweetness of an existence without anxiety or bitterness. In the midst of this tragic evocation of her misfortunes, a question continually nagged her.

What will be the consequences of the meeting between Vallières and my father? If my noble friend's suspicion that this appointment is some conspiracy organized against me, he could fall victim to my enemies. The more I learn, the deeper the mystery. I shouldn't have let him substitute for me, or at least forbade him from walking alone into danger. Maybe I still have time to keep him here or at least persuade Roger or Jacques, if he returns, to accompany their uncle?

With these intentions, Jacqueline intended to leave her room. Suddenly she remained frozen on the spot. As she was moving from the window, she saw a shadow, or rather a man wrapped in a black cloak, slip into from the garden. He soon disappeared behind a clump of trees. An intense fear overwhelmed her.

It's a man. Who is he?

In the moonlight that enveloped the park with mystical clarity, Jacqueline became convinced that she had seen this fantastic shape at the mill of Les Sablons.

Almost instantaneously, a name came to her lips.

"Jacques de Trémeuse. It can't be him. It's impossible."

Although she questioned her suspicion, an irresistible doubt had been cruelly born. Incapable of understanding the source of this fearsome drama, she still sensed its gloomy emanations. She felt the sensation of being caught in a frantic whirlwind that drew her towards the gulf of oblivion.

He face turned white as despair crushed her heart.

"I'm in love with my father's persecutor. As horrible as it may be, I do love him. The truth can't be so monstrous. I must be the victim of an illusion. What can I do? I can't be plagued by doubts. I need to know."

In thrall to a burning fever, she ran from her chambers towards the room with the terrace. She banged on the door.

"Vallières! Vallières!"

No one answered. Crazed with anxiety, Jacqueline was incapable of mastering her fear. Opening the door, she reluctantly entered the dark room. Not hearing any noise, she turned on the electric lamp.

The room was empty and the bed still made. She recognized the frock-coat of Vallières on a chair. On the desk was the formal top hat. A drawer had been left ajar. Inside was a gray wig and a false beard.

Viewing this evidence, Jacqueline felt that she had lost her mind. Dizzy and exhausted, she gave a cry, or rather a groan, that expressed the confusion of her tortured soul.

"*Mon Dieu!*"

She was about to collapse in a chair. Her brain felt drained. She was too terrorized to think. She wished that the uncertainty of the unexplained had never been usurped by the harshness of reality.

"What's wrong, my child?" said a sweet voice.

It was Madame de Trémeuse. Attracted by Jacqueline's calls for Vallières, the grand lady had just entered her son's room.

"You!" exclaimed the banker's daughter. She found refuge in the outstretched arms of the Comtesse. "I'm afraid! I'm afraid!"

"Tell me what's happened." questioned the grand lady.

"I was at my window. I saw clearly a man in the park. The man resembled a figure that I believed to have only seen in a dream. I dare not pronounce his name. I went to get Vallières. When there was no reply, I entered this room. No one was here."

She pointed to the clothing, the beard and the wig.

"I found this."

"My poor child," said Jacques's mother.

These simple words sufficed to enlighten the brain of Jacqueline. In a second, all veils were torn away. This was the moment of revelation. With dazed eyes, Jacqueline's quavering voice spoke slowly.

" Vallières... Jacques... Judex!"

The banker's daughter did not faint under this terrible shock. Instead she had the admirable strength to resist the deadly impact of this knowledge. She could have died from shock. If she lost her consciousness, Jacqueline feared that she would never awaken. Summoning all her energy, she willed herself to live. Clasping her hands, Jacqueline looked imploringly at Madame de Trémeuse. The older woman's face generated maternal compassion.

"Madame, I beg you, tell me the truth."

"Come, my daughter," said Julia Orsini.

Jacqueline walked in a jerky fashion. Supporting the distraught woman, the Comtesse entered her private chambers. Seating Jacqueline on a couch, the Comtesse sat beside her. The older woman spoke with the same sweet voice which she had used with her sons before tragedy had demolished their happiness.

"My dear child, listen to me. You deduced the truth. Vallières, Jacques de Trémeuse and Judex are one and the same."

"It's horrible!" cried Jacqueline.

"I feel your pain," resumed the Woman in Black, "because I know that you're in love."

"Madame..."

" Cry, yes, cry as you listen to me. As I will cry... As I have always cried. For we will overcome our ordeal together. Both of us have a cross to bear!"

Madame de Trémeuse became more beautiful due to their shared suffering. Vengeance had been forgotten. Absolution was triumphant.

"To defend my son, I will be forced to accuse your father. You may not wish me to do so, but it's necessary for you to comprehend your own heart."

"Speak, madam! I will listen with all the strength that I can muster."

"Thank you! My dear husband and I lived us happily with our sons. Nothing threatened our love and our prosperity until a man appeared. He desired me. He tried to seduce me. I rebuffed him. In revenge, he ruined my husband... and drove him to suicide."

"And this man was my father!" screamed Jacqueline tearfully. "It's one more crime to add to the others. I beseech you to forgive him."

"I already forgave... for you... for your child... for my son...," said Julia Orsini. "Before, I had wanted to avenge myself. When my fortune was restored, I consecrated all my life to the preparation of my vengeance, I raised my two sons with this sole goal. I proudly fashioned them in my image. I successfully infused within them all my values and beliefs. The hour arrived! I wanted the verdict to be merciless.

"It would have been if not for you! Your father owes his life to you. My son would not have weakened if you hadn't succeeded in melting my hatred. I, who had sworn to be implacable! Yes, you taught my son the pleasures of mercy. Your innocent child kissed my forehead. Every day, I came to know you better. I finally read in your heart a secret that you wouldn't admit to yourself. I, a woman and a mother, guessed it. My hate felt placated. I now knew that my vendetta had wrongfully included you. That realization made me gradually forgive my husband's slayer. Do you now understand why I ordered my son to punish your father?"

"Madame! Madame! I no longer know what to believe. This feud is horrible. Was it necessary for my father to provoke it? Why must I be forever the victim?"

Madame de Trémeuse nobly answered.

"Be joyful and proud. It is you who have conquered all. My sons and I are sworn to restore your father to you. I don't know how he will react to our mercy. However, we no longer pursue him It is you, my dear child, who will finalize this miracle of redemption and peace. I have no doubt that you are up to the task. As for me, my conscience is my punishment. My heart will always the regret having inadvertently hurt yours."

"And mine will never forget your affection for me, and the clemency extended towards my father."

A long embrace, maternal on the Comtesse's part, and feverish on Jacqueline's, sealed this mutually beneficial pact.

However, Jacqueline trembled! The fears that she had for Vallières were now transferred to Jacques de Trémeuse. In his efforts to deliver Favraux, was he heading towards disaster? The criminals had seized the banker to serve as an instrument of blackmail, or at least as bait for a trap. What would prevent them from treacherously murdering Jacques? Forgetting her father's peril, she thought only about the danger facing the man she loved.

Wildly running towards the window, she looked outside. The night was serene and silent. No gush of wind passed through the palm trees. The moonlight illuminated the sea. Far away, a handsome sailing ship was anchored. It rested motionless on the sleeping waters.

Jacqueline wondered if this setting of exquisite poetry didn't mask a brutal tragedy. She dreaded hearing the final cry of Judex as he was fatally stuck by a bullet or a knife!

Placing her forehead against the edge of the window. Her shoulders shook as tearfully stammered.

"Protect him, my Lord! Save him, I beseech you."

As Madame de Trémeuse approached her, Jacqueline rose with burning tears flowing down her face.

"I am unworthy of his love!"

Completely exhausted, she fainted into the arms of the Comtesse.

IV. The Rendezvous

After Judex passed through the villa's gate, he met his brother.

"Are you going to this rendezvous?" asked Roger.

"Yes."

"Alone?"

"Alone."

"You're taking a grave risk."

"Why?"

"You said it yourself. Favraux's letter to his daughter was certainly dictated, or at least inspired, by Diana Monti with the intention of ensnaring Jacqueline in order to eliminate her once and for all."

"That's my belief."

"They'll seek vengeance for your constant frustration of their schemes."

"Quite probably."

"Let me accompany you."

"Impossible."

"Brother!"

Judex had mastered a cold rationality due to his brushes with danger. He solemnly explained his decision:

"If we both appear on the harbor pier, the suspicions of these criminals will be aroused. Put on their guard, they'll avoid any contact with us. They will retreat to plot some new deviltry. But if they see me alone, without you or Kerjean nearby, they will come out into the open. That's my plan." Judex cryptically smiled. "I'm sure that 15 minutes of discussion, maybe less, will accomplish my objective."

"You're dealing with people who will stop at nothing to achieve their vile goals."

"I'm prepared."

"Are you armed?"

"No."

"Jacques, you're scaring me. What are you thinking? Exposing yourself like this. Your love for Jacqueline is affecting your reason."

"I have never been more sane."

"At least, take my gun."

"I have at my disposal something that's more potent than a pistol."

"What?"

"This." He pulled out a checkbook. "This is an argument that outlaws like Diana Monti and Moralès can't refute. Our immense fortune allows us to negotiate royally Favraux's ransom. I'm confident that I shall secure his release. It may cost me a million or maybe more."

"Be careful!" said Roger. He knew that it was futile to challenge his brother. Once Judex made a decision, nothing to the world could dissuade him.

The two brothers exchanged a warm handshake. While Roger, far from assured, returned to the villa, Jacques advanced towards the harbor.

He had been preceded there by Cocantin. Right after dinner at the Trémeuses' villa, the sleuth pretended to have a headache. He had told his hosts that he needed to take a little night air before retiring,

After strolling in the park, he surreptitiously left by a side door. His heart beat faster as he thought about the "splendid goddess" with whom he had an assignation. Never had Cocantin felt so passionate. All day long, the vision of the gorgeous swimmer appeared before him. This modern Amphitrite rising from the waves was a graceful mirage that he couldn't forget.

There is no one more beautiful, he thought. *What charm! What physique! What style! What curves! So seductive! And she loves me! If this enticing Daisy wasn't in love with me, she never would have granted me so easily this divine tryst!*

Having packed his Napoleonic bust from his Paris office, Cocantin had installed it in a place of honor in his room at the villa. Glancing at the statue earlier, the detective made a pronouncement:

"I'm sure that the Emperor was just as moved by his first rendezvous with Josephine."

It was in this frame of mind that Prosper Cocantin arrived on the deserted pier.

"She isn't here!" he said with disappointment.

Pulling out his watch, he realized that it was only a quarter to 10. Like all true lovers, he was early. Sitting on a bench, he was lost in a dream of romance. The director of the Celeritas Agency patiently awaited his beloved.

The minutes seemed to him like an eternity. As the desired hour approached, he alternated between hope and despair. A burning question had seized control of his brain:

Will she come?

Soon, he was filled with joy. His ears heard a noise. He looked up. A feminine outline appeared in the distance. An astral light seem to form a halo around her. She was here. Daisy was here!

"She has to be in love!" whispered Cocantin. Writhing nervously, He ran towards his conquest. He delivered a banal traditional greeting. "It's nice for you to come!"

"I was anxious to see you, my dear Cocantin." With a spontaneous frankness characteristic of a lover, she added an observation. "You may not be pretty…"

"I have no illusions!"

"…But you are such an honest man."

"One does what one can."

"I like honest men at lot. You're a good fellow."

"And I, your good fellow," said Cocantin charmed by this declaration, "finds you very pretty. I like pretty girls a lot."

"Pretty girls!"

"Come with me, my pretty girl." Cocantin passed his arm around the supple waist of the attractive swimmer. "Daisy! You have conquered my heart. I love you. Kiss me!"

A distant noise unfortunately resounded.

"Damn! Someone's coming!" shouted Prosper Cocantin. He led Daisy to the old side of the pier. "Let go to the lighthouse. We can talk undisturbed as we contemplate the sea."

Daisy agreed to the request. She always felt for the gallant Cocantin a cordial affection that was more enduring that an intense passion. She was an independent woman whose honesty and fearlessness had won her many admirers.

They walked towards the lighthouse, continuing to flirt under the stars. They exchanged their confidences in front of the Mediterranean that was filled with silvery reflections of the moonlight. The sea contrasted strangely with the azure darkness that formed a fluid veil of charm and mystery.

Behind them, a constant noise resounded from the flagstones of the piers. Upon arriving at the foot of the lighthouse, Cocantin yielded to his natural curiosity and turned around. Next to the area that they had just left, he glimpsed a figure standing in the moonlight. It was a man in a large cloak whose characteristic profile was unmistakable.

"Judex!"

"Judex!" repeated Daisy. "What's that?"

"It's nothing," answered Cocantin. "Actually, it's the name of a friend. A very good friend of mine."

"Do you think that he saw us?"

"No… and we have nothing to fear. He's a very discreet man."

"Do you want to introduce me to him?" mischievously proposed Miss Torp. "That's probably the polite thing to do."

"No! No!" Suddenly Cocantin's attention was no longer diverted by his romantic obsession. He grasped the reality of the situation. "We won't bother him. It's better that way. We must hide."

"You think he also has a rendezvous?"

"Yes."

"Of love?"

"Daisy, don't question me."

"What's wrong, Prosper. You seem distracted."

"I am indeed."

"Why?"

"Because… because I love you."

"Truly?"

"I adore you!"

In order to prove to Daisy his sincerity, Cocantin was about to hug her tenderly when the sound of oars striking water distracted him.

"Wait here, Daisy."

Cocantin moved away from the swimmer to conceal himself behind a wall. His gaze shifted towards the place where he had noticed Judex earlier. The shadowy figure sat on a large stone. He seemed to be serenely waiting for something to happen.

A rowboat, filled with several men, had left the anchored brig-schooner and steered towards the pier. When the boat stopped next to Judex, he didn't budge.

He scarcely turned his head when a young sailor jumped of the boat and headed for him.

Thanks to the magnificent moonlight illuminating the bay, Cocantin observed all these events clearly. He had watched impassively, but then his reaction changed.

A young sailor struck Judex lightly on the shoulder. Judex stared at his interrogator with paramount scorn.

"*Diable!*" exclaimed the director of the Celeritas Agency.

"What's happening there?" questioned Miss Torp, rejoining her suitor.

The detective appeared distraught. "We're witnessing something extraordinary!"

V. The Trap

When Jacques de Trémeuse had pretended to be oblivious to the movement of the rowboat, the sailor had shouted: "*Bonsoir*, Monsieur Judex!"

Despite his phenomenal self-control, Judex couldn't suppress a slight shiver. Quickly regaining his composure, he confronted his opponent, He recognized the derisive voice vibrating in his ears.

"Diana Monti! Our battle is spiraling out of control..."

The adventuress wore her sailor disguise with a sort of cynical grace. The cutthroats in the boat were ready to rush to her assistance at the first signal. Emboldened by her allies, the ex-governess of Les Sablons mocked her nemesis.

"Can I ask what you're doing on this pier tonight? You wouldn't by chance be composing some sonnet to the stars?"

"No," said Judex. "I'm waiting for Favraux!"

"So! You're waiting for Favraux? And why, please?"

"What are you doing here?"

Despite the security that the presence of her companions inspired in her, Diana was unnerved by her arch-enemy. She answered Judex's question:

"I was entrusted by Favraux to bring his daughter and grandson to our boat."

"And I came to prevent you from murdering them," said Jacques de Trémeuse.

Diana was furious to have her plans frustrated, but she decided to bluff.

"Is that what you're think I'm planning? Murder this woman and her child? You must be mad!"

"You have made earlier attempts."

"I don't understand."

"You don't?"

Judex pulled off Diana's beret. The long dark hair of the adventuress came undone and fell on her shoulders.

"Enough of this needless farce, Diana Monti! Now that we're face to face, let's be frank with one another."

Suddenly, the mistress of Moralès pulled out the gun that she had concealed behind her back. She pointed it at Judex. Without deviating from his calm demeanor, the cloaked avenger spoke authoritatively.

"You're losing your nerve, Mademoiselle Monti. If you knew why I'm here, you wouldn't be trying to kill me."

Responding to Diana's surprise attack, Jacques de Trémeuse hoped to conquer his foe with an unexpected maneuver of his own.

"I harbor only peaceful intentions," he continued. "You see that I came unarmed. I am simply here to negotiate Favraux's ransom."

"The ransom of the banker Favraux!" exclaimed the astonished Diana.

"Exactly"

Shocked, Diana responded only with silence. Judex attempted to overcome his adversary's distrust. "Do you want to discuss the terms?" he asked.

"Gladly, Monsieur."

Jacques de Trémeuse spoke as if he was discussing his financial dealings with a solicitor.

"I have no use for subtleties. In business deals, I make it my principle to go straight to the point. You must accept that this is nothing more than a business deal. If we reach an agreement to my satisfaction, not only will I forget the circumstances under which it was concluded, but I will erase from my memory all knowledge of your criminal activities. This declaration should completely satisfy you."

"In that case, Monsieur, let's hear your conditions."

"Wouldn't you rather tell me yours?"

"I haven't had time to reflect. As you said, this is a business transaction."

"A very large one."

"I need more time."

"We need to move quickly."

"I'm not alone."

"That shouldn't matter."

"This is rather embarrassing..."

"Do you want me to make an offer?" said Judex.

"Gladly."

"Permit me to speak with a bluntness that might be offensive. However, you have enough intelligence to realize that such candor is essential..."

Diana was developing an instinctive admiration for the extraordinary man in front of her.

"You, sly devil" she said. "You are handsome as well as strong. If you try to cheat me, you will find yourself mistaken. I will prove to you that Diana Monti has the ability to strike back."

She then adopted a more conciliatory tone.

"Your rather original way of making an entrance generated my mistrust. I was prompted to take defensive measures."

Putting her gun back inside her jacket pocket, she tempered her hostility by smiling. "Your subsequent behavior has placated me. Your offer does merit a hearing. Speak, Monsieur, I shall listen."

"Neglecting all the detailed circumstances that have placed us in this drawn-out conflict, I want to focus on the present question, namely the ransom of Favraux. First, why did you remove the banker from my custody? To marry him and then seize his fortune by killing his daughter and grandson. Do not protest! I warned you that I would discuss unpleasant matters. Much better to dispense with untruths at the start. This way, we avoid any misunderstanding that could ruin our negotiations. Hear me out. I guarantee that you won't have any regrets."

Diana became more intrigued by the twists of this unique chat. "Continue."

"Your plan can't succeed anymore," declared Judex

"You really believe that?" punctuated Diana.

"I'm sure. To achieve your ends, you resolved to eliminate Jacqueline Aubry and her son. Your motive is more than seizing their inheritance. They have become troublesome witnesses capable of exposing your schemes to Favraux. The unveiling of the banker's eyes would demolish the scaffolding that you erected to ensnare him. Thanks to a fortunate combination of events over which I won't linger, you didn't succeed in executing this important part of your plan. Tonight, you have failed once more, and you will always fail if I don't return alive to my villa."

"You have nothing to fear," asserted Diana. She was very eager to hear her opponent's proposal.

"So much the better for us all!" exclaimed Judex. "Let me summarize my terms. You have to abandon your designs on Favraux's millions and any plans to publicize that he is still alive. For the moment that the banker tries to reclaim his fortune, his daughter will stand between you and him. While you can accuse me of abducting him, Jacqueline can accuse you of trying to murder her and his grandson. It's in both our interests that Favraux remains in his grave. When all is said and done, only you, Moralès and I know that he's alive. For I assume that you weren't careless enough to fully confide the details of this affair to your other minions?"

"Of course, but there remains Favraux's daughter."

"She's under my protection!"

"Still…"

Judex was too honorable to lie, even to a criminal of Diana's caliber. He responded with annoyance.

"I repeat that she's under my protection. You must plainly see that everything can be worked out to the betterment of our common interests."

"Perhaps!" The adventuress began gradually to yield. She was sharply impressed by her opponent's arguments.

"What will you do with Favraux?" said Judex. "He's only an encumbrance to you. You will find it impossible to completely isolate him. Sooner or later, he'll escape or be discovered. If he's in my custody, there's nothing to fear. I guarantee you that, this time, my precautions will be so strong that no one, not even you, will be able to trace him. Relinquishing your prisoner, I repeat, is in as much your interest as mine."

To overcome any final doubts the adventuress might have, Judex stressed one salient point in a hushed voice.

"A million francs for you if you accept right away."

Upon hearing these words, Diana became briefly giddy.

"A million francs…"

Swayed more by the large sum than by Judex's arguments, she was about to accept when suddenly the truth dawned on her.

I clearly see his game, she thought. *He's in love with Jacqueline. There can be no doubt. In order to marry her, Judex must reunite Jacqueline with her father. As for the million he's just offered to me, he might not allow me to spend it. He could deliver me to justice, or rather his justice. Judex may intend to strike at me later…*

Why risk such a questionable bargain when he's my prisoner? I can do whatever I want with him. Instead of deli-

vering Favraux to Judex, I can deliver Judex to Favraux. And then we shall see if Jacqueline and his child are as unassailable as Judex claims.

"Monsieur," she resumed after a brief silence, "I have considered everything you said. I concede that you are extremely persuasive. I'm ready to make a deal that gives you Favraux in exchange for the million, but I have one condition."

"Name it."

"I've already told you that I'm not alone in this enterprise…"

"You mean, Moralès?"

"Yes, Moralès. There is also Favraux. The first will be easy to convince, but the second…"

"I don't understand."

"You're not unaware that the banker has lost his reason?"

"Yes, I know!"

"A this moment, he's haunted by an obsession to see his daughter and grandson."

"Well?"

"As long as he hasn't seen them, he will refuse to leave the boat. If we insist too harshly, I fear a violent incident might erupt. There's only one thing to do. You can send for Madame Aubry. However, you will assume that I still want to entrap her…"

Judex remained silent. A odd glimmer appeared in his eyes. A reflection of incomparable nobility illuminated his features. His love for Jacqueline inspired him to make a sublime counter-proposal.

"Would you take me to Favraux?"

"What?" said Diana confounded by such audacity.

"I already told you. I'm unarmed."

Diana repressed her wild delight. Her enemy was acceding to her own secret designs. Her restrained ferocity caused her answer to be delivered in a quivering voice:

"Yes! Follow me!"

283

Moments later, the small rowboat moved away from the quay. Jacques de Trémeuse stood in the middle of it. As large clouds gathered on the horizon to veil the Moon, his high stature dominated the brigands with whom he was about to engage in the ultimate fight for supremacy.

Cocantin had just had a long and mysterious consultation with Miss Torp. Leaving their hiding place, the detective advanced towards the harbor. With a worried expression on his face, he watched the small boat move towards the *Eaglet*. He entrusted his deductions to his American friend.

"It's her! It's that Monti woman, I'm sure of it. She's taken him, She must have tricked him just as she tricked me! The swine! Daisy, I have to do something! When I saw Judex climb in that rowboat, it was like seeing the departure of Napoleon for St. Helena. I have the premonition that disaster awaits my friend. And there's no way to reach him. I can't take a ferry. I don't have a dinghy, a canoe or even a raft. If only I had learned how to swim!"

Hearing these words. a mischievous expression formed on Daisy's pretty face.

"Do you like this Judex?" she asked.

"He has a brave heart!" said Cocantin sincerely.

"Well, don't fret!" declared the fearless American. "I'll free him. Leave it to me. I'm sure that I'll succeed."

The charming lady removed her hat, her coat, her dress and her shoes. On the pier, she was attired only in the same black silk bathing suit that she wore in lieu of an undergarment, a common practice among American swimmers.

"Daisy, what are you doing?" questioned the detective.

"I'm rescuing Judex," announced the swimmer just before executing a masterly dive in the sea. She swam towards the brig-schooner which was awaiting Jacques de Trémeuse.

"If you save him," yelled Cocantin, "I'll make you my wife!"

"I accept your proposal!" shouted Daisy back.

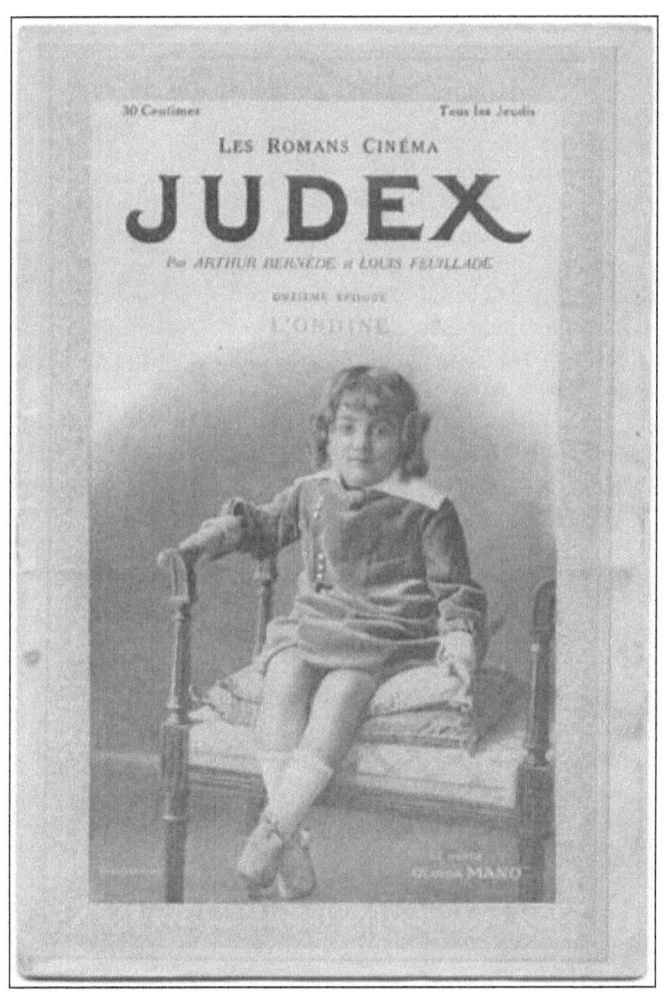

Part Eleven: The Water-Sprite

I. Aboard the Eaglet

When Judex set foot on the brig-schooner, the *Eaglet*, he had not lost his admirable serenity. He showed no concern about walking defenseless into the den of his enemies.

Confident that his logic had convinced Diana Monti to surrender Favraux, Judex never doubted for an instant that a ransom agreement had been concluded. Unaware of the banker's restored sanity, Jacques de Trémeuse never feared for his own safety. He trusted in the success of the plan that he had so audaciously conceived and so energetically executed.

He was sustained by the immense love that he shared with Jacqueline. Their love already had accomplished a miracle that he had long believed impossible. Their romance had melted a heart that was once closed to any other feeling besides vengeance. The once stifled feelings of human kindness and Christian charity has been revived inside Madame de Trémeuse.

Judex's special education had indoctrinated him with mysticism. In the fervor of his passion, he drew into his soul the chivalry of another age and time. He believed that an invisible and tutelary power empowered his actions, watched constantly over him, and was ready to protect him against the attacks of his enemies.

At this moment, he was no longer the patient and secret judge that surrounded himself with safeguards, subterfuges and disguises to conceal his identity and actions. He was solely an apostle of love who desired to successfully romance the essential woman in his life.

As soon as he was on the bridge, Diana Monti affected a courteous deference that was almost timid. She approached Judex and pointed to a stairway that led inside the boat.

"I must descend to the banker's cabin while you wait here. I have to prepare Favraux to accept your presence and my decision that he should accompany you. That will be difficult, but you can rely on me. We are in complete agreement. You found the best solution to our dispute."

Diana summoned the captain who had been lurking in the shadows. She demonstrated her total authority over the leader of the smugglers.

"Martelli, escort Monsieur Judex to my cabin. Don't give any orders concerning him before conferring with me."

More and more certain that his negotiations with the outlaws had been fruitful, Judex followed the captain. Meanwhile, the adventuress sought out Moralès. Dressed as a sailor, he been hiding behind a rope pile during the docking of the dinghy that had brought back Diana Monti and Jacques de Trémeuse. Kerjean's son had instantly recognized Judex. Whatever his surprise, he had carefully decided not to intervene. He dreaded both the tyranny of his demanding mistress and the resourcefulness of his infernal nemesis.

Moralès was anxious to hear the explanation of this new enigma. Once Diana was near his side, he questioned her.

"What happened?"

Rather than provide an explanation, she forcefully reprimanded him.

"Be quiet!

Seizing Moralès by the arm, Diana pulled him into an isolated corner where she proceeded to speak in whispers. More than ever the slave of this terrible woman, Moralès was satisfied to react to the words of his mistress with nods of approval. Both of them disappeared below deck into the cabin reserved for Favraux.

Having recovered all his intellectual faculties since his moving encounter with Jeannot, the banker had again succumbed to depression. Nevertheless, he had been succored by the certainty that he had regained his freedom as well as by the anticipation of being reunited with his daughter and grandson. With a feverish impatience, he awaited the results of the mission entrusted to Diana Monti. Favraux considered the ex-governess his liberator. Fueled by gratitude, his excessive passion for her had returned.

"Did everything go well?" he asked upon the entry of the adventuress and Moralès into his cabin.

"My friend," say the ex-governess, "I can tell you that both your daughter and Jean are safe. There is no cause for concern, but you won't see them tonight."

"Why?" The banker's face darkened.

"Because your daughter never received your letter."

"Did your envoy contact her?"

"No!"

"Why?"

"He was prevented from doing so."

"By whom?"

"By Judex."

"Always this man!" shouted Favraux.

"Don't torment yourself, my friend," said Diana. "Your situation is better, much better. If you fell ill again, I wouldn't be able to help you recover your lost fortune. Calmly listen to me. You shall soon notice that all goes well."

Reassured by the seductive words of the perfidious creature, Favraux took her hand.

"You are my loyal friend. You proved it to me. I will not forget."

Lowering her eyes, Diana behaved with false modesty.

"My brother and I were only too glad to snatch you out of your enemy's clutches. For my part, I am amply rewarded by your presence close to me."

"Thank you! My friend! Thank you with all my soul!" said Jacqueline's father. "You're right, my dear friend. I must be calm... very calm. My mind is not yet whole. There are gaps in my reasoning. I must let you guide me. Continue, I beseech you."

With a Machiavellian dexterity, the adventuress was enacting a plan that she had conceived during her confrontation with Judex on the pier.

"I must repeat. Madame Jacqueline Aubry and Jeannot are perfectly safe! Judex recently brought them to Sainte-Maxime. They are living in his villa. He sees to all their needs, but he's using them as hostages."

"They must be freed."

"My brother and I are devoted to that outcome."

"Judex is a terrible opponent."

"He no longer is to be dreaded."

"How so?"

"He's in our hands."

"What are you saying?"

"Judex is here. He's in Captain Martelli's cabin. Judex arrived at the harbor to bargain for your ransom. He offered me a million francs to return you to him. I pretended to agree. Believing that I have yielded to his arguments, he did not hesitate to follow me aboard the *Eaglet*."

"I want to see him!" demanded Favraux imperiously.

"You're sure about this?"

"Absolutely."

"I didn't wanted to upset you." declared the adventuress hypocritically.

"I want to see him!" insisted Favraux. "I demand it."

"Very well. I shall take you."

"Right away!"

"As you wish. However, my friend," insinuated the clever schemer, "let me warn you against the deceit of this man. He'll lie about my brother and me. He'll seek to smear us in your eyes. He'll unleash the most cowardly slander."

"Rest assured, I'll know how to answer him."

"He's very skillful."

"I don't fear him," asserted the banker. "Both of you will be here to defend me."

The adventuress was sure of her influence over Favraux.

"Henceforth, Judex belongs to you," she said. "He's at your mercy. I could have gotten rid of him straight away, but I wanted to give you the satisfaction of personally taking your revenge. It's now your turn to pronounce the verdict, your turn to be merciless. Your judgment will be faithfully executed."

The ex-governess ascended the heights of hypocrisy.

"Be aware, my friend, that if you want to live peacefully with your family, Judex must disappear from the face of the Earth."

"He must indeed," confirmed the banker.

"You must be without pity."

"I will be!"

Dominated by the infernal woman, the banker felt his instinctive brutality revive in him.

"He will die! Yes, he will die! My only regret is that I can't strangle him with my bare hands."

"Come!" said the adventuress. Her face triumphantly radiated evil.

II. Truth and Deceit

Assured of her success, Diana Monti was about to deliver the supreme assault with all the cynical composure of a poker player holding a royal flush. Opening the door of the cabin where Judex waited, she made a theatrical announcement.

"Monsieur Favraux, here's your tormentor. Here's the man who holds your daughter hostage."

Hearing these words, Judex replied only with an ironic smile. He deduced everything that had transpired. The adventuress had unleashed her counterattack. This development didn't totally displease him. Judex didn't display the least worry in his retort.

"The battle is joined" he said. "So be it."

Judex's noble demeanor contrasted with the wild hatred of Jacqueline's father.

"Monsieur," Judex told Favraux, "this woman's assertions are false. Madame Jacqueline Aubry and her son are not my hostages. I merely offered them the hospitality of my home where they are perfectly safe. My intention was not to imprison them, but to shield them from the criminals intending to murder both of them." He forcefully pointed at Diana and Moralès who had followed Favraux into the cabin. "These are the real criminals."

"I won't lower myself into giving a denial," replied the adventuress.

"I accuse you, Marie Verdier," resumed Judex, "and your lover, Robert Kerjean..."

"My lover!" laughed the ex-governess.

"Yes, your lover!"

"Enough!" interrupted Favraux. "I know only one thing. You're accusing those who restored my liberty and saved my life."

"If you don't believe me," declared Judex, "come with me to Sainte-Maxime. Your daughter will tell you that I decided to release you. You will also hear my accusations against these two ruffians."

"I won't go with you!" shouted the gilded merchant.

"Why?"

"Because I won't fall into the trap that you've set."

"I haven't set any trap!" exclaimed Judex. "The proof is that I only came here with a checkbook. In exchange for your liberty, I was ready to pay a million francs to this woman. She actually holds you in her power. She will commit any crime to steal your fortune."

"I don't believe you!" proclaimed the banker completely under the spell of the infernal temptress.

"If your daughter was here," argued Judex, "she would shout the truth at you."

"Really!" roared Favraux. "I look forward to that."

"Yes," interjected Diana, "she'll be here soon."

"If you recovered your sanity, Favraux," said Judex, "you should understand that your daughter's place isn't with these people. Besides, she'll never get this far. These miscreants will find some way to kill her en route."

"You see," noted Diana, "he can't prove anything he says. If Judex wants you, it's not to reunite you with your daughter, but to lock you again into another inescapable prison. He hoped to buy you with a million, but he didn't count on my devotion to you. Now, my friend, you have in your hands all the pieces of the puzzle. It's your turn to judge. Condemn him! Just as we are here to protect you, we are here to avenge you!"

"Favraux!" shouted Judex, "can't you see that this woman breathes only lies and crimes?"

Addressing Moralès, Judex continued vehemently:

"And you, Robert Kerjean, you know the truth. I saw you shamefully beg for forgiveness in the arms of your father. In front of me, you swore that you would once again be an honest man. You're insane to place yourself again in the power of this woman, You should help me make the truth prevail against her lies. Instead, you are descending the ladder of crime until you reach the last rung of damnation. You think that you're her accomplice, but you're merely her blind instrument. This miserable sinner will drive you to the guillotine!"

On hearing this diatribe, Moralès grew pale. Was it anger or shame? Judex didn't have the time to notice.

Pulling a whistle out of her pocket, Diana made a sharp noise. Before Judex could defend himself, Martelli and two sailors burst into the cabin. The trio treacherously grabbed Jacques de Trémeuse. They tied him to the central post supporting the cabin. Then they gagged him and put a thick, black, eyeless hood over his head, which served as a blindfold.

After giving a secret sign to the captain, Diana climbed back up onto the bridge with Favraux.

"What is your decision?" she asked the banker.

Before hearing his response, she hammered home her arguments:

"You know that I'm right! This man is a demon incarnate. Now that he's in our power, no one will be able to save him. We will make him undergo, increased by a hundredfold, all the sufferings that you endured."

"Marie!" shouted Jacqueline's father. He was completely dominated by the bewitching she-devil.

Favraux ceased speaking. Broken by emotion, he staggered. He leaned on the boat's rail.

"I wonder if I'm dreaming. Maybe I'll awake suddenly in that awful prison where I almost went mad. Marie... it's awful... awful!"

"You can rest, my friend. Sleep soundly. Your awakening will not be disrupted by any unfortunate surprise. Far from it! You will find me at your bedside, smiling with and only thinking of my devotion to you."

She showed him the sailors being directed by the captain to drop the sails in preparation for departure. Diana talked to the banker with a seductive voice that concealed her unfathomable perversity.

"We'll take Judex out to open sea where we can safely settle accounts with him. Then we'll return to search for your daughter and grandson. Go, my friend, go. Let this night be the sweetest of your life. It shall be the preview of the pure happiness that we shall share together!"

The banker's trembling lips skimmed Diana's forehead. She escorted him to his cabin. Leaving him on the threshold, she gave him a kiss.

Climbing back onto the bridge, she made a cynical announcement.

"Let's go! All is well! Now we'll be able to act undisturbed!"

She went to Moralès who was standing behind a empty chest.

"What are you doing?" she said roughly.

"I'm waiting."

"For what?"

"For you to finish your love duet with Favraux!"

"I shall ignore your stupid jokes. You know our goal. We must attain it by any means. So be quiet."

"I said nothing."

"But your thoughts challenge my authority."

"Nevertheless, Diana, I have served you well in this enterprise. This time, you have no reason to criticize my actions."

"I admit that you behavior was adequate," said the adventuress.

"At last!"

"However, when Judex talked to you abour your father, you became pale. You began trembling so much that I thought that you were going to crack again. Also I wonder…"

"What?"

"Nothing!"

"Say what's on your mind."

"Do have the guts to throw Judex overboard?"

"Judex again. Diana, you will drive me…"

"…To the guillotine?"

"No, to Hell!"

"There's no more time for eloquence, my little Moralès. Can I count on you?"

"You know you can."

"Then I love you!"

One long kiss sealed this infamous pact as the *Eaglet* sailed into the night.

As the clouds shifted to reveal the bright Moon, different people witnessed the slow movement of the boat.

Having seen Miss Torp execute her masterly dive, Cocantin remained on the pier. The bold swimmer moved towards the brig-schooner. Never before had Cocantin regretted his inability to swim.

The detective thought of the joys that he missed by not accompanying his beloved on this watery raid. He also weighed the risks that she was taking to assist Judex.

"It's clearly idiotic for parents not to teach their children to swim!" he ranted. "No diploma should be granted to a person who can't swim. No one should be allowed to run for public office if they can't swim. The government should impose a fine of 500 francs on anyone who can't swim."

Cocantin gazed with despair upon Daisy's discarded hat, coat and shoes.

"Why don't I know how to swim? Why?" Suddenly another question rose inside his troubled mind. "And the Emperor? Did he know how to swim? With all his courage and audacity, he couldn't escape from St. Helena. Since he didn't do that, he must not have known how to swim."

Somewhat consoled by this illustrious example, he spoke with resignation. "If only I had known that my rendezvous would be foiled by water!"

Meanwhile, in a window on the upstairs floor of the Trémeuses' villa, two women watched the boat in the bay. They were Jacqueline and Madame de Trémeuse. Jacques's failure to return had deeply troubled them.

They didn't exchange their suspicions. They didn't want to frighten each other. Yet the same alarming thought invaded their minds. Jacques must have fallen into a trap!

They used powerful binoculars and saw the rowboat approach the anchored boat. With the clouds no longer obscuring the Moon, Jacqueline had spotted the characteristic profile of Judex illuminated by the silvery light. She couldn't stifle a cry of surprise.

"I see him!"

"My son?"

"Yes, Jacques."

"Where?"

"In a small rowboat next to the schooner. Maybe my father's kidnappers are holding him there? Monsieur Jacques must be searching for him…"

Quickly Madame de Trémeuse took the binoculars, but the rowboat had already disappeared behind the schooner. "I see nothing," she declared.

"Perhaps I was fooling myself," said the banker's daughter.

When the *Eaglet* dropped its sails and slowly made a majestic wide turn, Jacqueline had a premonition of the truth. She felt her heart ache. It seemed that this boat was stealing all her hopes.

"God... save him... protect him," prayed Jacqueline.

Dark and silent, the daughter of the Orsinis contemplated the sea.

III. Cocantin's Fiancée

Miss Daisy Torp was one of those women whose courage knew no bounds.

The reader must have noticed that the history of this charming lady has, until now, only been sketched despite the important and even decisive role that she shall play in this narrative. To do justice to her beauty and bravery, her full history will now be provided.

Daisy Torp was the only daughter of a rich industrialist from Chicago. Destined to inherit an immense fortune in the United States, she had been groomed by her parents to be the bride of some important European nobleman whose lofty title was likely offset by a depleted bank account. Her extremely independent character rebelled against this fate. Instead, she indulged her enthusiasm for athletic sports.

Not only could Daisy Torp swim like an undine, but she also rode a horse like a jockey, piloted an automobile like a professional racer, and handled a sword like d'Artagnan. A financial disaster had ruined her parents. Her father found a modest job in a bank to support his twilight years. Daisy became a typist at a movie studio. She only worked there eight days.

She was thirsty for the freedom to travel. The restraints of working on a typewriter from 9 a.m. to 6 p.m. depressed her.

She made a grand resolution. "I want to leave for Europe to make my fortune. With my talents and energy, I cannot fail."

With her parents' blessing and her small savings, Daisy Torp booked passage on a steamship bound for Saint-Nazaire.

Rather than exploiting her beauty for easy profit, the young American was determined to achieve success through hard work.

An extremely practical businesswoman, she had not taken this decision blindly. Daisy had a precise plan based on her phenomenal athletic talents acquired during her former opulence. Once in Paris, she quickly began to implement her strategy.

First, in order to gain publicity, she entered the swimming race scheduled along the Seine from Charenton to Point-du-Jour. Beating by 20 strokes Toto Lemoine, the famed English swimmer, she finished first. In a single stroke, she had broken all records to win the World Championship.

Some days later, she won a second victory, no less stunning, in a famous car race in the Auvergne. Maneuvering her vehicle along the dangerous curves of a difficult course, she successively passed all her opponents.

The career of Daisy Torp was launched without paying a penny for advertisements. Then she opened a fencing school for women at the Boulevard Malesherbes in Paris. Students flowed in droves to enroll.

Yielding to the entreaties of the manager of a big Parisian circus, she accepted a large fee to perform nightly iat that famous establishment. Her death-defying dives gave the audience an extreme case of goose bumps. This was her ultimate consecration. All alone in France, Miss Daisy Torp had prevailed.

Deciding to take a vacation on the Mediterranean, the accomplished American had been spotted by Prosper Cocantin as she reveled in the blue waves like an exquisite and svelte water-sprite.

Such was the woman who, prompted by her devout love for the detective, had not hesitated to rush to the rescue of his friend, Judex.

She swam gently and silently in the water in order not to attract the attention of the rowboat's occupants. When they had reached the brig-schooner, she had observed the passengers from the sidelines. Once everyone had set foot on the bridge, and the dinghy had been moored to the ship, Daisy swam close to the *Eaglet* in order to climb aboard.

How to execute this feat without attracting attention?

Daisy was not a woman to remain indecisive for long. She grabbed the end of a rope hanging from the ship's rail. Holding it with a vigorous grip, she placed her feet against the hull of the *Eaglet*. She hoisted herself to the height of the bridge when voices from the interior reached her ears.

She heard the name pronounced by Cocantin: "Judex!"

A porthole was opened very close to her. She quickly approached it and looked inside. Thus she observed the confrontation between Judex, Favraux, Diana and Moralès. Clinging patiently to the rope against the side of the boat, she fully understood the sinister implications of the dramatic meeting. She saw Judex bound and gagged to the post. When the criminals left the cabin, Daisy realized that it was up to her to free Cocantin's friend. She formulated a plan to deliver Judex from his enemies.

With infinite care, she climbed alongside the ship's rail. Staying vigilant, she reached the portside and cast her eye on the bridge. The back of the ship was deserted. Located there was the cabin where Diana and her accomplices had secured Jacques de Trémeuse. Assembled in the front of the vessel, all the sailors listened to their captain's orders. On the other side, Favraux and Diana seemed to be having an intimate conversation. Miss Torp also spotted Moralès hiding in the shadows.

She didn't hesitate. With an athletic leap, she landed on the bridge. With the nimbleness of a panther, she reached the stairway to the cabin. As she descended the steps, a possible obstacle flashed through her mind. *What if they've locked the door?*

She soon breathed a sigh of relief. Believing themselves undetected and their victim securely bound, the criminals had no thought to take that extra precaution. Promptly, the young woman opened the door. Waking straight to Judex, she removed the black hood covering his head. Seeing this unexpected vision of a damp woman in a black bathing suit, Judex was taken aback. His surprise turned to hope when Daisy Torp identified herself.

"Don't be afraid. I'm Cocantin's fiancée. I'm here to rescue you."

Daisy recognized that time was critical. She couldn't afford a lengthy explanation. Right away, she searched for an instrument to cut the ropes binding the prisoner. Not spotting anything immediately, she became frustrated. Then, she spotted an alcove inside the cabin containing the captain's bed. Hanging from a coat rack was a leather jersey with two wide pockets. Searching the pockets, Daisy found a knife and a gun.

"All right! Now everything will work out."

Returning toward Judex, she hurried to remove his gag and cut his bonds. Putting on the captain's jacket, she handed the gun to Judex.

"I'll keep the knife," she said. "This way we'll both be able to defend ourselves."

Scarcely had she had pronounced these words than a sound came from the stairway.

"Someone's coming!" said Judex. After nearly losing his life, Jacques was once more ready to engage his enemies. He concealed himself in a corner. The door opened revealing Moralès. After consulting with the *Eaglet*'s captain and Diana Monti, he had come to check on the prisoner.

Kerjean's son didn't even have time to yell. Scarcely had he set foot in the cabin than Judex jumped him. With the butt of the gun, the avenger delivered a tremendous blow to Moralès' temple. Diana's lover staggered. Losing consciousness, he fell into the arms of Jacques de Trémeuse. Removing his cloak, the son of Julia Orsini fastened it around the unconscious criminal's shoulders.

"Mademoiselle Torp, help me tie this rascal to the post."

Daisy was delighted to find herself allied with a man who was a sportsman in every sense of the world. Moralès was quickly bound and gagged in Judex's place. Judex placed the same black hood that Diana had employed as a cruel refinement over his enemy's head. The ropes looped around Moralès pressed the cloak over the front of his body. His sailor clothes couldn't be discerned.

Judex counted the cartridges in the gun.

"Thanks to your opportune intervention, Mademoiselle, I shall soon be in command of the *Eaglet*. You didn't tell me your name?"

"Miss Daisy Torp."

"I suspect that we shall have other visitors. We must hide. Follow me, Miss Torp."

"Yes, captain!" said the young American, smiling.

Judex went into the alcove that contained Captain Martelli's bedroom. Dressed in Martelli's jacket, Cocantin's fiancée was behind him. With a sense of legitimate pride, she breathed a sigh of relief.

"If my dear Prosper was here, he would say that we've turned a corner. Yes, a tight corner!"

IV. Honorable Revenge

While Moralès had gone to execute her orders only to be ambushed, Diana leaned against the ship's rail and congratulated herself on the success of her schemes.

Long had she lusted for Favraux's millions. The banker's wealth appeared no more than a distant mirage whose uncertain conquest was fraught with peril. Her tremendous efforts were about to bear fruit. The money was out there, very close to her. She only had to reach out and grab it. No obstacle would stand between her and this colossal fortune, her heart's desire.

The sails of the *Eaglet* were inflated by the breeze as her thoughts focused on the future.

Judex will shortly disappear in the sea. Tomorrow, I shall kill Jacqueline and her child. The half-mad Favraux will never suspect my roles in their deaths. Besides, once we are married, I can cause him to lose whatever sanity he has left. As for Moralès, despite his failures, he has served me well.

With a perverse exquisite delight that knew no bounds, an indefinable half-smile formed on her lips.

I enjoy being loved by a man who is a willing slave ready to risk his life for my kiss.

As she became engrossed in these reflections, the *Eaglet* continued to head for the open sea. Soon the coastal lights appeared in the distance only as tiny flashes.

Diana contemplated the sea which would soon be her silent partner in a murder. She then shifted her attention to the captain.

"Martelli! The moment has arrived to fully execute our bargain."

The Mediterranean pirate laughed before answering.

"I'm ready, but…"

"But what?"

"Doesn't this extra little task of yours merit me an additional bonus?"

"Didn't Moralès pay you?"

"2500 francs. All paid on time."

"So?"

"You'll soon be very rich. That fact alone should double my fee. This would net me a hefty profit that I don't need to share with my crew."

As the adventuress looked at him with an air of harsh contempt, Martelli continued:

"Lady, sending a man to the bottom of the sea is a separate job throughout all the corners of the world."

Anxious to liquidate her enemy, Diana was in no mood to haggle. Reaching into the pocket of her wool jacket, she pulled out a bundle of bills and handed them to the captain.

"I knew," said Diana sarcastically, "that we would fully understand each other. Thank you for your support." Then she asked: "Where's Moralès?"

"I saw him enter my cabin earlier," declared Martelli. "Do you want me to find him?"

"No, he's useless. His nerve must have failed. It's much better to ignore him. Now let's act."

Acting on her orders, the captain blew a whistle. Immediately, two men, two true buccaneers directly descended from the bloodthirsty pirates who infested the Mediterranean in centuries past, hurried to their chief.

"Fetch the prisoner, and do it quickly!" ordered Martelli.

With an alacrity that revealed their total servitude, the two sailors ran down the stairway to the cabin where, half an hour earlier, they had personally tied Judex to the central post.

Judex and Daisy remained hidden in the captain's bedroom as the sailors approached Moralès. They detached him from the post and climbed back up on the bridge. During the entire operation, the black hood had remained over Moralès' face.

Carrying their burden, the two sailors rejoined Diana and Martelli. The captain made only a simple gesture, but it was frightful in its implications. He designated the sea. Without the least hesitation, the two ruffians threw the bound man into the waves. The duo left in the company of their captain. They all had the air of men who had just performed a simple task.

Diana remained alone. She leaned over the ship's rail. Her crazed eyes fixed on the spot where the body disappeared. She gloated with a fierce joy.

"*Bon voyage*, Monsieur Judex! Enjoy your eternal rest. You thought yourself stronger than me, but I emerged the victor!" Her macabre laughter accompanied the last ripples in the water. "*Bon voyage*, Judex! *Bon voyage!*"

Suddenly, a shadow rose behind her. A hand clutched her shoulder. Abruptly the adventuress turned around. A cry of terror escaped from her throat. Judex stood before her! Dwarfing Diana with his height, his steely gaze crushed her spirit.

"You!" she gasped.

"Yes, it is I! Judex!"

"Who did I throw into the sea?"

"Your victim is your accomplice, Robert Kerjean, alias Moralès."

"Wretch! I shall have the last word. I am surrounded by loyal men. They won't let you murder me."

"We shall see," said Judex calmly.

"Help me! Help me!"

Martelli and his men rushed to her.

Holding the gun in his fist, Judex stood between them and Diana Monti.

"The first one to make a move," he announced unemotionally, "I'll blow out his brains."

The unexpected apparition of this amazing man who had just eluded death, with his bold attitude and admirable courage, overcame the smugglers. The crew of the *Eaglet* stood petrified. Hanging on to the ships rail, Diana was mad with fury.

Taking advantage of the effect that he had produced on these crude and savage seamen, Judex pointed at Diana, still foaming with rage.

"How much did this woman pay you to be her stooges?"

As they all remained silent, Judex moved his gun squarely on Martelli.

"Captain! Answer me!"

"5000 francs," said the *Eaglet's* captain whom Jacques de Trémeuse had easily bullied into submission.

"I shall pay you 50,000 francs plus a bonus of 1000 francs per man if you transfer your loyalty to me. Furthermore, I won't be asking you to murder anyone, but to help me save lives."

Hearing these words, a deafening clamor rose from the sailors impressed by the offer.

"Enough talk!" decreed Judex. "Choose!"

"What guarantee can you give us?" asked Martelli. The captain was dazzled by Judex's promises.

"I am Jacques de Trémeuse," said Judex, pulling his wallet out of his pocket. "I can give you a downpayment."

"That's acceptable," declared the pirate completely conquered.

"I can count on you?"

"Absolutely."

"And on all your men?"

"And on all my men."

"In that case, await my orders," concluded Judex authoritatively. He pointed to the vanquished Diana Monti. "I must settle accounts with Mademoiselle Monti first."

While Martelli and his delighted men returned to their duties on the ship, Jacques seized Diana by the arm.

"Come with me!"

"You'll kill me," said the wretched Diana.

"Come with me. Do as I say!"

With her head lowered in defeat, Diana allowed herself to be guided by Judex to the captain's cabin where Daisy awaited.

"Miss Torp," said Judex, "I entrust you with my prisoner. Watch her and make sure that doesn't attempt some dastardly move. I want to bring her back to shore alive."

Exhausted, Diana fell across a trunk. Not a single tear gushed from her eyes. Only the tightening of her features into a hellish grimace showed the agony plaguing this she-devil.

Now completely the master of the situation, Judex went back to the bridge and ordered the boat to return to shore.

The pirate captain hurried his crew to obey Jacques de Trémeuse. Martelli no longer had any desire to serve the interests of Diana Monti. His guiding principle was to sell himself to the highest bidder. Judex had immediately understood this salient fact and exploited it to make himself the master of the *Eaglet*.

I did well, he thought, *to follow my first inspiration. Jacqueline will be happy! I had done my duty by imprisoning his father. I shall fulfill my duty even more by returning him to her without being disloyal to my mother.*

While the boat sailed back in the direction of Sainte-Maxime, Jacques de Trémeuse went to the cabin of Favraux. He gently opened the door. Spread on a bunk, the banker seemed to rest calmly.

"Let's leave him," said Judex. "It's useless to disrupt his sleep."

As he was about to withdraw, the banker stood up on his bunk and made a hoarse cry. He sounded like a man in the grip of a terrifying hallucination.

"Him! Him! I see him! It's Judex! Judex!"

V. Judex!

"Yes, it is I, Judex," said Jacques de Trémeuse. He advanced towards the gilded merchant. Already terrified by the sight of his enemy, the banker felt his remaining sanity begin to slip away.

Judex spoke in a tone unknown to Favraux. The words of the self-styled judge were laced with the noblest mercy.

"Be calm, Monsieur Favraux, your worries are over. You no longer have to fear me. As I told you earlier, I have no intention of putting you back into a prison cell. Instead, you shall be returned to your family with the full freedom to act as you please. You should have listened to my declarations rather than the perfidious lies of Marie Verdier and her lover. Yes, her lover. You allowed yourself to be bound hand and foot by the falsehoods of these two scoundrels. You would have inadvertently sacrificed your daughter and grandson by luring them into a murderous ambush.

"This miserable temptress, Marie Verdier, alias Diana Monti, only wanted your millions. She would have engineered your death as soon as she came into possession of your fortune. When I was rendered defenseless by being tied to the post in the captain's cabin, she was convinced of the inevitability of her diabolical scheme.

"Favraux! Favraux! If you had only then looked on her face. It was a face of awesome hate, a face of deviltry triumphant, a face which shined with the glimmer of crime. If you had seen that face, you would have grasped the truth. Instead of reveling in the spectacle of my defeat, and the certainty of my death, you would have feared for yourself. You would have understood that it was really this woman who wanted to destroy you, and I who wanted to save you.

305

"Blinded by your resentment for me and your passion for this heartless creature, you observed the preparations for my death with a bestial ferocity. You were the guilty convict who was given the chance to punish with impunity the man who had sentenced him to life imprisonment.

"All your malicious desires, all your criminal instincts, that had previously dissipated due to the angelic and divine love of your grandson, were reborn. In a word, you reverted to being the greedy merchant, the brewer of merciless enterprises. You lowered yourself to the level of this loathsome adventuress. If she had put a knife in your hand amd told you to strike, you would have obeyed her, for your eyes reflected the same glimmer of crime. Yes, your eyes resembled hers. It's better that you failed. After savoring my fall, you would have become the unconscious executioner of your daughter and her child."

As Judex concluded his remarks, Favraux contemplated him with terror.

"God did not want these two innocents to be sacrificed to your cowardice and hate" Judex continued. "My chains were broken in time. I was saved despite Marie Verdier and despite you, Favraux! I shall now render my verdict. Don't tremble. I shall soon prove to you that you no longer have anything to fear from me."

"No! No!" screamed the banker wildly. "That's not possible!"

"Why isn't it possible?"

"Because I now know who you are."

"So?"

The gilded merchant bowed his head.

"Jacques de Trémeuse could never forgive me!"

"Of course," resumed Judex, "I had the right to be merciless. My brother and I felt heroic in our hatred of the man who killed our father and forever broke the heart of his loving wife, my caring mother. Nothing would have diverted us from the vengeance that we swore against you, if an angel had not come to your rescue."

306

"My daughter!" stammered the banker as he instinctively clasped his hands.

Due to the depth of emotion that Judex had demonstrated while pronouncing this last sentence, Jacqueline's father finally understood that his enemy was sincere. The banker no longer had anything to fear from him.

"Yes, your daughter!" stressed Jacques de Trémeuse. "While you await her confirmation of my accusations against the infamous Marie Verdier, let me describe your daughter. You never questioned your treatment of her. When she lived with you, you never deigned to cast a kindly glance towards her. You placed your own interests above hers. You only viewed her in the context of your financial ventures. You used her as a pawn to further your business successes. You were ready to relinquish her to a wastrel whom you knew was saddled with debts. Worse yet, the bridegroom of your choice was a rogue also capable of any crime. When I rendered justice unto him, he was about to commit a murder."

Captivated by these powerful words, Favraux listened without interrupting.

"I speak the truth," continued Judex. "Once I free you in the name of your daughter and your grandson, you will act towards me and everyone else with full independence. I will do nothing, you hear me, absolutely nothing to mitigate the consequences of my leniency. Perhaps these two human beings, who value your welfare, can inspire you with the moral courage to live a peaceful existence. I hope for your sake, more than for the others, that you will devote the remainder of your life to remorse, redemption and righteousness."

With a wide gesture, Jacques de Trémeuse indicated the horizon that began to display the first fire of dawn.

"Favraux, a new day awaits you. Are you worthy of the light that it brings you? Do you merit the happiness that it shall give you? I will only say this: the punishment that you underwent is nothing in comparison to your crimes. I wish only one thing for those who love you, for those who you will

307

now finally love, that your punishment will placate God as it has placated me."

Distressed by these words, the gilded merchant found himself conquered by a new, unknown feeling. Touched by regrets, he now understood what he had been, and what he should have been.

"If only I had known..." he whispered.

Meanwhile, lying on a bench in the cabin of Captain Martelli, Diana Monti had not ceased displaying the symptoms of a deep depression. She remained under the supervision of Miss Daisy Torp. Faithful to the mission entrusted to her by Judex, the American swimmer never took her eyes off the prisoner. Diana did not speak or move. Holding her head between her hands, as if she was afraid to look at the American, she was content to merely moan occasionally.

Thus the adventuress gave the impression of a woman resigned to her fate. She seemed incapable of offering any opposition because despondency had rendered her passive.

However, this tigress had not been tamed. She concentrated her thoughts on a unique goal: to escape Judex. The clever creature hadn't been dejected for long. In fact, a plan had already hatched inside her mind.

I will employ the same trick to escape from this boat that served me well at the mill of Les Sablons. Once the Eaglet *is close enough to shore, I will find a way to outwit my jailer. I will quickly climb to the bridge. Without hesitating, I will dive into the sea. I'm a rather good swimmer who can pull her weight. But what should I do after reaching land? I'll worry about that later... It's essential now to pull the enemy's claws. How to get rid of my jailer?*

Right away, Diana Monti realized that she was dealing with a formidable opponent. A frontal assault was out of the question. First, Diana probably wasn't the stronger adversary. Second, the noise of the fight would certainly attract Judex's attention. Third, the defection of Captain Martelli and his crew meant that she could count on no one else to defend her.

A ruse needed to be devised. Even on the boat with all the obstacles facing her, the ex-governess was confident of her success. Her plan was quickly conceived. All that remained was to execute him.

With an extraordinary calm, and an astonishing self-control that showed that she was still dangerous and in possession of all her criminal faculties, the adventuress calculated the time when the brig-schooner would be at a reasonable distance from the shore.

Once she was convinced that the ship was no more than 300 meters from the shore, she rose and pretended to be suffering from a sudden and irresistible pain. Touching her throat, her mouth contracted; her eyes contorted; foam formed on her lips.

"I can't breathe… I can't!…Help me… I'm dying."

Whirling in a dizzy trance, Diana collapsed heavily on the cabin floor. Daisy Torp instinctively rushed towards her. It was the instant that the she-devil had been waiting for.

When the American leaned towards her, Diana struck like a panther. Delivering a vigorous head butt into the middle of Daisy's chest, Diana sent Cocantin's fiancée plunging backward into the garret. Surprised by this treacherous attack, Daisy had no time to sound an alarm.

Diana's nervous vitality was multiplied tenfold by her burning desire to escape Judex. As quick as a flash, she ran to the door, opened it, scrambled up the steps, and reached the bridge. Heading straight for the ship's rail, she climbed up on the edge. In an audacious dive, she disappeared into the waves.

However, Daisy Torp had swiftly recovered from Diana's attack. The American swimmer reached the deck the moment the head of adventuress slammed into the sea. Reaching the ship's rail, Daisy saw Diana swimming away from the *Eaglet* towards the shore. Without hesitating, Cocantin's fiancée lunged into the sea in pursuit of the escaped prisoner.

Diana hoped to win through speed. However, she soon noticed the splendid American swimmer gaining on her. Soon the women were no more than a few meters apart.

A vicious fight without mercy soon commenced. For Diana, in a desperate moment, had resolved to fight to the death.

The modern water-sprite reached the adventuress. The two grappled with each other. Diana's hands grasped Daisy's throat. She was going to strangle the American.

Locked in a deadly embrace, they disappeared as the waves closed over them.

Part Twelve: Love's Forgiveness

I. Cocantin's Anxiety

In the expectation of the return of his lady-love, Prosper Cocantin had remained at the harbor. As time passed, his concern had transformed gradually into the most nagging anxiety, especially when he had seen the *Eaglet* move away from the shore in a swift and silent maneuver.

What's going to happen to her? he thought. *She was beautiful when she swam like a fish. In fact she swam better than a siren, better than an undine. But it's impossible for her to follow this boat after the wind accelerates its speed. Some accident, like a cramp or a mental blackout, could result in a fatal disaster. If such a catastrophe befell Daisy, I could never forgive myself. It's my fault, absolutely my fault. Poor Daisy!*

Soon a beam of light, a true ray of hope, shone in Cocantin's spirit.

Parbleu! Reaching her destination, she would have wanted to see what was going to happen aboard this vessel. Being clever, she could have hidden herself on the boat.

As we have seen, the director of the Celeritas agency had guessed correctly. This time, his sense of the dramatic had not led him to an erroneous conclusion. Scarcely had this thought occurred to him, than his anxiety became sharper.

What if the boat is headed for India or America? Her only clothing is a bathing suit. The poor girl! She must be cold!

Contemplating Daisy's clothing in front of him, Cocantin shouted in exquisite innocence.

"If only I could mail her these! My little Daisy! My poor Daisy!"

Shivering with anguish, he began pacing down the quay. He despairingly muttered to himself.

"My parents were guilty of not teaching me to swim. If not for that, I would have been with her. Instead, I'm hanging around here. It's freezing. I feel like a penguin! Everyone says that the Midi is always very hot. What legend! As soon as the sun disappears, a chill bites through your shoulders. What cold nights! Brrr! I have to walk to remain warm. I'm frozen, literally frozen. My poor little Daisy! How is she going to survive this cold!

"In cold fact, it's I who needs to worry about survival! What a night, my friends, what a night! I would be better in y bed. To thinks that I came here for an amorous rendezvous. It should have been a beautiful tryst." He sneezed twice. "I'm pinched. Tomorrow my nose will flow like a fountain. I'm catching a cold!"

Prosper Cocantin has a severe dread of the common cold. Faced with this affliction, the most famous doctors recognized their powerlessness. This pestilence has emerged victoriously over science past, present, and probably future. For Cocantin, the common cold assumed the proportions of an irreparable disaster.

Doubtless, the subtle microbe that so cleverly escapes all the attacks of the medical profession, found in Cocantin's nose a spacious refuge where it could, in complete security, perpetuate a large family. Often it took advantage of the generous hospitality involuntarily offered by Cocantin's nasal cavities. Sometimes, for several weeks, Ribaudet's wretched successor seemed to be transformed into a fountain whose continuous outpouring cost the detective half a dozen handkerchiefs.

Cocantin sneezed twice more. "I'm poisoned here. It's unbelievable. Why do we have doctors? There's not a single way to rid me of this abomination. What new Pasteur will deliver us from this blight? I'm not rich, but I would give 10.000 francs to the man who manages to eradicate the common cold." He sneezed. "What filth! It's disgusting!"

A sudden gush of wind sent Cocantin's cap rolling into the sea. The growing bald spot on his scalp was now exposed.

"I didn't need this! Now I'll be bedridden not for three weeks but six months." He continued to sneeze. In order to protect himself from the cool air, the distraught Cocantin put on the hat that Daisy had abandoned. The wind continued to harass him. Having already tied his fiancée's *chapeau* around his chin, Cocantin didn't hesitate to wear the clothing that she had discarded before diving into the sea. Dressed in this manner, he continued to pace on the pier. As he shivered, sneezed, groaned and grumbled, he uselessly probed the dark horizon with his binoculars. He was determined to remain there until Daisy's return.

In the early dawn hours, a young man and a small boy arrived on the pier. The youngster rushed towards Cocantin.

"Wow! Coconut, you're dressed like a shepherdess. Let me admire your costume."

In a comical pose, the Licorice Kid scrutinized Prosper Cocantin. In his odd, improvised attire, the detective looked like a participant in one of those grotesque carnival parades held on the Côte d'Azur.

Roger de Trémeuse joined them. Despite his anxiety over his brother's continued absence, he couldn't repress an exclamation of joyous astonishment.

"Monsieur Cocantin, why are you disguised? Are you shadowing some criminal?"

"Not at all," rectified Cocantin as he continued to sneeze. "I passed the night on this pier, to await my… my fiancée."

"Your fiancée?"

"A charming American, Miss Daisy Torp. I love her and she loves me."

"Coconut," observed the Licorice Kid impishly, "you've been keeping secrets from us. This is great news!"

The detective explained.

"I've just been through a very cruel ordeal. It's painfully cold. The wind blew my cap into the sea. I started to catch a cold. So I put on my fiancée's hat and clothing to keep warm."

"She's running around in her underwear?" said a gawking Roger.

"Well, yes," asserted the detective. "She dived into the water to chase the rowboat that took your brother to that schooner. It was called the *Eaglet*. I saw its name through the binoculars."

"What are you saying?" exclaimed Roger. Judex's brother wondered if Cocantin had gone insane. The Licorice Kid had the same concern, but he expressed it in very blunt language.

"Are you crazy? Has the cold made you a numbskull?"

"*Au contraire*, I have all my faculties," asserted Cocantin gravely. The detective assumed his customary Napoleonic solemnity. "Monsieur Roger de Trémeuse, I have important revelations for you."

The director of the Celeritas Agency gave Judex's brother a detailed account of the events of which he had witnessed during the preceding night. Interrupted by constant sneezing, he praised the bravery and loyalty of Daisy Torp. Cocantin finished with a sentence that he felt equaled the inscriptions on Napoleon's Tomb:

"I know Miss Torp has done her best. As for me, I regret to not have done more."

Roger had listened with undivided attention. He viewed the situation as extremely serious. Despite his brother's prudence and valor, Roger wondered if Judex's offers had been rebuffed by the banker and the others aboard the *Eaglet*. Had Diana Monti decided to exploit the situation in order to eliminate a dangerous opponent?

"Whatever the courage of this young American woman, Cocantin, I doubt that, if my brother was in danger, she would be able to help him."

Roger's heart ached at the possibility that the admirable being that was Judex had possibly succumbed at the moment when he was going to realize his sublime mission of love and clemency.

Suddenly the Licorice Kid cried out. Having borrowed Cocantin's binoculars, he noted an important development on the horizon.

"There's a ship coming!"

Cocantin looked through the binoculars. "I recognize it. It's the *Eaglet*. They have returned. They are safe. Safe! I'm so happy!"

Prosper Cocantin began executing a frantic dance in his strange outfit. He then resumed his vigil with the binoculars.

Once the *Eaglet* had thrown its anchor within distance of the pier, a rowboat left it. The profile of Judex could be seen standing in the middle of the small boat. Seated in the back was a man lost in deep melancholy with a trace of fear. He was the banker Favraux, Jacqueline's father. When the sailors had moored the dinghy to the quay, Judex signaled to Favraux. The banker docilely followed him.

Cocantin rushed towards Judex. "And my fiancée? Where is she?" he shouted.

Hearing these words, Judex shuddered.

"Miss Torp, to whom I owe both my freedom and my life, swam in pursuit of Diana Monti who had fled into the sea."

"Did she return?"

"No, but be calm. I sent a small boat to search for her. I'm sure that it will find your valiant fiancée."

The terrified Cocantin could no longer listen to Judex. Followed by the Licorice Kid, Cocantin ran towards the rowboat. The Kid was thrilled to be part of this new adventure.

"Take me over there!" insisted Cocantin. "I want to look for Daisy. I want to help her."

"Do what he wishes," ordered Judex.

Captain Martelli, who had remained in the small boat, obeyed. While the oars of the *Eaglet*'s sailors rowed away from the wharf, Favraux was escorted by Judex and his brother to the Trémeuses' villa.

II. Towards the Ultimate Test

During the journey, not a word was exchanged between the two brothers and Jacqueline's father. As they approached the villa, the banker became more and more hesitant. Not completely released from the hypnotic influence that Diana Monti exercised over him, a question remained in the far corner of his mind. What if she was right? As he reviewed that question, his mind began to be plunged back into a captivity from which nothing could release it. Would Judex cast him once more into the horrible cell of the caverns of the Chateau Rouge?

Upon arriving at the front gate of the Trémeuse property, Favraux recognized Pierre Kerjean behind the bars. The old man had waited for the return of Judex. A feeling of insurmountable dread overcame the banker.

"My jailer!"

"No, Favraux," gently reassured Jacques. "This isn't a trap. I've already told you. We have forgiven you."

Although his soul still wrestled with the acceptance of such a sublime clemency, the banker allowed himself to be guided by Jacques and Roger into the house. Judex courteously showed him an armchair in the parlor.

"Please sit, Monsieur Favraux, I will inform your daughter that you're here."

Restraining his emotions, Judex withdrew. Favraux, remained alone. Judex's last sentence vibrated through his ears. *"I will inform your daughter that you're here."*

Everything was true! He was free! Free! He was going to recover his strength and influence. His gold beckoned him once more. In this burst of impetuous selfishness, all the cupidity of his past reawakened, with an irresistible desire of ambition and revenge. Once more master of himself, he craved that tremendous lever that is wealth. He experienced an unspeakable exhilaration.

Forgetting all his past remorse, he plotted crimes to reestablish his financial domination with the same insolence that

317

had formerly been so devastating. Not only did he believe that he had recovered the power of the past, but he persuaded himself that he had never ceased being the gilded merchant, one of the kings of modern finance. This was a minute of joyous frenzy where he forgot all: families, friends and enemies. He forgot Diana, Judex and Kerjean, His sole contemplation was a sparkling river of gold that flowed towards his cash registers.

The door opened to admit Jacqueline holding Jean by the hand. She had replaced her mourning clothes with a simple white dress that enhanced her grace and tenderness. Her sight pulled the banker out of the moral drunkenness that had devoured him since Judex's departure.

"My daughter!" he cried.

"My father!" shouted Jacqueline. In a filial moment of love, she rushed towards Favraux, who had already embraced Jean.

On the threshold, Judex contemplated this reunion. He had wanted to view the joyful consequences of his clemency. Nevertheless, a cruel worry plagued him. But not having consulted the Comtesse de Trémeuse, he was unaware of her discussion with the banker's daughter.

When Jacqueline learns the truth, he wondered, *what will be her feelings towards me? Will she forgive me? Will she see in me only Judex, the man who struck down her father?*

He went to see his mother.

"Favraux is here," he said. "I left him with his children." His voice trembled slightly. "Now, we no longer have to wait for the supreme decision!

Madame de Trémeuse read her son's heart.

"I don't know what the banker will do," she said.

"It's unimportant." declared Judex nervously. "I just know that I've done my duty, my entire duty. I don't fear the consequences."

"I like this proud response," retorted Julia Orsini. "She is worthy of you, worthy of us. I must review my attitude towards this merchant. If he insists on challenging our family, I am ready to confront him openly. I am ready to accept, before all the world as well as God, the responsibility for my vengeance. However, I shall make a prediction. I have the absolute conviction that Favraux will dare nothing against us. For his daughter will always be there to forestall him."

"Really, Mother!" exclaimed Jacques of Trémeuse in a flight of exuberance. "You believe that Jacqueline will force her father to change?"

"I'm sure of it."

"What gives you such certainty?"

"Jacqueline knows all."

"My God!"

"She knows that Judex, Vallières and you are the same man."

"How?"

"With all the strength that I could muster, I revealed the truth to her. Jacqueline is fully cognizant of the feelings that she inspired in you."

"And, Mother…?" questioned Judex apprehensively.

The Comtesse de Trémeuse made a loving smile. Her face formed the charming and divine expression that belongs only to mothers. "I need only say one thing, my son. Jacqueline knows all, and she loves you."

"Mother!"

Such was the only word that gushed from Judex's lips in a jubilant cry.

"Yes, she loves you!" repeated Madame de Trémeuse. "Love is stronger than hate. This was written in Heaven, and I have no right to bear a grudge against God."

However, the face of Jacques darkened. The flame of hope in his eyes became extinct.

The Comtesse was surprised.

"What's wrong, my son? Why this sudden melancholy? What do you fear?"

Judex kept silent, but Julia Orsini insisted.

"Do you think that my maternal feeling has caused me to inadvertently exaggerate?"

"Mother, I have too much respect for you not to be convinced that everything you've said is an accurate reflection of reality…"

"Then what's the problem?"

"What about Favraux?"

Scarcely Judex had pronounced this name than a woman's cries interrupted them.

"Help! Help!"

Recognizing Jacqueline's voice, Judex rushed to the door. Followed by his mother, he entered into the parlor where he had left the young woman with her father. While the banker's daughter came towards him, conveying hopeless distress, Judex saw Favraux spread on a couch. He wasn't displaying any signs of life. A tearful Jean knelt praying next to him.

III. Redemption

"What happened?" asked Judex.

"My father seemed happy to be reunited with Jeannot and me," explained Jacqueline. "He started questioning us. Sitting on the couch, he was holding his grandson when, suddenly, he became very pale. His eyes contorted. His head oscillated. He fell over backwards. He remained there motionless. Despite all my efforts, I couldn't revive him." Jacqueline's eyes enlarged with terror. "I fear that he's dead!"

Judex approached the banker. He gently removed the child who kept repeating the same words over and over: "Grandpa, it's me, Jean. Answer me."

Leaning over the body, Judex placed his ear over the chest.

"It's only a fainting spell," he announced. "Be assured, Madame, that your father will live. I didn't return him to you so that he could leave again. There's no reason for concern."

Judex moved away. Jacqueline grabbed the hands of her father and rubbed them. As for Jean, he found refuge with Madame de Trémeuse. Placing the young boy on her knee, she consoled him.

320

As he promised, Jacques promptly returned. He had a flask containing a powerful restorative that he handed to Jacqueline.

"Have your father breathe this. There is no need for my mother and I to be here. It's better that he only sees you when he recovers. Assure him that he has nothing to fear from me. He is free, completely free."

The banker's daughter thanked Judex with a long glance that seemed to reflect her entire soul. While Jacques and his mother went away with Jean, Jacqueline unstopped the flask and placed it under the nostrils of her father. She made a sigh as his eyes half-opened and his lips stirred.

Some incoherent sounds gushed hoarsely from his throat as a mask of terror spread over his features. Soon, the sounds became words.

"Father, how do you feel?" asked Jacqueline. "Fear nothing. I'm here, next to you." Her harmonious voice vibrated sweetly in his ear. It appeared to calm the banker. His voice became less feverish.

"Is that you, Jacqueline?"

"Yes, Father, it's me. I'll never leave you again."

As she leaned over him, she seemed like an angel of redemption. This messenger of mercy consoled the sinner. "You no longer have anything to fear," she said. "Your terrible nightmare is over."

"Is that true?" murmured Favraux,

His tearful daughter smiled at him. "Yes, Father, it's true."

The face of the gilded merchant slowly relaxed. He began to accept the reality of his freedom. He wiped the sweat from his forehead.

"It's horrible! What I just endured. Horrible!"

"Be calm," counseled Jacqueline. "Rest."

"No. I must talk to you," implored the banker. "All the time we were together with Jean, an unspeakable malaise assailed me. I heard a ringing of bells. A funeral veil spread over my eyes. I didn't hear anymore. I didn't see anymore. Death was stalking me. My body seemed to be disintegrating. I had the hideous sensation that my soul was being taken away from me. My spirit was fleeing despite all my efforts to keep it. I experienced the same feeling once before, at the Chateau des Sablons. It was during your engagement dinner, just seconds before I was stuck down by the mysterious hand of Judex!"

Favraux spoke as if he was trapped in a empire of fear.

"I believed that I died for the second time!" The banker's face became pale. "I was certain Judex had played a cruel jest. I suspected that he dangled before my eyes the prospect of happiness only to cast me once more into the abyss. Was this a refinement of his cold-blooded vengeance? During my first pangs of consciousness, I feared awakening in an even more horrible prison than Judex's underground cell. Perhaps I was now condemned to the horrendous torture that he had initially reserved for me. I would find myself in a coffin, buried alive!"

"Father!"

"But it wasn't true. You were here. You *are* here. Your sweet words made me realize at last that I have nothing to fear from Judex, or anyone. Thank you, my child. Thank you with all my soul. I can completely confide in you. Where's Jeannot? Call him quickly. Yes, call him. We have to leave straight away. I don't have the right to remain any longer in this house, It belongs to the man who hates me. He released me only because you knew how to deflect his venom."

"Father, let me talk to you."

"Listen, my daughter, I beg you. I implore you. My mind is in turmoil. Any thought about my enemy contaminates my brain with nightmarish visions. I don't want to be driven mad. I want to keep all my faculties. I must restore to you and your son the beautiful life which we once had. Judex told me that, yielding to his mysterious threats, you had donated your inheritance to the Public Assistance."

"It's true!"

"I applaud your generous gesture. However, I have now recovered my freedom. As soon as we return to Paris, I shall assert my rights. My fortune shall be returned to me. Then we shall see if Jacques de Trémeuse dares to attack me again!"

"My father," resumed Jacqueline solemnly, "neither Jacques de Trémeuse, nor his mother, nor his brother, will ever do anything against you."

"But they will!"

"No. They have forgiven you. Their souls are appeased. I can vouch for them."

"That's well and good!" shouted the banker whose brutal selfishness still remained.

"I ask you not to take offense at what I am about to say," said Jacqueline. "I must now tell you my true feelings. Yes, I must unburden my heart. Despite my reluctance to offend you, my love for my child and my fellow man forces me to follow the dictates of my conscience. I must talk to you as a mother, a daughter and an honest woman."

"Speak," invited Favraux. His face began to resume his former expression of hardness.

The banker's daughter called upon all her courage.

"I won't judge you. Therefore, no reproach will escape my lips. In this hour, as in any other, I have the strict duty to remember that you're my father. Nevertheless, it's also my duty to warn you that I know how your fortune was accumulated."

"What are you saying?"

"I saw the stark proof of the means used for your enrichment. I know everything. Spare me the ordeal of repeating the details to you."

Favraux made an impatient gesture close to anger. Jacqueline, remaining divinely sweet and merciful, continued:

"I saw all the documents."

"How?" said the gilded merchant as he began to sweat.

"Vallières."

"He was the traitor!"

"He's also Jacques de Trémeuse."

"That was him!" yelled Jacqueline's father. "I understand how he was able to exercise his vengeance so easily.

323

He's very cunning, this Jacques de Trémeuse. Yes, very cunning, much more cunning than me."

The banker started to rant incoherently.

"What if I declare war on him? What if I decide to take the revenge to which I am entitled? Soon I will have recovered my power. When that happens, I will crush him as I crushed so many others. For I will neither be as weak nor as stupid as him. I will not retreat. I will not relinquish my weapons. I will not falter in the duel to the death between us. He may have pitied me, but I swear to have no pity for him!"

"Father!" screamed the young woman. She was incapable of restraining herself. "Father, have you forgotten everything?"

"So! You want to say something more?"

"Yes, I entreat you to forget his act of vengeance and remember only his gesture of forgiveness."

"Do you know how I suffered?"

"And him... And that poor woman, Madame de Trémeuse."

"You dare defend them!"

"I tell you father: I know everything! Every ounce of my being deplores the frightful hate that threw you against one another. Despite the ties of blood and affection that binds us, I can't forget that it was only you who provoked this feud!"

"You dare take a stand against me!"

"I'm protecting you from yourself."

"To vindicate himself in your eyes, Judex doubtlessly invented some idiotic history!"

"Do you deny that after trying to seduce his mother, you drove his father to suicide?"

"It's a lie."

"Father, are you provoking me into a debate from which you can never emerge victorious?"

"Jacqueline!"

"Calm down. Be reborn as a generous man of virtue."

"Be silent!"

The madness seized Favraux again. His eyes became red with blood. His whole body shook with rage.

"I want to see Judex. I want to speak him. I want to scream my hate at him. I want to kill him. Yes, kill him with my bare hands."

Rushing towards her father, Jacqueline screamed her agony.

"Do you want me to die?"

The plea from the soul of the heroic young woman produced an instantaneous reaction from the banker. He refrained from any further actions. He looked at his daughter without any fury in his face.

"Your death? No, no! I don't want that!"

He dropped into an armchair. His hands pressed against his head.

"I no longer know myself! I no longer know!"

Jacqueline rejoined him. Gently she sat close to him. Leaning against him protectively, she was determined to succeed in her tragic and sublime mission. She had undertaken to extract from the banker's ulcerated soul all the malign instincts that had made him a criminal. Gently, without violence, only using persuasion and kindness, she began her task. It was the noblest of tasks, the salvation of a father through his child.

"Listen to me, Father. There's no longer any need for harsh words between us. You're beginning to understand me. I see it. I feel it. You will understand me completely. Father, believe me, we can be so happy. Yes, so happy without this curse of gold, the cause of all your misfortunes and the reason for all my tears. My health has returned. I will be able to work. You are rejuvenated. After some rest, I'm sure that you will also want to work. We will go abroad to America. I don't doubt for a moment that, thanks to your admirable qualities of intelligence, energy and willpower, you will succeed in promptly rebuilding your fortune. It shall be as large as the first, but more solvent and enviable because it will be achieved by the most honorable means.

"It's not necessary that the banker Favraux reappear. Let him sleep for eternity in the tomb where the world believes him buried. You must be another man. I want a new father. Yes, a father that I can cherish and respect all at once; a father of which I have the right to be proud; a father for whom I will never have enough love; a father whom I want to be surrounded by the purest happiness during the lengthy years that remain in his life. Tell me quickly that you want the same thing as myself?"

At these words, the banker separated the hands that hid him the face. Jacqueline gave a shout of joy. She instantly recognized her victory.

In fact, not just remorse shined in the gilded merchant's eyes. They also reflected benevolence. He had been transformed completely into a new man, the new father so eagerly awaited.

In a long embrace, the redeemer and the redeemed mixed their tears in an intimate communion of their souls united by the shared feelings of duty and honor.

Then the banker spoke to appease his child:

"My daughter, I will never forget what you did for me. You did more than open my eyes, you healed my heart. Already I know how to be the good man of your dreams. I glimpse new joys that are infinitely superior to those sensations that trapped me in a revolving whirlwind. I understand the happiness that I noticed formerly, with a despising smile, on the face of the common man. I recognize the foolishness of ambition that left me always insatiable. I condemn and curse avarice from every corner of my being. Thanks to you, my soul has been illuminated by the true light. Be blessed, my child. You have nothing to fear from me. I recognize the full scope of my duty. Repair the past, remake the future, but always be in the right with justice and honor."

"Father, kiss me!" shouted Jacqueline. "I've never been so happy!"

After a long embrace of his daughter, Favraux was transfigured with the beauty of sincere penance and recovered honor.

"Now, my dear child, help me accomplish the first step of my pilgrimage of expiation." He looked at Jacqueline with paternal affection. "Take me to Judex. I must ask his permission to see Madame de Trémeuse!"

IV. Cocantin the Savior

"Let's go, my old Coconut. Don't fret. We'll find her. She's a duck that floats like a cork. The sea won't drown her."

With these words, the Licorice Kid consoled his friend as they took their places in *The Eaglet*'s rowboat in to search for the intrepid Daisy Torp. As the dinghy left the shore, the anxiety of the Celeritas Agency's director grew. Fastening his eyes to the binoculars, he scanned the beautiful horizon of the emerging dawn. He saw an empty sea. It was absolutely empty. There was no sign of Daisy. Not even the smallest wake of a swimmer was present on the waters. Cocantin became pale with the frozen face of anguish.

"She could have been pulled towards the high sea by some current. How horrible! The thought makes me sick. I'm going mad!" He questioned the sailor at the helm. "Are there a lot of currents near here?"

The helmsman was an old sailor with swarthy skin and thick eyebrows. His cunning eyes were the color of seaweed. Before answering, he chewed tobacco between the three or four teeth that remained at the far end of his mouth.

"There are sometimes, but they can be avoided."

"And fish," asked Cocantin. "Are there dangerous fish? Like sharks?"

"Sharks in the bay of Saint-Tropez? I've never seen any."

Cocantin decided to get a second opinion from a cabinboy who was rowing with remarkable vigor.

"And you, Paulo, have you ever seen a shark on the coast?"

"No! Never!"

"What have you seen?"

"Scorpion fish."

"Scorpion fish!" shouted Cocantin. He completely lost his head since he had a very vague knowledge of marine biology. The mere nature of this aquatic creature's name caused the detective to break out in a cold sweat. His immense nose shook with anxiety.

"What's a scorpion fish like?"

Winking at the cabin boy, the old sea wolf at the helm replied.

"It's bad! The isn't a more briny beastie in all the Mediterranean. It's very bad."

"As bad as that?"

"More even!"

"What's it like?"

"It's not pretty to look at," explained the cabin boy. "It has a big head with sharp bristles and protruding eyes. It's got a wide mouth that swallows its prey in a second."

"*Mon Dieu*!" signed Cocantin

"On its back," continued the cabin boy, "there a large bunch of pointed spines that stick out when it's angry."

"Don't tell me anymore," interrupted Prosper Cocantin. He was overwhelmed with horror by this picturesque description. "My poor Daisy! I hope she wasn't devoured by a scorpion fish!"

Hearing these words, the sailors burst out with laughter.

"What kind of men are you?" chided the indignant detective. "There's nothing funny about this!"

"Devoured by a scorpion fish!" repeated the sea wolf at the helm. "Devoured by a scorpion fish! My poor man, don't fear for your lady. You can be calm. it is more likely that she would devour a scorpion fish."

"What are you telling me?" asked Cocantin angrily. He had the distinct impression that *The Eaglet*'s sailors were mocking him.

Chewing his tobacco, the helmsman's eyes crackled with mischief.

"Tell me, Monsieur, have you ever eaten bouillabaisse?"

"Bouillabaisse? "

The sea wolf elaborated with the precision of the author of an acclaimed cookbook.

"It's a country dish made by cooking fruit in water or white wine and adding a lot of garlic, parsley, saffron, fish and bay leaf."

"I know this dish." The director of the Celeritas Agency recalled his experiences with cuisine. "I ate it on the harbor in Marseilles. It was very good. I also ate some in Nice. It was just as exquisite. What does the scorpion fish have to do with bouillabaisse?"

"Bouillabaisse is made from scorpion fish."

"It's a small fish?"

"Yes, a very small fish."

"You were pulling my leg!" shouted Cocantin. If not for his concern for his fiancée, the good-natured Cocantin would have been the first to laugh at being the butt of the sailors' joke. He was about to retrieve his binoculars from the Licorice Kid when the small boy yelled.

"Hey! Coconut, over there. A little to the right. I see something stirring. Stirring in the water. "

Grabbing the binoculars, Ribaudet's heir looked through them. After some seconds of silence, he shouted:

"It's her! I can't see her that well. But that means nothing! I'm sure. It's her. My heart tells me right away."

Without recognizing that he was mimicking the Chevalier des Grieux in Jules Massenet's *Manon*, he made a dramatic outburst while striking his chest.

"My heart is not mistaken! Daisy! Daisy! I've arrived just in time to save you!"

Immediately the rowboat shifted towards the moving object seen in the distance. They could see ripples that could be caused by the movements of a swimmer.

Their goal became clearer. Cocantin and the Licorice Kid had not been mistaken. It was Miss Daisy Torp. Still supple and graceful, but weakened by fatigue, she balanced herself on the waves.

Spotting the small boat that came to her rescue, the young woman tried to reach it. However, she had exceeded her resources. Clearly exhausted, she raised her hands in the air.

"Hold on, we're here!" yelled the Licorice Kid.

The swimmer disappeared under the waves.

"Too late!" yelled Cocantin. "We've arrived too late! I'll never forgive myself! Never!"

Scarcely had he pronounced these words than a cry of hope burst from him.

"It's her. I see her. I see her. Daisy! My fiancée! My woman!"

He had just seen Daisy's opulent hair floating very close to the small boat, within reach of his hand. His arm grasped a bunch of blonde hair while the sailors leaned outside the boat to successfully seize the young woman's arms. Daisy was saved! In a flash, she was pulled from the brink in time.

The audacious water-sprite was extremely weak. When the rowboat regained the harbor, Cocantin, helped by the Licorice Kid, massaged his beloved while murmuring gentle words of affection.

After a few minutes, the American beauty regained her power of speech. Waiting for her first words, Cocantin stared at her.

"Thank you," she stammered with a barely audible voice. "I feel better. A lot better. I wanted to recapture that woman! Tell your friend Judex that she'll never bother him again. I guarantee it!"

Closing her eyes, Daisy Torp fell into a stupor, an inevitable consequence of the exhaustion from the superhuman effort she had made.

We shall not wait for Miss Torp to regain consciousness before narrating to our readers the brutal underwater battle in which Diana Monti and the American beauty had been the combatants.

Emboldened by desperation, the adventuress had grabbed the swimmer's neck, hoping to strangle her in a tremendous outburst of rage. Being nimble and sturdy, the American hadn't yielded to the force of her adversary's onslaught. Daisy had broken the hold. Realizing that they were in a true duel to the death, the two opponents returned to the surface. They grasped each other in a furious embrace. Now fully aware of her enemy's murderous intentions, Daisy took the initiative in this merciless combat. She caught her enemy in the grip of a debilitating bear hug.

Squeezed in a vice, Diana was completely dominated by the valiant Daisy. Despite her repeated efforts, the ex-governess felt her strength depleting. Paralyzed by the destructive hold, she was incapable of further countermoves. As a final howl of hellish rage escaped her lips, she lost consciousness. Held in the arms of the triumphant swimmer, Diana was little more than a limp rag waiting to be swallowed by the sea.

However, the fearless Daisy had resolved to bring her prisoner back alive to the *Eaglet*. She wanted her victory to be complete. With her arm supporting the head of the miserable criminal above the water, Daisy swam towards the boat that had begun to maneuver towards the coast. Soon, however, she realized her severe miscalculation.

The currents, without presenting any danger, were a tiring hindrance, which forced her to modify her intended trajectory. Slowing down her pace, she became separated from the *Eaglet*. Cocantin's fiancée then understood that it would be fatal to persist in her original intention. Her priority was to preserve her own life at all costs. She resolved to return alone to the boat.

Released by her conqueror, the unconscious Diana Monti disappeared beneath the waves. As Daisy was adjusting her course, she gasped in shock. The *Eaglet*, all sails extended, now speeded rapidly back towards Sainte-Maxime!

As for the small boat that Judex had sent after the swimmer, it misjudged the direction that Daisy had taken during her pursuit and subsequent struggle. Therefore, it searched for her futilely in another direction.

Daisy's only course was to swim back to shore. But did she have the strength? In any case, she would try with all her indomitable energy. As we have seen, Cocantin had arrived at the very moment when, despite her indomitable courage, Daisy's phenomenal prowess was about to fail.

When the small boat reached the harbor, she opened her eyes. She saw the Licorice Kid looking at with deep admiration and sympathy.

"Who is this child?"

"He's my son," said the gallant Cocantin. He hugged the young boy.

The graceful water-sprite smiled. "Then he shall also be mine."

"What luck!" exclaimed the Licorice Kid. He kissed the swimmer. "A Papa and a Mama all in the same day. The only thing missing is for me to inherit a fortune. This is what I get for being a good boy!"

V. Absolution

Yielding right away to the request of the banker, Judex had taken him to see his mother.

Madame de Trémeuse was sitting in her parlor. With her son Roger, she was in the process of consoling Jean. After leaving his Mama and his Grandpa, the young boy had finally been soothed by the kindly Comtesse.

Seeing Jacqueline and his grandfather, Jeannot left Madame de Trémeuse's arms and ran towards his mother. The young woman wanted to spare her son the painful scene between her father and Judex's mother. She was about to take him outside when Favraux intervened.

"Stay, my daughter. Stay with my grandson. He, as well as you, must observe what transpires here. He must remember it forever in his spirit and his heart. I want him to fully understand. I want him to witness my remorse! He must never yield to the same evil temptations as I did. If he hears and sees what transpires here today, he will understand that there is only one true road on Earth to follow: the path of integrity, justice and honor!"

While hearing these words, Madame de Trémeuse rose. The words of this unscrupulous criminal had rendered her speechless. This swindler had mercilessly crushed anyone whom he considered an obstacle to his fanatical ambition. This man had spread around him shame and misery. Due to him, countless families had been decimated, countless souls had been driven to despair, and countless hearts had ceased to beat. At last, he recognized all his wrongs in a humble attitude of expiation and sorrow!

He was transformed! No longer was he the gilded merchant, the cruel tyrant whose millions had corrupted the conscientious, the honest, the noble and the heroic.

At present, Madame de Trémeuse had before her a man deeply hurt. He was humiliated, but it was a humiliation without baseness. He was tortured, but only by regret. He was now resolved to lead a life of sacrifice and suffering. More than anything, he craved forgiveness, not so much for himself, but for the two innocent beings whose divine grace had opened his eyes to the light of goodness and love.

How sincere he was at this moment! How much he wanted to buy back, with every ounce of his blood, all the crimes that he had committed! How fully he understood the hideousness of his sins!

Falling on his knees in front of Madame de Trémeuse, Favraux shouted his plea:

"Madame, for many years, I was a miserable sinner. I cowardly struck at you! I broke your happiness! I committed an abomination! I humbly admit it. I beg your forgiveness, Madame. Yes, I beg forgiveness with the life that remains in me. Like the first Christians of the Church, I really want to confess all in public. Such a demonstration would inflict my disgrace on the guiltless. I don't want two innocents to bear the weight of my sins. The banker Favraux is dead. He shall not return. He will not take advantage of your clemency to resume in this world a place to which he never had a right. He declares himself forever chastened. He will disappear. He will begin a new life of honest toil, and will strive to obtain, fairly this time, for his daughter and grandson, the affluence that they deserve."

Madame de Trémeuse made her declaration:

"My presence in this parlor is proof that I forgive you."

In this supreme instance, she still had to struggle to accomplish this final of mercy. Her quavering voice her internal conflict.

"Rise, Monsieur… all between us is obliterated."

"I am not finished," resumed Favraux with clasped hands as if he was thanking an angel of forgiveness who had just descended down to Earth. "You must know that I no longer hate Judex. I thank him. Yes, I proclaim it. Your vengeance was legitimate. I add that it was even sacred. You had the right, the duty, to strike me. You refused to see your task to the end. You had pity. You are blessed!"

"Jean, my child, kiss your grandfather," shouted Jacqueline. Her face was illuminated by the purest happiness that she had ever known. Hugging his grandfather, the young boy didn't fully grasp the tragic meaning of this confession, but he felt its magnitude.

"My little one!" shouted Favraux. "At last, I will be able to love you and your mother!"

"But, Grandpa, we always loved you!" replied the child before kissing his grandfather's feverish forehead.

"Favraux," said gravely Madame de Trémeuse. "The kiss of this angel is your absolution!"

The banker endured a long eruption of tears before replying: "Now, it only remains for me to leave with my family. I must not impose on you my presence."

However, Madame de Trémeuse directed him to turn towards Jacques and Jacqueline whose eyes mutually betrayed the dear secret of their souls.

"Look at them, Monsieur Favraux," said the widow. "Do either of us have the right to break these two hearts? My forgiveness sprang from their love. It was inside them because God put it there. Do not tamper with the designs of God!"

"O holiest of women!" murmured the banker. "I must unite their hands as they already united their hearts. I shall leave them in peace! That way, they will be happy forever!"

"And my son?" asked a trembling Kerjean of Jacques de Trémeuse.

With an expression of deep commiseration, Jacques grabbed the hands of the old miller.

"He could not escape justice! It was his destiny to be punished. While seeking to murder me, he perished in my place."

A painful sigh erupted from the chest of the ex-convict.

"Although this affair has ended, my friend," said Jacques, "you will always remain close to me. My work is not finished. My own personal happiness is not a reason to despicably retreat into selfishness. Once united to the woman I love, my work will continue. She supports me in this. Thanks to my immense fortune, I will be able to remain Judex, the judge who punishes and rewards. This is a superb task—a tremendous task that attracts me even more since I have already tasted the thrill of adventure. I need you, Kerjean, and I ask you to remain with me."

"Thank you!" said the ex-miller of Les Sablons. He kissed the hands of his benefactor.

The next day, Kerjean wandered melancholically on the beach facing the sea that had served as a tomb for his son. He thought sadly that, if not for that miserable adventuress, Diana Monti, his son would be here, ready to assist Judex in the new task that he was about to undertake. Confronted with that harsh reality, a deafening rage smoldered inside. He gave voice to a bitter despair.

"If I saw this woman, I would kill her in a second!"

At his feet, the waves flooded the pebbles with foam. The advancing waters twisted and tossed a dark mass towards which the father of Moralès was instinctively drawn.

With a shock bordering on horror, Kerjean recognized this mass as a human body, the corpse of the woman who had been his son's evil genius. The sea had rejected her carcass and deposited it at his feet as if Providence was saying: "You are avenged!"

The following night, the remains of Diana Monti, collected secretly by Judex, rested at the bottom of a deep hole in a deserted field near the coast. The earth was shoveled over her corpse. No cross marked the location of this mysterious grave. Hell had reclaimed its she-demon!

Epilogue

Faithful to his word, the banker Favraux secluded himself under an assumed name in a remote villa.

Cocantin got ready to marry Miss Daisy Torp and adopt the Licorice Kid. Having resolved to mimic his beloved, the sleuth cautiously performed swimming exercises on his parlor table to the comic delight of the pretty American and the Licorice Kid.

The dream of Jacques and Jacqueline had become the most ideal reality. They prepared to take a honeymoon trip to Italy. They would return to devote themselves to the grand cause of justice.

Perhaps one day, this aftermath will be told.

The Continuity and Chronology of Judex

One of the challenges of adapting *Judex* into English was all the continuity glitches present in the original French text. Most of these problems probably resulted because the novel was serialized in 12 installments like its cinematic doppelganger. However, Arthur Bernède could even have major inconsistencies between chapters in the same installment.

The most glaring anomaly was the spelling of the sinister banker's surname. In Part One, the financier's name was Favraux. This is also the name used in the film. However, the last letter was changed in Part Two onward. Favraux was transformed inexplicably into Favrauz. I have used Favraux consistently through the English text.

There were inconsistencies involving titles of nobility. César de Birargues and Amaury de la Rochefontaine both held the title of marquis when they were introduced in the French text. In a single sentence, César became a baron. Probably Arthur Bernède simply confused the Marquis de Birargues with the phony Baron Moralès. I restored César's original title. However, I made the opposite decision concerning Amaury de la Rochefontaine. Bernède demoted him to a Vicomte at one point. Since it was somewhat confusing to have two dissolute marquises allied with Diana Monti, I made Amaury a Vicomte to distinguish him from César.

A further contradiction involved the abduction of Pierre Kerjean from the Chateau Rouge. The French text had Amaury getting out of the car with Moralès at the Chateau Rouge. Amaury was then inexplicably teleported to Diana's house. My adaptation always has Amaury at Diana's.

The height of the evil Dr. Pop was also inconsistent in the original text. He was short in the grave robbery sequence in which he first appeared, and then suddenly became tall when questioning Marianne Bontemps. I deleted the reference to Pop being short.

Bernède would have characters privy to vital pieces of information without explanation. When Judex learned about Marie Verdier's visit to the boarding house, he immediately recognized her as the notorious Diana Monti. Bernède never explained how Judex came by this knowledge. The most likely explanation is that he investigated Marie Verdier's background when they knew each other at the Chateau des Sablons. When Pierre Kerjean was reunited with his son at the mill, he realized that the female criminal was Diana Monti. How did Kerjean know about her? The original text didn't indicate the obvious explanation that Judex had briefed him about Diana. In the scene where the Licorice Kid and Roger de Trémeuse accosted Prosper Cocantin at the shore, the detective knew that the *Eaglet* was the name of the vessel boarded by Judex. Although Bernède doesn't identify how the sleuth came by this knowledge, he probably saw the vessel's name through his binoculars. I have inserted these logical rationalizations into my adaptation.

When Diana transported Favraux from the villa to the *Eaglet*, she only identified herself as Marie Verdier to the banker. Nevertheless, the French text had Favraux sometimes addressing her as Diana. Since there was no logical reason for Marie to disclose her Diana alias to Favraux, my adaptation only has the banker addressing the ex-governess by her real name.

When Captain Martelli complained that his fee was too small, the French text gave that fee as 500 francs. Diana then doubled it. Therefore, he should have been paid 1000 francs. Yet an intimidated Martelli told Judex that Diana paid him a total of 5000 francs. I made the original fee 2500 francs rather than 500 to be consistent. Doubling 2500 would give us the sum cited by Martelli during his conversation with Judex.

The hours listed in the chapters involving the two ambulances also required modification. In the French text, the references to when the vehicles arrived at Loisy was not consistent with Diana Monti's preparations to manufacture a fake ambulance. When the counterfeit ambulance arrived at the mill, Bernède totally forgot about Crémard. He disappeared from the scene without explanation. I added a scene in which Diana ordered Crémard to ditch the ambulance and return after nightfall.

Judex utilized several dogs in his operations. The majority of these canines are Vendean hounds. However, three dogs are distinct breeds. There is Vidocq, the "police dog" (probably a German Shepherd), Maxime the poodle, and an unnamed fox-terrier. At one point in the original French text, Maxime was referred to as a fox-terrier. I corrected this inconsistency. Probably Bernède originally intended for the poodle and the fox-terrier to be the same dog. However, he must have realized that it was impossible to have the same canine present at both Jacqueline's awakening and Diana's emergence from the tunnel.

The French text clearly identified Favraux as the driver of the car that ran over Pierre Kerjean. No one else was mentioned in the car. Later, Favraux told Vallières that Reste Martial, the chauffeur, was aware of the supposed accident. Where did this chauffeur come from? In the original movie serial, the chauffeur did make an appearance. He was inexplicably seated in the passenger seat when Favraux attempted to murder Kerjean. The cynical filmgoer must have wondered if the chauffeur was teaching Favraux how to drive. Therefore, my adaptation has the chauffeur seated next to Favraux and provides an explanation for his presence.

When Daisy Torp jumped into the sea to rescue Judex, the original text had Prosper Cocantin mumbling to himself that he would ask her to marry him once she returned. There was no formal proposal. Nevertheless, Daisy identified herself as Cocantin's fiancée aboard the *Eaglet*. Furthermore, Cocantin referred to himself as her fiancé on the shore. Therefore, Cocantin's proposal and Daisy's acceptance appear in my adaptation.

The chapter in which Judex overcame Moralès on the ship ended differently in the original French text. Announcing his intention to take over the *Eaglet*, Judex started to ascend the stairs towards the upper deck with Daisy following him. Totally forgetting this detail, Bernède has Judex and Daisy hiding in the captain's bedroom in the next chapter. The hero then appeared on deck after Moralès' demise. Therefore, my adaptation has the earlier chapter concluding with Judex and Daisy going into the captain's bedroom. When Judex does eventually reach the upper deck, he referred to his American ally as Miss Daisy, even though she has only described herself as Cocantin's fiancée in the French text. I added some brief dialogue in which she told Judex her name.

In the film, Judex removed his cape and put it on the unconscious Moralès. This is necessary to hide the crook's sailor suit when he was tied to the post in the captain's cabin. The French text doesn't mention this important detail. I added it to my adaptation.

There is another example of Bernède's sloppy editing in the chapter in which Jacqueline redeemed her father's soul. Bernède originally had Favraux asked his daughter to take him to see Comtesse de Trémeuse before she meets Judex. Yet a subsequent chapter had Favraux requesting Judex's permission to see his mother. My adaptation removed this contradiction.

Diana Monti's constant changes of addresses caused some minor confusion in the original text. After leaving the Chateau des Sablons, Diana moved into Moralès' bachelor apartment, utilized the remote villa where Jacqueline was imprisoned, and returned to Paris with Moralès—presumably to his apartment. She then checked into a hotel without Moralès, moved into Amaury's apartment, and ended up in a house that she owned. When Moralès returned to Paris from the Chateau Rouge, he sought out Diana at this house. Bernède noted that they lived there together. There is even a reference to them dining together at a restaurant prior to their quarrel. This is probably the same restaurant that they went to after their visit to the Celeritas Agency. The logical conclusion is that Diana and Moralès didn't return to the latter's apartment after the assault of Judex's hounds on the villa, but moved into her house. My adaptation reflects this assumption.

When we are introduced to Comtesse de Trémeuse, she was shown looking at a photograph of Jacques and Roger when they were respectively 14 and 12 years-old. This photograph appeared in the original film, and it was obviously that photograph was taken around the time of Count de Trémeuse's suicide. Since Madame Chapuis described Judex as being between 25 and 30, Judex would seem to be the latter age. However, the original French text, as well as the serial, contained references that that the Count died 20 years earlier . I viewed the 16 year interval as more logical and made the corresponding alterations.

Some names and addresses are different in at least the English version of the movie serial. For example, the Callyx Bar from the novel is the Calyx Bar in the film. In English, a calyx is defined as the sepals of a flower or part of the kidney. However, Callyx is a variant of the Latin name Callis (meaning "chalice or "goblet").

The exact year of the events of *Judex* have been debatable due to telegrams and other documents that appeared in the film. These documents are dated during April-May 1917. This would imply that *Judex* transpired during World War I. However, there is much in the storyline that contradicts such a chronological placement. Would Jacques and Roger, men of honor, be pursuing a personal vendetta when they should be fighting in the war? Why would Robert Kerjean (alias Baron Moralès) consider seeking redemption by joining the French Foreign Legion? He would have decided to join the French army and take a trip to the trenches along the Western Front. The 1963 remake of *Judex* recognized this fact by revealing in the closing frame that the story happened in early 1914 before the outbreak of the war.

Bernède's novel never specified the year in which it was set. Furthermore, the novel began in June, not April. The nov-

341

el also mentioned summer when Judex arrived at the mill after the Kerjeans are reunited. Most likely, the novel was set sometime between 1911 and 1913. If I could view the novel in isolation, I would choose 1913. However, there is a 1918 sequel in both film and book form, *La Nouvelle Mission de Judex* (*Judex's New Mission*). I'm not sure if a complete copy of the second *Judex* serial survives. In March 2006, only the first 9 of the 12 chapters were shown during a Louis Feuillade retrospective at *La Cinémathèque francaise*. The corresponding novel has apparently not been reprinted since 1934.

Reading a single book in a series could lead to radically different chronological conclusions than reading the entire opus. An excellent example is Gaston Leroux's *Le Mystère de la Chambre Jaune* (1908). The text explicitly placed its events in 1892. However, the third book in the series, *Rouletabille chez le Tsar* (1913) shifted the events of the first book to 1902.

The film version of *La Nouvelle Mission de Judex* was set not long after the original serial since Jean Aubry was still played by child actor Olindo Mano. Other characters returning from the first film included Roger, Jacqueline, Cocantin, Favraux and Pierre Kerjean. The title of the first chapter, "Le mystère d'une nuit d'été" ("The Mystery of the Summer Night"), suggests that *La Nouvelle Mission de Judex* began in the summer.

While I decline to explicitly assign an exact year to the event of *Judex*, I will note these chronological observations based on the novel:

1) Pierre Kerjean was born 60 years before *Judex* began.

2) Prosper Cocantin was born 40 years earlier.

3) When she was 20, Julia Orsini married Pierre de Trémeuse.

5) Jacques de Trémeuse (Judex) was born 30 years prior to the events of the novel. His brother Roger was two years younger. Robert Kerjean (Baron Moralès) was born about 28-30 years before *Judex* began.

5) Pierre Kerjean was sent to prison 20 years earlier.

6) Count Pierre de Trémeuse committed suicide 16 years earlier.

7) His widow purchased the Chateau de la Ferté 15 years earlier.

8) Jean Aubry was born four and a half years earlier (the novel rounded up his age to five in his initial appearance).

9) Posing as Vallières, Judex became Favraux's secretary a year earlier. In the same time interval, Diana Monti became Jean's governess in her real identity of Marie Verdier.

10) The novel began in June, and probably concluded in either August or September.

There are some unanswered questions in the novel. One revolves around that fact that two chambermaids called Mariette appear in the novel. The first worked for Gisèle de Birargues. The second later labored in the house which Judex maintained as Vallières. Are these two women the same person? Probably Bernède just carelessly reused the name. Another possibility is that Bernède originally intended the de Birargues to play a larger role in the novelization. Jacqueline initially suspected that she was in the care of the de Birargues family when she woke up after the ordeal at the mill. A theory could easily be constructed where Mariette leaves the de Birargues household to work for Judex. My adaptation merely noted the similarity in names.

The mystery of Mariette is not the only instance of a common name raising questions. Is Prince Martelli, Diana's deceased lover, related to Captain Martelli, her smuggling partner?

The exact number of Judex's agents remains unclear. We know about his brother, Pierre Kerjean, and an unnamed chauffeur, but who were the trio of "acolytes" who assisted Roger in rescuing Jean. Presumably one was the chauffeur who drove Roger to Loisy, but was he the same chauffeur who Judex summoned to rescue Kerjean? Another could have been the valet from Roger's bachelor apartment. Were there any female "acolytes" in Judex's employ? Did Gabrielle Fleury, Vallières' housekeeper, know that he was really Judex?

A curious enigma surrounds Vallières. Is he solely a fictional identity or was there a real Vallières whom Judex was impersonating? Jacqueline mentioned that Vallières gained his position through a letter of recommendation written by William Simpson of New York. There could have been a real Vallières who worked for Simpson in New York. In Maurice Leblanc's Arsène Lupin series, the master thief often impersonated a Frenchman who died aboard. Lupin would cover up the death and gain possession of the deceased's papers. Judex could have done the same.

Considering that Favraux entrusted the false Vallières with the location of his incriminating documents, the corrupt banker must have considered his secretary to be thoroughly unscrupulous. He must have been given this impression by Simpson. The New Yorker must have been a complete scoundrel. Perhaps Simpson was even Favraux's subordinate. Favraux clearly had an organization active in the United States. The banker was able to sabotage the de Trémeuse mines in the United States. There was also the cryptic reference to Favraux's role in the horrible fire at the docks of the fictional New-City (this name appears in English in the original French text). New-City sounds like an alias for New York City. Therefore, Simpson could have been Favraux's chief agent in the United States. Simpson could have transferred one of his employees, the real Vallières, to France to act as Favraux's secretary. In unknown circumstances, Vallières perished. Judex then gained possession of his papers. The death of the genuine Vallières would have happened a year before the events of *Judex*.

Judex could have spent years in the United States battling Favraux's American allies. Jacqueline's first husband, Jacques Aubry, was involved in Favraux's illegal enterprises. He perished in an automobile accident in America. Could Aubry and Judex have been acquainted? In the movie serial, Jacqueline had been a widow for four years. The book implies a different interval.

If the film was correct, Jean Aubry would have been less than a year old when his father died. In the book, Jean's has vivid memories of his father's leaving for America. The child also recalled how his father dressed for the races. These memories suggest that the youngster was more than a year old when the tragedy occurred. Jacques Aubry's death probably transpired two or three years before the events of the novel.

The movie serial differed substantially from the book in other ways beside chronology. The book has a grimmer tone. The Licorice Kid, a completely comic character in the film, disclosed that he had been beaten by Fagan-like criminals.

Judex's pack of Vendean hounds are as threatening as Walt Disney's Dalmatians in the film. They merely knocked Crémard down by running between his legs. The dogs are as lovable as the *Hound of the Baskervilles* in the book. They threatened to rip Crémard apart.

Perhaps the most notable difference is the underwater sequence with Diana and Daisy. In the film, Daisy never caught up with Diana. Recognizing that the waters were dangerous, Daisy turned around. Diana was then drowned by accident. The book gives us a vicious catfight where Daisy made a conscious decision to kill Diana. The 1963 remake featured the climactic catfight, but shifted it to the rooftops of Paris.

Despite the more brutal tone of the narrative, Arthur Bernède kept all of the comic relief sequences involving Prosper Cocantin. In fact, Cocantin is an even more humorous figure in the book. One scene was so ridiculous that I felt obligated to modify it for the English adaptation.

In the film, Diana and Amaury threw down their pistols in disgust when the Licorice Kid arrived in place of Judex. In the book, an unarmed Cocantin adopted a Napoleon stance to browbeat the two conspirators to drop their weapons. The formidable Diana Monti came off like a total fool in that scene. Therefore, my adaptation fashioned a compromise between the film and the French text. Amaury dropped his weapon in anger permitting Cocantin to use it to disarm Diana.

Rick Lai

Judex and The Shadow

The similarities between Judex and the American pulp hero, The Shadow, have always been readily apparent. Both wear black hats and cloaks. Both have distinct profiles. In fact, the resemblance between the two fictional characters was so pronounced that the American comic strip adventures of The Shadow drawn by Vernon Green and distributed by the Ledger Syndicate in the 1940s were reprinted in France with the hero's name changed to Judex!

The parallels between Judex and the Shadow may stem from a common literary inspiration, Gaston Leroux's *The Phantom of the Opera*. Leroux's classic novel was first serialized in 1909-10, more than six years before Judex debuted on film. In an enigmatic sequence from Leroux's novel, there was a mysterious figure called "the shadow" and the Man in the Felt Hat. Like Judex, he wore a cloak and a black felt hat. This throwaway character may have inspired Louis Feuillade and Arthur Bernède to fashion their own "mysterious shadow."

Writing as Maxwell Grant, Walter Gibson didn't pen his first Shadow novel until 1931. Although Gibson was primarily influenced by Maurice Leblanc's Arsène Lupin and Frank L. Packard's Jimmie Dale, there are distinct traces of Leroux's novel in The Shadow from his initial exploit. However, Gibson's creation has more in common with the title character of the novel than the obscure Man in the Felt Hat. Erik, the Phantom of the Opera, was a recluse whose ugliness prompted him to live a clandestine existence. In *The Living Shadow* (April 1931), Gibson's hero debuted with strong suggestions that he was a disfigured World War I veteran. In *The Black Master* (March 1932), a Fantômas-like mastermind unmasked The Shadow and made the cryptic remark that the crime fighter had no face. In both *The Shadow's Shadow* (February 1, 1933) and *The Black Falcon* (February 1, 1934), criminals were terrified upon viewing The Shadow's true face. Unfortunately, Gibson abandoned all these hints because he gradually concluded that a disfigured hero was too gruesome. This orphaned concept later influenced Sam Raimi to make his movie *Darkman* (1990).

Gibson's Shadow has very little in common with the cinematic version of Judex, other than a penchant for a hat and cloak. Judex is much more fallible than his American counterpart. Gibson never would have let The Shadow walk into a trap armed with only a checkbook. Furthermore, Judex wore his hat and cloak rather openly rather than skulk in the dark. Ironically, the French novel has greater similarities between Gibson's hero and Judex. The scene where Judex as a living shadow follows Jacqueline reads like a passage from Gibson's early Shadow novels. Since he's no longer a character in a silent film, Judex was given the opportunity to terrify Favraux with maniacal laughter. The Shadow became famous by using the same technique to frighten criminals. While Judex rather nonchalantly introduced himself to Cocantin in the film, he melodramatically arose from the shadows in the book. However, it is highly unlikely that Gibson had any exposure to the novel. The most likely way for Gibson to have been exposed to the French hero would be through film.

Was *Judex* ever shown in the United States? In the silent film era, it was easy to market films aboard since dubbing was not an issue. It's hard to find exact dates for the releases of Louis Feuillade's serials in the English film market, but film historian David White has found definite proof that the Fantômas films, *Les Vampires* and *Tih Minh* (retitled *In the Clutches of the Hindoo)* were distributed in the United States. English versions of both *Judex* and *La Nouvelle Mission de Judex* (translated as *Further Exploits of Judex*) were shown in Japan during 1921. It's hard to imagine that the Judex serials didn't reach American shores.

There is one Shadow's novel by Gibson, *Crime at Seven Oaks* (August 1, 1940), that is slightly reminiscent of *Judex*. In this pulp novel, The Shadow teams up with a Great Dane named Vulcan. There is some similarity between Vidocq, Judex's dog, and Vulcan. However, American dime novel heroes frequently used dogs long before Judex appeared in celluloid. Gibson's Vulcan probably had more to do with Nick Carter's Cuban bloodhound, Pedro, than Vidocq. Since Nick Carter was popular in France, one could even speculate that Pedro, who first appeared around 1906, inspired the creation of Vidocq.

Although there is very little commonality between Gibson's Shadow novels and the film, the case is far different with another pulp writer associated with the American avenger. In 1936, Street and Smith, the publisher of *The Shadow*'s magazine, hired Theodore Tinsley as a backup writer to Walter Gibson. Also employing the pseudonym of Maxwell Grant, Tinsley wrote 28 Shadow novels that had sharp differences with Gibson's work and intriguing parallels to Judex's first exploit.

Tinsley's Shadow was more fallible than Gibson. In Tinsley's hands, The Shadow walked into traps as obvious as the meeting with Diana Monti at the pier. Tinsley liked extremely bloodthirsty and passionate female criminals to populate his Shadow stories. These *femme fatales* often quarreled with their male associates. In other words, a lot of the villains resemble Diana Monti and Moralès.

The most formidable mastermind fought by Tinsley's Shadow was Benedict Stark, a respected financier who destroyed people for slighting him. Stark had the same *modus operandi* as Maurice-Ernst Favraux. In both the film and the book, Favraux ruined the de Trémeuse because the Comtesse refused his advances. Both Favraux and Stark drove men to suicide and impoverished their families. Stark appeared in four novels, *The Prince of Evil* (April 15,1940), *Murder Genius* (July 1, 1940), *The Man Who Died Twice* (September 15, 1940) and *The Devil's Paymaster* (November 15, 1940).

The most intriguing innovation that Tinsley made to the Shadow was the creation of a scientific torture chamber that appeared in *The Prince of Evil* and *The Devil's Paymaster*. In this chamber, The Shadow imprisoned Stark's henchmen and forced them to divulge their secrets using a combination of light and sound. This torture chamber could have been inspired by Judex's underground jail cell with its electronic mirror and fiery letters.

Having made the case that Theodore Tinsley might have been influenced by Judex, let me now provide the counter-evidence. Tinsley was a good friend of Norvell Page, the principal author of The Spider, the leading pulp rival of The Shadow. The Spider often committed grievous errors in his war on crime. Therefore, the fallibility of Tinsley's Shadow could be attributed to The Spider rather than Judex.

Tinsley was also a contributor to *Black Mask*, the cornerstone of hardboiled detective fiction. He must have been familiar with Dashiell Hammett's *The Maltese Falcon* in which a female criminal feuded with all her male associates. Tinsley's scheming women probably owe more to Hammett's Brigid O'Shaughnessy than to Diana Monti.

The likely inspiration for Maurice-Ernest Favraux was Baron Danglars, the corrupt financier in *The Count of Monte-Cristo* (1844). Holding Danglars responsible for his father's death by starvation, Edmond Dantès kidnapped the banker. Imprisoned in a jail cell, Dantès starved Danglars until he signed away his fortune. The Danglars episode could have independently influenced Tinsley to create Stark. The scientific jail cells utilized by Judex and The Shadow were modern extensions of the prison employed by Dantès. Under the influence of Dumas, Tinsley could have independently conceived a futuristic form of solitary confinement that resembled the plot device conceived by Louis Feuillade and Arthur Bernède.

Graves Gladney's cover or the first Benedict Stark novel, *The Prince of Evil,* illustrated The Shadow tormenting one of Stark's underlings. The artistic depiction of that villain resembled Louis Leubas, the actor who played Favraux in *Judex*. Gladney drew the crook covering his face in terror.

350

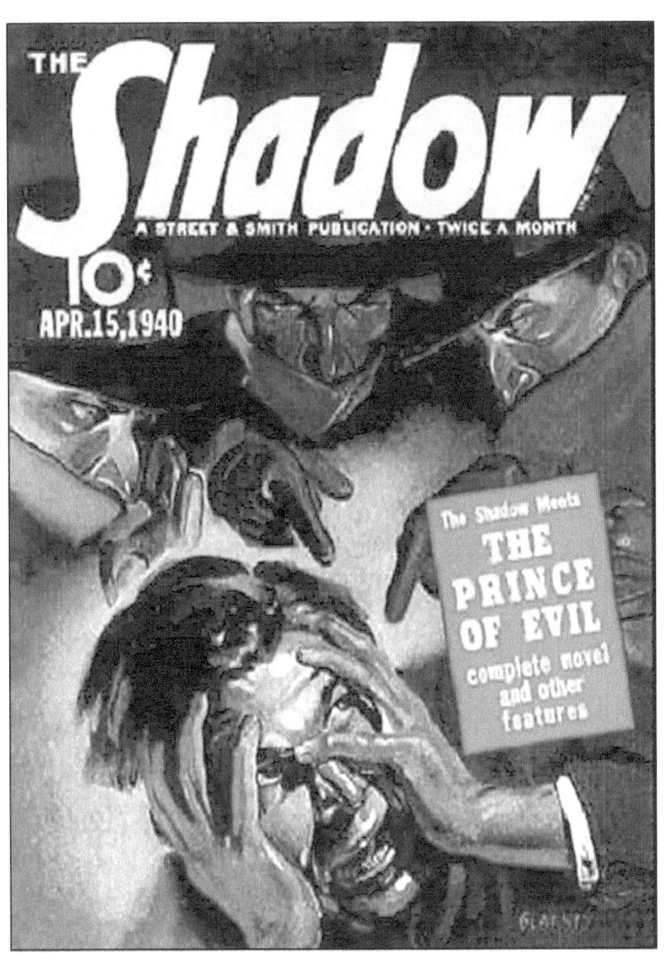

Favraux made the same gesture in the classic film sequence where Judex sentenced him to life imprisonment with fiery letters. What are the odds of that being a coincidence?

Actually, the odds are very good that it's a coincidence. I checked with Anthony Tollin, a scholar with vast knowledge about the artists employed by Street and Smith to illustrate The Shadow. The novel would have been submitted nearly a year before Gladney got the cover assignment, Furthermore, Gladney wouldn't have had any contact with Tinsley but with the art director of Street and Smith. Gladney generally used models for his covers. It would be unlikely for Street and Smith to give Tinsley a still from a French film made over 20 years earlier when all that was needed was a frightened male face similar to many others that graced detective and horror pulps. Thus, Gladney probably used a model for the terrified criminal rather than worked off a photo of Louis Leubas.

The argument that *Judex* influenced *The Prince of Evil* remains unproven.

Rick Lai

A List of Judex Pastiches

Judex has had many adventures penned by other authors. Every story has at least one crossover to another series. Some of these stories follow the 1917 references in the film, while others operate under the premise that the story took place around 1913. The majority of the pastiche writers have only seen the film versions. The original movie serial sometimes had different names and addresses than the novel. This divergence is reflected in at least one pastiche. Every story listed here has at least one crossover to another series.

1) ***Tales of the Shadowmen***, anthologies published by Black Coat Press, edited by Jean-Marc and Randy Lofficier. Some stories do not feature Judex, but supporting characters or fictional locales associated with him.

Volume 1: The Modern Babylon, 2005
Baugh, Matthew, "The Mark of the Monster." Judex teams up with Jules de Grandin and Inspector Maigret to battle the Frankenstein Monster and Dr. Cornelius.
Roberson, Chris, "Penumbra." In conjunction with The Shadow, Judex saves the Wayne family from persecution by the Vampires (from Louis Feuillade's other serial).

Volume 2: Gentleman of the Night, 2006
Lofficier, Jean-Marc, "Judex: Lost and Found." Illustrated by Fernando Calvi. Judex becomes involved with the Maltese Falcon.

Volume 3: Danse Macabre, 2007
Robinson, Robert L., Jr., "The Two Hunters." Judex joins forces with Tarzan.

Volume 4: The Lords of Terror, 2008

Newman, Kim, "The Mark of Kane." Story only features Favraux. This is a delightful parody of the 1967 film version of *Casino Royale*. Charles Foster Kane's French Casino is destroyed by a battle between various fictional characters.

Volume 5: The Vampires of Paris, 2009

Bigot, Michelle, "The Tarot of the Shadowmen." This is an illustrated Tarot Deck with text. Judex is the Judgment Card

Volume 6: Grand Guignol, 2010

Eckert, Win Scott, "Is He in Hell?" A 1795 ancestor of Favraux runs afoul of the Scarlet Pimpernel.

Volume 7: Femme Fatales, 2011

Baugh, Matthew, "What Rough Beast." Judex and Hugo Danner battle the Colossus of Ylourgne.

Dennison, Matthew, "Faces of Fear." In this horror story, there is a brief battle between Freddy Krueger and Judex (or at least a dream version of the character).

Eckert, Win Scott, "Nadine's Invitation." Story features a 1795 version of the Calyx Bar (the movie serial used that spelling while the Callyx Bar appears in the novel).

Volume 9:Agents Provocateurs, 2012

Eckert, Win Scott, "Marguerite's Tears." In 1798, the Calyx (Callyx) Bar is briefly mentioned.

Gallagher, John, "Book of Shadows." Posters for hypothetical movies include a serial pitting Judex against Belphegor, Arthur Bernède's other great creation.

Lofficier, Jean-Marc and Lofficier, Randy, "The Affair of the Queen's Necklace Revisited." Richard Benson (alias the Avenger) is assisted on a case by Judex.

2) Other Pastiches:

Lai, Rick, *Shadows of the Opera, Book One: The Mark of the Revenant,* Wild Cat Books, 2010. A series of short stories in which Julia Orsini, Judex's mother, is a major supporting character. The Callyx Bar and Pierre de Trémeuse also appear. The stories imply that the Phantom of the Opera was indirectly responsible for Judex and an unnamed American pulp hero taking up the hat and cloak.

Maumejean, Xavier, *The League of Heroes,* Black Coat Press, 2005. Judex is one of many fictional heroes in this ambitious work with a clever twist that should not be mentioned.

Power, Dennis, "The Judex Codex." (2006). http://www.pjfarmer.com/woldnewton/Judex_Codex.pdf. In this internet text, Judex is linked to a magical ring very familiar to fans of heroic fantasy.

SF & FANTASY

Henri Allorge. *The Great Cataclysm*
Guy d'Armen. *Doc Ardan: The City of Gold and Lepers*
G.-J. Arnaud. *The Ice Company*
Cyprien Bérard. *The Vampire Lord Ruthwen*
Aloysius Bertrand. *Gaspard de la Nuit*
Richard Bessière. *The Gardens of the Apocalypse*
Albert Bleunard. *Ever Smaller*
Félix Bodin. *The Novel of the Future*
Alphonse Brown. *City of Glass*
André Caroff. *The Terror of Madame Atomos; Miss Atomos; The Return of Madame Atomos; The Mistake of Madame Atomos*
Félicien Champsaur. *The Human Arrow*
Didier de Chousy. *Ignis*
Captain Danrit. *Undersea Odyssey*
C. I. Defontenay. *Star (Psi Cassiopeia)*
Charles Derennes. *The People of the Pole*
Georges Dodds (anthologist). *The Missing Link*
Harry Dickson. *The Heir of Dracula*
Jules Dornay. *Lord Ruthven Begins*
Alfred Driou. *The Adventures of a Parisian Aeronaut*
Sâr Dubnotal *vs. Jack the Ripper*
Alexandre Dumas. *The Return of Lord Ruthven*
Renée Dunan. *Baal*
J.-C. Dunyach. *The Night Orchid; The Thieves of Silence*
Henri Duvernois. *The Man Who Found Himself*
Achille Eyraud. *Voyage to Venus*
Henri Falk. *The Age of Lead*
Paul Féval. *Anne of the Isles; Knightshade; Revenants; Vampire City; The Vampire Comtesse; The Wandering Jew's Daughter*
Paul Féval, *fils. Felifax, the Tiger-Man*
Charles de Fieux. *Lamékis*
Arnould Galopin. *Doctor Omega*; *Doctor Omega & The Shadowmen*
G.L. Gick. *Harry Dickson and the Werewolf of Rutherford Grange*
Edmond Haraucourt. *Illusions of Immortality*
Nathalie Henneberg. *The Green Gods*
V. Hugo, P. Foucher & P. Meurice. *The Hunchback of Notre-Dame*
Michel Jeury. *Chronolysis*
Gustave Kahn. *The Tale of Gold and Silence*

Gérard Klein. *The Mote in Time's Eye*
Jean de La Hire. *Enter the Nyctalope; The Nyctalope on Mars; The Nyctalope vs. Lucifer; The Nyctalope Steps In*
Etienne-Léon de Lamothe-Langon. *The Virgin Vampire*
André Laurie. *Spiridon*
Gabriel de Lautrec. *The Vengeance of the Oval Portrait*
Georges Le Faure & Henri de Graffigny. *The Extraordinary Adventures of a Russian Scientist Across the Solar System* (2 vols.)
Gustave Le Rouge. *The Vampires of Mars*
Jules Lermina. *Mysteryville; Panic in Paris; To-Ho and the Gold Destroyers; The Secret of Zippelius*
Jean-Marc & Randy Lofficier. *Edgar Allan Poe on Mars; The Katrina Protocol; Pacifica; Robonocchio; Tales of the Shadowmen 1-8*
Xavier Mauméjean. *The League of Heroes*
José Moselli. *Illa's End*
John-Antoine Nau. *Enemy Force*
Marie Nizet. *Captain Vampire*
C. Nodier, A. Beraud & Toussaint-Merle. *Frankenstein*
Henri de Parville. *An Inhabitant of the Planet Mars*
Gaston de Pawlowski. *Journey to the Land of the 4th Dimension*
Georges Pellerin. *The World in 2000 Years*
J. Polidori, C. Nodier, E. Scribe. *Lord Ruthven the Vampire*
P.-A. Ponson du Terrail. *The Vampire and the Devil's Son*
Henri de Régnier. *A Surfeit of Mirrors*
Maurice Renard. *The Blue Peril; Doctor Lerne; The Doctored Man; A Man Among the Microbes; The Master of Light*
Jean Richepin. *The Wing*
Albert Robida. *The Adventures of Saturnin Farandoul; The Clock of the Centuries; Chalet in the Sky*
J.-H. Rosny Aîné. *Helgvor of the Blue River; The Givreuse Enigma; The Mysterious Force; The Navigators of Space; Vamireh; The World of the Variants; The Young Vampire*
Marcel Rouff. *Journey to the Inverted World*
Han Ryner. *The Superhumans*
Brian Stableford. *The New Faust at the Tragicomique;The Empire of the Necromancers (The Shadow of Frankenstein; Frankenstein and the Vampire Comtesse; Frankenstein in London); Sherlock Holmes & The Vampires of Eternity; The Stones of Camelot; The Wayward Muse.* (anthologist) *The Germans on Venus; News from the Moon; The Supreme Progress; The World Above the World; Nemoville*
Jacques Spitz. *The Eye of Purgatory*

Kurt Steiner. *Ortog*
Eugène Thébault. *Radio-Terror*
C.-F. Tiphaigne de La Roche. *Amilec*
Théo Varlet. *The Xenobiotic Invasion; Timeslip Troopers* (w/André Blandin); *The Martian Epic* (w/Octave Joncquel)
Paul Vibert. *The Mysterious Fluid*
Villiers de l'Isle-Adam. *The Scaffold; The Vampire Soul*
Philippe Ward. *Artahe*
Philippe Ward & Sylvie Miller. *The Song of Montségur*

MYSTERIES & THRILLERS

M. Allain & P. Souvestre. *The Daughter of Fantômas*
A. Anicet-Bourgeois, Lucien Dabril. *Rocambole*
A. Bernède & L. Feuillade. *Judex*
A. Bisson & G. Livet. *Nick Carter vs. Fantômas*
V. Darlay & H. de Gorsse. *Lupin vs. Holmes: The Stage Play*
Paul Féval. *Gentlemen of the Night; John Devil; The Black Coats ('Salem Street; The Invisible Weapon; The Parisian Jungle; The Companions of the Treasure; Heart of Steel; The Cadet Gang; The Sword-Swallower)*
Emile Gaboriau. *Monsieur Lecoq*
Steve Leadley. *Sherlock Holmes: The Circle of Blood*
Maurice Leblanc. *Arsène Lupin vs. Comtesse Cagliostro; Lupin vs. Holmes (The Blonde Phantom; The Hollow Needle)*
Gaston Leroux. *Chéri-Bibi; The Phantom of the Opera; Rouletabille & the Mystery of the Yellow Room*
Richard Marsh. *The Complete Adventures of Judith Lee*
William Patrick Maynard. *The Terror of Fu Manchu*
Frank J. Morlock. *Sherlock Holmes: The Grand Horizontals; Sherlock Holmes vs Jack the Ripper*
P. de Wattyne & Y. Walter. *Sherlock Holmes vs. Fantômas*
David White. *Fantômas in America*

SCREENPLAYS

Mike Baron. *The Iron Triangle*
Emma Bull & Will Shetterly. *Nightspeeder; War for the Oaks*
Gerry Conway & Roy Thomas. *Doc Dynamo*
Steve Englehart. *Majorca*
James Hudnall. *The Devastator*

Jean-Marc & Randy Lofficier. *Royal Flush*
J.-M. & R. Lofficier & Marc Agapit. *Despair*
J.-M. & R. Lofficier & Joël Houssin. *City*
Andrew Paquette. *Peripheral Vision*
R. Thomas, J. Hendler & L. Sprague de Camp. *Rivers of Time*

NON-FICTION

Stephen R. Bissette. *Blur 1-5. Green Mountain Cinema 1*
Win Scott Eckert. *Crossovers* (2 vols.)
Jean-Marc & Randy Lofficier. *Shadowmen* (2 vols.)
Randy Lofficier. *Over Here*

HEXAGON COMICS

Franco Frescura & Luciano Bernasconi. *Wampus*
Franco Frescura & Giorgio Trevisan. *CLASH*
L. Bernasconi, J.-M. Lofficier & Juan Roncagliolo Berger. *Phenix*
Claude Legrand, J.-M. Lofficier & L. Bernasconi. *Kabur*
Franco Oneta. *Zembla*
L. Buffolente, Lofficier & J.-J. Dzialowski. *Strangers: Homicron*
Danilo Grossi. *Strangers: Jaydee*
Claude Legrand & Luciano Bernasconi. *Strangers: Starlock*

ART BOOKS

Jean-Pierre Normand. *Science Fiction Illustrations*
Raven Okeefe. *Raven's L'il Critters*
Randy Lofficier & Raven OKeefe. *If Your Possum Go Daylight...*
Daniele Serra. *Illusions*